THE
SISTERHOOD

HELEN
BRYAN

amazonpublishing

Published by Amazon Publishing
PO Box 400818
Las Vegas, NV 89140

ISBN-13: 9781611099287
ISBN-10: 1611099285
Library of Congress Control Number: 2012920046

For My Family

ACKNOWLEDGMENTS

No matter how difficult, rewarding, frustrating, enjoyable, compulsive, or exhausting the process of producing a manuscript, writing is essentially a singular occupation for the author. Turning that manuscript into a polished book, however, requires a huge collective effort on the part of others. I am grateful to so many people who have had a hand in getting *The Sisterhood* onto the bookshelf. One and all, they have given the book and its author the benefit of their unstinting attention and professional expertise.

First of all I would like to thank my agent, Jane Dystel at Dystel & Goderich, who has been a constant source of support, generous with her time and input, and whose experience and professionalism have smoothed the manuscript-transformation process for everyone concerned. And given my rashly optimistic approach to deadlines, it was particularly helpful that Jane had a better view than I did of the time it takes, realistically, to deliver a manuscript. I am grateful to Jane and to her partner, Miriam Goderich, for the time they spent on the manuscript and their thoughtful editorial advice. I have to say, they were generally right.

A gifted editor will often understand a book even better than its author and have a sixth sense how editing will produce the best possible version. That was certainly the case with developmental editor Charlotte Herscher. Aside from the fact that it was a pleasure to work with Charlotte, her focus, sure professional touch, and clarity worked wonders on a long and complex manuscript. From her first perceptive comments, I knew I could rely on her advice. Editing *The Sisterhood* was a big project for both of us, and I am grateful for the way she transformed the book.

Author-centric Amazon Publishing was, as ever, a joy to work with. From an author's perspective, everything at Amazon Publishing runs on well-oiled tracks with never a glitch. Senior editor Terry Goodman employed his considerable author-charming skills by e-mail, kept the publishing schedule on target, and made sure that what was supposed to happen, happened. Jessica Poore and Nikki Sprinkle of the Amazon author team couldn't be more helpful and are always available in case of queries. And thanks are due to copy editor Katie Parker, who expertly smoothed the final version and tied up loose ends.

Finally, I am grateful to my wonderfully supportive family: Roger, Cass, Michelle, Niels, Bo, and Poppy, who, rightly or wrongly, profess themselves amazed by all my efforts. Above all, thanks are due to my husband, Roger Low, who understands my need, when writing, for a degree of quiet and privacy that, according to him, is not so much Virginia Woolf's "room of one's own" as it is "lockdown." In our household this is only achievable because in addition to everything else he does, Roger can hold the fort through any known domestic crisis. Best of all, when writing is done for the day, I can leave my imagined world with its fictional inhabitants for my lively and loving real one.

PROLOGUE

From the Chronicle of Las Sors Santas
de Jesus, Las Golondrinas Convent,
Andalusia, Spain, June 1552

It is midnight, but only the orphanage children sleep. At sunset a
messenger came from the valley to warn the Abbess. Like wolves
slinking toward the sheepfold, the Inquisition tribunal are drawing
closer and will soon be upon us. All in the order, from the youngest novice to elderly bedridden Sor Augustina, are awake, praying
the queen will intervene, and for courage if she does not. We must
remember the example of our beloved Foundress in her hour of
trial.

I, Sor Beatriz of the Holy Sisters of Jesus, servant of God and
scribe of the convent of Las Golondrinas, make my last entry in this
Chronicle I have kept for over forty years. Tonight this Chronicle
and our Foundress's medal, our order's two most precious possessions, must leave the convent to be out of the Inquisition's
reach and to keep her spiritual legacy alive. Our Foundress's plan,
revealed to us over the years, is to send them to Spanish America,
and we pray that our obedience to her wishes will allow them to be
rediscovered one day.

Since the earliest days of Christianity our order has born witness to a female tradition of spirituality that men of the church have suppressed and replaced with doctrines that refashioned God and religion in their own image. Centuries ago, the Emperor Constantine called disputing bishops to the Council of Nicea to agree on church doctrine. By consensus, and one curious result, Mary the mother of Jesus was declared the ever-virgin mother of God—despite the fact that Jesus never claimed divinity for himself, and our Foundress was living proof to the contrary regarding Mary's perpetual virginity.

These man-made doctrines swept all before them, drowning out the voice of women, indeed the voice of reason and experience. Resistance became heresy, regardless of the truth. Deaconesses, so active in the early church, saw their authority curtailed, then extinguished. Before long, men of the church were debating whether women, like animals, were incapable of having souls. Secure in their spiritual supremacy, men of the church easily believe women's enforced submission is genuine.

Outwardly compliant to the church, our order has continued to bear witness to the truth. We have preserved the evidence of it in our Gospel and our Foundress's medal, evidence that is more important than ever now.

Since the *Reconquista*, the Inquisition has unleashed a wave of religious terror to strengthen the Christian monarchs' hold on Spain. A growing network of Inquisition familiars watch, whisper, and denounce—setting neighbor to spy on neighbor and servants to watch their masters and mistresses; reporting who closes the curtains of their house on Friday, who will not touch pork or shellfish or mix meat and milk, who hides a nine-branched candlestick, who prays toward Mecca, who fasts for the month of Ramadan, who celebrates the Passover Seder. People are accused of hideous crimes invented by fevered imaginations, and dragged away to the torturers, the rack, and the stake. All are suspect. All live in fear of accusation.

Now a Franciscan zealot, Fr. Ramon Sanchez, claims the Blessed Virgin appeared to him, weeping because secret Jews and Muslims masquerade as nuns, profaning convents by their presence and plotting the overthrow of our Christian monarchs. He swears the Virgin bids all who love her to seek out and destroy this abomination without mercy, to purge convents of heretics and unbelievers for the glory of God. Alas, so much evil done in a woman's name! By a lunatic perhaps, but with the willing help of men none would call mad.

And they say Fr. Ramon is both ignorant and mad, a dangerous combination. He cannot read or write, has fits, fasts continually, and his habit is streaked with filth and blood from a *cilice* round his waist. He screams in his sleep, tormented by demons who would have him loosen it. Yet he exercises a strange power over those who come into contact with him, and mobs are swayed to violence by his sermons, and they roar in approval when he speaks of "purifying" convents. The Abbess believes the tide of favor must turn against him soon—the Jesuits of the Holy Office will not be led by a crude peasant forever. But until this happens he is as dangerous as an adder in spring.

Last year the Holy Office of the Inquisition notified the Abbess it would begin an investigation to discover whether there was merit in Fr. Ramon's claims. Their tribunals would visit each convent in Spain, a work that would take many years to accomplish. At each convent the tribunal would require a list of possible heretics to be drawn up for examination.

For the Abbess and for all of us, death is preferable to such betrayal. The first rule of our order was laid down by our Foundress, and requires we protect girls and women from the violence of men. From the earliest days of our community, when the first sisters lived in caves, women of the mountain villages found a refuge with us when their men beat and abused them. Our first Abbess decided men must be required to give something of value to us as pledge for their future good behavior before their women would return. Since the men of these mountains have always regarded the women of this place as having special powers, whether of healing or supernatural forces, it has proved an effective tactic.

The obscurity of our order and its distant location have been advantages in our work. For centuries the church scarcely acknowledged our existence save for supplying us from time to time with an elderly priest to say Mass and live out his declining years under our care. After the *Reconquista*, Queen Isabella made a special pilgrimage here, to honor a Christian convent sustained under Moorish rule. She particularly approved of our seclusion from the world, believing it a safeguard of our spirituality and virtue. For that reason she favored us with her patronage.

The sinful world, however, sought us for the selfsame reasons of distance and obscurity. Courtiers who attended the queen on her visit endowed an orphanage within our walls for purposes of their own. And this has had the curious effect of shielding us from the Inquisition, even as the Inquisition has grown in power and influence.

The rigid Catholic morals at court have created new victims, the endangered *escondidas*, the "hidden girls": illegitimate daughters of courtiers and their mistresses, often aristocratic ladies. There are also offspring from lusts of the vilest kind—fathers and brothers and uncles who have gotten children on their own daughters, sisters, and nieces. Grandees must conceal the fruit of such lusts or jeopardize their positions at court.

The girls are spirited away to us in secrecy, usually when they are weaned. They say that someone prominently placed at court arranges their removal through a chain of middlemen who do not know the mothers' identities. The mothers never know where their daughters are bound, only that it is to a convent far away. Save for the courtiers who endowed the orphanage, few others could trace the children to Las Golondrinas.

The hidden girls bring religious dowries, the price of their parents' guilt. The children never know any life outside the convent, and in due course all become nuns. The pious justification is that giving these girls to God expiates the parents' sin. The truth is darker, and the reason we agreed to the orphanage. It is frequently the only means of saving the lives of these children. Inconvenient infants are helpless victims, quickly smothered or drowned like kittens.

But while the orphanage girls are a sensitive matter, what endangers us with the Inquisition are the five older girls who found their way here to be hidden in the convent—Esperanza, Pia, Sanchia, Marisol, and Luz. Preparations are nearly complete for four of them to leave tonight, to seek refuge and husbands in Spanish America. If the Inquisition finds them, they will be subjected to hideous interrogations that would quickly yield three "heretics," one girl hunted like a white doe because her existence threatens the throne itself, and the poor little heiress Luz who must be protected from her father at all costs. Luz, so gifted with her needle, who worked the beautiful altar cloth sent as a gift to the queen, must stay behind. She would endanger the others on the journey. As she cannot speak, perhaps they will have mercy on her.

Perhaps.

The Abbess's widowed sister, the beata Sor Emmanuela, will accompany the four girls as chaperone. As a lay sister, Sor Emmanuela is not bound by the church's rules on enclosure that confine nuns to the convent and prevent their going abroad without special letters of permission.

The Abbess believes the safest plan is to divide the responsibility for the medal and the Chronicle between Sor Emmanuela and the eldest girl, my assistant Esperanza. Sor Emmanuela will wear the medal, but the key to its meaning is hidden in our Gospel, copied into our Chronicle. Esperanza will take charge of the Chronicle. The Abbess has charged her with keeping a record of the journey, just as I would have done, and I have showed her our Gospel, written in Latin and concealed in its middle pages. She reads Latin easily, but more importantly she will understand how it points to those shared beliefs between Jews and early Christians, and later Muslims, that should be a basis of peace, not persecution, between the different faiths. If some mishap befalls the Chronicle on the journey, Esperanza's memory is as excellent as her understanding, and she has sworn to memorize and rewrite if necessary.

Even as we wait, the Abbess prays for deliverance, that the queen will be moved by Luz's gift to protect us and stay the Inquisition's hand. But we cannot wait longer for miracles or influence. A beata has come, weeping with fright. There are arrivals at the gate, despite the early hour of morning. Surprise is one of the Inquisition's weapons.

Farewell to the Chronicle. May it and our Foundress's medal find a safe haven and one day, God willing, be returned to this holy place. Let those who read this pray for those who take our treasures to exile and safety, for those who remain, for those who may return in the future, and for the soul of the scribe Sor Beatriz.

Peace be upon you and God's mercy and blessing.

Deo gratias. God is great.

CHAPTER I

Pacific Coast of South America, Spring 1983

The first signs appeared in December. By *Navidad* the warm seas yielded dying fish to the fishermen's nets. Anxious women crowded into the churches, to light candles and beseech God, the Virgin, and all the saints to stay the hand of *El Niño*. The peasants clung to their superstition that naming the capricious atmospheric phenomenon after the Christ Child might appease it. But this time *El Niño* came in the guise of the Devil, *El Diablo*, to turn the noon sky a strange color. People looked skyward uneasily and crossed themselves, muttering prayers as midday turned black as night, the wind rose, and a hard rain began to fall. The sky sank lower and lower and the wind gained strength, and people called on older, darker gods before abandoning prayers altogether to shout for their children and run for shelter.

The hurricane, the worst in a hundred years, was known afterward as the *Mano del Diablo*— Hand of the Devil. It struck with terrible ferocity. A screaming wind set shutters banging, then tore them away and sent them flying, followed by anything it could reach—doors, roofs, trees, bicycles, cars, and trucks, tossed and smashed like toys. Rain lashed like a hail of bullets, hard enough to kill chickens and goats and babies. Peasants on the road or in their fields were swept away in the storm's merciless grip. And as

1

for the poor in the shanty towns, where could they go? Mudslides swallowed flimsy shacks with their inhabitants, and the sea came rolling in towering waves to seize boats and fishermen from shore. Roof tiles and trees and people were tossed, sucked up, hurled down, buried alive, crushed, swept out to sea.

After two days of roaring winds and thudding debris, collapsing buildings and landslides, the aftermath was eerily quiet, broken by the feeble cries and muffled shrieks of survivors, the muttering of the dazed and bereft, the wails of children, the shrill yelping of dogs in pain. People struggled to understand what had happened. The living scrabbled with bare hands to reach the trapped and injured, their families and neighbors, while cries for help from under the rubble grew fainter. The emergency services were pitifully useless, with no heavy-moving equipment, no sniffer dogs. Injured survivors screamed invisibly, and many of those who were found died nonetheless for want of medical supplies, food, and blankets.

It took a week to reopen the airport, and by that time the air was fetid with death. The world's press arrived with the international rescue teams who had been delayed by red tape and chaos. When aid eventually trickled in, reporters had no shortage of horror stories to back up an international appeal to help victims of the crisis, though hardened correspondents familiar with the region knew the greater part of disaster funds would be siphoned off to private accounts in Switzerland.

On the ninth day amid the carnage and destruction, a single item of good news emerged. A little girl had been found alive and uninjured by a navy ship making a final sweep along the coast. The sailors onboard had nearly abandoned the search at nightfall when they heard crying. Throughout the night the crying continued as they swept searchlights back and forth over the sea, bumping bloated human and animal carcasses aside.

Finally, at dawn, they located the source of the sound in a fishing boat caught between a logjam of smashed timber and a dead mule. It looked empty, but two young sailors climbed aboard to look. Then they gave a shout. The girl, perhaps two or three years old, naked except for a chain looped round her neck several times with a medal strung on it, was found trapped under a nest of fishing nets too heavy for her to escape. It seemed unbelievable that she had not perished from exposure or been drowned by a wave, but she was crying and sucking her fist.

The story of the little survivor appeared briefly in the press, with pictures of the child, the boat, the medal, and the two grinning sailors. But news has a short shelf life and by then the foreign press had moved on. There were wars and celebrity divorces to cover elsewhere. The little girl disappeared into a local orphanage, the only record of her existence a sheaf of yellowing press clippings.

In the Shadow of the Andes, Spring 1984

A year after the *Mano del Diablo*, a battered car with "Taxi" painted on its side wound its way into the oldest part of the old provincial capital, which was still scarred by the disaster. Finally the potholed streets narrowed too much for the car to continue. The driver stopped and pointed. A middle-aged American couple got out of the backseat, shading their eyes against the sun to look around. "They said it was in the old part of the city," the woman said, looking at her map, "and this part looks old, alright. It's practically falling down." She was a plump lady in a neat Liz Claiborne skirt, matching cardigan, and low-heeled pumps, and she patted her coiffed hair nervously.

Her husband, a large man perspiring in a button-down shirt, bow tie, and plaid sports jacket, adjusted a camera around his neck—a cheap one, because he had been warned to leave his expensive one at home. He clutched a guidebook and, incongruously, a large teddy bear sporting a pink bow under his arm. He took his wife's elbow protectively. "Come on, Sarah-Lynn. Hang on to your pocketbook," the man muttered, glancing at the driver who was slumped back in his seat rolling a cigarette.

The *Norte Americanos* were conspicuous in that neighborhood. Men in vests and women in cheap print dresses watched from balconies that sagged on peeling houses and peered from lean-tos beneath crumbling arches. Ragged children with big bellies crowded to peek through iron gates. The couple pushed past old cars and donkeys and beggars, and rattling cars whose brakes screeched and whose drivers spat and shouted insults at each other, banging the sides of their vehicles for emphasis. The couple skirted makeshift stalls selling fried fish and *arepas*. A prostitute on a broken chair in a doorway called to them in mocking Spanish, raising a cackle of laughter from her companions. Women shouted, babies cried, children were scolded or slapped. The streets stank of frying oil, urine, tobacco, sweat, exhaust fumes, rotting garbage, animal dung, and fear. In the distance the snow-capped Andes rose clean and remote against a hard blue sky.

The Americans turned their map this way and that, looking around, ignoring the people around them. "There! I recognize it from the posters!" exclaimed Sarah-Lynn suddenly, pointing ahead to a whitewashed bell tower, one that was featured on a famous travel poster of the 1970s when trains still ran to this remote corner of South America. Then, souvenir sellers had done a brisk turnover in clay swallows, cheap silver bracelets, and gourds decorated in the native style.

Now the tourists were long gone, but a few old men still waited hopefully under the convent walls, shabby old merchandise spread on dirty blankets. "Hello! Nice souvenir?" they wheedled.

"That's definitely the bell tower, Virgil. I guess we found it... Oh, what a smell!" Her nose wrinkled as a gust of open sewers engulfed her.

The man calmly opened his guidebook. "Oldest convent in Latin America, *El Convento de las Golondrinas*, home of *Las Sors Santas de Jesus de Los Andes,*" he read, testing out his newly acquired Spanish. He sensed an undercurrent of violence in the air, ready to be ignited, and instinct told him on no account to show fear, or to hurry, or these people would be on them like vultures. So he stood his ground, acting casual and interested in the sights, a tourist. "Lotta birds, listen to that racket! No wonder they call it Convent of the Swallows. *Las Golon...Golondrinas.*"

Feeling the eyes boring into his back, he planted his feet firmly and stopped to turn a guidebook page, as if he hadn't a care in the world. "Says here, there's an old superstition about swallows, because of how they migrate back and forth to the same places every year. In the olden days sailors got swallow tattoos for luck so's they'd make it home after going off, same way as the birds. And if they died at sea, they believed swallows would fly down and carry the souls of the tattooed ones straight to heaven. Ain't that something? Big, isn't it?" he remarked, refusing to be hurried. He took a pocket-size Kodak from his pocket and fiddled with the distance setting. "Must be the size of a city block. Wonder where the entrance is?"

Sarah-Lynn was folding up the map and looking around for the gate. Virgil was going on and on like a travelogue because he was nervous. She understood; she was edgy as a cat herself. She jumped as a tray of shabby merchandise was thrust under her nose by an old man with no teeth, muttering "Cheap! Cheap!"

"Virgil, tell that man we don't want any souvenirs!"

Her husband shook his head at the souvenir seller and, taking Sarah-Lynn's arm, pulled her away to have her photo taken in front of the gate. He kept talking. "Before the Spanish came, the Incas had some kind of women's building in this same site, the Virgins of the Sun or some such heathen thing. Had a garden inside, made all out of silver with gold flowers."

He kept talking, loud and conversational, while he snapped pictures. "Yep, the Spanish tore it down, reused the stones to build a convent for missionary nuns who came here from Spain. They had them a school and a hospital for native girls and an orphanage. Lotta illegitimate babies, the Spanish men and the Indian women—the nuns would take the children in and see they got baptized and saved. There was even a women's jail in there…"

"I don't want to hear about jails, Virgil! We're about to go in and get our child and we have to decide once and for all what her name's going to be!"

"I thought we planned we'd name a girl after your mama, like you wanted. And if it was a boy, Virgil Walker Jr." Sarah-Lynn patted her husband on the arm. He had wanted a son.

"God's sent us to this little girl. I know she's special. Where on earth is the gate?"

"That's it behind you. I'll take a couple of pictures for that scrapbook the adoption worker told us to make for her. Then we better hurry. We don't want them thinking we've changed our minds about the adoption."

Inside the convent, Mother Superior was waiting behind her desk with its ancient black telephone. Light slanted through barred windows set high in the wall, and the room was crammed with solid old-fashioned furniture in dark carved wood. The walls held the convent's collection of portraits. Dark-eyed girls with heavy eyebrows dressed in fine clothes and jewels, holding flowers, stared down at Mother. They were long-dead *monjas coronadas*, crowned nuns, girls about to enter a convent. Portraits of a daughter betrothed to Christ had been a status symbol among the Spanish colonial families of the sixteenth and seventeenth centuries. In their *salas grandes*, where visitors were entertained, they were hung conspicuously higher on the walls than the betrothal portraits of daughters engaged to mere men. It had been customary to eventually donate the portraits to the girls' convents. Mother found the silent company of the portraits restful, and often sought their imaginary advice in convent matters.

As the parlor clock ticked, Mother began to wonder if the American couple had changed their minds and were not coming for Isabelita after all. She sighed and looked up to argue the case for the adoption once more with her serene companions. She reminded them there was another civil war brewing—stories of atrocities and foreign-trained paramilitaries with plentiful supplies of weapons had reached the convent. And she reminded them of Sor Rosario's claim of having a vision last year, shortly before the hurricane.

Sor Rosario, the youngest nun and somewhat giddy at the best of times, had been hurrying across the cloister, late as usual for compline, when a "vision" had halted her in her tracks. Mother had been skeptical and questioned her closely, fully expecting the vision would resemble a Renaissance statue of the Madonna to which Sor Rosario was particularly devoted. The statue had its own small chapel in the convent church, built by a conquistador's widow to house her husband's tomb. The daylight poured through a window above, as if from heaven, on a Madonna who was slender and blonde with gold stars on her blue gown, a red cloak trimmed with ermine, a filigree crown, and pointed golden slippers peeking from the hem of her gown.

Sor Rosario said, "She was tall, with dark hair down her back. It had bits of gray. She had dark eyes that looked directly into mine. Black eyes. Heavy eyebrows that met over her nose. The evening wind was just beginning to blow and her dress and cloak billowed behind her—she looked like she had wings! She spoke of a warning, a promise, and a reminder. Her voice was not soft or gentle—she spoke loudly, as women do when they intend to make men listen whether men want to or not."

"Indeed!" It didn't sound like any vision of the Madonna Mother knew of.

Sor Rosario nodded. "Naturally I knelt and began saying the *Ave*, but she stamped her foot and held up her hand for silence, saying there was no time for all that and to pay attention. A terrible storm was coming. The sky would be ripped apart and the angel of death would spread its wings above us. But a blessing or a gift would come from the sea, something would be found…we must save something…but her voice began to fade and I couldn't hear her every word, and she stamped her foot again, looking angry, but I think that was because she had not finished what she had to say and—"

"*Stamped* her *foot*, Sister? Perhaps you were dreaming." Mother sighed, closed her eyes and tried to massage away the beginnings of a headache. The more emotional nuns often claimed to see visions, particularly when there wasn't enough to eat. Usually they were of Santa Teresa and roses.

"Oh no! She was real as anything, Mother. Her cloak was brown." Sor Rosario's voice was tinged with disappointment. She had loved pretty frocks once. "Plain brown. You would think, blue, perhaps a nice rose pink, but no…a kind of grayish brown. Rough fabric, stained white around the hem, as if it had been dragged through something and dried. She began fading away, still talking, shouting almost, but the sound was fainter—something about...fools of men...the Sors Santas de Jesus must protect... something—the Chronicle. That was it—protect the Chronicle! Because it explains something to do with the gift, the one from the sea."

"The Chronicle? We haven't seen that in over half a century; how are we supposed to 'protect' it?" Mother was exasperated. The order's Chronicle was an ancient volume that had supposedly come from their mother house in Spain, wherever that might be, like the medal that had supposedly come from the same place but disappeared during the 1932 civil war. It had been hidden as a precautionary measure by an elderly and forgetful nun, Sor Agnes, when the convent was attacked by a revolutionary mob, inflamed by legends of Inca treasure supposedly buried in the convent's chapel crypt. The convent's stout gates had held against the mob then, though the stories about hidden Inca treasure had survived and resurfaced periodically. Mother suspected it was only a matter of time until the gates failed.

When the army crushed the revolt in 1933, the nuns of the day searched for the Chronicle in vain, and the then–Mother Superior beseeched God for patience with Sor Agnes, who died unable to recall where she had hidden it, whispering only that it was in a secret place.

With the Chronicle missing, the nuns passed their traditions on to younger nuns by word of mouth, but as time passed they recalled less and less. When Mother herself was a young novice, only the very oldest nuns remembered actually seeing the Chronicle before it disappeared. They told the novices that they would know it at once; it was an old leather-bound volume with vellum pages and a faint gilt imprint of a bird on its cover.

Mother asked crossly if Sor Rosario's "vision" might have revealed where the Chronicle was hidden, if it was so important. Sor Rosario shook her head. Mother had sighed and asked if the vision explained whether she meant a political storm or a weather storm was coming. What kind of blessing was coming from the sea? And what were the nuns supposed to do about it? But Sor Rosario only shrugged apologetically. Mother despaired of getting any sense out of her and sent Sor Rosario back to her chores.

In a matter of days the *Mano del Diablo* answered the first question.

In the convent's orphanage, nuns and lay sisters made up extra pallets and readied their meager collection of medical supplies, their stocks of patched nightdresses and underwear and threadbare pullovers for the traumatized and injured children that began arriving—brought by the makeshift rescue services, the police, the army, neighbors, and strangers.

The arrivals stretched the convent's resources to the limit. Once, patrician nuns' dowries—land, gold and silver and emerald mines, and vast sums of money—had enriched the convent, but as centuries passed the convent's wealth diminished with vocations. When Sor Rosario, their last novice, came begging to be admitted, her dowry was two squawking chickens—all she had in the world. So the burden of the orphanage fell on the shoulders of a dwindling population of aging nuns and equally elderly lay sisters. And the children orphaned by the disaster cried all night, from pain and for their lost families. They wet their beds and had nightmares. Those who could not cry desperately needed specialist help, but there was no one to give it. Sor Rosario hitched up her habit and scrubbed pots and floors, boiled sheets, set older children to look after the younger ones, and watered the maize gruel and the dwindling contents of the last bottles of iodine, until the tincture was no longer red but barely pink.

Soon both nuns and lay sisters were tottering with exhaustion, but with so much extra work the afternoon siesta was abandoned until Mother finally insisted that everyone—children, nuns, lay sisters, even the elderly odd-job man—was not to stir for an hour after lunch, regardless.

That brief interlude of tranquillity was broken one afternoon by the sound of running footsteps coming down the corridor. "Mother!" shouted Sor Rosario, racing round the corner, skirts still hitched from her morning's work and beads swinging at her waist as she hurried round the cloister toward Mother Superior's office. "Mother!" echoed the old nun hurrying behind her. Her high-pitched voice, wobbling with excitement and breathlessness, was shrill. "The key! You must come at once!"

At her desk Mother had sat up with a start and straightened her wimple, realizing she had fallen asleep again over the orphanage accounts. The convent was desperately short of money, the roof over the crowded dormitory was sagging, and food was in short supply and more expensive by the day. The intake of children orphaned by the hurricane had strained resources to the breaking point. The children often went to bed hungry. There were not enough blankets, and though the children bundled three and four to a bed for warmth, they shivered at night. As for clothing and sandals...Anxiety and despair always made Mother sleepy. Her glasses had slid down as she dozed, and now she pushed them back up and scolded, "Sor Rosario! Sor Maria Gracia! The siesta! No need for *running*! Most unseemly!" Mother tried to sound stern, but really, how did they have the energy? "What key?"

Sor Maria Gracia was wheezing too badly to speak, but Sor Rosario gasped, "Sailors, two...sailors...visitors' parlor...the key... open the *locutio* gate!"

Mother was shocked. "The *key*? *Open the locutio gate?* Sor Rosario! We never open that gate! The *locutio* symbolizes our separation from the world, and—"

"Mother," Sor Maria Gracia piped up, "the world has sent us a gift!"

11

Sor Rosario nodded earnestly, big eyes wide. "I told Sor Maria Gracia it is just as the vision promised…" she began, ecstatically.

"Vision indeed!" snapped Mother, thinking Sor Rosario was an impressionable peasant and Sor Maria Gracia was wandering in her wits. Then Sor Maria Gracia leaned forward and murmured in Mother's ear.

Mother started back and stared at her. "Two sailors with another child, who was wearing *our* medal? And the portress thinks I must deal with it?" Mother reconsidered Sor Rosario's vision, whose warning, she had to admit, had been accurate so far as the hurricane was concerned.

"The portress is surely mistaken!" The portress was old but sharp-eyed. "After three hundred years, the likelihood this is our medal is small. Nevertheless…"

Mother set off with a surprisingly quick step for the visitors' parlor, fingering the heavy key ring she wore on her girdle. The two nuns hurried after her. By the time they reached the parlor, Mother had extracted a large, rusty cast-iron key decorated with a cross and a symbol of a bird with a forked tail, and she struggled to fit it into the lock.

On the other side, two young sailors shifted from foot to foot while the nuns gathered behind the *locutio*. The gate in the middle shook as if someone was growing impatient and rattling it. A woman's voice muttered something that sounded like a profane oath. One sailor, holding a small malnourished girl sucking her thumb, raised his eyebrows at the other, who shrugged and shook his head. The sisters seemed to be behaving strangely.

The two sailors knew they had done what they should. They had taken the child to a side door of the convent, where for hundreds of years there had been a latticed hatch where abandoned babies and children were passed to the portress on the other side.

They had knocked on the hatch; the portress had come. "Take off the medal first so it doesn't get caught in the hatch and choke her," said the sailor holding the child to his companion. The companion unwound the chain and pushed it and the medal through the hatch and was about to set the child down when inside the portress shrieked, pushed the medal back, and said they must take the child and the medal to Mother Superior, before slamming the hatch closed.

Now they could hear a breathless voice behind the *locutio*— "Oil from the kitchen, Mother"—and a pale hand wearing a thin gold ring was visible through the ironwork, rubbing a cloth feverishly on the lock. Creaking loudly on its hinges, the iron gate was prized open.

"Well?" demanded Mother imperiously. She was a tall woman, and more formidable than ever because she was gaunt from the general shortage of food in the convent. She barely tasted what there was on the pretext of fasting, in order to leave as much as possible for the children.

The two sailors stepped back nervously. "We've brought her to the orphanage; we found her at sea a week ago," began the one holding the child. "And she was wearing...show them, Juan." The other nodded and held up a greenish disc on a length of tarnished gold chain. Mother peered, picked it up to examine it more closely, and turned it over. "Where...did...you...get...this?"

The other sailor said, "She was wearing it when we found her. She was all alone in a fishing boat, the only thing alive for miles. The chain was looped round her neck many times, Mother, as if someone hoped the medal would save her. And it must have—it's a miracle she survived."

Mother gazed at the medal, not quite believing her eyes. The old stories about the convent's medal, its description, and where it had come from had been kept alive in the order for centuries even though the medal itself had disappeared. But now she was holding a medal that fit the description—a swallow on one side and a female figure on the other. Could it really be? *"Deo gratias,"* she finally managed. "You have done well." She took the little girl and told Sor Maria Gracia to find the child some clothes at once and to take some money from the poor box and send a lay sister for milk.

Sor Maria Gracia tottered off in the direction of the poor box and Sor Rosario made cooing noises and held out her arms. Mother gave her the child and examined the medal closely. One of the sailors finally cleared his throat to get her attention. Mother looked up. Instinct told her it was essential that the bishop hear nothing of this. "Please say nothing about medals and miracles to anyone! It would only bring curiosity seekers to the convent and we have our hands full just now. It's only one child more for the orphanage."

"Yes, Mother."

"God bless you," she said in a perfunctory way, and pulled the creaking gate shut and relocked it.

Inside Mother leaned against the wall for support. Responsibility settled heavily on her shoulders. What next? "Send for Father. The child may have been baptized, but we cannot be certain. We will give her the name Isabella Salome. But say nothing about the medal to him."

Then Mother did the only thing a nun could: pray. She went back to her parlor, closed the door behind her, and sank to her knees on her prie-dieu, presented to an early Mother Superior by a Spanish vice-regent's wife. It was a heavy wooden piece, solid and immobile as a throne, elaborately carved in the style of the early seventeenth century with angels and human skulls. She prayed as she never had before for inspiration about where the lost Chronicle might be hidden. It was essential they find it—it had the whole story, it *must* be somewhere…She closed her eyes, gripped the lectern hard in her fervor, praying to all the saints in turn, "Please, please guide us to the Chronicle…"

She was startled when a panel on the side of the lectern suddenly loosened under her grip. Mother stopped midprayer. She bent sideways and looked at the section of wood beneath her hand. She pressed harder and there was a click as the panel sprang open, like a door. A secret compartment? Mother tentatively put her hand into what should have been a cavity, but behind the panel it was solid. Then she realized that was because something was wedged tightly inside, bulky, wrapped in coarse material.

It took both hands to maneuver it through the opening. Mother hardly dared breathe as she removed a cover of oiled wool and another of desiccated silk. Then, there it was—an old leatherbound book, rather large, like a ledger, with a blackened gilt clasp and the barely discernible outline of a bird with a long forked tail in faded gilt. Inside were pages of vellum, thin as tissue paper, filled with neat and clear writing, in ink that had faded to dark brown but was surprisingly legible. Mother saw the book was mostly in Spanish, but in the middle, the section in Latin! The Gospel! "*Deo gratias*," she whispered. "Sor Agnes's hiding place! I have found the Chronicle!"

She thought again about Sor Rosario's vision and its warning about the hurricane and a "gift," and now in the space of a few hours the medal and the Chronicle had been restored to the order. The child must have been connected to them somehow, but God moved in mysterious ways and they needed to wait to see how. Meanwhile they had to keep this news within the convent. There would be no end of trouble if it attracted the attention of the church authorities.

Unfortunately, the two young sailors disobeyed Mother's injunction to say nothing. A bored American journalist overheard them talking in a bar about the child and her miracle medal and thought it was a good story. He loosened their tongues with cachaca and a little cash that was a fortune to boys on naval pay. They told him everything while he made notes, and his story about the *Mano del Diablo* "miracle medal" was rehashed by a number of wire services months after the event.

As Mother had feared, the bishop got wind of it. He wrote a stern letter to the convent, reminding the order that for centuries suspicions of heresy had hovered around the *Sors Santas de Jesus* like a noxious cloud, and he intended to investigate this matter of the miraculous medal and report to Rome. The Catholic Church had enough of priests accused of abusing children to deal with; it could do without more trouble or controversy just now. He ordered Mother to turn the medal over to him at once. He would interrogate the child Isabella personally, then send her to Rome with his report and the medal.

Mother temporized. She replied in vague terms that ever since the *Mano del Diablo* the convent was overwhelmed, everything in disorder, and finding one small medal would be like looking for a needle in a haystack. Disingenuously, she asked the bishop to describe the medal in question, so that she would recognize it if it were found. Finally she protested that Isabella was only three years old and therefore unlikely to provide much assistance to a formal inquiry.

Mother had no intention of relinquishing the medal, nor did she intend to send Isabella to the Vatican. But the nuns could not fend off the bishop forever, and she had no idea what to do next.

The answer came via a phone call from an American missionary organization. She was telephoned by the regional chief of Christian Outreach—*Southern* Baptists, the man on the telephone emphasized. That didn't tell her much. Mother had no idea what distinguished one Protestant sect from another, just that their missionaries were said to hand out pocket Bibles and chewing gum and make a show of baptizing converts en masse in rivers. The man from Christian Outreach went on to say their churches had launched a fundraising appeal in the US for the victims of the *Mano del Diablo* disaster. Would Mother allow a photographer into the convent to take pictures of orphans for the appeal? Christian Outreach would donate some of the appeal funds to the convent.

Mother agreed—the convent was now so desperate for money that two nuns were being sent to beg in the town square each day. And the missionaries' photographer spotted Isabelita at once, pretty and photogenic, with big wistful eyes. She became the face of the appeal.

The Southern Baptists donated generously, and two months later Mother almost fainted when she opened a money order large enough to replenish the dispensary; buy a year's food for the entire convent, and blankets, shoes, and clothes for each child; repair the dormitory roof; and buy equipment for the schoolroom. Even toys. And there was a promise of more money to come. She reasoned that if God chose to work wonders through the Baptists, it was not for her to demur. If anything, it confirmed Mother's secret conviction that the world had enough trouble without insisting all worship God the same way. There was room before the Throne for everyone who served Him—Baptists and the Hindus, Seventh Day Adventists, Muslims and Jews, as well as Catholics. That this was a wide departure from the Church's teaching meant Mother had often struggled to fit her conviction into some recognized doctrinal framework. Though it did not fit, and the bishop would have been appalled, it remained a conviction.

Then the regional chief of Christian Outreach rang again, this time with the news that an American couple had seen Isabella's photo at a church fundraiser and been so taken with it that they wanted to adopt her. He explained that on the heels of the *Mano del Diablo* appeal, the church had lobbied Washington in support of its "adopt an orphan" project, and the US government had temporarily relaxed immigration rules to allow these fast-track adoptions for a short period. Mother asked to think it over.

The nuns held a convent meeting to decide and Mother urged, "Neither Isabelita, nor the medal, nor the Chronicle are safe here. The Marxists are whipping the peasants up with the old stories about churches hoarding Spanish gold while the people starve, and on top of that, the bishop is determined to get the Vatican involved with the medal. The Vatican has appointed an official investigator and if they learn that we have found the Chronicle as well..."

"They will send the Inquisition," muttered Sor Rosario rebelliously.

Mother ignored her and continued. "What better place to hide our medal and Chronicle than with Isabelita in an ordinary small town in America, where she will grow up quietly among the Protestants? I can lay a false trail with the adoption papers so it will be hard to trace her. Besides, adoption in America is a rare opportunity for one of our orphans."

The nuns couldn't disagree with that. Unless an orphan discovered a vocation—it had not happened in many years—the best the nuns could do when she turned sixteen was to turn her out into the world armed with a new set of clothes and a glowing letter of recommendation to enable her to be hired as a servant.

The nuns had many questions—whether the couple was trustworthy, and how would Mother ensure the medal and Chronicle were not lost once they left the convent. Mother promised she would insist on meeting the couple before she signed the papers. As for the medal and Chronicle, Mother explained her idea, and the nuns murmured their cautious approval—but everything depended on the adoptive parents.

Waiting for the Americans, Mother had nearly decided that their nonappearance meant it was God's will that Isabelita, the Chronicle, and the medal remain in the convent, when Sor Rosario appeared to say Señor and Señora Walker had arrived and ushered the couple in.

The Walkers said *"gracias"* nervously one after the other and Virgil Walker pulled his phrase book out of his pocket and began trying to make a sentence in labored Spanish. Mother managed a stiff smile and said, "Please be seated. We can speak in English." She had learned English as a girl, and though hers was rusty, recently she had practiced on the telephone with the people from Christian Outreach.

"Thank you, ma'am," he said, relieved. "We tried to learn some Spanish, took one of those crash courses, but right this minute, just when we need it, I can hardly remember a word." Mother smiled again, less stiffly. The couple were as nervous as she was. It reassured her, that and the teddy bear.

She glanced down at the couple's file open on her desk, even though she knew its contents by heart. Sarah-Lynn and Virgil Walker, thirty-seven and forty years old, married for eighteen years, during which time they tried but failed to have children. There was a letter of recommendation from the pastor of their church that said they were a fine upstanding couple and good Christians, that Mrs. Walker was a housewife and homemaker, member of the garden club, and active in her church Bible study group. There was another from their congressman saying they were pillars of their community. There was one from the Chamber of Commerce of Laurel Run, Georgia, confirming Virgil Walker owned a successful plumbing business there and was an active member of the Rotary Club. Mother had looked up Laurel Run in the convent's atlas, one that had been printed in 1930 and showed the state of Georgia divided up into counties. She found Laurel Run at last, a tiny dot in Bonner County, east of Fulton County where a much bigger dot said *Atlanta*. Mother was sure that she had heard of Atlanta. "I hope you found us without too much difficulty."

"Yes, ma'am, thank you. Sorry we're late. We were taking pictures outside. Children adopted under the new program are supposed to have a scrapbook for later, with photos and mementoes of where they came from. And speaking of pictures, Sarah-Lynn here has brought some to show you of our house, and the bedroom we've fixed up for our little girl."

Sarah-Lynn Walker opened a big leather handbag that matched her shoes, took out a manila envelope, and removed a sheaf of photos. "This is our home," she said, putting the first one on Mother's desk. "It's what they call a colonial ranch style, brand new when we bought it eight years ago," said Sarah-Lynn. The white brick and clapboard house with a pillared porch and surrounded by a lawn and flower beds was a small palace, all clean and new. "I do all the housework myself," said Sarah-Lynn, the hand with the pictures shaking slightly with nerves. "And the gardening. We put a swing and a sandbox there in the back so the neighbor children can come over to play. And here's her room." The bedroom was painted in pink and white, with a small four-poster bed and other child's furniture painted with flowers. It looked as if an entire toy shop had been emptied into the room, filled with stuffed animals and dolls and a large dollhouse that took up one corner. "I hope it's alright," Sarah-Lynn said nervously. "We did it real quick, as soon's we got the go-ahead. I forgot to get a picture of her bathroom, but it's decorated to match."

"Very nice," Mother said. Her own bathroom?

"Here's our town." There were more photos: tree-lined streets where every pristine house was surrounded by a similar neat lawn, bushes, flower beds, and trees. There was a photo of the brand-new Baptist church they attended, the town square, and the old-fashioned courthouse. It looked quiet and safe. There were pictures of the local elementary school and the high school, and both Walkers were emphatic their daughter would go to college. "We got us a real good junior college in Laurel Run, kind of old-fashioned and ladylike, and the state university is thirty miles away. Then there are more colleges than you can shake a stick at around Atlanta. I'm what you might call a self-made man, but our little girl will have every opportunity!"

"My husband's a hard worker. He built his business from nothing," Sarah-Lynn interrupted proudly. "He started off as a plumber when we got married and now he owns a plumbing business with five branches, doing work all over the place, clear to Atlanta where there's lots of new homes going up. Got eighteen people working for him now."

"Here, this is one of my trucks," said Virgil, pulling out his wallet and extracting a business card that showed a sleek dark-green van with classical script on the side: GET A QUOTE FROM VIRGIL. "Latin teacher at the high school's an old army buddy—this was his idea."

"Virgil, honey!" Sarah-Lynn nudged her husband. "Tell about our church."

"Well, ma'am, we belong to the First Baptist Church, we go every Sunday, and on Wednesday night for a prayer meeting and a potluck supper." Virgil talked on about vacation Bible school, and the Little League baseball team he coached, and the Brownies— things that Mother had never heard of but were evidently children's activities.

Gunfire in the distance, then an explosion, interrupted them. Both sounded closer than usual. The Walkers jumped.

Mother gathered up Isabelita's file, with the newspaper clippings. "Here is all we know about Isabelita. We can only speculate who her parents might have been—almost certainly local people and certainly dead. They may have been from one of the fishing communities on the coast, or trying to escape."

The Walkers both nodded and Virgil took the file. "Our adoption worker has stressed that adopted children need to know where they came from. Especially when it's a foreign adoption. It can turn into a big issue when they grow up. So we'll make sure she knows."

Mother took a large parcel from her desk. "I understand. And since Isabelita will have so little to go on, here are two keepsakes from the convent. One is a medal she was wearing when she was rescued. You will see a photo of it in the newspaper stories in the file. We were extremely surprised to see it as our convent had one like it once. We felt she should have it.

"And this book is for her, too. It is very old, some old records of our convent. Our nuns were always educated, and the convent always had a scribe to keep the records. Perhaps Isabelita will want to read it someday if she remembers her Spanish. There is a section in the middle in Latin, too, but I know children do not learn Latin in school as they did in my day. Still, it is all we have to give her. Before I consent to the adoption I require your solemn promise to give her both these things on her sixteenth birthday." Mother felt an acute pang of regret that they had been unable to read the Chronicle properly before sending it away. Various nuns had made a start during the past year, but God alone knew where the convent's old Latin dictionary was. No one's Latin was up to much, and in any case there was so much work to do in the convent there hadn't been enough time, even to read the Spanish.

Sarah-Lynn Walker leaned forward earnestly. "That's lovely! Of course we promise, don't we Virgil?"

Her husband nodded. "Yes, ma'am, I give you my word. We'll see she gets these things. And our local high school still teaches Latin in the honors program; it helps kids get college scholarships so the PTA won't let them drop it. So we'll do our best to see she takes Latin, too. Virgil Walker doesn't go back on his word," he added and instinctively stuck out his hand to shake on the bargain. Startled but quick on the uptake, Mother reached out her own frail hand for his firm handshake. She believed him.

"Very well. I approve the adoption." Mother nodded at the Walkers and pushed the parcel over to Sarah-Lynn, who whispered, "Thank you." Mother rang a little silver bell and Sor Rosario appeared so quickly Mother knew she had been listening outside the door. "Please bring Isabelita."

Sor Rosario took her time. Mother made polite conversation while they waited, proudly pointing out the portraits of the crowned nuns, saying she thought they were quite special and certainly old, explaining that on feast days the orphanage children were allowed into her study to see them as a special treat. Convent life was rather spartan for the children, and a visit to Mother's parlor to hear a story about the crowned nuns was one of their few luxuries. Mother explained to the Walkers how she would give a little talk about these extraordinary girls, who were dressed in beautiful clothes with flowers and jewels and elaborate crowns as they prepared to become nuns. "Isabelita loves these paintings. When I asked why, she said they smiled at her." Mother smiled herself. "Perhaps they do. But mainly the children look forward to these occasions because afterward they have hot chocolate and almond pastries, like the ones offered to girls entering the convent, as a symbol of the sweetness of a cloistered life dedicated to God."

The Protestant Walkers looked dazed by this information, so Mother politely changed the subject.

"Let's see, what can I tell you about Isabelita to help you know her a little? She is a very good girl, very obedient, says her prayers and tidies her clothes. Her health is good. She's never been ill or at all naughty, although when Christian Outreach was so generous we were able to buy toys for the children—we've never been able to afford toys here." Mother shrugged apologetically. "Isabelita was so excited by the crayons and coloring books that she decorated the walls of the dormitory and some of the missals in the chapel before we could stop her."

"Bless her heart, the child was just happy to have something to play with!" exclaimed Sarah-Lynn.

Virgil grinned. "We got a new refrigerator, plain white, could do with some decorating," he said. "I'll get her the biggest box of crayons they make and she can draw on that all she likes."

Then there was a knock at the study door and the three of them turned as the door opened. Sor Rosario was holding the hand of a beautiful little girl, her dark hair neatly braided, wearing a spotlessly clean, carefully darned white pinafore, white socks, and new white sandals. Mother repressed thoughts of sacrificial lambs. After saying *"Buenas tardes,* Mother," the child smiled shyly from under her long eyelashes and wished the Walkers *"Buenas tardes."*

"Well hey there." Virgil smiled.

Sarah-Lynn whispered, "My precious baby!"

Mother beckoned the child to her side and took her face in her hands. Speaking in slow Spanish so the Walkers could follow she said, "These good people were lonely without a little girl of their own and have chosen you to be their daughter. Your parents in heaven are watching over you and are happy that God has sent them to be your new mother and father. You will leave the convent and go with them now. But wherever you go, our prayers will follow you every day." She spoke earnestly, looking deep into the child's eyes, which were neither brown nor black but a dark, inky blue. Mother's word was law. The child nodded obediently. "Good girl," whispered Mother.

Mother unscrewed an old-fashioned fountain pen. "Now the paperwork must be completed. The full name on her baptismal certificate is Maria Salome Isabella Luz de los Angeles—the 'light of the angels' surname we give to all our orphans whose surnames are unknown, but what of her first names? Do you wish to give her another?" Mother strove to sound casual.

Virgil looked at his wife. Adoption counseling stressed the need to respect ethnic origins. Would it seem disrespectful to change this rather exotic name? He said tentatively, "That's a real nice name, just a little unusual—not many girls named Salome, what with John the Baptist and that business with his head—"

"A more American name, perhaps? Brenda or Marjorie or... Nancy?" Mother suggested, racking her brains for American names. "Susan?"

Virgil breathed more easily. "Those are nice but, we always had a name picked out for a daughter if we had one. Menina Ann Walker."

Mother looked up in surprise. In old Castilian "Menina" meant a young lady-in-waiting to the queen.

"Where we come from, it's a custom to call children by names in the family. Sarah-Lynn's mother was Menina. She passed shortly after our wedding. Ann was my mom's name. How does that sound to you?"

"Menina Ann Walker—sounds very American. Very nice." Mother took her time laboriously signing the official adoption papers in handwriting she had practiced over and over, until it was so embellished with curlicues as to be almost but not quite indecipherable. "Just one more form, for the convent records." Now Mother filled in the names of the adoptive parents as Mary and John Smith, place of residence, Chicago. She wrote Isabelita's old and new names illegibly. She shook a large blot of ink onto the new one for good measure and replaced the pen in the inkwell with a smile of satisfaction. Then the Walkers signed everything—too nervous to bother reading the papers, let alone translating them. Anyone looking for Isabelita would find themselves on a wild goose chase.

"Isabelita, from today you have a new name, Menina Ann Walker. It is God's will," said Mother in Spanish. She sat up very straight, pushed her spectacles back up her nose and frowned at Sor Rosario, who was dabbing her eyes suspiciously. Sor Rosario gave a little sob and bent and hugged Isabelita hard, then Mother came round her desk and bent down stiffly and hugged her, too. "Remember, always be good." She said again in the child's ear, "Be a good girl. A very good girl. God bless and keep you. *Adios.*"

"Don't y'all worry," Virgil told the nuns. "We'll bring her up right. And keep our promise," he added. He bent down and held out the teddy bear to the child. She looked at Mother for permission. When Mother nodded, her face broke into a huge smile as she walked to him and took it. He scooped her up and said, "Hey, whose little girl we got here?" The child giggled and buried her face in the bear. "Menina honey, Mama and Daddy are going to take you for some ice cream, *helado.* You like *helado?*" The child nodded. She had no idea what helado was, but that seemed to be the right response. "And after that, we're going to get on a big airplane and fly away. This family's going home!"

Sor Rosario opened the door and followed them out, sniffing loudly. Mother listened as their footsteps faded down the corridor. Alone again, she looked up at the *monjas coronadas.* "May God guide and protect her, but I am convinced we have done the right thing. *Deo gratias,* for the Walkers, sisters. *Deo gratias.*"

CHAPTER 2

Laurel Run, Georgia, March 2000

The force of Mother's parting admonition to *"Be a good girl"* stayed with Menina long after her memories of Mother, Sor Rosario, and even the convent faded into a hazy recollection.

"Be a good girl! Be a very good girl!"

She was. Everyone in the small town of Laurel Run agreed that Menina Walker was a credit to her adoptive parents. She was polite, a straight-A student since first grade, sang in the choir of the Baptist church, helped her mother without being asked, and in high school had been one of the girls with a "good" reputation. She had never sneaked cigarettes, smoked pot, come home drunk, or experimented with sex at the drive-in. Laurel Run mothers who despaired of their own teenage daughters' behavior wondered how Sarah-Lynn Walker had managed to raise such a lady, and held her up as an example to their own girls.

The girls often felt driven to retort that it wasn't like Menina had had much chance to be anything but good. The pretty child who returned from South America with the Walkers had gone through a gawky adolescence, taller than her classmates since the age of twelve, afflicted by braces on her teeth and a reputation as the class brainbox, teacher's pet, and model of good behavior. The scrawny duckling had only emerged as a swan during her final year in high school, and by then boys saw her as the class valedictorian, not someone to date.

But she had blossomed, strikingly. At nineteen she was tall and slender, fine featured, with a smooth olive complexion and dark hair that offset her beautiful sapphire eyes. Up close, despite her ready smile, a certain tentativeness in her manner and a slight shyness in those lovely eyes betrayed the fact that her beauty was a recent development—one she was still getting used to.

Even now she didn't quite believe how she'd changed, whatever her mirror and her doting parents said. Not that she spent much time worrying about how she looked. She had had to develop the good sense not to and besides, she knew she was a bit of a nerd— she had learned long ago that the best antidote to feeling plain and left out of the giggling cliques of her girl classmates was to bury herself in her schoolwork. It made her parents proud when she got all As and was at the top of her class and the star of her high school honors program. And she actually really, really enjoyed school.

But not being popular left her with time to fill. So she found a way to do that, too.

No one had ever disparaged Menina's Hispanic origins, and indeed, the Walkers had always stressed that she should be proud of them. When they gave Menina the medal and the old book on her sixteenth birthday, just as they had promised Mother Superior they would, Virgil had made a little speech about how important her heritage was and how her birth parents might have put the medal round her neck, hoping it had some miraculous power to save their child. Menina had taken his words to heart.

But she had gleaned early on that, as a *Mano del Diablo* orphan and the Walkers' adopted daughter, she was privileged. She was uncomfortably aware of the local prejudice against Mexicans and the other Hispanic immigrants, with their battered trucks full of shabby kids, and their willingness to sweep hardware stores, pump gas, and do heavy yard work for less than the minimum wage. There was a lot of local resistance when money was donated to build a Hispanic community center on the outskirts of town, and a joke made the rounds at the high school. "What do you call a Hispanic maid? Answer: Spic and Span." When Menina heard it she was angry. That very afternoon after school, she had ridden her bicycle to the center.

She found the director's office—a small room smelling of plaster where workmen were putting up a large brass plaque noting the community center was the gift of the Pauline and Theodore Bonner II Charitable Trust—and offered to volunteer. Soon Menina was tutoring children in English and helping their parents with advice and referrals and forms for practical things like health care and food stamps. She enjoyed feeling useful, and she began to relearn Spanish in the process, though when she tried to test her Spanish on the old book from the convent, she found the book just too difficult. The *s*'s all looked like *f*'s and it just seemed to be about nuns. A convent record, like her parents said. Not all that interesting.

When the time came for college, Menina preferred not to leave home. She won a scholarship to study art history at a local all-girls junior college called Holly Hill. It was, the old ladies of Laurel Run thought, a ladylike choice, which only raised her in their estimation. As did her choice of subject.

Holly Hill was one of those anachronisms that survived in southern states. Founded by two bluestocking spinsters late in the nineteenth century as a "female academy," it had offered girls Latin, history, and sciences at a time when flower arranging, embroidery, and a smattering of French were all that was thought necessary for a young lady's education. The founders' motto was "If a girl can read Cicero she can read a recipe," and Latin, which Menina had once been uncool enough to admit she loved, had remained an entrance requirement. Thanks to wealthy alumnae, the college had added an outstanding art history department.

Being ladylike had its rewards. In her first year at college Menina had caught the eye of handsome Theo Bonner III. When Theo's sports car began to appear in the Walkers' driveway in the evenings, the whole town took note of the fact. Theo was the only son of one of the oldest and wealthiest families in Georgia. He could have been a trust fund layabout, but instead was finishing law school at the university, planning to work for a law center for the indigent instead of joining one of the prestigious Atlanta law firms, and was generally approved of as a "boy with his feet on the ground who'd amount to something." There was speculation he would go into politics, because the Bonners had been involved in state politics behind the scenes for generations.

And in a scandalous age when single women and men lived together to see if the relationship worked before getting married, Theo had done the old-fashioned thing and proposed within a year of meeting Menina.

In coffee mornings, at Bible class, garden-club luncheons, and church suppers the Walkers' friends congratulated and envied Sarah-Lynn who never tired of regaling them with the story of how Menina and Theo first set eyes on each other.

At college Menina had continued to work twice a week at the Hispanic community center, and a few weeks into her first year at Holly Hill she was rushing to one of her tutoring sessions with no time to change from paint-spattered jeans and an old sweatshirt full of holes she had worn for studio work. To her mortification, the center's director called her into the office and introduced her as their hardest-working volunteer to Pauline and Theodore Bonner, who had come to see the center in operation. Feeling awkward, Menina shook hands with a distinguished gray-haired man, a slim and well-dressed older woman, and then their son, Theo Bonner III, who shook Menina's hand and said he was in law school and had come along to see if the center's users could be referred to their free legal-advice sessions.

Theo was taller than Menina, handsome in an agreeably scruffy way, tanned with sun-bleached hair that looked like it needed cutting, and wearing a frayed sport coat that must have been inherited from a fraternity-house grab bag. The director asked Menina to give the Bonners a tour and Menina did, flustered by Theo's presence, unable to stop herself sneaking glances at him. Something about Theo made her feel like she had an electric current running through her bones. She tried to behave normally until Theo caught her looking at him, grinned back, and winked at her. When the Bonners left, Menina cursed the fact she looked like she had crawled out of a garbage can. Then she sighed and told herself not to be an idiot. Theo Bonner was way out of her league.

She was dumbfounded when he called a week later, saying he'd wormed her number out of the director, and asked Menina out. At Christmas the following year, Theo had proposed. Menina, dazzled and in love for the first time in her life, felt sure it was all a dream—of course she said yes.

Out of Sarah-Lynn's hearing the ladies speculated that Menina was engaged because she had heeded her mother's advice not to have sex before marriage, which would have been along the lines of advice given by their own mothers: "Men think, why buy the cow when I can get the milk for free?" Pretty, ladylike and deserving—Menina moved in an aura of romance and approval.

The only person less than thrilled that Menina was getting married was Menina's best friend, Becky Taliaferro, though she hadn't had any time alone with Menina to say so since Menina called her with the news she was engaged. Becky thought Theo was nice and definitely attractive and Menina seemed to be in love, but she'd never dated anybody else, so what did she know about men?

Besides, Becky and Menina had always planned to travel and discover the world after college. Becky frankly hoped Menina wasn't going to wind up as a housewife, even a rich one—Menina was too smart for that. Not just because she got As, but smart as in she liked ideas. She thought about stuff, really thought. Menina was the only person Becky knew who had a sort of scholarly streak—it was just who she was.

But loyally, she was going to be Menina's maid of honor in June. Now three months before the wedding, she had come home from college specially to choose her maid of honor dress. The two girls slouched on loungers in the Walkers' sunporch, with iced tea and a plate of cookies between them. It was a comfortably shabby room—a repository for old rattan furniture, sun-faded cushions, and back issues of *Good Housekeeping*—and had been Menina and Becky's playroom ever since the day Becky's family moved next door to the Walkers. Seven-year-old tearaway Becky had grown tired of teasing the cat, ripping open packing boxes and driving her mother crazy, and climbed the fence to make friends with seven-year-old Menina. Before long, naughty, irrepressible, blonde Becky and shy, dark-haired, well-behaved Menina were inseparable, always together at one house or the other. The Taliaferros stopped referring to Menina as "that nice little Walker girl" and nicknamed her "the Child of Light" because around Menina, evil little Becky behaved beautifully.

As children the girls had built tents with card tables and blankets in the sunporch, had rainy-day picnics; as preteens they huddled over a forbidden Ouija board; in high school they pushed the card tables back and practised for cheerleader tryouts. In their senior year they sat at the card tables filling out college applications together. At the time, Becky teased that Holly Hill was a dull choice, while Menina quipped that Becky's eagerness to embrace a hectic social schedule and join a sorority with hundreds of other students at the University of Georgia filled Menina with dread.

Neither imagined how quickly their choices would lead them in different directions. If Menina was on the road to matrimony in short order, Becky had seized the opportunity to spread her wings. Abandoning her preschool teaching course, she had surprised everyone who knew her by being accepted to the Grady School of Journalism where, between boyfriends, she had become surprisingly focused on a career as a foreign correspondent, like Marie Colvin or Christiane Amanpour. So people would take her seriously, Becky compensated for her pretty face, wide blue eyes, and blonde curls with a gold stud in her nostril, a tattoo on her shoulder, and her current boyfriend's motorcycle jacket. All of it, from journalism to the jacket, gave her mother fits.

Together again in their childhood haunt, for a minute it seemed impossible to be discussing such grown-up concerns like weddings and careers. How, both wondered, had they got to this stage of their lives already? Then Menina said, "You haven't seen this yet. Look! Isn't it beautiful?" and banished their childhood ghosts. She had twisted her engagement ring—a big diamond flanked by sapphires—inward, saving up for the big moment. Now she twisted it back and fluttered the fingers of her left hand at Becky. The setting sun shone through the dogwood trees into the sunporch, sending little sparkles from the diamond dancing on the wall.

"Oh Child of *Light*!" exclaimed Becky, leaning over from her lounger. "It's amazing! Did Theo choose it or did Mother Bonner point him in the right direction?"

"Theo chose it. He said sapphires matched my eyes! Isn't that sweet? But 'Mother Bonner'—*please!*" Menina laughed. "Just between us, Mother Machiavelli's more like it! I had no idea until I got to know her better. Don't you remember, she was in that *Vogue* feature last year about women who are 'Old Southern Money, New Southern Politics and the Power behind the Throne'? That woman is politics all the way."

Becky munched sugar cookies. "Why doesn't she just cut out the middleman and run for office herself?"

"Oh, you know, she can go all fluffy and talk about politics being a man's game, but I think she likes the string pulling, fundraising dinners and stuff. Thanks to her the Bonner family's got political contacts up the ga-zing. I don't know whether Theo really has ambitions, anyway. He talks about it, but he's only just passed the bar exam. He wants to spend a couple of years working at the legal advice center."

"The indigent's friend? And speaking of indigent, are the two of you planning to live on what he makes there? You'll have to get a job won't you?"

"Well it is peanuts, but Pauline took me to lunch after we got engaged at Christmas and explained that Theo's trust fund would support us. Don't look at me like that! I have plans, of course I'm going to work! It's just that it'll be a help if I don't have to work full time while I write my scholarship thesis."

"A junior college and you practically have to write a master's dissertation. Sheesh!"

Menina nodded. "Yeah, it's harder than I thought it would be when I applied." Her scholarship had been a big one—with its small classes, well-equipped studios, and high ratio of teachers to students, Holly Hill was expensive—but it had a condition attached that meant few girls applied for it. The scholarship was the gift of an art-loving Holly Hill alumna in the late nineteenth century. She wanted to encourage Holly Hill's "lady" scholars to contribute to the study of art history without engaging in unseemly competition with men. Recipients signed a pledge to write an original thesis on an original art-related topic of their choice after they graduated—the scholarship included a special grant for travel if further research was necessary. These theses were then privately published by Holly Hill and available to the academic world at large. The stinger was in the penalty clause. If a scholarship recipient failed to deliver her thesis within a year of graduation she had a legal obligation to pay back her scholarship.

Menina had been so excited about giving her parents the good news about her scholarship she hadn't mentioned that part and she still hadn't.

"Sure focuses your mind," said Menina, "but once that's out of the way, I'll finish my degree at the University of Georgia. Then maybe graduate school. I really like art history, and I'm planning to work in a museum someday. We'll see. There'll be a lot to juggle with classes, a part-time job, cooking dinner, all that stuff, but Theo's pretty busy so I have time. We saw some cute apartments near the campus, in that section of old houses. A lot of Theo's married fraternity brothers live in the neighborhood, and everyone takes turns to have the others for dinner. Mama's already copying recipes for this and that for when it's our turn."

Menina didn't mention that she had come away from her lunch with Pauline with a rather different view of Menina and Theo's married life. To Menina's dismay, then irritated astonishment, Pauline had made it clear that Theo was working on building his electable image for the future. As Mrs. Theo Bonner III, Menina would join the Junior League, do volunteer work, and attend charity lunches to network with the wives of prominent businessmen, the kind who made large political contributions. Menina knew it would be waving a red rag at a bull to repeat Pauline's words to Becky. She would just have to think of a tactful way to stick to her own plans.

Menina sighed and crunched the ice in her glass. "The hardest part was finding an original topic, but at least now I've got one. When they were cleaning out the library at Holly Hill a few months ago, the librarian gave me an old book nobody wanted and I found it in there. It was privately printed back in 1900 and had some portraits by an artist called Tristan Mendoza, painted in Spain in the sixteenth century. The portraits are all women, dressed up to the eyeballs, no low necks or anything, like in those English portraits of royal mistresses that have their bosoms practically in your face. These ladies have rosaries and prayer books, but then while you're looking at them, they start to look different—well, sort of hot and come-hither like the bosomy ones. Pornographic; it's hard to explain. None of my teachers had heard of Tristan Mendoza but they saw what I meant, and said the Spanish court was pretty straitlaced at the time—the Christians had just defeated the Moors and the Moors were puritanical in some ways so the Christians had to out-puritan them to prove they were superior. But you want to hear the most interesting thing?"

"I'm all ears." Becky sighed.

"I got the magnifying glass to take a closer look at the reproductions, and under Tristan Mendoza's signature he drew a bird! A little swallow exactly the same as the swallow on my medal!"

"Why?"

"That's what I wondered, and from the research I've done nobody else seems to know. So—original thesis subject Tristan Mendoza and the swallow. If the swallow meant something to Tristan Mendoza, maybe it meant something to my birth parents. I just have to find out. My dad says they must have been Catholics, and believed it had miraculous powers or something." Menina's eyes filled with tears like they always did when she thought about her birth family hoping the medal would save her life. She tried not to think how much she wished they could know the wonderful man she was marrying or see her in her wedding dress. She rubbed them away hastily. "And get this, the Prado is the only museum with any of Tristan Mendoza's work, so I actually have to go to the Prado! The scholarship even pays for it. I'm thinking I should take the old book the nuns gave me to the Prado. It's pretty old and just sitting in a drawer in my room. They must have an old manuscript department, or if they don't they'll know who does."

"Madrid!" Becky reached over and they high-fived. "Fabulous! I hope you find out what you want to know. Now, it's getting dark, I better go; a guy's supposed to call me about a project that I hope will get me a summer internship at the *New York Times*."

"Oh Becky! I talk too much! Tell me!"

"OK, remember that local guy, Junior, kind of dumb kid who dropped out of high school, used to work at the gas station and then got the death penalty for killing a couple? Well he's on death row trying to win an appeal or get a retrial—you know, he had a fuckwit public defender, evidence full of holes, et cetera, miscarriage of justice, and his new lawyer's keen to get some publicity but till now Junior won't talk to anybody. But I got in touch with his lawyer and Junior remembered me from when I used to fill up Mama's car and said since I was the only girl not too snooty to talk to him then he'll talk to me now. His lawyer's supposed to call and give me a date to come to the penitentiary."

"I bet you haven't told your mother you're going to the penitentiary!"

"Er, no. I'll surprise her. Gotta hop."

They hugged. "*Hasta la vista*, Child of Light," called Becky as she disappeared over the fence.

"Becky hasn't changed," muttered Sarah-Lynn darkly, closing the door. "What possessed her to stick that thing in her nose? Please tell me she'll take it out for the wedding. What color dress does she want, the blue or the lavender?"

"Oh, sorry, Mama, forgot to ask her! We got carried away talking about other stuff. I was telling her about my thesis and—"

"That thesis again! Honey, it'll have to wait; there's a little matter of your wedding dress fitting and we've got to decide on a silver pattern and finish the guest list before the invitations can go out."

"Later, Mama." Menina escaped to set the table. She knew she ought to care more about dotted swiss versus tulle, flower arrangements and silver patterns, and all the things that brought joy to her mother's heart, but she didn't. The bride thing wasn't the big deal, the big deal was living with Theo—she couldn't wait. Aside from the fact they could *finally* have sex, it would be heaven to wake up together, knowing that she'd see him every evening, too. She hugged herself thinking about it.

While she knew for a fact that other girls had a flourishing sex life without a scarlet *H* for harlot appearing on their foreheads, she wasn't exactly brimming with sexual confidence. Menina had indeed listened to her mother's warnings about sex before marriage and all that stuff about cows and free milk. And Theo, who could have picked any girl in the world, had picked her. Deep down Menina thought maybe her mother had been right. She had been too terrified of losing him to risk finding out.

CHAPTER 3

Laurel Run, Georgia, April 2000

Menina and Theo hadn't decided about their honeymoon. They were thinking of a week in Venice, another in Paris—Theo's choice, not that Menina was complaining, but if they could extend their honeymoon another week it would be fun to go to Madrid together. She could visit the Prado, see the Tristan Mendozas there, and find what other information the Prado had. She was quite excited by the idea and sure Theo would like it.

Meanwhile she drove her mother crazy by slipping away to the library when she was supposed to be doing some wedding task or other. She could only find one reference book that mentioned Tristan Mendoza, who had been born around 1487 in Andalusia, studied in Italy, and returned to Spain where he was hugely successful until he abruptly abandoned court. It wasn't because he had died—a later contemporary reference referred to "the great artist Mendoza, now the poor pilgrim and wretched mendicant."

The only other bit of information that proved he hadn't died at court was a signed work from this later period, documented as having cropped up in England before World War II. It was a painting of a woman in a cloak, bearing Mendoza's signature with the characteristic small bird beneath, and bought at a Sotheby's auction by a wealthy English collector in London. Unfortunately that painting no longer existed. During the Blitz, a German bomb destroyed the collector's Mayfair house. After the war, an inventory of the contents of the London house, including the art collection, was found in papers kept at the collector's country house. The inventory referred to a painting of "an unknown holy woman, a rare, late work of Tristan Mendoza."

The reference book suggested there might be more of his work in private Spanish collections if they hadn't been looted or destroyed in the Spanish Civil War in the 1930s, but his only known paintings were in the Prado. Menina thought this was pretty convenient, and if the Prado did know something about private collections, they could put her in touch.

Menina planned to ask Theo about Madrid the following weekend. The Bonners were holding a special dinner party that Theo said was important for them to attend.

When he came to pick her up that night, she was excited and nervous. Pauline had called to tell her the dinner party included the governor and his wife, an elderly state legislator, and some important and influential campaign contributors. Menina had gone shopping and was feeling glamorous in a new scoop-neck black dress with a sassy ruffled skirt, and Sarah-Lynn's pearls. Her hair swung over her shoulders, and her engagement ring sparkled on her left hand. She kissed her parents good night and the couple left hand in hand.

In the car Theo was preoccupied, so to fill the silence Menina chatted about wanting to go to Madrid. He muttered something about being too busy.

Too *busy*? For a honeymoon or for Spain? She took a deep breath and reminded herself that her scholarship debt was her problem, not his, that she was the one interested in the swallow, not him. She would be a good sport about it. "Oh. It's OK. I understand. I'll manage by myself and go later. The scholarship will cover it."

Theo interrupted, "The thing about tonight's dinner is, we're both on show." He took one hand off the steering wheel and put it on her knee. "Things are moving sooner than we expected. Old Tubby Gaines who's been in the state legislature forever is retiring after one more term—and that's created an opportunity for me. Tonight they want to discuss precampaign strategy. It depends on whether voters will see me as a solid citizen, not a rich kid. If I get elected, a couple of terms in the state legislature would pave the way for a Senate race in the future. How about that? Exciting, huh? In fact, everything hinges on you tonight."

"Me?"

"You. Because I'm a Bonner it's easy to discredit my bid for the nomination; they'll say I'm a young rich guy dabbling in politics. But with a lovely wife and a young family, bingo, I'm John Kennedy. You're beautiful and smart without being a ballbuster or a pushy career woman. You go to church and, well, you're such a lady that I could be an ax murderer and you'd make me look good. And with your background, you know, your adoption, being Hispanic, your volunteer work at the Hispanic center, you'll draw the Hispanic vote. That's the crucial demographic these days. So brush up your Spanish, honey, and you can translate my campaign speeches." He gave her knee a squeeze.

"Mmmm." Menina looked out the window, feeling deflated. Her own plans had just been swept aside like dust.

Nevertheless, at dinner Menina did her best. She made polite small talk until dessert, when Theo's mother steered the conversation toward her female guests and the volunteer activities that filled their free time and offered such wonderful networking opportunities. The women responded with a chorus of offers. One said the symphony fund-raising group could use someone young on their committee. Another offered there was a vacancy on the board of her children's charity that she was sure would be perfect for Menina. A third insisted Menina should come and talk to her about a museum trust that had been run by old ladies from the same families for too long. When Menina tried to think of a way to refuse politely, Theo's mother pointedly told Menina, "Women wait years for invitations to joint these very high-profile causes."

Menina rebelled. She managed a tight smile and said that she wouldn't take on any new commitments; she had plenty of commitments of her own between her thesis and finishing college. The governor overheard, raised his eyebrows. Theo scowled at her and shook his head slightly and his mother asked sweetly if Menina's little projects couldn't be put on hold. Shouldn't a wife put her husband's career first? Menina stabbed her spoon into her peach melba, but was too polite to argue in public.

On the way home Theo asked why couldn't she see that the ladies were doing her a favor.

"Doing you and your mother a favor, you mean! My 'little projects!' Please!"

"Menina, be reasonable. My mother's going to pull strings so you don't have to write the damn thesis, because you won't have time to go running off to Spain or burying yourself in the library. We need to look for a house—my parents will buy it as a wedding present—and you'll have to decorate it and then entertain. I know my mother's talked to you about stuff, like the Junior League. And the other thing is, we should start a family soon—maybe not within nine months, people will start counting, but we could have a baby by the end of the first year. Voters want to see a candidate's family on the campaign posters. It was one thing to mess around with art at college, but now you need to grow up!" he said irritably. "It's only a medal, not a divining rod to locate your birth family."

Menina couldn't believe her ears. "Your mother will do *what*? And start a family? I won't have a baby just so people will vote for you! I understand what's important to you, but something's important to me, too! And…and…for your information, I'll go to Spain, with or without you!"

Theo slammed his foot on the accelerator and the sports car skidded and nearly slid off the road, scaring Menina. Maybe she hadn't thought about the future as much as she should have. His words conjured up a picture very different from the ideas she'd had about living together in a student apartment, having their friends to dinner, telling each other about their interesting days, maybe planning a few more foreign trips before children tied them down. Instead it seemed she'd be up to her ears in ladies' lunches, home decoration, charities, and children she would probably have to raise all by herself because Theo would be so busy with his important life.

How could they have such different ideas about their marriage? Maybe she didn't know Theo as well as she thought she did.

"Theo?"

No answer.

"We need to talk."

No answer.

"It's not just about a trip or a baby. It's about us, our lives together, how we get what we both want out of life. It matters."

No answer.

Menina took a deep breath. "The wedding's picked up steam like a runaway train and we haven't had time to ourselves since you proposed, but now let's talk this over calmly."

No answer.

What on earth was going on? She had never seen him taciturn and hostile like this, not the Theo she loved but an angry stranger. It frightened her, enough to blurt out, "If we can't talk, we should postpone the wedding until we can."

Silence.

She expected Theo would drive past the lake, but at the last minute he braked hard, sending the car into a skid as he turned off the road. He pulled up at the edge of the lake and turned off the engine, still silent. It was a lovely night with a full moon reflected off the water's surface, and cicadas were singing—a marked contrast to the poisoned atmosphere in the car. Finally Theo let out a big sigh and touched a button to recline their seats slightly. He lowered the armrest so he could put his arm around Menina's shoulders. Menina felt stiff and miserable.

"Menina, I'm sorry. Mad at me?" he asked, nuzzling her ear, then just underneath her ear and down her neck.

"Yes, I am," she muttered, trying to ignore the way kissing that spot always sent a jolt down her spine.

"You're right; we need to work this out now," he murmured, nuzzling her neck until she finally relaxed against him, feeling the knot of misery loosen. Still they needed to talk now, not make out.

"You're upset. Kiss me and then we'll talk," Theo said in her ear, then kissed her, long and deep, in the way that always left her breathless and less interested in talking.

"I wish we were married now," she whispered when she came up for air. They kissed again and Theo pushed the button and reclined the seats even more and his kiss became more urgent. "It's hard to talk lying back like this," Menina protested.

"Let's just do it!" he muttered in her ear, nudging a knee between her legs. "C'mon," he said, "then a good girl like you will have to marry me and we won't need this discussion."

"I want to Theo, but…but it's not long now and I'd rather be in a bed where we have all night, not a car on my way home. And we really need to discuss things and anyways, this seat's not all that comfortable and the gear shift is—his breath tickled and she giggled. "Theo, stop it! No!" she said, trying to push him away.

But Theo was breathing heavily in her ear and didn't seem to hear what she was saying. He certainly didn't move away. He was a lot bigger than she was and she couldn't seem to move; he was pinning her down. Then he was doing something else that made her push as hard as she could. "Theo! No, Theo! Stop!

"*Theo!*"

Then she was fighting him. "No...no, no! Stop, Theo, stop!... Theo, don't! Not like this. No, no, no! *Please stop! I don't want to!*" Her voice rose to a frantic plea. He couldn't be doing this! He *wouldn't*—but he didn't stop. Not even when she screamed. He clamped a hard hand over her mouth and she choked and fought to breathe, blind panic lending her strength, but it wasn't enough. He was bigger and stronger and rough, but the shock of what was happening was worse than the pain.

When Theo finally moved, Menina struggled upright. Her breath came raggedly and she began to shake. Too shocked to cry, she heard herself making a dry whimpering sound, and a monster with Theo's face was saying, "Menina! Come on, what's the big deal, really? It doesn't matter, we're getting married! In a couple of months we'll laugh about this. Who knows, we may even have started that first baby." He zipped up his fly.

Doesn't matter? Laugh? She could still feel his hand on her mouth and the rest of her felt as if she had been beaten up and turned inside out. "Take. Me. Home," Menina said with as much dignity as she could summon through her gritted teeth while trying to straighten her clothes.

"Honey, don't make a big thing out of sex before we're married! Lighten up! You'll enjoy it next time. I promise."

Wedding? Next time? Was she hearing right? Was he trying to persuade her that rape was OK? She felt dizzy. Then doubt began creeping in. Sarah-Lynn always said a girl was in control. Had her dress been too sexy? Menina had thought it was pretty, and she would hardly have made it out the door past Sarah-Lynn if she hadn't looked ladylike, but had she sent out the wrong message? And she had acted passionate, kissing Theo the way she had—maybe he took that to mean yes. Was getting raped *her own fault?* Uncertainty eroded the last shreds of her self-confidence but didn't mend her shattered heart.

When they pulled up in front of her house Theo said, "OK, we'll talk if you want and everything will be fine." Menina didn't try to answer, just flung open her car door, tore her engagement ring off and hurled it into the distance. Then she raced for the house.

"I'll see you tomorrow, when you've calmed down," he said, rushing after her.

"I n-n-never w-want to see you again!" Menina slammed the front door and locked it, then ran to her room, threw herself onto her bed where she buried her head in her pillow to muffle her screams and cried herself into a fitful sleep.

She woke early with a heavy head, her life in ruins, and the bleak certainty that she must never, ever let a word of what happened cross her lips. A girl who brought an accusation of rape invited trouble from the accused's friends, who as often as not joined forces and told the police the girl was a lying slut. That she had a reputation of being hot for sex, all the time, with anybody. Theo had a lot of friends, an entire band of fraternity brothers, plus there were the Bonners—they had power to do anything they wanted. Who knew what that would be if she accused their golden boy of rape, what stories they would make sure were circulated? If Sarah-Lynn heard Menina publicly called a cock-teaser and a slut, it would break her heart. Virgil would go after Theo with his shotgun, and end up in the electric chair for murder. Sarah-Lynn would be widowed and people would whisper that after all they had done for her, Menina had been trash who ruined the Walkers.

No, she could never, never tell anybody—not the police, not her parents, not even Becky. A turmoil of emotion and doubts and shock swirling in her mind, she grabbed scissors and cut all her clothes from the night before into tiny shreds, then flushed them down her toilet. Afterward she stood sobbing in a scalding shower, scrubbing and scrubbing at her body until the water ran cold. Numbly she pulled on her clothes, and went to face her parents.

At the breakfast table the Walkers were reading the Sunday papers before church. Virgil said, "You coming down with something, honey? You don't look too good."

Menina wanted to scream the truth, but made an effort and confined herself to crumbling a piece of toast with shaking hands, her engagement ring conspicuously absent. "Theo and I broke up."

There was a shocked silence.

"Broke up! How could you break up?" wailed Sarah-Lynn, while Virgil put an arm around her shoulders.

"What happened?" he asked.

Menina stammered out that Theo didn't understand what was important to her, then trailed off into silence, tearing a paper napkin to shreds under the table.

"I still don't understand!" said Sarah-Lynn incredulously.

"Mama, *please*..." Menina croaked hoarsely.

"Well, what's everybody going to think?"

Menina hadn't thought she had any tears left, but now it seemed that she did. Virgil hugged her tighter and poured her a cup of coffee. "Drink this," he said.

The telephone rang. Virgil answered and mouthed, "Theo," muffling the receiver in his shoulder. Menina's hand holding the coffee cup started to shake, and coffee spilled everywhere. She shook her head and fled back to her room. She refused to talk on the telephone or see Theo later when Virgil knocked at her bedroom door to say he was at the front door, wearing a sorry expression.

"Make him leave, Daddy! Please!"

Minutes later Virgil came back and closed the bedroom door behind him. "You want to tell your mother and me what's going on? This isn't like you."

"I don't want to see him. Ever."

Virgil looked at her shrewdly. "Are you pregnant? Honey, it's not the end of the world. So what if you two have a baby less than nine months after the wedding? We always wanted to be grandparents; a little sooner is fine with us."

Menina stared at him in horror. *Pregnant?* She hadn't thought about that horrible possibility! Had Theo *wanted* to get her pregnant?

"No!" Menina exclaimed, crossing her fingers and praying that was true.

"I'll try and calm your mother down," said Virgil after a minute.

Theo kept calling but Menina refused to speak to him. Pauline Bonner called Sarah-Lynn, mother to mother, trying to find out what the trouble was. She understood there had been an argument, but Theo wouldn't tell her anything. She hoped "the children" would work things out soon.

Alerted by her mother that something was wrong at the Walkers', Becky cut her Monday classes and drove back to Laurel Run. Menina was lying on the bed in her darkened room with the curtains closed at midday. Becky walked over a sea of used tissues on the carpet to the bed. "Menina?"

"Go 'way, I'm sleeping," was the answer, in the kind of croaky voice hours of solid crying brought on.

Becky pulled open the curtains and brought her a glass of water from the bathroom. "You can run but you can't hide, Child of Light. Drink this and talk to me."

Menina sat up and Becky smothered an exclamation of dismay. Menina looked awful—hair tangled, big shadows under her eyes, and a haggard expression Becky had never seen before. She flinched when Becky hugged her but wouldn't say what was wrong, just that she and Theo weren't getting married.

"Oh Menina! Was that Theo's idea?"

"No."

"Is it another girl?"

"No."

"His mother? She's a bossy bitch."

"Not her."

"Well, um…is he gay? Sometimes men don't realize it themselves—"

"No," said Menina stonily. "Don't talk about it."

"Are you pregnant? Really that's not such a big deal these…"

Menina moaned and buried her face in the pillow. "NO!"

"Did he give you…some kind of disease?" Becky's stomach lurched with fear. Menina *couldn't* be HIV positive? Menina was the only girl Becky knew who bought her mother's line about no sex until she got married. She *couldn't* have caught anything. Buried in her pillow Menina was shaking her head. "Did he hit you? I don't care who he is, if he did we're going to call the police and have him arrested," said Becky.

"No police! Forget it, Becky. Go back to college. I'm tired of talking." Menina curled up in a fetal position, pulled the quilt over her head, and wouldn't say anything else. Becky left the room quietly and shut the door.

Outside in the hall Sarah-Lynn was bringing a plate with a chicken-salad sandwich, Menina's favorite. "She won't eat," she whispered to Becky. "Hasn't touched a bite for two days. And next week there's a bridal shower and a big luncheon and all those invitations to address. You reckon it's just wedding nerves?"

Becky cautiously said, "Maybe. Mrs. Walker, give me that sandwich." She took the plate and marched back into Menina's room. She pulled the quilt off her friend's head and said firmly, "Whatever happened, you've got to get away from Theo and your mother and his mother and the wedding craziness while you figure things out. The scholarship lets you travel if you want and you're going to use it."

"What? I don't want to go anywhere. I…"

"Yes, you do." Becky handed her a Kleenex. "You want to go to Spain and you're going to Spain. Next Saturday…"

Menina sat up slowly and said, "*What?*" again, like she wasn't hearing well. Then she started crying incoherently again. Trying not to show how this behavior alarmed her, Becky said firmly, "Here's the deal—there's a three-week trip organized by some big cheese art professor at the university leaving for Madrid next weekend. It was supposed to be just for the art history graduate students, but they're advertising spare tickets in the campus newspaper because they haven't filled up all their places. The flight and a place to stay are all included, a YMCA hostel or something. They're doing the cultural crap—museums, cathedrals. Your idea of a good time. And yes, you *are* going! It's a chance to go to the Prado like you wanted."

"Oh Becky, I can't…there's packing and my parents…you know…they'd worry…" Menina waved her hand feebly at nothing.

"Oh, I can totally see it's better to sit here crying in a dark room in broad daylight—that doesn't worry them in the least. A few more days of it and they'll have your ass in a loony bin, drugged to the eyeballs. Besides, when you hear what your mother's got lined up, it won't be pretty when she starts canceling things. So eat while I call to grab one of those spare tickets for you, then I'll tell your parents."

Menina stared at her blankly, then picked up the plate, looked at the sandwich, and sighed. "They won't like it." Her stomach hurt. Maybe she should try and eat.

Becky snorted. "The professor who organized the tour is a woman, Professor Serafina Somebody, Spanish, which is why she's guiding the tour. Probably a dried-up old bag with the kind of ideas about being ladylike that your mother would love. Anyway, you got a better idea?"

The sandwich stopped halfway to Menina's mouth. "No." She took a small bite.

"Didn't think so. That sandwich better be gone when I get back. Then we'll pack."

Menina ate her sandwich like chewing hurt, but she ate it. She was distractedly filling a suitcase with jeans and sweatshirts when Becky returned from a difficult conversation with the Walkers. "Not that stuff!" Becky exclaimed, emptying the suitcase. She tried to sound upbeat. "Get with the program. In Madrid, you go out all night. They never sleep." Becky held up skirts and tops and trousers against each other and squinted critically to see what matched up.

"Never mind that stuff. I won't be going out."

Becky stuck her head out of the closet. "You need to go out; you never dated anyone but Theo. There are other fish in the sea, you know."

"I don't care!" Menina snapped. The thought of men caused a surge of stomach pain that doubled her up. She rushed to the bathroom to find the pain she'd had all afternoon was cramps; she had got her period. Relieved not to be pregnant, Menina took a shower and dressed, and after Becky had gone, she sat down to supper with the Walkers, trying hard to act normal and not cry. She made it to dessert and fled back to her room.

For the next week everything was strained at the Walkers' house. Sarah-Lynn prayed it was just wedding nerves. She turned the house upside down for things that might come in handy on the trip, and stuffed them into the backpack Virgil had ordered for Menina express from L.L. Bean.

Becky drove back to Laurel Run especially to deliver a large brown envelope with plane tickets, the itinerary, and information from the organizer. Menina emerged from her fog of misery long enough to realize Becky must have canceled her interview at the penitentiary.

"Oh Becky, I'm so sorry!"

"I'm rescheduling it. Don't worry, it wasn't that important," said Becky unconvincingly. Menina felt worse than ever—she was a terrible friend to Becky.

A woman from Sarah-Lynn's Bible study class brought over an old-fashioned guidebook to Spain, published by a Christian publishing house, for Menina. Menina thanked her lethargically and put it on her bedside table. *That* was staying here.

Virgil stopped making jokes the way he usually did, while Sarah-Lynn's avoidance of anything to do with weddings was painful. Menina was too depressed to look forward to the trip, but by the end of the week she thought Spain couldn't be any worse than home.

On Saturday afternoon the Walkers drove her to the Atlanta airport. Menina boarded and slipped into her window seat, and after the plane had filled up, a last-minute arrival flung herself into the aisle seat. Menina was glad to see there was a vacant seat between them. She didn't feel like being elbow to elbow with another person. Soon the Atlanta airport was rolling by outside Menina's window—slowly, then faster, then dropping away as the plane lifted off, banked and climbed. Menina watched the evening lights of greater Atlanta grow smaller and smaller below, feeling cut adrift from everything she knew. Before long a flight attendant came down the aisle pushing a drink cart. "Would you like something to drink?"

Menina managed a tight smile and said, "A Coke, please. No. Wait...maybe...bourbon. A big one." Virgil drank bourbon. When Sarah-Lynn wasn't watching.

"Big bourbon it is. And a splash?"

"Oh. You mean water. Thanks." The attendant smiled and rattled ice cubes into a glass, emptied two miniatures into it and added a little water from a big bottle. She handed it over with a handful of extra little bottles and a conspiratorial wink. "You must be with the bachelorette party. Like I told the others, might as well start the party now." Menina had been about to refuse the miniatures. Now she took them and forced a smile. "Thanks. How did you know?"

"Spain's real popular for bachelorette parties, you know—sightseeing, great bars, great shopping." The attendant grinned. "And a *long* way from anybody who might care what they're up to. Y'all have a great time." Then she turned her attention to the woman in the aisle seat, who waved her away.

Menina stared at her glass. She had drunk perhaps a dozen glasses of wine in her life and didn't care for alcohol, but the smell of bourbon reminded her of her father. She took a big gulp, then gagged. The vile taste seemed appropriate. Menina poured another two miniatures into the melting ice, and downed them determinedly. After a while she had another miniature.

She shook her head when dinner was offered. She felt better—but worse, too; everything was blurry. She must be drunk. She drank the last two bourbon miniatures straight from the bottle. She no longer cared about anything. She could no longer taste anything. Becky had been right, this was a good idea, Menina thought, and passed out cold.

She came to, disoriented and feeling worse than she ever had in her life. Sun streamed through the plane window and Menina blinked, piecing yesterday together with a growing sense of horror. The pilot said they were holding to land at Malaga airport. She turned to the woman in the aisle seat and croaked, *"Malaga?* Aren't we going to Madrid?"

The woman looked up from something she was writing and gave Menina a funny look over the tops of the wire-rimmed glasses that had slid halfway down her nose. She was middle-aged and rather striking, with a distinctive streak of gray in her black hair. Despite a night on the plane, she looked elegant in a black cashmere sweater and jersey skirt, accented with a modern silver necklace and bracelets. Menina realized to her horror this was the tour organizer. Her photo had been on a welcome message with the tickets. Professor Serafina Lennox, professor and author, the Spanish art expert—the one person in the world, in fact, who might know about Tristan Mendoza. Her heart sank. "You're Professor Lennox, aren't you?" she asked weakly.

The woman raised her eyebrows as if to ask what on earth Menina was doing on the tour, extracted a card from her handbag, and gave it to Menina. "Yes. So nice to get acquainted with students. I don't recall you from any of my classes. You are...?" Menina mumbled her name as she put the card in her jeans pocket, wondering how to explain what she was doing here. She couldn't think of a good way to do that just at the moment.

Professor Lennox said, "We've been diverted to Malaga because of bad weather. You were...er...asleep when it got rough, so I pulled your seatbelt tighter and I noticed your lovely medal. Is it old?"

"Actually I don't know much about it. I'm sorry." It hurt to talk, and Menina didn't feel up to explaining about the medal or her thesis. She turned away and peered out the window. After the storm, the air was clear and bright and below them dark-blue mountains were topped with snow. As the plane descended, Menina could see the coast in the distance, and beyond it, the gray-blue Mediterranean. Her hand closed nervously around her medal as the plane sank lower and lower, the wheels hitting the tarmac with a thud that made her aching brain bounce.

"Welcome to Spain," said Professor Lennox dryly.

CHAPTER 4

Spain, Holy Week, April 2000

Malaga was airport hell. Menina lost track of Professor Lennox, the only person she recognized from her flight. At the information desk where Menina tried to find out when her flight to Madrid would leave, a harassed young woman threw up her hands. "Nobody knows about your charter. Is *Semana Santa*! I don't know. Maybe it doesn't go today. You must wait over there." She pointed vaguely toward the departures hall, another heaving mass of people. Menina felt she either had to lie down and die from her hangover or get herself to Madrid somehow and meet her group at the hostel.

"Is there another way I can get to Madrid—a train, or a bus?"

"Trains impossible this week unless you have a reservation, is *Semana Santa*, but you can take a bus from the airport. There, past the telephones. Longer than train but nice sceneries. You get there tonight."

Next Menina tried to call her parents on a pay phone. It wasn't easy. The operator's lisping Spanish sounded different from the Latin American accent she was used to, and when she couldn't understand the operator finally hung up. An elderly woman stopped and showed her what to do, and finally there was a ringing tone and her father answered. Sleepily. "Menina? You OK?"

No, not really. "I'm fine. Sorry, I forgot about the time difference. It must be four thirty in the morning…"

At the other end Virgil yawned. "Naw, it's OK, honey. Glad you got to Madrid in one piece. Make the most of it. Go shopping with that new Visa card. Get your mother a pocketbook; I hear they got nice leather in Spain. Don't worry about anything else. By the time you get home the whole mess will have blown over."

"OK, we'll cross that bridge when we come to it…but I'm not in Madrid yet, Dad. There was bad weather and we got diverted to Malaga. It's kind of crazy at the airport, and nobody knows when there'll be another plane to fly us up to Madrid. Rather than sleep on the airport floor I'm taking a bus up to Madrid. I'll get there tonight."

"You be careful. Don't go talking to strange men!"

"Strange men!" Menina couldn't help laughing. "I'm not five years old."

"By the way, speaking of strange men, last night after we got back from the airport a man and a woman, nice couple, rang the doorbell, looking for you. They'd seen that article in the paper—well, you know the one, it was in yesterday—anyhow, they had had something to do with the Catholic Church and the adoptions of you hurricane kids. Your mother served them cake and coffee and we showed them your file for old times' sake. They said they'd love to see your medal, it was supposed to be real old, and asked when you'd be back. I told them not for a while, you'd just gone off to study some old painter in Spain, and they…"

The phone made a pipping sound. Menina found she had no coins left.

"…They had some idea our last name was Smith, asked when we moved here from Chicago—don't know where they got that—but we straightened that out and…"

"My money's run out! Bye, call you when I..." and the line went dead.

Menina hung up and picked up her backpack. It weighed a ton. She hadn't paid attention to that in Atlanta, but now she opened it to see why. In case the airline lost her bag she had put in a sweater, a spare T-shirt, a change of underwear, clean socks, tampons, and the velvet bag that contained the old book from the nuns because she really didn't want to lose that if her suitcase went missing. She had tossed in the small Latin dictionary she had used in high school, too, in case she needed to tell the people at the Prado what the Latin part was—it seemed too short to be a prayer book. They could figure out the Spanish part themselves.

She dug deeper and found the miniature toiletries, and aspirin, some small towels that expanded when wet that Menina had once used at summer camp, and a new travel bathrobe, all stuffed in by her mother. Then she exclaimed, "Oh no!" At the very bottom, her mother had hidden the heavy old guidebook to Spain that Menina had tried to leave behind. In the side pocket Sarah-Lynn had put in a couple of spiral notebooks, ballpoint pens, and Menina's favorite Hershey bars. In another side there were two bottles of water Menina had bought at the airport in Atlanta.

The woman who sold her a bus ticket said, "Is *Semana Santa*," and everything was crazy; there were no direct buses. She would have to go toward Ronda, then change. She gave Menina a bus schedule, pointing at a stop where she would have to transfer. And Menina mustn't miss it; there was only the one bus a day to Madrid from there.

The bus driver, a swarthy man whose stomach hung over his waistband, stood by the open baggage hold sucking a toothpick. Menina showed him her ticket and the name of the place she was supposed to change buses for Madrid. "*Sí! Le dire.*" I'll tell you. The driver smiled, flashing a gold tooth before throwing her suitcase in. He held out his hand for the backpack but Menina shook her head. She'd take it to her seat and read her guidebook.

Menina found two seats to herself, took two aspirin and fished out the guidebook. Fifteen minutes later the bus pulled out of the airport, going west along a coastal highway dotted with construction sites and new holiday villa developments. Out to sea an oil tanker hovered on the horizon, sun danced on the waves, and a gleaming white gin palace motored closer to shore as they wound along the coast.

Then the bus turned inland and the villas gave way to new-planted fields and an occasional old farmhouse with wooden lean-tos added on the back. Sun shimmered on the silvery leaves of olive trees planted in rows on walled terraces. Plodding horse-drawn carts laden with firewood, women in black stockings and cardigans and faded headscarves carrying loaves of bread, an elderly couple leading a donkey with wicker-clad wine jars on its back across a field where wildflowers rippled in the breeze.

Menina opened her guidebook. Andalusia, it said, was derived from Arabic, "Al Andalus," and traces of the Moorish civilization that flourished in the Iberian Peninsula between 711 and 1492 could be seen everywhere. "Look closely and you will see the footprint of the Moors—terraced fields, fountains and arches, orange and almond trees, and even churches that contain traces of the mosques they once were. The modern road follows an ancient way linking the mountains to the coast. It is possible to see the white stones that mark it, and it is still used by people who live in the mountains. Archaeologists have found shards of pottery stained with the purple dye from Tyre, and half-buried altars dedicated to the Phoenician goddess Astarte, suggesting the Phoenicians had traveled into the mountains from the coast before the Romans colonized the Mediterranean. This pre-Roman route continues east into the mountains, probably to France."

The guidebook drew the reader's attention to the white villages clinging to the mountain face. These dated from the time of the Moors. Even so many hundreds of years later, old customs, legends, and superstitions lived on in them.

Menina found something soothing and reassuring about this history, about the fact time moved on, life moved on. Maybe eventually it would move on for her, too.

She read on about the *Semana Santa* celebrations that had drawn travelers and pilgrims to Andalusia for hundreds of years, still held in many of the villages. They were part religious, part fiesta, and part drama, designed to advertise the Christian triumph over the Moors to the populace. Most involved decorated floats, some centuries old, that carried images of the crucified Christ, the Virgin Mary or saints, or sometimes saints' relics—bits of bones, dried blood or desiccated body parts, often believed to have miraculous powers—in jeweled containers. Everyone joined in the procession: priests and acolytes and local dignitaries in their medals and decorations at the head, followed by religious brotherhoods called *confraternidads*, nuns, laypeople, and often a special contingent of children. Processions usually took place at night, through torchlit streets and with all the participants carrying candles. Afterward, fiestas went on until dawn, with wine and singing and dancing, special food, and people dressed up in traditional costumes. Gypsies traveled from near and far, setting up market stalls, selling horses on the side, and singing, adding to the ceremonies with their unique laments for the dead Christ and his grieving mother, another centuries-old tradition dating back to the *Reconquista*.

Had *Semana Santa* been celebrated this way in Tristan Mendoza's time? Menina put down the book to think about it and watched a bird of prey circling the sky over the valley. It drifted on the thermals, around and around. Watching it was hypnotic, and Menina drifted off.

An hour later she woke with a start when the bus halted, thinking the stop must be the place where she'd change, but the bus driver looked back and shook his head no. She pushed her window open and leaned out to see they were in a plaza before a whitewashed church. The plaza was full of people, many wearing Andalusian costumes—women with ruffled skirts and high combs in their hair and men in braid-trimmed jackets, some on horseback. There were tourists who looked plain by comparison, holding cameras and moving slowly through a market set up in the center, where swarthy men and women jostled to sell carpets and lace and copper utensils spread out on blankets to the tourists. Somewhere the smell of food cooking, like a barbecue or sausages, filled the air.

Then a slow insistent drumbeat made itself heard over the noise, and the people in the square fell silent as the drumbeat grew louder, moving aside to leave a path through the crowd. A somber chanting sound came with the drums, like someone was on a microphone. Then a procession passed slowly in front of the bus, led by a priest in black robes carrying a tall pole with a crucifix draped in black gauze. A group of boys in robes followed behind him, chanting responses to the microphone.

Then Menina caught her breath. A huge black-draped float bearing a larger-than-life plaster image of the grieving Madonna appeared, swaying above the crowd and dwarfing the grimacing, sweating men who carried it on their shoulders. Beneath an enormous silver-filigree halo, a wimple and black veil framed the Virgin's white, grief-stricken face. A rosary of outsize black pearls with a silver cross swung from her hands raised in prayer. At her feet lay the tortured, twisted body of the dead Christ, red blood dripping realistically from his wounds. The image dominated everything in the square, and some of the women selling carpets began to sing in a shrill, keening harmony, a primitive lament raw with grief and suffering that sent chills down Menina's back.

The next part of the procession was even stranger. Behind the swaying Madonna, also walking in slow time to the drumbeat, came figures in purple robes and tall conical hoods that covered their faces completely save for narrow slits for their eyes. They held what looked like whips made from barbed wire. Every few steps and in sync, the hooded figures swung the whips onto their backs, ritually beating themselves. A few had faint red patches on their shoulders. Then with a roll and a final thud, the drumbeat ceased and the procession halted. The singing stopped. In the silence an order rang out and the men carrying the float shifted their weight in unison and lowered it down on the plaza. The float bearers, wearing thick pads where their shoulders took the weight, rubbed their necks and wiped their brows. The hooded men took off their hats and many lit cigarettes. Wine and coffee were produced.

"*Están practicando*," announced the driver, half turning his head toward the passengers and gesturing with his thumb. Practicing. The driver leaned out his window and exchanged laughing comments with some of the men before slapping the side of the bus and starting the engine. As they pulled away Menina stared back, feeling shaken. In Laurel Run, Easter was lilies at church, colored eggs, and ladies in new hats. What she had just seen was raw and visceral—about death and blood and terror and the iron grasp of religion.

Menina thought they must be getting close to the place where she would change buses. When it didn't happen she began to wish she had bought some food at the airport. By three, with her stomach grumbling, she stood up to retrieve a Hershey bar from her pack. Just then the bus swung wide round a precipitous hairpin bend, throwing her off balance. Grabbing the baggage rack with both hands, she felt the bus turn again as it wheezed slowly up a narrow street leading into a white village that hung over the valley, then stopped at the edge of a plaza with a large tiled fountain, a white church with a red tiled roof, orange trees in bloom, and a café with tables outdoors in the sunshine.

The driver stood up and announced they would stop for *"la comida"* for one hour. He pointed at his watch, and said to be back on the bus on time. People should take all their possessions with them; Spanish people were honest but even this high up there were many Africans and other illegal immigrants nowadays who stole things. He winked at Menina, patted his stomach and beckoned. She busied herself with her backpack and handbag and ignored him. After she ate she would have a look inside the church and avoid the driver like the plague.

In the café, a boisterous group of men stood round a bar laden with wineglasses and bottles even though it was only lunchtime. The driver's gold tooth flashed as he moved over to make room for her beside him. Menina turned quickly and went to sit outside at one of the tables under the orange trees, took her pad of paper out, and began sketching the church, the flowers, and what looked like the ruins of an old castle on the rocks above. She was dying for a cheeseburger or a club sandwich, but the waiter shook his head. He would bring her something. She didn't understand what, but nodded and wolfed down the dish of small black olives that arrived with her Coca-Cola. Then she ate a large potato omelette with herbs and peppers. After she paid the bill she felt too full to get up and visit the church right away.

The people from the bus were still inside the bar and the plaza was deserted. The only sounds were the swallows flitting overhead, and the fountain in the center of the plaza. Little bursts of sweet scent drifted her way from the orange blossoms, bees buzzed, and the hot sun on her back felt relaxing. Menina laid her head on her pack on the table and closed her eyes for a minute.

A jolt on the back of her chair woke her. Struggling to remember where she was, Menina saw a boy sprinting away down a narrow gap between the houses. It was late afternoon and the plaza was in shadow now. She shivered and reached for the handbag she had hung on the back of her chair. To her horror it wasn't there. She sprang to her feet, looked around her and under the table but the handbag with her money, passport, and airline ticket home, as well as her new Visa card, was gone. With a sinking heart she knew the running boy must have stolen it. Surely the driver would still let her back on the bus, he had seen her ticket…but the place where the bus had parked was empty. It had left without her and her suitcase was on it. "No," she whimpered. "No!" Her stomach knotted in dismay.

And then she was afraid. The square had filled up with the workmen she had seen drinking in the café earlier, now hammering together some large structure at the edge of the plaza. Seeing a young woman by herself, a few came closer. "You are friendly girl, no?" one asked in Spanish, with a furtive smile that revealed bad teeth. His friend whistled softly and raised his eyebrows. The men raked her body with their eyes and exchanged a joke in a guttural language Menina did not understand, but the gist of which was all too clear. One of them rubbed his fingers together in a universal language for money. "A little drink, yes?" said a man. Laughter.

There was menace in the air and only some instinct for preservation made her force herself to behave calmly, not to act like a victim. Across the plaza a sign said *Policia*. Thank God. Pointedly ignoring the men, she forced herself to sling on her backpack in an unhurried fashion and then walk calmly past the leering men across the plaza, feeling their stares on her back. She was seriously in trouble with no money or passport, but the police would help her call the American consulate in Madrid about getting a new passport, and—much as she dreaded the explanations that would be necessary—she could phone her parents to wire her money. But how stupid of her to get into such a mess!

The door to the police station was unlocked. Menina walked in calling, *"Hola?"* She didn't see anybody at the front desk. She wandered down a corridor to the only room with a light on. Inside was a single policeman at a desk covered with files, absorbed in reading something. He looked up with surprise when Menina knocked at his open door. Menina was relieved to see it wasn't some teenage rookie. The policeman looked thirty-ish, with a mustache and thick dark hair. The collar of his uniform was unbuttoned.

"Señora? ¿qué puedo hacer para usted?" What can I do for you? He stood up at once, buttoning his collar hastily as if embarrassed she had caught him relaxing. He was as tall as Menina, heavy but fit, with an air of authority that was reassuring under the circumstances.

She struggled to explain in Spanish. "Excuse me; I have to report a crime. I fell asleep in the square and my bag with my money and my passport was stolen. My bus left. My suitcase was on it...the men in the square were...pretty unpleasant." She was hyperventilating and suddenly dizzy. "Could I sit down, please?"

The policeman eyed her narrowly. He introduced himself as Captain Fernández Galán and to Menina's surprise his polite expression altered to one of disapproval. He pulled a chair to his desk for her and said in English, "Please. You must fill out an *informe del crimen.*"

She shrugged off her backpack and sat. He pushed what he had been reading so intently to one side, and sighed. Looking distracted, he checked several drawers before finding and retrieving a form. He put it and a pen down in front of her. "Can you read it?"

Menina nodded.

"English?"

"Americana."

"Mrs.?"

"No, *señorita.*"

"Please, I speak English," he said abruptly. "Fill out your name here," he said, pointing to a box on the form. He frowned as she wrote "Menina Walker." At least he wasn't leering at her like the bus driver and men outside. She looked back down at the form, her lips moving as she read and reread the questions in Spanish. Still shaken by the encounter in the plaza, she found her mind had gone suddenly, totally blank. After a minute he pulled the form back impatiently. "Mees Walker, explain to me what happened and I fill it in. Otherwise we are here all night."

He sat down, clicked his pen, and wrote while Menina told him her age and what was in her bag. Her passport—no, she didn't have the passport number—about six thousand euros in travelers checks, a thousand or so in cash, her return plane ticket, and a Visa card. She didn't have the Visa number either. She explained about the tug on the back of her chair in the square and the running boy and then realizing her bus had gone.

He gave her a look that said just how stupid he thought she was, and asked where was she going.

"I was going to Madrid from Malaga, and the lady who sold me the ticket said to take the bus I was on, then change at the stop after Ronda, for the one to Madrid. The bus driver promised to tell me when to get off."

Nervously, she trailed to a halt midsentence. She could hear the men outside hammering something and shouting to each other. What was she going to do when it was time to leave the police station?

"Place of birth?"

She told him and he looked surprised. "Why did you say that you were American?"

"I am. I was adopted."

"Occupation? No, don't tell me, is it 'model' or 'actress'?" he asked. Menina thought he sounded sarcastic.

"I'm in college."

His heavy brows gave him a stern expression. *"Mees Walker,* in a few days, we have some tourists who come for the *Semana Santa* procession, but not many rich ones. We are just an old village in the mountains. At this time of year some British retired people and the Catholic tourists who want to see our religious festival in a few days come but"—he spread his hands expressively—"nothing is here for *muchachas de la llamada."*

"The what?"

"Expensive girls—what is the English expression? The polite one, I think it is 'call girls'—in southern Spain, for the yachts, the rich men. The most expensive ones can pass for convent girls. Like you, for example."

"What?"

He slammed his hand on the desk. "Oh please, Mees Walker! I am a policeman—you cannot fool me. You think you are not obvious? Following the rich Arabs, the drug smugglers, the people who deal in arms, with their parties on the yachts where a beautiful girl is always welcome. But here in the mountains is mostly poor foreign workmen who find work at Easter to build the *Semana Santa* floats, because most men in the villages are away working or getting too old. Or maybe you have problem with the drugs and any men with even a little money will do. Though I admit, you do not look like you have a problem with the drugs. Yet."

Menina's mouth dropped open. He had called her a *prostitute?* And a drug addict? She had been in the police station less than twenty minutes—what had she done to make such a terrible impression? "I'm not a…a…call girl," she stammered. "Or a drug addict. I've never even seen a drug that I know of. I just want to go to Madrid to…"

"Madrid? Is *this* the road to Madrid?" he interrupted and swept his hand toward the window and a view of the mountains.

"How would I know? It's my first time in Spain!"

"I wish, Mees Walker, whatever you are, that you had not come here. Because now someone must take care of you, and I cannot because I am too busy."

I hate Spain, Menina thought bitterly. It had begun to dawn on her that she might be in more trouble than she thought. No one knew where she was. *She* didn't know where she was. And if this horrible policeman thought she was a prostitute, then the men in the square must have come to the same conclusion. That would explain the hissing and the comments. She was so worried now that she hardly heard the captain asking her another question.

"I said, why do you go to Madrid?"

"I need to go to the Prado. I have to write about an artist for college…"

"Picasso, I expect?"

"Picasso? Of course not!" Mention a Spanish artist and people always said Picasso, but there were no Picassos at the Prado. Though it might be better not to say so.

"Ah, so you think Picasso is not at the Prado?" The captain raised his eyebrows.

"No the Picassos are at the Reina Sofia Museum!" Menina snapped. This man was not just rude, he was irritating. He probably knew perfectly well where the Picassos were! "The artist I'm studying is older, Tristan Mendoza, you won't have heard of him, most people these days haven't. He was a portrait painter—his only work is in the Prado. I have a medal with the same…"

Menina knew she had gone on long enough. "Look, never mind, you don't want to hear about all this. May I *please* use your phone to call my parents? I'll reverse the charges of course, but they'll be worried and my father can wire me some money and—"

Captain Fernández Galán had gone quiet and was looking at the ceiling. "An old artist?" he asked, as if this was the strangest thing he'd ever heard.

"Y-Y-Yes!" she stammered.

"Hmmm." Clearly he was trying to think of another sarcastic response. What a horrible, horrible man! It had been a long, hard day and Menina suddenly felt very tired and teary. She searched in her pockets for tissues but they were in her handbag. And that was gone. Gone! Everything was gone! She was an idiot, had messed up and she was frightened and, oh God, what was she going to do? She was unable to stop tears rolling down her cheeks, and swiped her sleeve across her eyes like a child.

There was a light touch on her arm. "Please." She raised her head to see the captain offering her a white cotton handkerchief. It even looked clean. She took it warily and muttered, "Thanks." She wiped her eyes and nose, and thought the captain looked less irritated. More resigned. "Tristan Mendoza, eh? Was when? What did he paint?"

"Oh—" Sniff. "Probably mid- to late sixteenth century." Sniff. Did the man want an art history lesson? "Portraits. Women mostly. But he might have also—"

"And you have really studied old paintings?"

"Well, not *every one* ever painted," Menina couldn't resist retorting. "But yes, in college."

"OK. That is different. Is only one thing to do now."

"I know; let me make some phone calls *please!*"

The captain shook his head, spread his hands and shrugged expressively. "Unfortunately I regret it is not possible to call anyone. I have a cell phone but it is no use up here, no connection. And we have a few telephones in the village but the line is out of order—this often happens in Spain, especially in the mountains. Now is *Semana Santa*, and no one can fix until after Easter. No Internet, no e-mail, no phone. Believe me, that is a big problem for me too at the moment."

"OK, can you please give me a ride to somewhere with a working phone, someplace with a hotel? Then I'd be out of your way."

In her pocket she still had Professor Lennox's card. Thank heavens. She would call Professor Lennox and beg her to get her out of this mess.

He shook his head. "No, I am sorry, but I cannot leave the village for the time being. Not until after Easter. So, unfortunately, you must stay here till then."

This was a whole new problem. *Semana Santa* had only just begun. And it would be another week before she could let her parents know she was OK. They would be frantic. And where was she supposed to stay?

He seemed to read her mind. "Is somewhere you can stay but I must take you up there myself."

"I can pay for a hotel when my father wires money," she said, trying to regain some kind of control.

Captain Fernández Galán shook his head and stood up. Now he looked faintly amused. "No wires here. No hotel either. But money is not necessary where I take you."

This was more worrying than anything he had said so far. But it was the policeman or the men in the square. She bent to struggle into her heavy backpack to find the captain had already reached down and picked it up and was holding the door open for her. Outside he strode away from the square, leading her up narrow winding streets between whitewashed houses. Aromas of onions and garlic frying in hot oil filled the chilly evening air. She heard women talking and the clatter of dishes. Normality. But hopes of a spare bed in one of these homes faded as they left the houses behind. The captain was leading her up a steep rise that had once been terraced. They followed a narrow path between some olive trees. In the distance, the last pink and orange glow of a spectacular sunset was fading behind the mountains. He stopped and pointed to the dark bulk of the ruined castle above them. "We are going there."

"Oh?" Menina looked for lights, some sign of habitation, but it looked deserted. And ominously dark at the end of the path. They reached an arched gate in the wall and stopped. It had two heavy, iron-bound wooden doors with a latticed hatch. Was it a prison? There was no sound but birds. How could she have been stupid enough to come to a totally deserted spot with a man convinced she was a prostitute? An armed man at that.

"Where are we?" Menina asked warily, starting to back away. She was fit—she could outrun him, get back to the village. But what then? Would someone in one of those houses they had passed take her in?

The captain seemed to sense her mood. "Do not be frightened. This is a convent, very old convent, maybe oldest in Spain. No one knows the real name; people call it *Las Golondrinas* because, listen, the *golondrinas.*"

The captain pulled a rope and Menina jumped as a bell clanged loudly over their heads and disturbed the swallows who rose in a noisy, scolding crowd. "No one knows when the first nuns are here. But was before the *Reconquista*. It was a Moorish village, but when the Moors are in Spain, there are many Christians, many Jews. They must pay a special tax and not make trouble against the Moors, but is OK to be Christians and Jews. And nuns make no trouble. Once they go in, the nuns they never leave the convent. Tax is no problem either—convent was rich, and girls bring money when they come to be nuns. The girls, they come here as babies and they become nuns.

"Oh that sounds…as babies? Why? How did they know they wanted to be nuns if they were babies?"

"Was orphanage. They have no parents, maybe they have no choice. I don't know."

He gave the bell another tug. "The nuns make medicines and cakes and sweets." He pointed to the window covered by dark iron latticework. "They sell there, to pay the religious tax. And because it is very old, very holy convent, there were many pilgrims coming here, people sorry for their sins. There was a kind of hospital—sick people come, too, Muslim and Jewish sick people, nuns treat them as well as Christians, and an orphanage."

"Sounds busy." Menina's feet hurt and she was so tired by now she was ready to lie down and sleep under the olive trees. But what if the men in the plaza found her?

"Yes, great ladies, queens even, they make the pilgrimage here because it is so old, so holy. In the chapel is a tomb of a princess from the north, from Leon, was Christian, who came here to be a nun in the time of the Moors, and behind the convent are caves in the mountain where nuns were buried, like the catacombs in Rome. But now"—he shrugged—"is not so important, no one comes. Is only a few old nuns. They still make sweets to sell to the tourists at *Semana Santa*. This does not make a lot of money. Nuns are very poor now, poor and old. Is hard for them. They get sick. People in the village still help, bring them food so they don't starve, and wood for the fires but in winter is very cold."

He pointed up and Menina squinted in the dusk. She couldn't see much. "Windows broken. Everything broken. They say it will close when the last nun dies. Terrible to think there will be one old woman all alone here, all the rest dead. Is many years ago, when I was a boy, a few pilgrims were still coming, but no more for a long time. But there are rooms where pilgrims and travelers could stay. Is why I bring you."

"Maybe it wasn't a good idea. No one's answering the bell," Menina said anxiously. She couldn't decide whether it was better to take refuge inside such a creepy place away from the men in the square or whether there was no way she was setting foot in it. "Let's not bother them."

"Don't worry, nuns are there, only a little deaf. Always it is necessary to wait and ring for some time before they hear." He rang the bell again. "Besides, it is good for them if a visitor knows about paintings."

"Why?"

"Because the old convents, the old monasteries, like this one, they have paintings. If you stay here you can help, see if you think any paintings are worth money, so the nuns can sell. They could have heat, the sick ones have nurses and medicine, they can fix some broken things."

"That sounds like a good plan, but really, I'm no specialist. Look, I'm only in junior college! You need an expert." She felt for the card in her pocket. "But there is an expert, a famous one, on our tour, Professor Lennox. She's half Spanish. I think. And I could call her if I could just get to a phone," Menina wheedled. How could there be absolutely no phones? "I have her cell phone number."

"But I told you, is no phones. No electricity even, here. But please, try. Is good if you find something, but if not, then you cannot. Don't worry. Sor Teresa speaks a little English. She learned as a girl, so you can ask her."

No phone, now no electricity. Great! But he'd said please…

Just then the latticed window opened from inside. A high-pitched old voice exclaimed, "Aha!" and demanded crossly to know who was ringing the bell, saying something about having no *polvorónes* at this hour.

"Ah, Sor Teresa," said Captain Fernández Galán, removing his cap and sounding suddenly polite and respectful. He wished the speaker good evening, called her "*Tía*"—aunt—and launched into an explanation in rapid Spanish. Menina caught enough to understand he was saying there was a nice American girl with him who had unfortunately been robbed and missed her bus, a very nice girl who needed a place to stay until after Easter and couldn't she use one of the pilgrim's rooms.

The lattice slid closed and there was a sound of a bolt being drawn back, then the heavy wooden door was opened by a bent old woman in a nun's habit, carrying a lantern. She muttered grumpily, "*Deo gratias*, Alejandro," by way of greeting. She didn't seem happy to see them. Something about them interrupting the evening vigil.

The captain explained. Menina tried to follow, catching a word here and there—her name and the words "Madrid" and "Malaga" and "student." He was getting around to the paintings in the convent when Sor Teresa interrupted, as if she were scolding a small boy. Her thin old voice replied in staccato Spanish, something that sounded to Menina like no, they weren't having another of his women...the last one had...going and coming at all hours...a great disturbance...shocking...cigarettes...short skirts. Menina heard her spit a word that sounded like "hippies."

Sor Teresa paused for breath and Captain Fernández Galán resumed his plea, apologized if the last girl behaved badly...on his parents' grave he had never seen Menina before this afternoon. A nice girl.

Menina was surprised to hear the captain defend her as a "nice girl." An hour earlier he had called her a prostitute. And it sounded like the captain parked his girlfriends at the convent? How odd. But she needed a place to stay. Menina leaned forward to assure the nun in the best Spanish she could muster that she wasn't a girlfriend or a hippie, she didn't smoke, didn't want to go anywhere, she wouldn't cause any problems, please, please, let her stay until the next bus to Madrid. Sor Teresa stared at Menina as if she were looking straight through her, then opened the gate wider and, none too gently, grabbed Menina's arm, and pulled her in.

The captain was adding something again about showing Menina the convent's *pinturas* and please could Sor Teresa speak

English—but Sor Teresa ignored him, and began to swing the gate closed. He just managed to shove Menina's backpack in before it slammed shut, snatching his hand back just in time.

Sor Teresa bolted the gate and turned to Menina. "You stay," she snapped in English, "inside convent. Not going out of the convent with mens! No mens."

"Yes, ma'am!" said Menina, wearily picking up her backpack. Nothing suited her better than no men. "Of course...*sí*... *comprendo*."

Sor Teresa made a "humpff" sound as if she didn't believe it and hobbled ahead surprisingly fast, holding her lamp high. The lantern threw a bobbing pool of light around them, as she led Menina down one corridor after another. Menina saw broken floor tiles and closed doors, but beyond the light everything was pitch black and nobody else was about. There was a powerful smell of mildew and dust, and a mouse or something scampered past.

Finally Sor Teresa stopped in the corridor and creaked open one of the closed doors. She held up the lantern. "Here," she said, in Spanish. The room was a small, musty whitewashed cell, with a crucifix askew on the wall and a wooden stand for kneeling beneath it, a shuttered window and a bed made up with yellowed linen sheets, a folded blanket, and patched embroidered cases on the pillows. There was a chair and small table under the window. On the table was a glass hurricane lamp. Sister Teresa dusted off the table with the hem of her habit and said, "*Por alimento*." She felt in the pocket of her habit and retrieved two part-burned candles and a matchbox. She lit one of the candles and put it in the lamp, then handed the other candle and matchbox to Menina who said "*Gracias*," trying not to sound as dismayed as she felt. Sor Teresa beckoned for Menina to follow her back into the dark corridor. Sor Teresa pushed another creaking door open. "*Servicios*," the old nun said. "Toilet."

"Oh…" Menina faltered. She held her candle up and could just make out a hole in the floor, a pile of old newspapers, and a rusty pump over an ancient stone sink on legs on the far wall. No electricity and now this! Sor Teresa had disappeared. Since by now she needed a pee in the worst way, she used the primitive toilet and tore off pieces of newspaper she guessed was meant to be toilet paper. The pump needed a lot of priming before it groaned loudly and regurgitated icy water over her hands.

As she groped her away back along the dark corridor, a draft made the candle flicker alarmingly, and her shadow jumped creepily along beside her. She was relieved to see a feeble glow from the open door of her room and she saw a tray covered with a linen cloth had been left on the table. Someone had brought her supper! Beneath the cloth was an earthenware bowl of pungent garlicky soup, bread, cheese, and a little carafe of red wine. Menina realized she was very hungry. The soup had an egg in it, poached by the hot broth. It was delicious and she mopped the last bit up with the bread and washed the cheese down with the wine.

She undressed and put on the travel robe her mother had put in her backpack. It was made of lightweight fleece, welcome in the dank room. The mattress, on the other hand, was thin and lumpy. She shifted about to get comfortable.

She shut her eyes and was drifting off when down in the village slow rhythmic drumbeats started again, and then the same kind of wailing singing she had heard earlier that day began, too. She would never sleep now. She sat up and reached for her guidebook, the only thing she had to read. She hoped the candle in the lamp wouldn't go out before morning. How was she going to survive a week of this?

She woke, slumped against the wall with the book open on her lap. Her watch said six thirty. Slowly she focused on the bare little room, trying to remember why she was in it. In the early light she saw that her supper tray had been taken and another tray left on her small table. This time it was coffee, hot milk, and warm almond bread. She felt guilty—her parents would have a fit if she let old ladies wait on her like room service.

Just then, she heard voices whispering something. She went to the window to see if anyone was on the other side, then there was a knock at the door. Menina turned from the window and gasped. In the middle of the floor a group of girls in somber wide-hooped skirts and white ruffs of the sixteenth century sat grouped together as if for a photo. They stared at her with pleading eyes. "*Sala grande...locutio sala...sala de las niñas...jardín de peregrinos*," whispered young voices.

"What? *Qué?*" Menina rubbed her eyes and looked again, but there were only dust motes floating dreamily on the slanting rays of sun. Stress and jet lag did funny things.

Sor Teresa hobbled through the door, barking, "*Deo gratias.*" She said that Menina could join them for Mass while she was there—the convent chapel had an entrance door, and every morning it was unbarred for the old ladies who came to Mass. Menina could sit with them.

Menina declined, explaining she was not Catholic. Before she could offer to carry her tray to wherever the kitchen was and wash her dishes, Sor Teresa snatched the tray and snapped that she must get back to the vigil.

Menina retrieved an airline toothbrush and toothpaste, and Holiday Inn soap, braved an icy wash from the pump, and dressed. Then she tried to read her guidebook some more, waiting to see if Sor Teresa or someone came to talk to her about the paintings, but soon Menina decided. She couldn't just sit in a small space with nothing to do. Maybe she could find the paintings herself. She wished Becky were here.

CHAPTER 5

Las Golondrinas Convent, Spain, April 2000

The convent was a maze of corridors. The mountain wind whistled through the gaps between the walls and ceiling, and birds flitted in and out, chirping and making nests under the roof. The only light came from small barred windows set high in the thick walls. When her eyes adjusted to the gloom, Menina saw the walls were crowded with faded religious cards, dried flowers, garishly colored Madonnas, Saint Teresa of Avila, the Sacred Heart, lithographs of various popes, and badly executed paintings of saints. Menina guessed most of the artwork was mid-nineteenth or early twentieth century, and of little value. She knew enough to know her limits, but Holly Hill had trained her eye. This stuff looked like junk.

She went along one corridor after another, past doors that hung open to reveal other rooms like hers, with a narrow bed and a table and chair and crucifix on the wall. They must have been filled with pilgrims once. Menina's nose wrinkled. She had never smelled anything like the dank odor of age and mildew and rot.

She hoped she would find the chapel or see one of the nuns, but the corridors were deserted. She emerged into a room with deep stone sinks around the walls and an old-fashioned iron pump. Patched nightgowns hung drying on a wooden rack. She opened a door to a larger room with tiles on the walls and floor and another stone sink, a pump, and a few pots and pans hanging crookedly on iron hooks in the low ceiling. There was a huge fireplace at one end and a scarred wooden trestle table. On it were wicker covered jugs labeled "*Vino*" and "*Aceite de oliva*"—wine and olive oil. There were ropes of garlic and onions, a basket of eggs, another of baby artichokes and another of potatoes with dirt still on them, some lemons, and a piece of honeycomb on a plate. Some bunches of dried herbs hung by the fireplace, and there was a stack of wood, and an iron pot simmering on the embers. She bent and lifted the pot's lid, and a garlicky steam rose from whatever was cooking that made her realize that she was very hungry indeed. The sweet bread at breakfast had been delicious but there had only been one piece. She replaced the lid and looked for something, anything, to nibble on.

Under the sink she spotted a large basket labeled "*pollos*." It was full of bread in various stages of staleness from slightly dry to hard as a rock. Menina found a large broken loaf fresher than the rest. Feeling guilty, she dipped a piece of it in the honey and ate it. She broke the rest in two and stuffed the pieces in her jacket in case there was no lunch, then went on with her exploration. The kitchen gave into a larger whitewashed room with a life-size cross of dark wood. Beneath it was a lectern with a book propped open and three long tables with benches. The nuns' dining room?

Beyond that, a door gave into another dim, silent, low-ceilinged room. Menina entered, then cried, "Excuse me!" The room was full of people. Unnaturally quiet people, all wearing hats and holding perfectly still—then she realized not people but plaster saints, with chipped halos. Crocheted antimacassars hung raggedly on the arms of chairs, and dusty glass cases covered with old spiderwebs lined the walls.

Weird. Like everything had been frozen in time, Menina thought. The dust made her sneeze and it sounded very loud in the silence.

A blue-and-white enameled medallion of the Madonna and Child hung over an empty font for holy water, set low in the wall. Looking around, she saw the walls were full of small carved images—Madonnas, angels, putti. She wished that she had brought one of her notebooks and a pen, to make a list. There were a few tapestries, dirty and moth-eaten, and a few paintings dark with age—she could make out a baby Moses in the bulrushes, another with cherubs playing with a lamb, a fat baby John the Baptist wading in ankle-deep water holding up a tiny cross, and a large composition of the Virgin and two other women watching a group of children playing at their feet. Childhood seemed to be the theme here—had this room been part of the orphanage?

She swiped away cobwebs and dust and pressed her nose against the first glass case to see what was inside. It was stuffed with toys. A host of dolls with blank faces and glassy eyes stared back at her. Most were dressed in nuns' habits of one kind or another, and there was another case of dolls of different sizes dressed in plain gowns that had once been white, each with a wimple held in place by a tiny brown scrap of something that might have been flowers. Brides of Christ dolls. To Menina, raised in the Baptist church, they were foreign, exotic, and a little bizarre.

The lower shelves held doll-size dishes, plates, and cups. On closer inspection, what she thought were dolls' tea sets were miniature altar fittings—small silver and gold crucifixes, chalices, and monstrances. There were small altars of marble and alabaster with miniature altar cloths, doll-size confession booths and fonts for holy water, and miniature images of Christ and the Virgin and different saints designed to screw onto a small replica of the float Menina had seen in the procession the previous day.

Another case held ivory-covered missals to fit a child's hand, dolls' rosaries of seed pearls, small palm branches, tiny scourges, and whips of tarnished silver with thorns so tiny they were nearly invisible. There were little gilded altar screens a foot high—Menina thought they were called *reredos*—painted exquisitely, and miniature gilt candlesticks holding wisps of real candles that leaned crookedly.

The last case held what looked like jewelry. Then she recoiled. Tiny crystal caskets and urns, trimmed with blackened silver and gold and dusty jewels, held tiny relics in ivory and ebony—skulls, a severed hand in miniature, a human heart, John the Baptist's tiny but grotesquely bleeding head...reliquaries, she knew they were called. She soon saw where these had been used. The big dark shape in one corner was a dollhouse-size chapel.

All these things conjured up child nuns. *Child nuns?* It gave Menina the creeps and she left the *sala*, relieved to see sunlight at the end of the passage. There she found an arch that led into a cloister garden. Weather-beaten gargoyles with broken noses crouched above a Romanesque cloister. Bees buzzed in overgrown beds of herbs between paths of faded red and blue tiles, and a fountain on a pedestal splashed feebly. It was a garden out of a medieval Book of Hours, gone to seed.

Menina perched on the low cloister wall as the convent bell broke the silence with twelve strokes for midday. Lunchtime. She broke off a piece of bread. In the sunlight it was an unappetizing gray color. She should return to her room in case there was lunch. If only there were someone to ask which way her room was. Then she heard footsteps and looked up to see a nun walking swiftly behind the arches through the shadows on the far side of the cloister. Menina called, *"Momento, por favor!* Then *"Hola!"* but the nun must not have heard because her long black skirts whisked out of sight as she disappeared back into the convent.

Menina crammed the bread back in her pocket and hurried to catch up. She heard the nun's footsteps ahead of her, reassuring after the silence and spirits of the morning. The brightness outdoors made it hard for Menina's eyes to adjust to the dimness inside. She felt along the wall for a light switch, and then remembered the convent had no electricity. Then she could no longer hear the nun, and the fact that she couldn't see sharpened Menina's other senses. She smelled something sweet and faintly musky, like Sarah-Lynn's beeswax polish. She put out a hand and felt air, then a door frame. She felt her way along a wall, then stumbled over a large object. "Oh damn, now what?" she muttered, rubbing her shin while her eyes adjusted enough to make out a dark rectangular shape. She groped her hands over it. It felt like a chest with metal bands. Menina felt her way round the edges and made her way into the room. Daylight seeped in from under the eaves, where swallows were making their usual noises, and she saw it was another low-ceilinged room. It smelled of woodsmoke and there was an iron candelabra holding pale half-burned candles, suggesting the nuns actually used this room. She looked on the table, hoping to find matches.

A little iron box indeed held matches. Menina lit two of the candles and looked around. In the flickering light she could see high-backed chairs, a table, and a large black crucifix over a fireplace. The tile floor was uneven and sunken in places, and one wall of the room was an iron grill, like a prison cell, with a curtain pulled across on the other side. There were shelves, empty save for a collection of baskets that Menina discovered held sewing, and an alcove where firewood was stacked.

And on the walls were picture frames holding paintings blackened with age, much dirtier than the ones in the orphanage room.

Menina took a candle from its holder and held it close to the nearest picture. She squinted through the dull reflection of the candlelight, her nose inches from the surface, and was rewarded by the faint outline of a face beneath the layers of age and dirt.

She'd found a portrait. Now what?

The bread in her pocket was what. She had heard it was possible to clean paintings using bread to absorb dirt. It wasn't a good way to do it; modern packaged bread had a lot of chemicals and bleach that would cause damage. But the bread in Menina's pocket wasn't Wonder Bread; it was gray, so maybe it was unbleached. Should she? Probably not, but no one had paid any attention to these paintings in years, and unless she did something, no one would. In the font she rinsed her hands in holy water, then rubbed them hard on her jeans to get them as clean as she could. She tore a piece away from the crust and worked it with her hands until it was pliable. She blew on the surface of the painting to dislodge any loose dust, then pressed the softened bread carefully at a corner of the dark canvas.

The bread turned black as it picked up dirt, and the frame looked like it was gilt.

"OK, let's see what you look like." Menina started on the face with another piece of softened bread, pressing gently. Heavy eyebrows over dark eyes and the bridge of the nose emerged, then slowly a face, dark eyes staring into hers. Menina moved from side to side and saw the artist had been skillful enough to paint eyes that followed the viewer. Definitely worth seeing the rest of the portrait.

As the dirt came away, Menina was surprised to find it was not a saint or the Virgin Mary, but a young woman in fine clothes. Under the dirt she could just make out an elaborate sleeve, a smudge of a flower in her hand, a sort of embroidered shift, and jewelry. And though muted by grime, the colors were crude enough to make an impact—red and black and green and blue. Obviously a portrait of a wealthy young girl, there was something exotic or *primitif* about it that made Menina doubt it was European.

"Where did you come from?" Menina asked the portrait to break the silence and jumped when Sor Teresa's voice cackled,

"Aha! There you are!" Menina whirled around. "You should not be here, is only for nuns," said Sor Teresa accusingly from the doorway. "When is visitors, women from the village, they come and sit there." She pointed to the grille. "All people not nuns, they sit on the other side. What are you doing?" There was no mistaking the suspicion in her voice.

Menina felt like a naughty child caught off limits. "It was Captain Fernández Galán's idea! He said I must look for paintings that might be valuable, to sell, and we can take them to—"

Sor Teresa drew herself up, and there was an indignant rapid-fire response in a mixture of Spanish and English. "How dare you accuse Captain Fernández Galán! Alejandro is not thief! It is you who want to steal from us! Bah! You must leave the convent!"

"No, no, no! We don't want to *steal* anything. The captain thinks the convent needs money and he wanted me to find a painting you could sell."

"Humpff!" There was another torrent of Spanish and English about Alejandro and his bad ways, she never knew what to think of him nowadays. Menina was startled to see she had hit a nerve. Sor Teresa had a lot to say about the captain, the life he led, that he had been...something disgraceful...ever since he was a little boy, not to mention he was no better now...something, something in fast Spanish about chasing shameless girls who spent their lives attracting attention and enticing men. Alejandro attracted exactly this kind of girl. They threw themselves at him; no wonder he wasn't married—all he knew were *putas*. Menina's eyes opened wide in surprise. Sor Teresa had just called the captain's girlfriends *whores*! Including Menina? Well, she was just sick to death of people calling her that!

"I'm *not* a *puta* or a girlfriend! I only met him yesterday! He made it clear he thought I was an idiot to take the wrong bus and have my things stolen—he was really rude. But since you let me stay here, I thought I should try and help like the captain asked. Sorry about being in your private area, but I couldn't find anybody to ask. But why not let me see your paintings? Like I told the captain, I'm only studying art history at college. I know a little but not much. What I can do is clean some of the dirt off, with stale bread, and make a note of anything that looks valuable. Then a real expert can take a look and advise you about selling."

"Humpff! We will see. Maybe we do not like to sell our paintings. Now come. You must eat and I must return to the chapel."

"Was this room the library?" Menina asked, following her to the door.

"Old scriptorium," said Sor Teresa.

"Scriptorium? A writing room?"

"Yes, a nun was always writing there. Convent always had a writer—a scribe. Many books, was a library, too, very special, because is not so many books then, books very precious. Not so many people could read. But in this convent all the nuns were educated, could read, so is many peoples come, want to know what books say, the scribe will find the books and tell them what they want to know."

"Look it up," said Menina.

"Yes. First people must get permission from the Abbess but if she give they can go to scriptorium. You see there is a *locutio* in here, just like in the Abbess's parlor. The church says nuns must keep behind the *locutio*. So there is bars, like prison to keep nuns and the world apart. Is long time ago. Now we don't write but sit there and work. Not too many windows broken. And fireplace is good, nice and big because scribe cannot write if too cold. Scribe is good job I think!" Unexpectedly Sor Teresa chuckled.

"I found a portrait of a girl. She didn't look like a nun. Why would her portrait be in the convent?"

"A girl?" Sor Teresa chuckled again and shook her head. "Of course is girl! Is many girls come to Las Golondrinas long time ago. People do not remember now, but once so many girls come, we help them, save their lives sometimes," she muttered, leading the way down the corridor. "The world was dangerous place for girls if they are alone. But it is a long story. Everything at Las Golondrinas is a long story. And old. Too old. Soon all our stories, about the nuns, about our order, about the girls, are forgotten. Unless is a miracle, no one will know what happened here. You are the last girl, I think. Ha! Maybe you can tell our stories, no?"

"Maybe you can tell me the old stories and I'll do my best," said Menina, hoping to placate Sor Teresa. What sort of stories would those be, she wondered.

CHAPTER 6

Madrid, Winter 1504

The household of the Defensor del Santo Sepulchro family was in mourning. In the center of its great hall stood an elaborate bier draped in black and gold and surrounded by thick beeswax candles. On it lay the body of a woman in her thirties, her waxy face just visible under a shroud of black Brussels lace. A rosary of large black pearls with a diamond-and-gold crucifix was wound in her fingers. The countess had died a week after her stillborn son, and his tiny coffin with a lamb on its lid lay by her side. The bodies had lain in state for nearly three days, surrounded by the family and a host of nuns, friars, and priests who maintained a continuous vigil, praying for the souls of the departed. The next day there would be a procession to the Church of Saint Nicholas de los Servitas for a requiem Mass, followed by internment in the family vault.

The only daughter of the family, fifteen-year-old Isabella, knelt alone on one side of her mother's bier, her father, six brothers, and the priest on the other. If her clothes indicated wealth and her posture piety, it was her face that made her interesting—attractive rather than beautiful, intelligent and alert, with regular features and dark-blue eyes beneath heavy brows. In the flickering light shed by the tapers and candles, melancholy shadows devoured Isabella's black mourning dress, throwing her pale face and stiff white ruff into relief. The pearls dangling from her ears glowed softly in the light, as did her dark-gold hair beneath the mantilla covering her bent head. Once or twice her gaze flicked up and she saw the priest watching her narrowly. She dropped her eyes again to her clasped hands, her heart and mind racing.

She knew that her father and the priest were locked in a battle of wills over her future. Her family was an ancient one, and her pedigree outweighed even the huge dowry she would bring to a convent or a husband. Isabella was a vessel of *limpieza de sangre*, a pure Catholic bloodline untainted by intermarriage with Moors or Spanish Jews throughout the hundreds of years Muslims had ruled Spain. Since the *Reconquista*, *Cristianos Viejos*, Old Christians like the count's family, had risen to even greater wealth and prominence. Their name meant "Defender of the Holy Sepulchre." For centuries the family had secretly channeled money under the noses of their Moorish rulers to reclaim Jerusalem from the infidels. When their Catholic Majesties Isabella and Ferdinand swore to return the country to God and the Catholic Church, their plan to purge the country of unbelievers—Moors, Jews, and heretics—was a cause already dear to the count, whose pride in his bloodline was equaled only by his devotion to the church.

Three of his sons, none very robust, were destined for the church and already at the seminary at Valladolid. The other three were betrothed to the daughters of other Old Christian families. Only Isabella's future still hung in the balance. She was lame from birth, and the priest had repeatedly urged the count to install her in one of the elite convents in Madrid, reminding him of the advantages to the family of having a daughter placed among nuns who had royal blood and close connections to the court.

This was true, and yet...the count suspected the priest's rise in the church rested on his ability to steer human prizes of wealth and breeding into its arms. But the matter of the bloodline had made the count hesitate. The family's ancient noble title could be inherited by female descendants. Should his sons die without issue, the title would pass to Isabella and through her to her children.

Shortly before being brought to bed with her last child, the countess had urged that Isabella's marriage would be an extra safeguard for the family name, and the count had begun negotiating for her betrothal with several families. Now as he knelt beside his wife's bier he vowed to conclude negotiations quickly. As soon as his choice was made, the marriage would take place without waiting for the end of the mourning period. The priest's machinations were beginning to tire him.

Isabella swayed on her knees, feeling faint. The bodies had lain in state for two days and she was sure she could detect a whiff of decomposition. Her sense of smell was keen these days and her stomach heaved. She quickly put her handkerchief to her mouth to stifle a retch and fumbled for the pomander attached by a gold chain to her waist. Holding it to her nose, she breathed in the scent of dried orange peel, cloves, and anise. But now that she had noticed it, the smell of death seemed to enfold her in its cloying embrace. She had to get away or she would be sick in front of everyone… She began to lever herself up from the velvet cushion on which she had been kneeling. Allowances were made for her disability and no one would censure her for withdrawing.

She shook her head at the servant who came forward to help her. She crossed herself again and turned toward the door, holding herself upright with an effort, demonstrating that she could manage without help, that she was stronger than she appeared. She knew that Alejandro was watching. From his place among the friars chanting in the shadows, she felt his eyes following her with love and concern though the hood was pulled low on his forehead. By this time tomorrow they would be gone. Together.

That the daughter of the proud Defensor del Santo Sepulchro family would link her fate to that of a tutor in the household was something that no one would have thought possible. That was why the two young people were able to fall passionately in love beneath the eyes of everyone.

With the countess too ill with her pregnancies to attend to her daughter's education, from an early age Isabella was sent to the schoolroom with her brothers. Their tutors were elderly scholars from a nearby monastery who tut-tutted at the presence of a little girl. What need had females for education? But the count was powerful enough to have his way in most things, and Isabella, hungry for attention and praise, proved the most conscientious student of the siblings and gradually won over the tutors by her studious application. They even forgot she was a girl.

Then, just before Isabella's fourteenth birthday, a new tutor joined the family.

Fr. Alejandro Abenzucar was a seminary student at Valladolid, a young man of twenty-four who had demonstrated a brilliant grasp of mathematics, and Greek and Latin philosophy. His reputation as a promising Catholic scholar had reached the ears of the count, who insisted on the best for his sons and prevailed upon the young man's superiors to postpone his final vows so that he might spend a year or two teaching the count's sons. The seminary's superiors felt nothing would be gained by revealing that the Abenzucar clan had been a Moorish family of influence and wealth with a large valley fiefdom in Andalusia, who had converted—most of them—to Christianity after the *Reconquista*, and that their youngest son had entered the church as proof their conversion was genuine.

Fr. Alejandro's superiors failed to take into account that the *converso* scholar was a handsome young man blessed with the rare combination of good looks and a kind heart, nor had they any notion how much he detested the idea of the priesthood and inwardly rebelled at his family's humiliating forced conversion. He was also desperately lonely. Few of the other seminary students went out of their ways to befriend a *converso*, prodigy or not.

As for Isabella, no one paused to reflect that she was no longer a child, but of marriageable age and, save for her limp, a lovely girl starved of affection a daughter had never merited in a family of boys. And no one asked themselves what use Fr. Alejandro's mathematics and logic would be to a fourteen-year-old girl. Isabella's presence in the schoolroom had long been taken for granted, and like any well-born girl, she was always chaperoned. Her duenna, a stern elderly woman, sat by Isabella's side and sewed or told her beads during lessons. Only Isabella knew the old woman had grown deaf as a post and often fell asleep bolt upright in her chair or on her knees. Isabella helped conceal her frailties. She nudged the old woman awake when it was necessary for her to appear alert, and in the cold months slipped a shawl over her shoulders when she slept.

Alejandro was disconcerted to find a girl in the schoolroom, but was quickly reconciled to her presence by the same qualities that had appealed to her other tutors—her quickness of mind and her careful and considered answers to the questions he posed, her attention, and thoughtful application of what she learned. Gradually he began to notice Isabella's small graces—her neat ways, her beautifully legible hand, her modest demeanor, and the kind attentions to the old lady by her side. Above all, he noticed the expression on her face when he addressed her, the blush of pleasure when he praised some piece of work, and the way she lowered her eyes bashfully, long lashes sweeping her cheeks.

He realized her presence illuminated the schoolroom each morning. He did not care that she had a limp. In fact, he had scarcely noticed it. Having no contact with young women in the seminary, he dreamed of girls constantly. Then he began to dream only of Isabella and her beautiful eyes.

To a shy girl who knew no men outside her family, Alejandro was as dazzling as Apollo in a fiery chariot, and Isabella was disconcerted when he spoke to her. Previously, she had never looked in the mirror longer than necessary to see that her hair was tidy, but she began to study her reflection more closely to see how she appeared to him. She began to dress carefully, deciding whether this or that color was becoming, completing her toilette with a few jewels, scenting her hair. Then she suffered agonies of nerves in his presence, in case he noticed her efforts.

Lodged in the tutor's room next to the family chapel, Alejandro spent less and less time there, crossing back and forth across the courtyard to and from the count's library, where he prepared his lessons. The courtyard was where Isabella liked to sit at her needlework each afternoon. As the duenna mumbled over her beads, they exchanged simple everyday pleasantries. Alejandro looked into Isabella's eyes, tried to think of something interesting to say, and stuttered, "The weather is very fine today," or "How loud the church bells sound." To the despair of the gardener, he distractedly plucked the best blossoms from the carefully cultivated plants in the courtyard to present to Isabella. "The color of your embroidery thread," he would say as his hand brushed hers.

Isabella would nod, accepting it, and give him a smile. It was sweet to be given a flower. Alejandro finally asked if he might read to her while she sewed—a devotional work of course. His choice was *The Divine Comedy*. "It is about love! An allegory of holy love," he exclaimed enthusiastically.

Love! Isabella blushed, staring hard at her sewing as if she had never seen anything so interesting in her life as blue silk thread. "As you think best," she murmured. "I have not read it. My Italian is insufficient."

"Ah, exactly! Then you will benefit doubly—in addition to its instructive discourse, it will improve your Italian." But its instructive discourse was of love and adoration. And discussing these interesting topics did indeed give them a chance to practice their Italian, which the duenna did not speak. But had her hearing been as sharp as it once was, she would have had no need of Italian to notice the passion with which they compared courtly love, which looked for nothing beyond adoration of its object, and profane earthly love, which looked for a good deal more. In fact, so much was said on the topic of love and its ecstasy with Alejandro close by her side that Isabella found it difficult to confine her mind to love's subliminal nature. Alejandro's presence by her side made the air sweet and bright, and the sound of his voice threw her into a turmoil of emotion, made her heart pound and her trembling fingers snare her needlework into a hopeless tangle.

"*La gloriosa donna della mia mente*"—"the glorious lady of my mind"—as Dante had called Beatrice, rang in Isabella's ears as she remembered how intently he had looked into her eyes when he said it. At night in her bed she whispered it over and over, at the same time reminding herself severely that Beatrice was pure and unattainable, and the phrase had to be understood chastely.

Then one afternoon in the middle of a highly charged discussion of the intensity of spiritual passion, the duenna went off to answer one of her frequent calls of nature and Alejandro exclaimed, "I must tell you or die!" He knelt at her feet and clutched her hands. "You are my angel and truly, the flower, the glorious lady of my heart. I will place my life, my soul, in your power and no longer conceal the truth from you. I am no Christian with celibacy in his heart but a Moor with blood in his veins. And I am not Dante, to live forever without Beatrice. I would prefer death to parting from you."

"An infidel!" Isabella exclaimed in horror. Alejandro rushed on bravely. A Muslim's love for a Christian was not dishonorable. Until the *Reconquista*, the Abenzucar family had intermarried with Christian and Jewish neighbors, and had enjoyed a long friendship with a Christian convent—the Convent of the Swallows, Las Golondrinas, that stood above the valley where the Abenzucars had their estates. The Abenzucar women would travel up the mountain to visit the nuns with gifts of dried fruit, spices, and almonds for the Christian feast days, while the nuns offered prayers when the Abenzucars suffered illness or the women gave birth, and shared the medicines they made with great skill.

Though she could not imagine such cordial relations between nuns and the infidels, Isabella's scandalized expression wavered.

"If you do not believe me, in your own father's library is a book that proves the truth of what I say. It is the recollections of a venerable Christian hermit, a true Old Christian like your family, who lived in the mountains hundreds of years ago and who praised the nuns of the Convent of the Swallows for their learning and peaceable relations with their neighbors."

"But you converted, and that changes everything," Isabella said sadly.

Alejandro's expression altered as he explained he had done so unwillingly. After the *Reconquista*, formerly powerful Muslim families like the Abenzucars were offered a stark choice—baptism, or exile and confiscation of their lands and wealth. But his elderly father had decreed some must go and some must stay. Several families of younger cousins fled to Portugal, but Alejandro's parents, brothers, sisters, and their families had to become Christians and stay to preserve their estate. Baptism was only a formality. The Abenzucars would remain Muslims in secret and hope for better times.

A mass baptism of the family and all their servants and peasants had been held at his parents' estate. A distressing matter of necessity, his father had thought, but one to which they need not give the slightest credence. How could they seriously embrace the blasphemous practice of worshipping three gods instead of Allah, the one God?

But the Abenzucars had not anticipated the way in which the church authorities would seal their conversion. Alejandro's eyes filled with tears and his voice faltered. After the ceremony, a large group of people from the valley, their friends and neighbors, men, women, children, and old people were herded together to a vast pile of wood and brush. Their crime was read out. They were apostates, baptized but practicing as Muslims in secret. The Abenzucars had been forced to watch the auto-da-fé that followed as the accused heretics were burned alive before them. Their screams and cries and pleas to Alejandro's powerless father were a warning of what awaited false Christians. And to remind them that those enemies of the church would pay the penalty as enemies of Spain. And so, Alejandro had entered the church to allay suspicion of the Abenzucars' conversion.

What was Isabella to do now? Alejandro should be the mortal enemy of any Christian Spaniard. But her heart overrode what her religion had drummed into her, and above all, Alejandro's story inspired pity for him and the poor victims.

"God is great! I love you. Betray me if you must. My life is yours to do what you will," Alejandro took her hand and kissed the inside of her wrist. Isabella thought she would faint.

The duenna returned muttering about her bowels and Alejando let go of Isabella's hand. "Your secret is safe. I will never betray you," Isabella whispered behind the duenna's back, longing for the touch of Alejandro's lips again.

In the schoolroom they hardly dared look at one another now, each felt so keenly the presence of the other. Alejandro found it more and more necessary to lean over Isabella's shoulder to point out a passage in a book. Isabella would murmur, "Is this the one? Or this?" pointing to she-hardly-knew-where on the page to keep him close as long as possible.

Then one day when they were alone in the schoolroom save for the duenna snoring in the corner, Alejandro kissed her bent neck. She shivered, her lips parting, and looked up. Then before the two young people knew it, their lips met. Isabella broke away first, whispering they had sinned. Alejandro whispered that he did not care and kissed her again, so firmly that this time Isabella, transported, did not protest. The duenna stirred and they leaped apart.

"Will you come to me tonight?" begged Alejandro in a whisper.

There was no time for Isabella to do anything but whisper "Yes!"

Isabella's duenna slept soundly in an alcove in her room, but in case she woke, Isabella took care to mound her pillows to look like her sleeping form. She donned an embroidered nightdress, scented herself with essence of roses from a little vial, then slipped soundlessly through an anteroom and quietly down the stairs through a servants' entrance to the courtyard where Alejandro swept her into his arms, as if it was where she belonged.

They were young and passionate lovers, meeting every night sheltered behind the great pots of flowers in the corners of the courtyard or in Alejandro's cell, where they huddled together on his narrow bed. Isabella's gold hair cascaded over her naked shoulders as Alejandro recited Dante's sonnets between kisses. But Dante's love for Beatrice was nothing compared to theirs.

"Dante and Beatrice had barely spoken to one another, then she married another and died leaving Dante with nothing but her shade to mourn. What is the good of such love?" Isabella murmured into Alejandro's shoulder, loving its warmth and strength, and pitying Beatrice.

Alejandro kissed the top of her head. "It begat a great work of literature." He sighed. "But I do not want to write a great work of literature. I want only never to be parted from you."

They risked everything for these moments of precarious happiness when nothing existed beyond the two of them, dreading the time when Alejandro would be obliged to return to the seminary and take his final vows, and Isabella's fate would be decided, one way or the other. Isabella knew that her father was considering several offers made for her hand, but she suspected that the priest would not easily abandon his machinations to have her enter a convent. Whatever the outcome, a future without the warmth of Alejandro's love seemed bleak and cold as death itself.

Then Isabella began to feel sick in the mornings, and one day in her bedroom she swooned while dressing for Mass. When she came to her senses she vomited weakly into her handkerchief. She sent her maid to fetch her a dish of lemons, sliced thin, which she suddenly longed for beyond all reason. Her maid brought them and said slyly that when she washed Isabella's underclothes there had been no sign of her monthly blood for some time; perhaps soon it would be necessary to let out the seams in her gowns. When Isabella looked surprised the maid shook her head and muttered something about how interesting this discovery would be for Isabella's future husband. Isabella remembered her mother's violent sickness when pregnant and her fondness, too, for lemons at that time. A terrible possibility presented itself.

The maid rattled on, saying that was Muslim *conversos* for you, anxious only to get under the skirts of Christian girls. "Fr. Alejandro, such a handsome young man for a priest…So diligent with your lessons," she simpered, and then mentioned that her uncle was a familiar of the Inquisition. The maid aspired to be one, too, and her uncle had set her a test, saying she must keep her eyes and ears open for anything to report and promised to have a word on her behalf. Only last week, the maid said dreamily, she had revealed to her uncle that the cook was a secret Jew and in league with the devil to kill the countess's baby when it was born, so it could be used in cannibalistic Jewish rites. The cook had been taken away, weeping with terror and protesting her innocence. A new cook had been hired. The old one was not expected to return.

Any day, the maid expected to receive her reward for this information. But how much greater the reward would be for the information that a *Morisco's* bastard would stain the honor of an Old Christian family! What a pretty bracelet Isabella was wearing. Silently Isabella unclasped it and gave it to her tormentor, then turned her head away.

When Isabella told Alejandro, he put his hand on her stomach and exclaimed in wonder, "A child! Now we *must* be married! Our decision is made for us. God is great!"

But Isabella could think of nothing except what would happen when her condition became known. She would be handed to the Inquisition examiners who would spare her nothing to extract a damning confession and evidence to condemn Alejandro. Then she would be walled up alive while Alejandro would be turned over to the Inquisition until a full confession was tortured out of him, and he was burned at the stake as an apostate like the unfortunate Muslims on his family's estate.

Alejandro said he had a plan. They would flee to his cousins in Portugal, before the maid tired of bribes and Isabella's condition became obvious. "But how?" a tearful Isabella asked. "And when?"

"Hush, beloved! Soon, when your mother gives birth and the household is occupied with the christening."

But it was the countess's death that provided the perfect opportunity. The requiem Mass would be one of the few occasions Isabella could leave the palace, in the company of her duenna of course, but the old woman was a small hindrance. Alejandro would wear a workman's clothes under his habit and Isabella would dress plainly under her cloak. Their plan was to slip away after the requiem Mass, to melt into the crowd when the family left for the internment in their private crypt. The crypt was a confined space and neither Isabella nor Alejandro was important enough to be present, and the count's palace was full of people on account of the funeral. It would be many hours before Isabella and Alejandro were missed from the throng. Alejandro's wealthy father had provided a purse of gold pieces for expenses at the seminary, and with it Alejandro had made the necessary arrangements. A farmer's humble covered cart, mules, and provisions for the journey would be waiting in a side street near St. Nicholas de los Servitas.

There was just one final detail—the place where they were to meet at the church the next day in case they were separated in the crowd. Alejandro had told her to meet him in the far corner of the courtyard at midnight; he had prepared a small plan of the church marked with their meeting place in one of the chapels, he knew of a small service door behind a tapestry. That door led into an alley. Alejandro would be waiting when she came out.

Isabella worried about meeting him with so many priests and friars in the house, but Alejandro assured her that after several long nights' vigils, all would be trying to snatch a few hours' sleep before the next day's funeral.

So while Isabella knelt by her mother's bier and prayed for the souls of her mother and baby brother, she also made guilty supplications for the success of their plan.

When at last she fled the hall and its smells, Isabella sent her maid away and undid her too-tight bodice with relief. How swollen her breasts felt. She reminded herself that she only needed to be patient until tomorrow. She waited until it was time to meet Alejandro, then wrapped a woolen cloak over her nightdress, and managed to negotiate the servants' steep narrow back staircase, clinging to the banister for support and hearing snores in the darkness coming from the great hall.

She waited, barefooted and chilled to the bone, fearing Alejandro had fallen asleep, too. At last she heard soft footsteps crossing the tiles. She hurried to meet him and threw herself into the arms of the hooded figure. "Oh Alejandro, warm me in your arms. It is so cold," she whispered.

But instead of embracing her, the hooded figure stiffened and drew back with a sharp exclamation of surprise. Shoving her roughly away he lowered his hood and Isabella saw not Alejandro but—the priest! Then another figure came from the shadows whispering urgently, "Isabella, we must be quick! The priest is awake but I was afraid you would take cold waiting..."

The priest shouted, "You would seduce the count's daugh ter? Villain, infidel, to insult the honor of this Christian house! Apostate! Devil! False Christian!"

Servants and friars appeared, rubbing the sleep from their eyes. "Seize him!" the priest roared.

Isabella fell at the priest's feet to protest it was her fault, but it was too late. There was an uproar and Alejandro was dragged away struggling in the grips of four men, crying out the fault was his, not Isabella's.

The count was informed immediately, and at first refused to believe that his daughter had been beguiled into a clandestine meeting with a lowly *converso* friar. Had he suspected how far the relationship had gone, he would have drawn his sword and killed Isabella and Alejandro on the spot. As it was, he had Isabella whipped unconscious, then locked in her chamber.

The next day he broke off all betrothal negotiations.

Her maid brought bread and water once a day and Isabella passed her time in pain and silence. A month went by and Easter approached. The welts on her back healed. She stopped feeling sick and her waist grew thicker. The sly maid whispered that since the winter had been mild, an epidemic of fever was spreading through the poor quarters of the city. She told Isabella that a great bribe from Alejandro's family had spared his life, but he had been sent to work in the infirmary for the poor, where the pestilence raged. With great relish the maid described the hell of filth, suffering, and death into which Alejandro had been cast, until Isabella covered her ears and gave the maid a brooch to go away.

The mirror told Isabella she had changed. Her soft cheeks had hollows; there were shadows under her eyes and her dark gold hair was dull and thin. She felt suffocated by a noxious pervasive smell as the weather grew warmer. The pestilence? Her maid hinted there were ways not to have a baby; there were potions and spells and old women who could "see to it." Isabella turned a deaf ear. She wanted nothing to do with spells and witchcraft and poisons that would conjure the baby from her body. She remembered the look of joy on Alejandro's face when she told him, and felt such an intense love for the baby it nearly choked her. The maid helped herself to Isabella's things with impunity—trinkets and clothing, gloves, a shawl, ribbons. Isabella scarcely noticed. She could think of only one thing—how to save the baby.

Alejandro managed to send Isabella a letter calling her his dearest Beatrice, his light in hell. She must forget him and think only of herself and their child; if she could find her way to the Valley of the Swallows, she might throw herself on the mercy of his family. Isabella kissed the paper and felt a glimmer of hope. Alejandro was alive. Perhaps they might yet escape to Portugal...The baby kicked, to encourage her. Could the greedy maid be bribed to help them escape? Isabella discovered cunning. She reminded the maid that the Inquisition had never paid her for her betrayal of the cook, while she would be well rewarded for aiding her and Alejandro's escape. The maid admitted this was true and agreed to carry letters between the lovers so they could work out what would be necessary—mules, food, and bribes for those who guarded Alejandro.

Then the maid returned with news that Alejandro was dead. He had succumbed to the pestilence, and his body had been thrown into a common grave in a lime pit behind the infirmary along with the corpses of the poor. Isabella betrayed no emotion, too bereft to weep. Had he died with her name on his lips? She longed for death, too, but she must live, at least until the baby was born. She knew she must find a way to escape the palace before she gave birth, and make her way to the Abenzucars. The sly and dishonest maid was her only hope. Then even that frail link was severed. A new serving girl who was deaf and dumb brought Isabella's food and Isabella never saw her former maid again.

Hoping for a reward, the maid had reported to the count that Isabella and the *Morisco* still corresponded and planned to run away. The count did not believe her and had her locked in the cellars without food or drink to prevent such a vile story spreading. There, with rats scrabbling in the dark for company, the maid knew that her only revenge was that the count's precious family line would be polluted with the blood of heretics! She perished miserably trying to suck moisture from the walls.

Isabella, equally trapped in the palace, only knew her situation grew more dangerous with each day that passed. Then, incredibly, it was the priest's intervention that opened the door for her escape. Despite the count's efforts to suppress it, rumors of Isabella's attempted seduction by an infidel had spread among Old Christian families. The priest advised the count that the best that could be done in the circumstances was to place Isabella in a convent far from Madrid, preferably among an insignificant order of nuns. Let the girl and the scandal she had caused die in obscurity.

When the count informed his disgraced daughter of her fate, Isabella heard him with downcast eyes and a submissive expression, masking the spark of hope his words raised in her heart. On her knees, she begged her father as penance that he allow her three days in his library, to choose a convent such as he intended. Her father, having no better plan, agreed and dismissed her curtly, taking little notice of the fact that her wide hooped skirts sat higher than before. Isabella's disability had always given her an awkward shape.

In the count's library Isabella hunted desperately for the book that mentioned the convent of the swallows above the valley where the Abenzucars lived. She finally found what she was looking for, a disintegrating volume with mildewed pages that made her sneeze. It had been written by a Christian hermit's acolyte during the time of the Moors. The young acolyte had joined the hermit in his cave in the Andalusian mountains, intending to share his master's privations and preserve his teachings for posterity. But the hermit kept such long spells of fasting and silence that the acolyte went in search of food and conversation with the mountain folk. Among them was a community of religious women living in what the Moors called the House of the Swallows, and Christians called Las Golondrinas Convent.

Isabella had never heard of the order, Sors Santas de Jesus— Holy Sisters of Jesus. According to the acolyte, local people believed the order had occupied the site before the Moors and even the Visigoths before them, possibly since the Roman occupation of Hispania. The order was skilled with medicines, and the convent was known for charity to the poor of the mountain villages, regardless of their religion. Mountain people believed the nuns had special powers given by God. They said the swallows that returned to the convent each year from their migration and gave the place its name were the souls of dead nuns, and the convent was haunted by a tall woman in a billowing cloak. The main thing was that it would satisfy her father's wish to hide her away.

Isabella cared only for the convent's proximity to the Abenzucars in the valley below. For the moment she had no plan beyond reaching that valley. What to say to Alejandro's family, whether they would take her in—she would worry about that on the journey. Could she manage so long a journey, concealing her condition? She must. Fortunately she was slender, and the swell of her stomach could be disguised by exaggerating her limp to make her skirts sway, or bending to lean on her walking stick.

The count had never heard of the order, but made his own inquiries. What he learned gave him a grim satisfaction. The convent had Old Christian associations, and was far from Madrid in the mountains, at the end of an old Roman route from the coast. He sent for his notaries to prepare the nun's dowry Isabella was to have. As soon as that matter was settled they left Madrid, Isabella concealed behind the leather curtains of the carriage. But her plan to go to the Abenzucars was now impossible. Her father was accompanying her on horseback.

Day after day, they traveled with agonizing slowness, Isabella willing the carriage to hurry, bracing herself against the cushions, counting over and over on her fingers the number of months. She thought they would reach the convent in time, unless the baby came too quickly. Her mother's troubled experiences of childbirth had been the subject of whispered discussions among the maids and nurses of the household, and Isabella had acquired more knowledge of pregnancy and childbirth than most unmarried girls. She knew there was not much time left. A mule grew lame. A wheel did not turn properly. They halted for salve and then repairs. Isabella questioned the coachman impatiently. How much farther? The coachman did not know.

The road into the mountains grew steeper. Fresh mules were hitched to the carriage and new drivers took over, local men. When she asked, they pointed to the mountain ahead of them and finally gave her the welcome news they would reach Las Golondrinas Convent the next day. Inside the carriage Isabella stroked her belly to calm the baby as it kicked. By the time the carriage stopped for the night at a mountain *refugio*, a dull pain had begun tightening across her abdomen and back. Throughout a long night it came and went, came and went. Isabella lay sleepless on her straw pallet, perspiring with fear.

CHAPTER 7

Las Golondrinas Convent, Summer 1505

The next day the mules panted and strained to haul the carriage up the last steep gradient before finally pulling to a stop. Nauseous from the twisting road, Isabella leaned out the window and took great desperate gulps of air that was clean and cool after the scorching heat of the plains. Gold and ruby earrings flashed in the sun as she turned her head for the view of Alejandro's childhood home. Below her spread well-tended terraces of olive trees and vegetable gardens and she could hear goats' bells and the distant calls of shepherd boys. In the distance, small white villages clung to the mountains.

Relief at reaching her destination and the scent of sun-warmed herbs and pine soothed her nerves and stomach. She craned her neck to look up at the convent gates and walls with their barred windows and flocks of swallows whirling and dipping around the bell tower. She squinted against the bright sunlight. Save for the cross on top of the bell tower it could have been another empty Moorish fortress standing with its back to the rock face of the mountain. They had passed many such fortresses and castles the Moors had built, then abandoned in the *Reconquista*. Yes, there, just as the book had described, the statue with her hand out to the stone swallows carved around her feet, carved so realistically they looked about to take flight. Isabella closed her eyes, and for a moment it was not the mountain breeze but Alejandro's breath on her cheek, and she was comforted.

Only for a moment. There were new trials ahead. The pain gripped again, harder and more insistently. She clutched her handkerchief tighter and her breath came shallowly. Small beads of sweat appeared on her upper lip. She glanced at her father who was discussing something with the groom who waited to take his reins. She bit down on her handkerchief. Trying to think of anything but the pain, she distracted herself recalling what the acolyte had said of this place.

Before the convent, heathen goddesses had been worshipped by women who had somehow found their way to this remote spot. The Phoenicians had left shards of votive pottery and amulets and a small stone with Punic writing claiming it as the shrine of the goddess Astarte. According to Pliny, Carthaginian women were abandoned here when Hannibal led their men over the mountains on elephants to attack Rome, and rededicated Astarte's altar to their goddess Tanit. In Hadrian's time adventurous young soldiers would undertake expeditions to search for a legendary colony of beautiful Carthaginian girls in the mountains. But the Christian God and the intercession of the Virgin had vanquished pagan associations...

The pain gripping Isabella receded and she abandoned her recital to wonder what was keeping her father talking to one of the grooms for so long. A few minutes later the hand resting on the carriage window tightened again on her wadded handkerchief. She *must* get inside. Soon.

Then the coachman was opening the carriage door and placing a block in front of the steps. "Come daughter," said the count sternly. She needed his help to descend, and, gathering her skirts bulkily in one hand, she gave him the other and tried not to grimace. Perspiration broke out on her brow. The baby's life depended on her giving no sign. She willed the pain to wait, just a little farther now...another step...another.

They reached the gate, and the count knocked loudly. A grilled window slid open and a woman's voice demanded to know who was there. The count gave their names and titles and after a moment the gate creaked open wide enough for a girl to enter. As the pain came again Isabella caught her breath and the smallest moan escaped her lips. The count was grimly pleased by her seeming reluctance to enter. But her hesitation was because something hot and wet gushed down her thigh. She bent her head and kissed her father's hand, seizing her opportunity for the only revenge available to her. "Farewell. From this moment on I leave the name of sinful Isabella in the dust at my feet. In your prayers remember me as Sor Beatriz, the name I will take when I am professed."

She let go of his hand, turned her back, and as she entered the gate, a pale hand in a nun's sleeve reached out to pull her inside. The portress bowed silently to the count and swung the great gate closed with a thud as Isabella clutched the portress hard by the arm and sank to her knees with a cry she could no longer suppress— because of the pain and because she was trapped. Her plan had failed. She would never reach the Abenzucars now!

CHAPTER 8

Las Golondrinas Convent, Summer 1505

Isabella lay panting on a hard bed as two nuns in black habits and a beata in a brown dress moved back and forth over her. Beyond the candles burning at the end of the bed, the room was dim. She had no idea how long she had been there, in the clutches of pain like a great beast that showed her no mercy, returning again and again to tear her in two. Isabella moaned through clenched teeth at its approach. As it subsided, she looked wildly about her, the plain bare room, the flickering shadows of the nuns. How did she get here? Everything was unreal, unknown—the bed she lay in, the people around her, her own body. She longed to sleep. Her father...a journey...the gate...It was hard to think, here it came again...she tried to resist the urge to scream. She gasped, then clenched her teeth. But in the end the scream poured out of her as the pain took hold, stronger than before.

When she finally drew breath, the beata wiped her brow again and told her to suck on a wet cloth that tasted of some bitter herb. The pain receded but she felt dizzy. What had happened? The portress, she recalled foggily. The portress had slammed the gate and shouted...the baby—oh God, here it came again...

Throughout the long night and the next day Isabella was help-lessly adrift in a nightmare, aware of nothing but the pain that came and went. When she opened her eyes she saw the nuns' worried expressions as they whispered to each other, pushed and prodded her. She tried to fight them off.

Then a steady, authoritative voice penetrated her exhausted brain, ordering her to push, *push now!* Over and over. The voice grew louder and more insistent, forcing Isabella to try to obey, but she had no strength left. Someone took her wrists and pulled her up, and another supported her back, and the authoritative voice came again but from a great distance, saying now, NOW...a hot, sickly smell of blood filled the room. Isabella saw her dead mother's face, only her mother had pushed aside the black lace shroud that had covered it, shouting, "Now! Now!"

Isabella made a mighty effort and fell back, knowing she was dying. She was shaking uncontrollably, growing cold, falling, falling away. They were forcing something into her mouth but she could not taste it. The baby...she twisted her head away to beg for mercy for the baby. But they were stronger, something filled her mouth and she could not speak, she choked...poison...She surrendered to darkness.

When she opened her eyes again, sunlight streamed through a narrow window and birds were making a great noise outside. Between her legs it felt very sore and raw, and she felt both heavy and empty in her stomach. Her hand groped feebly across its new flatness, now tightly swaddled. She was wearing a coarse linen nightdress and her hair was braided. Several nuns bustled around the room whispering to each other. One carried a basin of water; another had a casket open, arranging vials inside. By the window another nun jiggled a bundle in her arms. The bundle began to wail.

It sounds like a baby, thought Isabella. Then she remembered.

There was a swish of skirts and a *"Deo gratias!"* The voice approaching the bed was the same firm, authoritative one that had

109

ordered her to push. A nun with a broad, rather stern face with pronounced eyebrows, framed in a wimple, bent over the bed. A medal swung on a chain on the front of her habit, a rosary was at her waist, her arms were folded inside the sleeves of her habit, and she had a terrifying air of authority. "I am the Abbess. How are you feeling? Speak if you can, but if you cannot, rest and I will return later."

Isabella was filled with despair. The Abbess had come to take the baby away! She gulped miserably and looked hard at the medal swinging in front of her eyes. There was a small bird on the medal and if she just kept looking at it everything would..."Isabella! Look at me!" the voice commanded.

Isabella raised terrified eyes. "Reverend Mother Abbess...the baby is innocent."

"That's better! You can talk. You gave us all a terrible fright that the baby would not come out, but in the end, thanks be to God, you managed it. You have a daughter, whom we baptized Salome when we thought you would die without giving her a name. Don't you want to hold her? She has been crying for her mother for five days now. A wet nurse is all very well, but it is best for her mother to feed her."

Salome? Feed her? The baby wailed lustily and Isabella struggled to sit up a little and winced. She felt a pressure in her breasts and her nipples stung. "Oh! What do I do?" The front of her gown grew two circles of damp.

The Abbess nodded approvingly. "Good. Your milk is coming in. You will soon manage." With strong arms she helped prop Isabella up and beckoned the sister holding the crying baby. "Pull your gown down in front—that's right." The nun lay the baby in the crook of Isabella's arm against her breast. Feeling a nipple on her cheek, Salome turned at once to clamp her tiny mouth on it and shivered as she began sucking greedily.

Weak as she was, a smile of delight crossed Isabella's face as she stared down at the small pink scrap of humanity. "How beautiful she is! Look at her hair, so thick, and such perfect little fingers!" The baby opened one eye and stared up at her mother, as if to say, "Of course, what did you expect?" Then she resumed her noisy sucking. Isabella's arms tightened protectively.

"We assume your father did not know," said the Abbess.

"No," faltered Isabella.

"Humpff! Men see only what they wish. The portress could tell what the situation was at once, and took care to close the gate in a hurry." The Abbess's tone was dry. "You did well to conceal your condition until the last minute. It probably saved both your lives."

Isabella looked up and asked fearfully, "Will you send me back?"

"Do you wish it?"

"No."

"And the baby's father?"

"Dead," she whispered, stroking the baby's head. "Dead. He...I contrived to come here because his family lives in the valley—"

"The *Abenzucars*?"

Isabella nodded and held her breath.

The Abbess looked thoughtful. "Hmm. Their youngest son, I knew him as a child. He came with his mother and aunts to visit. A sweet-natured boy, clever. He went into the church, a kind of hostage after the family converted."

Isabella nodded. "He told me. He was tutor to my brothers. We planned to run away, to Portugal, and then when we were separated he told me I must try and reach his family, but my father decided to accompany me...and it was not possible. And now I see Alejandro's family would only understand that their son is dead because of me and hate me even if they agreed to take Salome, and we would be separated forever."

"My dear, I think you do the Abenzucars an injustice, but that said, if anyone outside the convent learns the truth, there will be terrible consequences for the Abenzucars, for the baby, and for you. I think it is in your interest to take your vows and remain here with the baby, sending no word to the Abenzucars."

Isabella murmured, "Stay? I can hardly take a nun's vow of chastity!"

"Hmm. We are all sinners, life is precious, and children are a blessing. And many great nuns, prioresses and Abbesses, saints of the church even, were also mothers. It is a holy estate. Men and women of the church see chastity differently. Men give it an unnecessary spiritual significance and use it as a tool to control women. But for religious women, freedom from family ties allows them to progress in worship, study, and a life of practical service to God. However, you are free to decide for yourself. You may make your full confession to me, and decide in time whether you wish to remain, and whether to profess or not."

This was stranger and stranger. "Confession to you? Surely to a priest?"

The Abbess rose and folded her hands. "Ah, our elderly priest!" she said dismissively. "We do, of course, *have* a priest, though he sleeps most of the time. The church takes care to provide our community of poor, feeble women with a priest, because men, even dribbling in their dotage, must hold spiritual dominion over women. Pah! The priests they send are always so old that we are obliged to care for them until they die. Fortunately the Abbess of Las Golondrinas may hear confessions and give penance and absolution."

Isabella stared at her, open-mouthed. The Abbess permitted herself a little smile.

"A special dispensation. Granted by Bishop St. Valerius of Saragossa before he was martyred in the reign of Diocletian, because our community was so isolated in these mountains. He hoped our example would encourage celibacy among mountain women." The Abbess rolled her eyes, as if she were asking heaven to give her patience. "I often wonder if men of the church would prefer procreation to cease altogether. So far no pope has revoked the dispensation, because we have powerful friends at court who—"

Somewhere beyond the room a woman shrieked loudly and the Abbess patted Isabella's hand and rose to her feet as a nun bustled into the room. "Here is a sister with some food. Try to eat and then rest. We will speak later. I must go. A local woman is about to deliver, with great difficulty I fear. Come sisters, don't forget the medicine chest and clean towels."

The four nuns swept out, leaving Isabella alone with an earthenware bowl of soup steaming on a stool beside her, bread, a peach, and a cup of wine. Salome was asleep. Isabella lay her carefully down and drank her soup. It smelled of herbs, and there was an egg poached in it, the most delicious thing she had ever eaten. She soaked the last drops of soup up with the bread, then savored the peach slowly, letting the juice run down her chin. She took a sip of wine. Her ordeal was over, the burden of fear and concealment she had borne for so long lifted from her shoulders, and though she could scarcely believe it, she and the baby were both alive and safe. Her relief was so great it brought tears and the certainty that she would stay. She held Salome tight and whispered against the baby's soft head, "We are safe, precious one. Your father led us here and his spirit will be with us. God is great, Salome. God is great."

CHAPTER 9

From the Chronicle of Las Sors Santas de Jesus,
Las Golondrinas Convent, Andalusia, January 1509

Peace on all who read this.

By the Abbess's command, I, Sor Beatriz of the Holy Sisters of Jesus, scribe of Las Golondrinas Convent, begin this Chronicle of our order. We trust that whatever befalls the convent, this record containing the Gospel of our Foundress and the traditions which guide our work will survive to bear witness to the truth at some future time.

The Abbess says that to begin, we must imagine a stranger to the order opening this book, perhaps many years hence. To introduce such a reader to the matters contained in the Chronicle, she thinks it helpful if I begin with my own consecration into the order, the reasons for my appointment as scribe, and the particular circumstances which led to the keeping of this book. Otherwise I would never venture to write of my unworthy self, first or indeed at all, but it is my duty to obey the Abbess in all things.

After three years as a novice following the birth of my daughter Salome at the convent, I took my final vows and the name Sor Beatriz on Salome's third birthday. She shared the joy of the day, and sat by my side at the feast of welcome in the *sala grande*. The other sisters fed her tidbits and sweets like she was a baby bird.

Salome shares my cell. The Abbess will not permit my child to be separated from me to live among the orphans, saying in her forthright way that at least one child in the convent shall have her mother. I hardly dared hope for such indulgence. The child keeps a nun's day, waking briefly when I rise in the early hours for Terce, then joining us in the chapel for Mass. She is very obedient, understanding that her mother and the others must have quiet at certain times as they examine their consciences or meditate, and that at other times we are very busy, so that she spends most of her waking hours with the orphanage children sharing their dolls and toys as I go about my work. The rest of the time she is petted and chided and prayed with and told stories of the saints by all the sisters. I share her with many mothers.

I expected to be assigned the lowliest tasks in the convent, but the Abbess wished me to assist elderly Sor Angela, who had presided over the scriptorium for thirty-five years. Though strong in her faith, Sor Angela was a fierce guardian of her domain. Under her direction I cataloged and dusted books and scrolls and manu-scripts, mixed ink and prepared quills, trimmed candles, kept the seals and wax in their places, made sure there was clean sand for blotting, and saw that each child in the orphanage had her own small missal and lives of the saints. The one thing which earned Sor Angela's grudging approval was my handwriting—she repeat-edly said it was a blessing I had at least been taught to write quickly and neatly. When Sor Angela died in her sleep a month ago, the Abbess said that I was best placed to assume her duties.

Until now the scribe dealt mainly with convent correspon-dence—business matters and requests for methods of preparing medicines or the arrangements in our infirmaries, as well as over-seeing the records and books and documents stored in the scrip-torium. Our Abbess, who is young and likes order and efficiency, has never liked the keeping of our records in a haphazard method on scrolls, and has always believed the convent should have a proper Chronicle, especially so there is a meticulous record of the times when our beloved Foundress has appeared to the convent in a vision. On these occasions the Foundress has always appeared for a particular purpose—to give advice or a warning. Her words were always dictated meticulously to the scribe, that they might be consulted when necessary.

The scriptorium was of course open to all the order—it has been our rule since the community's earliest days that knowledge is shared and all the nuns are educated, able to read and write, to know arithmetic and Latin. But Sor Angela allowed no one else to touch the scrolls, insisting that they be stored in a particular order that only she understood, in a certain alcove, behind a curtain. Even the Abbess hesitated if she wished to consult the scrolls, both because of Sor Angela and because locating anything was difficult. But while Sor Angela ruled the scriptorium nothing could be done.

Sor Angela did not know that it was also my duty to keep watch on her, as she occasionally knocked over a candle without realizing. Alas, had she set the scriptorium aflame, it could have done no less damage than her method of storage.

Last week as I was mixing ink to answer a letter, the Abbess came and wished to read the account of the Foundress's words when she last appeared in a vision, an event that had taken place over thirty years earlier. She would not have me stand and fetch it, so I directed her to the alcove where the scrolls were kept, and had just dipped my nib into the ink when the Abbess's screams shattered the peace. I dropped my pen and hurried to her as fast as my bad leg allowed, fearing she had disturbed a nest of vipers and had been bitten. Instead, behind the curtain, the alcove was a mess of ragged pieces of chewed sheepskin and shreds of vellum—the work of rats! The Abbess and I were quite overcome by the horror of it and wept together for the loss.

"Perhaps," said the Abbess, drying her eyes with her sleeve, "it is not quite so bad as it looks." But it was. Even without the rats, many scrolls had disintegrated, brittle with age or mildewed and illegible. Some crumbled to dust in our hands.

As we sifted through the mess the Abbess sighed. "A letter has come from the Holy Office of the Inquisition that makes me uneasy and I was seeking the Chronicle entry of the last time our Foundress appeared. I believe it was shortly after our Catholic monarchs Isabella and Ferdinand married, and she warned they had vowed to unite Spain under the Christian faith, drive the Moors out and, with the pope's blessing, would strengthen the Inquisition's powers to purge the country of heretics and infidels. The Foundress warned of terror to come and advised how to protect the Gospel. That is what I need to know. Because the letter says they will begin a systematic examination of religious houses like ours which enjoy the patronage of the royal family, as 'the involvement of the royal family requires regular confirmation of the purity of the faith and the absence of heretics.' They are looking for Muslims and Jews of course, and even if there are none, the Inquisition has methods that will discover them, or at least *conversos* who are automatically suspect. Bah! It is an evil thing the Inquisition does, to sow division among those who serve God and help the poor. Our order has lived peacefully under Romans and Visigoths and longest of all, our Moorish rulers. We have always held the Prophet Muhammad in great respect, and like both Jews and Muslims, the first Christians attributed all things to God's will. We have much in common, whether Jew, Muslim, or Christian, only God can judge among us. And yet the church sows dissention and bloodshed. And we must do what we can." She had made a pile of scraps while she spoke, but it was impossible to see how one of these shreds joined to one another.

Then I made a happy discovery—the most recent scroll, being newer, had fared better, chewed but still partly legible. "Here is something, Abbess. This piece fits with that one. See...one can make some sense of the writing...*In the reign of Abu l-Hasan Ali, Sultan of Granada, our Foundress came to us...*"

The Abbess exclaimed, "A miracle! *Deo gratias.* I believe it was in the reign of Abu l-Hasan Ali! Is the rest legible? Can you make it out?"

"Not yet. I will try and copy out what is legible and find the sense of it. But Abbess, I have an idea. Why not use this opportunity to begin a proper Chronicle of our order, as you have always wished? We could use the Abenzucars' gift."

The Abenzucars—a bittersweet name, even now—had sent us a very fine gift for the scriptorium: a large book of blank vellum pages, beautifully cured so they were almost translucent, superior to the old scrolls, which stank of goat. It is bound in leather and gold, and even has a gold swallow on the cover. It was sent in thanks for a healing balm of herbs from our garden, herbs that will not grow at a lower height, supplied to the Abenzucars when their youngest daughter would not heal after childbirth and they feared for her life. The girl recovered, *Deo gratias.* Salome's aunt. "The book will be easier to protect against rats than the jumble of old scrolls and will last for many years."

The Abbess nodded and rose to her feet, brushing the dust off her hands. "We must remember, God sends even disasters for a purpose. Yes, use the Abenzucars' book. It is large, and if you write small and close, it will hold a great deal. And of course, a single book can be protected—and transported—in a way the scrolls cannot. And I see another advantage. Our Gospel is disintegrating; it could be copied into the new Chronicle before it, too, is lost."

The Gospel! I had not thought of that, but the Abbess was right. Although the rats could not damage it where it is kept in a silver casket, time was destroying it. Though the nuns of course know the Gospel by heart, it is a custom of the order that on the eve of a nun's consecration, she has a special audience with the Abbess to receive the Abbess's blessing and words of welcome, and is shown our great treasure, the ancient Gospel. When my turn came I watched nervously as she lifted it from its silver casket. The precious document resembled a bundle of dry leaves, crumbling with age so that flakes of it fell on her lap. In truth its condition, even unchewed by rats, is little better than our poor destroyed scrolls.

The Abbess was right, our Gospel must be copied soon or it will be lost. But it must also be kept from the Inquisition, for the same reasons they must not find this Chronicle with its mention of the Foundress's appearances and the Abbess's medal. Both undermine the doctrines and power of a church where men have refashioned God in man's image, and denied women's true spirituality. Discovery would doom us all, and the destruction that would follow would prevent the truth ever coming to light, as the Abbess believes will happen someday.

The Abbess rose to her feet and brushed her hands together briskly. "Copy the Gospel into the middle of the book—in Latin, just as it is now—and let our Chronicle be written around it to symbolize our order's embrace of the holy book. And if everything is together it will make better sense if someone is to read it many years hence. Let the maid tidy the scriptorium, and tell her to put the scraps on the fire when you have finished with them."

Obedient to the Abbess's wishes, I worked by day and by candlelight to recover the following account of the Foundress's last appearance:

1470 Anno Domini. Peace...all who read...reign of Abu l-Hasan Ali, Sultan of Granada...the Abbess a vision...Foundress...news...Infanta Isabella of Castile defied King Henry...Infante Ferdinand...of Aragon... Spain...God's kingdom...Moors crushed and banished...Queen Isabella... pilgrimage to Las Golondrinas...the Carthaginian road...Beware the Inquisition will...remember the fate of the Cathars...Carcassone...Gran Canaria...a mission the Gospel...the medal.

The Abbess and I interpret this as a warning of the Inquisition's interest in Las Golondrinas, on the queen's account. Queen Isabella did make a pilgrimage here after the final defeat of the Moors, and vowed to be a patron of Las Golondrinas to honor the courage of a Christian order that kept the light of faith alive through centuries of the Muslim darkness. Royal ladies are still our patronesses and protectors, but the Foundress surely intended to remind us of the fate of the "heretic" Cathars when the "Catholic" army destroyed Carcassonne, burning and hanging all who would not recant. Was the Foundress warning us that to protect the medal and the Gospel we must establish a mission in Gran Canaria?

But when? And how?

Summer 1509

In spring and summer, when the road up the mountain is passable, the children come. We received two today. They have very fine clothes and are both about one year old. I record the amount of their dowries in the Dowry List. We have no more information to add to the records; they have no names other than the ones we give. They say arrangements are made for the children's removal from court in great secrecy through a chain of wretches who act as go-betweens, so that none will know the children's ultimate destination. Most come in the care of peasant nurses who can tell us nothing of their true identities.

Poor nameless innocents. Do the mothers, if living, long for their daughters? I think of being separated from Salome in this way and give thanks to God every day for our refuge. Word has reached me that my father now believes—possibly informed by one of the servants—that I was with child when he left me here. He has sworn to be revenged, but I trust in God's protection.

Winter 1510

It is a hard winter. Snow has fallen continuously in the mountains. Yet in the pilgrims' garden, by some miracle, the spring does not freeze.

Salome joins the other girls in the schoolroom and learns her prayers in Latin and her numbers. She plays at "writing" at a makeshift table of wooden planks. She wishes to copy me in everything and sits with her adorable face twisted in concentration, practicing her letters. Then Salome looks up at me and a smile lights her face—the way it once lit her father's when I entered the schoolroom each morning.

There have been wonderful occurrences. The sky was filled with shooting stars at Epiphany, three nights in succession. Despite the cold, an almond tree has blossomed out of season and local people report seeing a fiery dragon in the sky. There is much hunger in the villages, and the Abbess and the sister in charge of stores are eking out our supplies of grain, oil, and dried fruit to make sure all have something. The nuns, of course, fast as much as possible—faith is a great sustainer of life—but the children in the orphanage and the patients in our infirmary must eat. We fight a constant battle to protect the food stocks from the rats. May God preserve us all until summer and the new crops.

Spring 1512

A sudden spring thaw during Lent brought disaster to the village last week. As the snows melted, a landslide buried a lower slope where the village's goats and sheep were grazing. The animals were swept away and five men herding them have been brought to the infirmary, badly injured. The infirmary sisters struggle to save four of them, but the fifth will certainly die; he has a pregnant wife and many children who depend on him and whom we must help.

Our stores are nearly bare at this time of year and the Abbess has used the last of our hoarded sugar and flour to make *polvorónes*. The dying man's brother has volunteered to take them to sell in the city via the ancient but steeper mule track through the trees. At Easter our *polvorónes* are in great demand in the rich households, and the brother can buy as much food as they can spare in the Valley of the Swallows to share out among the hungry villagers. In the convent we are reduced to a thin gruel, but nuns can survive on prayer. Salome has most of my share. She is too thin and her skin has a translucent look.

Summer 1514

News reaches us that the Spanish governors of the island of Hispaniola are criticized for their treatment of the natives there, and in Seville many are dead of the plague. We pray for the priests who have condemned the violent treatment of the Indians and say novenas for an end to the pestilence, for the dead and dying. The Holy Office sent another letter emphasizing the faithful are required to report any suspected of being false Christians. The Abbess was bad tempered for the rest of the day.

The slope below the convent has been terraced, and the apple trees and new olive trees are thriving. Our chickens increase and peck among them, though we must be careful all are shooed into their enclosure at nightfall, on account of the foxes. We will have special Masses said for a good harvest this year.

Spring 1518

Two visiting friars sought permission from the Abbess to speak to me at the *locutio* in the scriptorium on a medical matter. They were seeking a remedy for the bite of a mad dog. They whispered through the grille in the scriptorium that they had heard there was an infidel remedy that was infallible, and they were desperate for their bitten brother. I ceased my work and went to find the treatise by Avicenna but their furtive urging made me suspect they were

Inquisition informers. Since Avicenna was a Muslim doctor, I told them that the remedy I copied out for them was given to us two centuries ago by a Christian hermit who had lived in a mountain cave nearby. Perhaps they had heard of the book written by his acolyte? A very holy man. The remedy had been revealed to him by San Hieronimo. I cautioned them, the remedy would only be efficacious if applied with a pure heart while special prayers to the Virgin and St. Anthony were recited.

The friars cannot read.

September 1520

Late this summer two royal princesses followed in the late queen's footsteps and paid a visit, accompanied by many noble ladies. Their entourage made a great spectacle. Their coaches were drawn by pure-white mules, and they were accompanied by outriders with colorful banners, a large mounted guard in livery, and many Jesuits. The princesses had a requiem Mass said in the chapel for their grandparents, Isabella and Ferdinand, and their widowed mother, Queen Juana who is confined to a convent in Tordesillas. The gossip among the ladies-in-waiting was that ever since being widowed many years ago, she keeps her husband's preserved corpse in her cell for company and is greatly disturbed in the mind. Others said that the story of her husband's corpse is a fabrication, that she is sound of mind and kept prisoner against her will. Poor lady, a woman is powerless against the might of the church and secular authorities who will declare her mad or weak or both to justify their disposal of her.

The princesses stayed for three days, taking part in the daily life of the convent at Mass, prayers, and meals, and even donning straw hats to pick vegetables in our garden. The orphanage children sang an anthem for them, quite beautifully we thought, and afterward they gave each child a gold coin, including Salome whom they assumed was one of the orphanage girls. The princesses renewed their grandmother's promise of patronage and made a generous gift to the convent before departing. The Abbess was quite exhausted afterward.

Salome sits by my side half the day. She finishes her lessons before the other girls, and grows restless. She is quick with her Latin and Greek and can read Italian and a little French. I require her to sit still and practice her writing, stressing the importance of a neat, even, and legible hand, with no ink blots—despite her tearful protests that this is impossible. She stamps her foot when I oblige her to recopy mistakes, but she is learning to write with a beautiful, even hand.

The Abbess assigns Salome small scribe's tasks, sharpening quills or preparing the ink, and since Salome is conscientious and always washes her hands before she touches a book, the Abbess allows her to look at our beautiful illuminated missals. Some very fine ones were donated by our royal patronesses, with gold lettering enclosing holy pictures in the most beautiful detail of saints and angels and the Virgin, castles and knights, animals so finely drawn that even their little whiskers are discernible, fields and forests, sun and moon and stars, a glowing glimpse of a heavenly world. Salome loves them as much as the Abbess and I do, and has developed a fine sensitivity to the paintings in the convent, too.

She dislikes many of those donated by the pilgrims—compared to our beautiful manuscript they are often quite badly drawn, a triumph of faith over skill, but the Abbess insists we must hang all such gifts. The dark corridor we pass through on our way to the *sala de las niñas* each morning is full of the worst ones.

But finer paintings occasionally come to us with an orphan's dowry, and Salome helps the Abbess choose which to hang in the *sala de las niñas*. There are paintings of the Virgin and infant Christ and of child saints, showing the gentle influence of the Italian school with lovely rich colors, sensitive faces, and exquisite perfect landscapes in the background exuding the warmth of divine grace. They make the *sala de las niñas* a kindly room for the orphanage children.

At fifteen Salome is tall for her age, with her father's dark-blue eyes and my gold hair, before it was shorn. She does not see why she may not have a novice's habit yet. I tell her all in good time, though my heart is in turmoil for her future. Although I have found peace and contentment as a nun, because I was in love once I perceive that my daughter has an equal capacity for passion. I would not like her to be obliged to take the veil like the orphanage children, yet I do not see how she is to experience life outside the convent, or marry. And of course I would not send her away alone. When I ponder what is best for Salome, I imagine Alejandro and I had managed our escape to Portugal. We would now be discussing the future of Salome and our other children by the fire of a long winter's night. But it is ungrateful to repine. Salome's life will be as God wills.

Summer 1521

Salome is sixteen and has finally acquired the novice's habit she longed for. She thinks it is a promotion from the schoolroom, and that it makes her the equal of the other girls who enter the novitiate at sixteen. She is lively and affectionate and full of mischief.

April 1523

Such a thing has happened! Yesterday evening the Foundress appeared to the Abbess in the cloister, so quickly that the Abbess scarcely had time to realize what was happening before the Foundress delivered her instructions and disappeared. The Inquisition will come to Las Golondrinas, though when is uncertain, and the Abbess must prepare now to send our medal and Gospel away for safekeeping. A mission convent of our order is to be established in Gran Canaria. The Abbess must select twelve to go: four professed sisters, four novices who have not yet taken their final vows, and four middle-aged beatas chosen for their health and good sense. The most senior nun shall be authorized to act as Mother Superior to hear confessions, and one of the party must act as a scribe and write an account of the journey. In due course, other members of the order would follow.

Dictating all this to me for the Chronicle, the Abbess paced the scriptorium. "I do not know whether we are meant to send the medal and Gospel at once or wait until the mission is ready and send them with a later party. What if they were lost because I acted too hastily?"

"Perhaps too cautious is the preferable course," I replied. "Remember the damage the rats caused here, and how we have had a special metal-lined casket built in the wall of the scriptorium to protect the Chronicle now. We should wait until we know there is a similar safe place to keep the Chronicle in Gran Canaria. Who knows what conditions the mission will find in Gran Canaria, or how they will find a suitable building. Perhaps it is best to wait for word that all is ready, and then the medal and the Gospel can go."

"Yes, I think that is best, Sor Beatriz. We will wait until the mission has prepared a place for them."

June 1523

The convent threw itself into the preparations, and two months later all is ready. The Abbess sent two men from the village to Seville to arrange passage for the missionaries on a ship bound for Gran Canaria. They returned with news that the ship's captain served with the explorer Columbus, and our party will be in good hands. Next came the matter of choosing who was to go.

The Abbess consulted her council of older nuns, then came to me in the scriptorium, looking grave. "We have come to a decision in the council, Sor Beatriz, but you must make a decision, too. The mission must have a scribe..."

"You wish me to go to Gran Canaria?" I was astonished. My leg now troubles me so that I am often unable to walk, and my writing hand is sometimes so stiff and swollen I cannot write at all.

The Abbess shook her head. Suddenly I knew what she was going to say next. The earth began to sink beneath my seat, my heart gave way in my breast, and I clutched the sides of the lectern for support.

"Salome is the most able and intelligent of the novices, and you have taught her a scribe's duties. Young as she is, she is best qualified to be scribe to the new house, and I need not tell you how the written word has helped to bind the order in sisterhood for centuries. Now it will continue to bind us across the sea. I will not send her without your agreement, but you will have seen her expression when we speak of the mission."

I had. Now the room around me dimmed and something tightened in my chest so I could not breathe. The suddenness with which life can change! I struggled to consider wisely, without thinking of myself. I knew Salome was not just ready to obey the Abbess but eager to go, though she tried to hide it from me. The Abbess waited quietly, not urging or pressing me, but my duty was clear. The order had given me and my child sanctuary and peace when I had thought there was none in the world, and now it was my turn to give the order something in return, as well as allowing my daughter the only chance she might have to experience life beyond the convent's walls. She is nearly eighteen and should take her final vows next year. I felt a premonition that I should never see her in her nun's habit.

I summoned my courage and consented. Salome came running in soon after, breathless with excitement. "Oh Mother! The Abbess says you have given your permission! I so long to go, but then, my heart breaks at the thought of leaving you!"

I promised God would watch between us and unite us in our prayers, and repeated the Abbess's words about the records Salome would keep. She threw her arms around my neck and promised breathlessly to write a full account of all she saw and experienced. "I can scarcely believe I am to be the scribe, Mother! And the Abbess has promised you will come with the next party of nuns as soon as it is safe for them to come, that my profession will not take place until you are there. We shall not be separated for long. Only until we have made our new convent comfortable for aged nuns and cleared a pathway for their litters, poor old dears!" Salome added impishly. "But I will perform my new duties faithfully and make you proud. And ships come and go to Gran Canaria, so I will send letters with a full account of our doings back to the convent, and they will entertain you so well you will wish I had gone sooner!" Then she was in tears at the thought of leaving me, and for the next few days was in a state of agitation, alternating between anticipation and grief.

So was the whole convent, from the servants to the oldest nuns. But, regardless, lists were made, instructions dictated, trunks were packed and repacked.

Too soon, all was ready, and the night before they were to set off the Abbess heard the confessions of the twelve who were going. The next morning, after a sleepless night, a special Mass was said and a quick breakfast eaten, or mostly not eaten. Our nerves were stretched to the limit.

The priest, who had fallen asleep after saying Mass, was shaken awake to read out a letter of approval from the bishop, blessing our undertaking to bring the word of God to the heathens of Gran Canaria and prevent the Muslim infidels spreading the poison of their faith. As dawn broke across the mountains, the carriages rolled away to Seville. Salome lifted the leather curtain to wave until they disappeared from sight.

The convent and my heart feel empty, but Salome will write when they arrive, and we all look forward to her letters and news of our mission.

I clung to that thought throughout the months that followed.

July 1524

No word has come from Gran Canaria, but the Abbess has had an unwelcome missive from the Holy Office. This letter was ominously different from their usual exhortation to guard against lust and gluttony and sloth and to adhere strictly to the requirement of enclosure to ensure we remain untainted by the world and its vices—. This one stated they have information that our convent harbors a *Morisco*'s bastard like a worm in an apple. They will send an investigator to determine her identity and punish those responsible for her presence. The Abbess is ordered to begin inquiries to identify possible suspects for the investigators to question at length.

I said that my father must have found an informer among the convent servants, though possibly not a very clever one. "How thankful we should be that Salome is no longer here. And she is gone with the special blessing of the bishop! I can truthfully say there are no *Moriscos'* children here," said the Abbess.

When she left I thanked the Almighty for Salome's deliverance from the scrutiny of the Inquisition and repent of my missing her. God is great.

September 1524

Deo gratias, the investigators have not come. We had heard terrible stories of their remorseless search for heretics in other convents, and knew that some of our order were bound to be taken to join the nuns in Inquisition cells. Our reprieve was due to an outbreak of a terrible illness, with coughing and fever, aching joints, and a burning rash. It has spread through our infirmary and then the orphanage, taking the oldest patients and the youngest children. Lately many of the nursing sisters have been ill as well, while two of the older nuns who caught it died. The Abbess had me write a letter warning the Holy Office that many men in the pilgrims' hostel had contracted it. It caused the men to suffer horribly in their private parts, and while the disease had caused blindness in some, it delivered others from carnal temptation, as they no longer had any hope of indulging their lustful urges.

We received the reply that God had surely visited this scourge upon the convent for our sins, but that the Investigator would postpone his visit for the time being.

With so much illness, we have neglected our gardens and the harvest has been poor. We fear for the winter. The good Abenzucars have made us a gift of olives, dried figs, and dates, together with oil from their harvest, which will mark the difference between life and death for many this winter. Little twin girls have arrived, beautiful children of two as finely dressed in silks and jewels as any courtesan. Their double dowry will be useful to purchase ingredients for our *polvorónes* in the spring, but oh, their mother! To part with one child must be agony. To part with two, must be like death itself.

A celebration to mark the profession of two of our older orphan girls took place in the *sala grande*, while another orphan seized the opportunity of the celebration to run away with a young man from the village, causing great scandal. We cannot discover how the young people were able to meet or form such a plan, as the girls are not allowed out of the convent. Yet my heart wishes them well.

There is no word from Gran Canaria. I pray daily, hourly, for our mission and for Salome.

May 1526

Now the weather is very warm and our flocks of goats and sheep have increased hugely this year. Their bells make a pleasant sound as they graze, and the swallows sing in the eaves once more. But the Chronicle—indeed all my work—is neglected. Since Salome left, an inflammation flares up repeatedly in my bad leg, preventing my sitting at my desk for long, and my hands trouble me so that sometimes I cannot write at all. If only I could find a suitable apprentice or assistant among the novices! But it is exacting work, and those who have the patience for it lack a good clear hand, while those who write beautifully have little patience.

August 1527

Though it has been four years, whenever the bell at the gate rings we pause in our work or prayer, hoping that at last it is a messenger bringing a letter from our mission. Instead the bell has rung because the summer has brought a great number of pilgrims and sick people. They say the plague has returned in the cities and we have many penitent pilgrims who fear the illness is God's punishment for their wickedness. Both the men's and women's hostels are overflowing and we pray most will recover before the roads are no longer passable and we have many more mouths to feed for the winter. It is the harvest season and all are hard at work from sunrise. The Abbess works as hard as any of the younger nuns. In addition to nursing in the infirmary, yesterday she was busy gathering onions and garlic to lay in straw in the cellars, and preserving our last under-ripe peaches in honey. But she grew breathless and was persuaded at last to leave this work to others.

June 1530

Hope for our mission is extinguished altogether. Each spring the Abbess has sent village men to inquire among the ships' captains in the harbor in Seville for what they know of Gran Canaria and a convent there of the Order of the Holy Sisters of Jesus. But though many sailors know Gran Canaria, none have anything to tell our messengers and say that our party have certainly been taken by pirates or drowned in a shipwreck. The whole convent mourns their loss.

October 1538

Yesterday a pilgrim came who claims to be an artist and swears to recompense us for his keep with a painting. This, we know from experience, means that he intends to stay a long time, as these paintings take months. The Abbess groaned that the number of penitent artists donating their work to the convent was truly marvelous—they must all lead very wicked lives. And as the paintings are usually terrible, the penance is usually ours. The Abbess says that most of it would send Salome into fits of laughter. Yet she feels we must hang it all somewhere. A few find their way to the walls of the *sala grande*, but most are hung in the darkest and oldest corridors. The Abbess insists only portraits may hang in the locution parlor and as there are few of these she is spared the worst.

March 1539

The sweet smell of *polvorónes* fills the convent night and day. The court has ordered a great many for *Semana Santa*, and wealthy families follow suit. All the sisters and beatas are taking it in turns to cook them, and the kitchen maids keep busy stoking the oven round the clock. I help in the kitchen as much as I am able. At least it is warm by the ovens, though standing makes my back ache.

September 1539

The swallows have flown away for the winter. My hands grow stiff and I often find it difficult to hold the pen. I think often on my sins, and notice the grayness of everything—the clouds, the weather, the dying light of autumn.

Spring 1540

Easter approaches again, the long dark days of the Lenten fast draw to an end, snow melts, and though it is very cold, in the cloister the sun warms the bones of elderly nuns like me while the convent waits for the warm wind to bring the swallows back from Africa. The Abbess has not been well this winter, and spends most of her time propped in a chair in front of her *locutio*. I divide my time between the scriptorium in the morning and assisting her in the afternoons with the day-to-day business of the convent. The Abbess's younger sister, recently widowed, has come to live at the convent as a lay sister. This beata, Sor Emmanuela, has made over all the wealth she inherited from her husband to us, and I have been cataloging her fortune and property.

I am often short of breath and I do not believe it will be long before I join the nuns laid to rest in a cave behind the convent, like the early Christians in the catacombs of Rome. And one of the orphan girls will fill my shoes. I long for a competent assistant.

CHAPTER 10

Las Golondrinas Convent, Spain, Spring 2000

"Girls! So many girls in the convent at once! Girls better then!"
Grumbling about modern girls and hobbling surprisingly fast, Sor
Teresa led the way back through the convent's shadowy passages
toward Menina's room where lunch was waiting.

Menina made her offer of help. "Really, Sor Teresa, you can't
keep bringing meals to my room. Let me eat with the nuns. I can
help cook and wash dishes. At home I—"

"No!" Sor Teresa shook her head stubbornly, reverting to her
combination of English and Spanish. "Pilgrims stay, we must take
care of them. Nuns' custom, we eat always by ourselves, and hear a
sister read from a holy book. If we talk, is about convent business,
is not for outsiders. In the old days, when pilgrims came, there was
a room for the men pilgrims to eat and another for the women, and
men and women listened to the holy books at meals, just like the
nuns. Now no pilgrims, we put broken furniture in those rooms.
Water is coming in, roof will fall down soon." Sor Teresa shrugged
despondently. "But we feed you, don't worry."

Menina exclaimed "Men? You allowed men in the convent?"

"Oh, poor men, sick men, dying men, men with penances, *pilgrims*, yes. They are separated from the women, separate refectory,
separate door into the chapel, separate infirmary even, with a big

gate. Gate is locked. Same thing in the chapel. So they can worship, pray, hear Mass, not see the women who the nuns nurse in
women's infirmary. Lay sisters, the beatas, nurse the men. If they
want to talk to the nuns they do it at the *locutio*, the one you see.
Only if priest or friar, the Abbess saw him face-to-face."

"Sounds kind of crazy...I mean, like a lot of trouble, keeping
men and women apart," said Menina. Though she had to admit,
however crazy it sounded, separation of the sexes suited her fine
just now.

"Is no men pilgrims now. Bah!" Sor Teresa shook her head
emphatically. "Men not so good today as before. Not so good then
either, is why so many have to come here and repent. But they
repent. These days people very bad, don't repent. Don't worry
about sins. Don't think about God, they think God is not watching them. They forget their religion. They forget their duty. Their
families. Get big ideas. Then who knows what they do."

Ahead of Menina, Sor Teresa suddenly stopped in the middle
of her diatribe, supporting herself with a frail hand on the wall as
if she needed to catch her breath, or something hurt.

"Even Alejandro forget. He was altar boy, carried the images at
Semana Santa. His father was old Republican, policeman here, had
many children, hated the church, would not speak to the priest.
But his wife, Alejandro's mother, she insist the children are baptized, confirmed. She is a good girl even if she marry a man who
hates the church. Then children grow up, one, then another, come
to the convent to say good-bye to Tia, say is too old-fashioned
here, no good jobs. They go to Madrid, to Zaragosa, three go in
Salamanca, one girl go to London for university and then is meeting a man, gets married."

"And Alej...the captain, why didn't he go?"

"Alejandro, the baby, is the last. He is born when his mother
thinks there will be no more children. Ha! She is surprised. But

she die when he is five years old, and when he is eighteen his father comes to me to ask, what to do with Alejandro. He is very clever in school, learn English, he find there is a way he can go to United States to school for one year, live with American policeman family. Then come home. I think this is not good idea but his father does not listen. And when Alejandro goes there is girl in the family, he like her very much. And after one year he tell his father, he will not come home yet, he will study in United States, is scholarship he can get for police college. Alejandro's father is very proud, says is big chance to study in America. He sit at *locutio* and tell me he will give permission, but I warn him no, do not give last child permission, he will stay in America. But Alejandro's father does not listen again, and he is sorry."

Menina thought anyone who refused to listen to Sor Teresa might well be sorry. She wouldn't waste time telling them why.

"Alejandro is there for five years. He is only coming home two times. Every year, his father thinks, now, he will come home and stay. But when Alejandro finishes the studies, his father is sad. Alejandro will stay in America. He can be policeman there, can marry his American wife. And then his father is dying. Alejandro comes home then and he is ashamed now, that he has left his father for so long. He promise his father he will stay. But when he does this, something is different…Alejandro is policeman, yes, but not policeman like his father. I think maybe, he learned bad things in America."

"Oh?" Menina ventured. "What kind of things?"

"Yes, I think he has too much money for a policeman. His father had big family, never had so much money, but no one has much money here, they manage. Alejandro live in his father's house, is lonely, parents dead, no wife, no children, no sister to cook, keep the house clean. He spend a lot of money on his father's house, says he makes it ready for his American *novia* who will come soon—no water from the well, must have it inside, must have bathroom, *three* bathrooms, have electricity, have new kitchen, make the house bigger, he is talking of swimming pool! Trucks come with many boxes, of tiles and pipes and even re…refrigerator, I think is called. Men work for months until the house is a palace for his *novia.* Village all wait to see her, she must be a princess, but even though house is finished, no *novia.* Alejandro go back to America, only for a little while, come back here. No *novia.* No wife. Is very unhappy, I think."

Hmm, thought Menina, maybe that was why the captain had disliked her on sight—because she was American, too.

"He buy fast car, have loud music, is even cooking his food himself in his new kitchen! Then he eats alone! Is very lonely. No longer speaks of *novia.*" Sor Teresa shook her head. "These things are not good! But worst is *girlfriends*! Pah! Now he has many girlfriends! Very bad girls in the high heels, skirts that are too little, showing all their legs. Their stomachs! Girls today have no shame. They smoke the cigarettes. Paint their faces. Show everything to everyone. Don't want to stay home, raise the children, look after the family. I think, such bad girls, Alejandro has become *playboy*!" There was sadness and despair in Sor Teresa's voice.

Captain Fernández Galán a playboy? The mind boggled. "But you don't leave the convent, Sor Teresa—how do you know all this?" asked Menina, stifling a giggle.

"Aha! How you think? Is old women in the village, they are coming for Mass every morning, they come to the *locutio* after. They watch everything, they tell me everything." She started to walk again. "Everything!" she repeated with satisfaction.

"I see." It would be easy to scandalize a lot of old women, and Menina felt a flash of sympathy for the captain, trapped here by his promise to his dying father. But she wondered if Sor Teresa was hinting he was a dirty cop, taking bribes? In this godforsaken place? From whom? For what?

"I am angry when Alejandro bring you," Sor Teresa continued, as they reached Menina's room. "I think, here is another bad girl. But then when you talk you don't sound like the others. So I say yes, because I know with my ears."

Menina shook her head at the non sequitur. By now they had reached Menina's tiny room where a tray with bread, cheese, olives, and an orange waited with the little carafe of wine. Imagine wine at lunchtime! She wondered how she could avoid being stuck in here for the rest of the day. It was a little claustrophobic. As Sor Teresa turned to go Menina asked, "Is there anywhere outside I could go? A balcony? Was there, um, something called the *jardín de peregrinos?*"

"No balcony," Sor Teresa said. "Aha! But yes! Pilgrims' garden. Come quickly, I show you now," and set off down another corridor, narrower and darker than the rest, with walls mostly bare except for a few frames that held what looked like faded woodcuts. The ceiling was lower and it stank of rotting wood, mildew, damp plaster, and small dead animals. Underfoot the tiles were shards and dust that crunched under their feet. "Is old part of the convent."

Yes indeedy, thought Menina, watching her step.

They stopped in front of tall wooden shutters and Sor Teresa stood on tiptoe to battle with an ancient rusty crossbar until Menina said, "Let me," and finally unhitched it.

The shuttered door folded partway back and collapsed on its hinges and stuck, crookedly open, letting daylight into the corridor. Outside, what appeared at first to be a jungle proved to be a small cloister-like garden backing onto mountain rock and overgrown with roses and jasmine and weeds. Several stunted orange trees were in blossom in the thicket, and Menina spied a weatherworn statue in an arched niche high in the rock wall.

"No one use for a long time," Sor Teresa said, and pointed in the direction of a moss-covered alabaster basin in the shape of a shell set in the rock beneath the statue. "Is a spring." There was a sound of trickling water.

Water? Menina was thirsty. The rusty pump in the bathroom brought up water that was a funny brown color and she didn't dare drink it, but if this water was clean she could fill her plastic bottle from the airport. "Is it safe to drink?"

"Of course, is from the mountain, is clean. Many wells here— I forget how many—and springs. Always, convent has water from the mountain. Before we have buckets, very heavy to carry. But then we modernize, pumps is easier," Sor Teresa said complacently. "Garden was for the women pilgrims," she explained. "To sit here, is quiet, can pray and meditate. Read holy books. Is special place. Is good to be here, I think."

Menina could see it had been a long time since anyone had set foot in this minijungle, and she hoped she wouldn't find the skeleton of a long-lost pilgrim in the high weeds, but at least it was outdoors. There was a marble bench around three sides to sit on. She tramped a path to it, then walked about flattening more long grass and weeds, making another path to the fountain, glad of her heavy boots. Her camera had been in her suitcase, so she couldn't take any photos, but she decided she would make a sketch of it to send her parents when she got to Madrid next week.

While she was tramping and thinking, Sor Teresa disappeared. Menina fetched her empty water bottle, and refilled it from the trickle under the statue. She held up the bottle and looked at the water, but it was clear, no particles or anything, no visible amoebae anyway. "Here goes," she said and drank, and went back to her room to eat her lunch.

The combination of unaccustomed wine at midday and jet lag made Menina sleepy again, and she curled up on her bed and dozed off. It was a restless nap, however, disturbed by the feeling someone was calling her, dragging her to the brink of consciousness before jet lag pulled her under again. She woke disoriented, rubbing her eyes and trying to remember what she was doing in a strange room where late afternoon sun made a pattern of iron grillwork on the floor. Was she in jail?

Then she remembered where she was, and she fell back with a groan, thinking of her parents and how frantic they must be by now. They were bound to have phoned the hostel and found that nobody had seen her or had any idea where she was, but there was absolutely nothing Menina could do about it. They would blame Becky, call the police and probably the FBI and God knew who else, but would it make any difference? How long before someone galvanized the Spanish police to look for her? And how would they find her if they did? Probably the Spanish authorities wouldn't budge until the holiday was over. This left the captain her only link with the outside world, and she was wary of him. What was so urgent he couldn't leave the village for a short time?

Menina decided she couldn't put off a wash in the dreaded bathroom any longer. From her backpack she retrieved miniature toiletries Sarah-Lynn had tucked in, and the spare set of underwear, the socks, the expanding towels, and even a sweatshirt she had forgotten. Bracing herself, Menina soaped in the icy water from the pump, then shampooed her hair. Shivering, she wrapped herself in the bathrobe, and did her laundry as well as she could. Back in her cell she draped wet clothes around and was trying to comb her hair dry when Sor Teresa and another old nun, whom she introduced as Sor Clara, appeared with supper and a fresh candle.

Sor Clara was a little dried-up cricket of a woman, even older than Sor Teresa, and from the way her mouth worked, toothless as well. But Sor Clara had a sweet expression and the network of lines on her face crinkled further into a smile as she quavered "*Deo gratias"* in greeting. She patted Menina on the cheek, telling her in sweet lisping Spanish that it had been a long time since they had had a young guest in the convent, and she was very welcome, and she hoped Menina's stay would bless her with peace and comfort.

Then the two old nuns folded their hands in their sleeves and Sor Teresa began to speak in slow, careful Spanish so both Menina and Sor Clara could understand. "I have discussed what Alejandro says about the paintings with the other sisters." Sor Clara nodded vigorously. "We have vowed to stay here until death but it is true, we need money. All we can do for money is sell *polvorónes.* And people help us when they can. We are the last of the order; these days no girls have vocations. Some of the sisters are older than Sor Clara and I, and cannot rise from their beds. Some are ill, and need medicine and warm blankets. We bear our discomforts as God sends them, but even a simple life has its necessities so that we can continue to serve God until the end."

Sor Clara piped up, "And if God has new work for us, we are ready." She nodded again, as if she were prepared to embark on a new mission right away.

"Why doesn't the church help? You know, they must have some kind of welfare fund. I can't believe the Catholic Church lets nuns starve," Menina said helpfully. "Haven't you asked?"

Sor Teresa thought for a minute before she answered, "Las Golondrinas is a very old religious house, maybe the oldest in the world, and maybe we have some…little disagreements with Rome, a long time ago. The Inquisition did not like our convent, but the queen of Spain protected us, I believe. But still, we are always careful not to bother Rome. Sor Clara says, maybe God sends you to help us now. So I will tell you, yes, the convent has many paintings. All are old, some maybe are good, I don't know; many look terrible, I think, but we never said no when someone gave them. The old scriptorium, and the *locutio* parlor are the only rooms in the Abbess's part of the convent we use. There are some paintings, some portraits there, maybe they are the best ones because the Abbess was looking at them. Now we sit in those rooms. Having the portraits is nice, portraits are company. And the *sala grande* has many other paintings crowded together, but we have not used the *sala grande* for many years so I don't know what is there. And the *sala de las niñas* has some, too, I think. Sor Clara will show you. She is the only nun left who had anything to do with the paintings; maybe she remembers something. If you find good ones, then we can decide what we do. You may take the chickens' bread for the cleaning."

At the mention of the chickens' bread Sor Clara chuckled, rocking back and forth and bobbing her head up and down. "Cluck, cluck!" she exclaimed playfully, imitating her chickens eating their crumbs.

Menina wondered how much help Sor Clara would actually be.

Then Sor Clara gave a yelp like something had bitten her. Her gaze was riveted on the medal Menina had left lying on the table in the circle of candlelight. Sor Clara tugged Sor Teresa's sleeve and muttered something in rapid Spanish that made Sor Teresa exclaim in surprise. "Sor Clara says you have a holy medal. You are not Catholic—how did you get this?"

"My parents adopted me from an orphanage. I was wearing that medal when the nuns took me in, and the nuns said I should keep it. Is it something special?"

Sor Clara picked it up, turned it over, and stared some more. Then she whispered again to Sor Teresa, who rubbed her fingers on the front and back, then whispered back to Sor Clara. Sor Clara's mouth dropped open and she stared at Menina.

"Aha! A convent? You did not say this," Sor Teresa snapped.

"Well, no. I didn't think it mattered…"

"Your name is Spanish, no? In Spanish your name means a lady servant—no not a servant, a lady-in-waiting. You know the painting *Las Meninas?* By Velasquez? The Infanta, and her companions, her '*meninas*' in the Prado?"

"Oh, that painting! Yes, of course I know it. It's so famous, everybody does." The Spanish conversation was exhausting, and Menina was feeling a little bewildered—how had they suddenly moved on from the medal to Velasquez?

"Aha! So you are a Menina! Hmmm, like in the painting. But Alejandro said you are looking not for Velasquez, but for Tristan Mendoza. When I told the others, Sor Clara knew that name."

"*What?*" Menina was definitely feeling confused.

"Yes. Sor Clara cannot remember things that happen this morning and is sometimes like a child, but what happened long ago, yes, she remembers very well. When Sor Clara was a novice, her work was making the list of paintings."

Menina reverted to English. "An inventory? Sor Teresa, I'm sorry, but I think I'm too tired to understand everything you say in Spanish."

Sor Teresa obligingly returned to English, too. "She is sure she write Tristan Mendoza in the ledger." Sor Clara repeated the name and said something. "Several times, perhaps, she is not sure," said Sor Teresa.

Menina thought Sor Clara's memory was probably playing tricks on her, but didn't want to be rude. "That would be… unbelievable. If the convent has one of his paintings it might be worth a lot of money, so we should definitely look for it. And you know, when Tristan Mendoza signed his name on the paintings, he painted a swallow underneath his signature, just like the little bird on the back of that medal. My dad says it's a swallow, um, a *golondrina* because of the forked tail. So I wondered why he did that and that's why I—"

Sor Teresa interrupted. "Is time for the vigil. Once all nuns keep the night vigil during *Semana Santa*, but now, we take turns."

She put the medal down, her hand shaking with age. "Come, Sor Clara," she ordered, reverting to Spanish.

Sor Clara obeyed meekly, and as they left Menina noticed how thin and frail both old ladies looked. Their habits were frayed and patched, ragged around the hem. Poor old things! Menina thought. There must be *something* here they could sell, and she had better find it because no one else was going to. It would fill the time until she could leave, and if she couldn't find something worth selling, well, she would have to think of some way of helping the nuns. Besides, what if there was a Tristan Mendoza in the convent? There was a thesis for you!

Hunger made her remember her food. She read the guidebook again by candlelight while she ate a cold vegetable omelette and drank the small pitcher of wine. She tried to save her bread, but was so hungry she ate that, too. Then she blew out the candle that had burned down low, but she wasn't the least bit sleepy. How did people manage before television or paperbacks? She tossed and turned, thumped the lumpy pillow, and wished it was tomorrow already. Then the singing and drums began down in the village. She wished she could see whatever was going on. Maybe there was a way to climb up the rock wall at the back of the pilgrims' garden and see from there. Besides, she was thirsty and her water bottle was empty.

Menina groped for the matches, relit what was left of her candle, and located the empty plastic bottle. She put on her boots, wrapped the blanket from her bed round her shoulders and peered out. The corridor was creepy, but if old ladies could navigate in the dark, there couldn't be much to worry about. She stepped bravely into the dark, trying to avoid broken tiles in the faint pool of light cast by her candle a step or two ahead. Hand on the wall for balance, she made her way to the shuttered doors now hanging open, around a lighter rectangle in the inky dark of the hallway. Outside the night was cool, but the air was sweet after the odor inside, and the stars shone bright overhead. She could smell bonfires and hear singing and people clapping an irregular beat to the music.

Menina felt the sloping rocks, still warm from the day's sun, as she groped her way to the little spout where water trickled into the basin. She filled her bottle and drank. Then she blew out her candle, wrapped the blanket tight round herself and sat in her cocoon looking at the stars, listening to the peaceful sound of water and the women's voices rising in the darkness. Was this what being a nun felt like—life going on beyond the walls, able to hear it, smell it, but never able to see it or be part of it? She hadn't thought about convents since she was little, when her parents showed her the photos of the place they'd found her. She remembered how sad they'd been when they talked about that place; apparently it had been attacked and some of the nuns had been killed by a revolutionary mob after Menina had left.

Otherwise, convents of course weren't mentioned at the First Baptist Church. It wasn't until she studied the Renaissance at Holly Hill that she learned more about convents—nuns ran schools and hospitals, managed property, and even acted, performing religious plays for an audience sitting behind the *locutio*. Well-connected nuns even influenced politics. They even commissioned art and music; some convents were great patrons of the arts. They had been an important force in society, even if they led a sort of parallel existence from the world.

Suddenly it occurred to her that with so much else to worry about, she hadn't thought about Theo since before lunch yesterday, on the bus. Sitting in the pilgrims' garden, separated from the rest of the world, Menina took a deep breath and probed the terrible memories, like probing an aching tooth to see how bad it made her feel. It hadn't gone away, but she was safe and at peace for the moment. Not wanting to break the spell, she sat watching the stars until the singers grew tired and the singing stopped. She knew she had better try to sleep. She stood and stretched, felt for her matches to relight her bit of candle in its glass. There was a faint rustling noise—a plant stirring in the wind, a salamander, or perhaps a mouse. She held the light up but didn't see anything. "Good night," she said anyway.

CHAPTER II

Las Golondrinas Convent, Spain, Spring 2000

Menina pulled the thin pillow over her head to muffle the noise, but it came closer and got louder. Sor Teresa shrilled *"Deo gratias!"* in her ear and banged the breakfast tray on the table. Menina forced herself to sit up and pushed her hair out of her eyes.

"Hi!" she muttered, groggily trying to think where on earth she was, what day it was, and what was making such an unholy racket. *"Gracias!"* She pushed herself upright. Tuesday. It was Tuesday. The dawn chorus outside her window was on speed.

"Good, you are awake now, so I tell you, you are going in one hour, after Mass," Sor Teresa said, "with Sor Clara to the Abbess's rooms, look at paintings. I must go open the gate to the chapel, let people in for Mass." Sor Teresa bustled out.

"OK, *sí*. Great. Thanks." Menina rubbed sleep from her eyes, reminding herself where she was. She sank back against the wall sipping coffee and eating her slice of almond bread as slowly as she could to make it last. Then she grabbed her towel and toothbrush and went down the hall to the bathroom. The first thing she would do when she got back to civilization was take a long, long hot shower.

When Sor Clara came, Menina grabbed a notebook and ballpoint pen and followed the little old nun this way and that through the maze of corridors, until they could hear the cloister fountain. Sor Clara led her along the cloister's colonnaded walk to the same doorway Menina had taken the day before, and then they were back in the dim *locutio* parlor. Menina felt she was starting to get her bearings in the maze of the convent.

Sor Clara tugged her arm and pointed to a huge basket on the floor holding broken chunks of bread. "Alejandro. *Pobres pollos*! Poor chickens!" She chuckled.

Menina needed light to work. "I can't see," she said in Spanish.

"Ah," said Sor Clara, looking surprised. "Is it dark for you?" She tottered over to the far wall and tugged at a piece of heavy fabric that looked like a curtain. The room brightened, and a breeze stirred up dust in a shaft of sunshine. Sor Clara sneezed.

"Perfect," said Menina, and sneezed herself. Pulling the curtain farther back and propping it there with a chair, she saw it was a heavy tapestry that had been hung from a pole. She looked at it closely. It was coarse wool, faded and frayed, though she could just see that it had been dyed bright colors once, and there was a pattern that looked like serpents and birds. There were several more like it hanging crookedly on the walls. All could use a trip to the dry cleaners.

"Nuns sit in this room in the winter," said Sor Clara. "It is warm. Alejandro and other men bring wood." She pointed to the pile of firewood stacked in an alcove. "We mend our clothes, read, say rosaries."

Menina murmured, "Mmm, how nice," anxious to get back to work on the girl's portrait. She rolled a piece of bread until it was soft and set to work. Behind a veil of dirt, a flat red-and-black background set off the girl's fine clothing and jewels that glowed faintly. She looked about fifteen or sixteen. Menina thought it must be an engagement portrait. The girl's dark hair was studded with pearls, and a gold-embroidered tunic was pinned on each shoulder with a jeweled clasp threaded with ribbon. Beneath that was a white underblouse with jeweled sleeves, there was lace at her neck and wrists, and she wore a necklace with a star pendant. The girl was the only thing in the painting; there were no background details, no chair, books, sewing frame, pets, horizon, clouds or sky. Just a draped curtain and beyond that, blackness.

In her left hand the girl held a tightly closed fan close by her waist. In her right hand, she held a carnation against her heart. It disconcerted Menina the way its eyes held her own in an imperious, determined way. Forget the flower on the heart and the fact the girl was all dressed up like she was going to get married, Menina had the overwhelming impression that this was a young girl with a strong personality—a will of steel, in fact. There was writing in the upper right-hand corner of the picture. Menina used more bread and was rewarded by the appearance of florid script and a date: 1590, in gold Roman numerals. She stepped back and squinted, trying to make out the inscription. Finally her eyes adjusted to the letter *s* looking like an *f*, and she read out loud that the portrait was of Maria Salome Beltran of royal Inca and noble Spanish blood, the daughter of Don Teo Jesus Beltran and Dona Isabella Beltran de Aguilar, about to enter the convent of Las Sors Santas de Jesus de Los Andes. Like an engagement portrait, only the girl was engaged to Jesus.

But a distant memory came back to her: pictures on a wall, special girls. Dressed up to be nuns. The taste of hot chocolate and sweet cakes…she couldn't pin it down, but it was definitely not anything she had experienced in the Laurel Run First Baptist Church.

Menina felt questions hanging in the air around the portrait. The girl looked beautiful and rich. But this convent she was going to seemed to be in the Andes, and she was part Inca. So how did a portrait of a nun-to-be painted in Spanish America nearly four hundred years ago get to the top of a mountain in Spain a million miles from anything?

"Aha!" exclaimed Sor Teresa. Menina whirled around. Glancing at her watch, she was startled to see she had been working for over five hours. There was a snoring sound coming from the chair where Sor Clara dozed. "Sor Clara!" Sor Teresa said loudly and reproachfully, and poor Sor Clara woke with a start.

Menina did her best to save Sor Clara from a scolding. "Sor Teresa, come and see the portrait I found! Perhaps you can tell me what it's doing here."

Sor Teresa squinted in Menina's direction. She rubbed her eyes, stepped back, and squinted some more. "I cannot see as well as I used to. Is too much light. I cannot make out much." Sor Teresa had turned her head as if to look at the painting, but was staring intently too far to the left. As if she couldn't really see at all. Then Menina saw what she had not noticed before—that the nun's eyes were filmy, the corneas opaque. Menina stuck a hand in front of Sor Teresa's face and moved it back and forth. The nun blinked, but her eyes did not follow. The poor old soul, thought Menina.

"Sor Teresa, you can't see it, can you?"

"God has dimmed my eyes that I may see better with my spirit," Sor Teresa snapped. "And I can hear. I see what I see."

"If you can't see, how do you know where you're going in the convent?"

"Oh the convent...I am here so many years; I know the way from when I could see. Now God guides my steps. And all your chattering makes me forget, you have a visitor. Come." She closed the discussion of her eyesight firmly.

"Fantastic! My parents got in touch with the American consulate." Menina breathed a sigh of relief. "Captain Fernández Galán must have got a phone to work after all."

"Yes, is Alejandro. He is your visitor."

"Oh." Damn! "Why?"

"You ask him. Come to the *locutio*, where you can talk."

"The what?"

"Nuns cannot go outside the convent. People visit, must talk to nuns though the *locutio*." She pointed to the wall of heavy iron grillwork. "Alejandro sit on that side, you sit on this side," ordered Sor Teresa. "Is locked. So nothing can happen. Ha! Alejandro not used to that!"

"I thought this place couldn't get weirder," Menina muttered. "What did I know?"

She heard footsteps and the captain drew back the curtain on the other side. "Good morning Mees Walker. I hope you survived your night in the convent."

"Hi. Yes. It's odd to be talking through iron bars. Like being in jail."

"I understand. Is not the Ritz, but what is important is, the gate is strong. Trust me, why I bring you here is not crazy and why you should stay there is not crazy. I will explain later, but I am in a hurry now. I only want to ask why did Sor Teresa tell me, find a lot of bread and bring it for Menina. I think, she cannot be so hungry!"

"The bread is for the paintings—really, you should have asked Sor Teresa's permission about that. She was furious when she found me looking for things. She thought I wanted to steal them. Or actually, she thought I was accusing you of putting me up to it."

"I tried to ask her! You saw how she slammed the gate in my face."

"Yes, well, whatever. You were right, there are lots of paintings and Sor Teresa agreed to let me have a look. I warned her that if anything looks promising an expert will have to look at it, but at this stage most of the paintings are so dirty I can't tell what they are. Stale bread is an old-fashioned way to clean them. It's not ideal but it's all I can think of at the moment. Just so I can lift enough dirt from the surface to get some idea—I'm trying to be really careful and not damage the canvas or cause the paint to flake.

"The stuff hanging in the corridors looks worthless to me, but Sor Clara says there are portraits in the Abbess's quarters," Menina continued. "That's where I'm looking now, and there're more in the *sala grande*. But you said something about convents being looted during the civil war in Spain—just before World War II, right, in the 1930s? Was this one looted? Because it's a mess in the convent, but somehow it doesn't look like rampaging hordes came through. Maybe whatever was here before the war is still here."

Alejandro was nodding on the other side. "You're right, it wasn't looted," he agreed. "Unusually. Convents and churches and monasteries in other parts of Spain were burned by the Republicans, because the church helped the Fascists. Many nuns and priests were killed, but nobody burn Las Golondrinas. But here it is different. Nobody kill the nuns, even though most people here were Republicans. They would not attack them."

"OK, I hope I find something that'll bring in some money. I can see they need it. The nuns' clothes are practically rags, and did you know Sor Teresa is blind?" Menina asked. "She needs to see a doctor; she may need a cataract operation or have glaucoma. And Sor Clara is just...old. One minute she's fine and the next she's confused. And they say they're the younger ones. I haven't met any of the others, but I think some older nuns are bedridden. There are lots of broken windows, so it must be freezing in winter. You can't just leave a bunch of helpless old ladies to starve and freeze. And old people can have bad falls. What if one of them breaks a hip; how can Sor Teresa pick her up?" Menina was feeling indignant by now.

Captain Fernández Galán sighed. "I know. Is a big problem. In the village we try to help. We bring them food and in the winter they have the fireplaces and braziers—you know what is a brazier? People bring them wood, charcoal, and…"

"Wood and charcoal won't heat a place as big as this! Besides, braziers are a fire hazard and charcoal fumes can kill you. Or a forgetful old nun will start a fire and the bedridden ones will burn up, starve to death, or die of hypothermia."

"Yes, I know these things but the nuns are stubborn and will not leave," he protested. "It is the life they chose. Is a matter of honor, a test of their faith to keep their vow to God to die here. In the old days there were always girls coming to be nuns or just to live in the convent and work, lay sisters they were called—didn't take the vows or wear the habits, but lived like nuns. There was an infirmary for the old ones, and lay sisters to care for them. But no more nuns, no lay sisters even, for many years. And even people who bring food and wood and things they need, these people are growing old, too. The young ones, like my brothers and sisters, they come back for the holidays sometimes but don't want to live in a village. They want city life, nice flats and cars, nice jobs and cinemas and holidays. Old nuns are not their responsibility." He sighed.

"Is that why you still live here?" she asked. "To look after the nuns?"

"Sor Teresa was my mother's favorite aunt. She saved my mother's life once. Now my father is dead and my brothers have gone away, is just a few old nuns, many are my mother's cousins. I am the only man from the family here, so yes, they are my responsibility. I have promised my father." Just as Sor Teresa had said.

For a minute Menina was touched. Then she reminded herself that might sound nice now, but he had been extremely unpleasant and rude to her. Though, OK, she had to admit, he had rescued her from those workmen who were looking at her like a piece of meat. But she didn't have to like him.

"I'll keep looking. I'd like to help the nuns, too, and anyway, it's kind of interesting. But don't forget the bread—first thing tomorrow, OK? I have to use a lot and I don't think the nuns have enough to eat as it is, so I don't like to take theirs."

"No problem. Is always leftover bread in the village, does not go to waste because they feed it to the pigs and chickens. I will bring it. See you then."

No, don't see me, just bring the bread, Menina longed to say. But didn't.

By the time Menina ate her lunch of bread and cheese and some kind of cold tomato soup it was late afternoon, and Sor Clara had said it was her turn in the chapel, so they would finish for the day. They would look in the *sala grande* tomorrow.

Menina checked the underwear she had washed the previous evening. It was still wet. It needed to dry in the open air. She gathered it up and went to hang it in the pilgrims' garden. She draped her clothes on a warm rock and filled her plastic bottle with water. Back in her room she picked up her notebook and wandered along the cramped little corridors Sor Teresa had said were the oldest part of the building. With the shutters to the garden stuck open, there was enough light to see what looked like two woodcuts, and between them a small portrait of a tonsured monk.

Peering closely, she saw the monk had a crooked nose, and wore a plain habit with a hood. Piggy little eyes squinted off into the distance, and a tight unsmiling mouth was pursed. Was the artist trying to show him as shortsighted? Or focused on something otherworldly or spiritual? She lifted it down to get more of the light on it. The longer she looked, the more she sensed he was looking at something that gave him a smug satisfaction. The longer she looked, the less she liked the monk. "Fr. Ramon Jimenez" it said over his head, and she was just able to make out the words *"Tribunal del Santo Oficio de la Inquisicion."*

She hung it back up and turned her attention to the woodcuts which were in the line of his gaze. There was a jolly feel to the first one, a fiesta or something. Excited people pointing and holding up their children, soldiers, the dais draped in some kind of banner, people in plain tunics holding tapers.

The companion woodcut was less jolly. It showed the crowd of people in tunics tied together with ropes on a bonfire and a girl with long hair on her knees, raising her hands in supplication to a woman on the dais. The fiesta was taking place around people being burned alive. And on the dais, the same monk from the Inquisition was watching.

The woodcuts, with their strange combination of innocent joy at the spectacle of horrible suffering, were powerfully disturbing. Reeling from their impact, Menina backed away and fled to the garden, into fresh air and the long rays of the setting sun. She sank down on the marble bench and put her head in her hands. She hadn't been expecting mere pictures to be so terrible. She knew what it was, the Inquisition burning heretics at the stake. It was a picture from a long time ago. The world was different now. Wasn't it? Why did it feel like it was happening before her very eyes?

Menina sat there while the sun set, then went in and felt her way back along the corridor, averting her eyes from the horrible woodcuts and the evil monk. In her room the candle in the lamp had been lit and the covered tray was on the table. She ate, changed into her robe, tried to read another part of the guidebook, and fell asleep wishing she had a paperback romance or a magazine or anything that was part of her clean, ordered American world. She fell into an uneasy sleep and began to dream.

She was in a crowd pushing forward to see some spectacle in the plaza ahead. "Look," said a man who turned out to be the fat bus driver. "See the spectacle, eh?" He pointed. At the end of the plaza was a great platform, full of priests and dignitaries, and some sort of festival seemed to be in progress. A religious procession filed past to assemble before the dignitaries on the dais. They were followed by another slower, drabber procession—barefoot men, women, and children, dressed identically in penitents' gowns and holding tapers. The crowd waved and called out to them, jeering, shouting. A beautiful girl about Menina's age looked at them, terror in her eyes. Names were solemnly read out and the people with the tapers began to cry out and weep. The girl Menina's age fell on her knees before the dais, pleading to a woman wearing a crown. She was a Jewess because she had never known another faith, but she was a loyal Spaniard, about to be married, have mercy…

"Heretics!" cried the bus driver. "Burn them!" He licked his lips as the soldiers began to prod the procession toward the center of the plaza.

"Now comes the fun," the bus driver exclaimed. There was a silence, then a roll of the drums and the fire was everywhere…her face hot from the fire, Menina woke to her own shriek of terror, twisting against the rope that bound her, desperate to escape the flames at her feet. She sat up in the narrow bed, trembling and rubbing her eyes to banish the nightmare. Just a dream, she told herself over and over, but to avoid it returning she lay awake, fighting off sleep the rest of the night.

CHAPTER 12

From the Chronicle of Las Sors Santas de Jesus,
Las Golondrinas Convent, Andalusia, Autumn 1548

Deo gratias, at last I have an assistant in the scriptorium. Not one
of the novices, but an eighteen-year-old girl who collapsed at our
gate before the autumn storms began. She wore a rough boy's
attire, was crawling with lice, ill, and very nearly unconscious. Her
companion, a mountain girl named Maria, must have dragged
her bodily up the olive terraces. Maria said the girl's name was
Esperanza, that she was in danger and begged the ladies of the
swallows to help her. Maria herself would not wait to eat or rest.
She was in a hurry to be gone, saying she hoped to be married
soon.

Esperanza spent many weeks in the infirmary before she could
tell us more. She was emaciated and weak, and then delirious with
a fever brought on by exposure to the cold. She rambled about a
secret that frightened her. I took my turn sitting by her side, trying
to soothe and comfort her, and assure her steadily that she was
safe. By the time Esperanza was well enough to rise from her bed,
I had grown fond of her. Somehow she has filled the empty space
in my heart left by Salome.

Esperanza went to the Abbess and produced a pouch of *reales,*
saying she could pay for her keep if she might be allowed to stay

until summer came. Meanwhile, she would willingly do any work, in the kitchens or laundry or anywhere at all that we might wish.

"My dear, you may stay as long as necessary. Our order is sworn to protect women, and I gathered that you carry a terrible fear of something—though even at your most delirious you would not say what," said the Abbess. "As to the matter of your work here..." The Abbess took Esperanza's hands in hers and, examining them, said that it was plain she had never scrubbed pots or clothes, and she doubted Esperanza would be any use at menial work. I quickly asked if Esperanza might act as my assistant in the scriptorium. I had spent enough time with her as she was recovering to learn that she was not only intelligent but well educated. I had her copy a letter or two out for me and her writing was exquisite.

"It is unusual for anyone not admitted to our order to have knowledge of our affairs...but Esperanza, you seem to have kept your counsel regarding your own secrets. Can I trust you to keep it regarding ours?"

Esperanza nodded. "I give you my word, Abbess."

"Very well." Then the Abbess reproached Esperanza for forgetting Maria, who had saved her. "Why not send some of your *reales* to her as a marriage gift?" Esperanza blushed and exclaimed, "Of course!"

When I showed her our library and scriptorium, Esperanza looked around her, sighed with pleasure, and began to make herself useful at once, paying close attention to every instruction I gave. What a pity she will not join the order; she would make an excellent scribe when I am gone! But she made a deathbed promise to her father to marry and is determined to keep her promises. She has recovered her spirits and passes the part of the day not spent in the holy offices, prayer, or meals working by my side, sometimes so lost in a volume that I must recall her sharply to the present. Increasingly I entrust the writing to her, and in particular the infirmary sisters praise her quickness in locating information from our medical texts.

Once Esperanza was settled into her duties, the Abbess was determined to discover what dangerous secret Esperanza had. If we were to protect her, it was necessary to know why. Esperanza finally agreed to tell her story, and after hearing a little, the Abbess insisted she write it in the Chronicle.

Esperanza was the only child of an advisor to the king. Her mother had died at her birth, and she led a lonely existence in Seville, in a somber house full of paintings, tapestries, books, and shadows. Esperanza was left in the care of a nurse, a girl in love with a soldier stationed in Seville, who seized every chance to attend services at the cathedral where her soldier stood guard duty nearby.

One day as her nurse brought Esperanza from Mass, there was a carnival atmosphere in the streets and trumpets and drums in the distance. A noisy crowd pushed and jostled and pressed forward to see some spectacle or other in the plaza ahead. "Master is away, we needn't hurry," said the nurse. "Let's have a little fun, poppet, eh?" She dragged Esperanza to the guardsman, who lifted the child onto his shoulder so she could see.

At the end of the plaza, a platform was crowded with priests and dignitaries, and as the drums grew closer a line of hooded friars entered the plaza, followed by another, slower procession—barefoot, dressed identically in plain gowns and this time under guard, men first, then women and children holding tapers. Among the children Esperanza caught the eye of a little girl her own age, holding the hand of a woman at the edge of the crowd, and waved. The woman and the little girl looked at her with frightened eyes and didn't wave back. Names were solemnly read out and the people with the tapers began to cry out and weep.

Cheeks flushed and eyes dancing, the nurse pointed. "Those are heretics, enemies of the church. False Christians who returned to their evil Muslim and Jewish ways!" She licked her lips as the soldiers prodded the procession to a great pile of faggots and straw in the middle of the plaza. A few of the people shuffling toward the great mound were pulled aside. Swiftly, soldiers looped a cord round their necks and pulled. The figures slumped to the ground and were lifted, and their limp bodies were tossed onto the pyre. There was a rumble of disapproval from the crowd.

"Garroting," said the guard, sucking air through his teeth disapprovingly, "for them as can afford it."

"They killed our Lord—make them suffer. Long live the Inquisition!" people around them shouted. The little girl and her mother were crying and clutching each other, and the mother was pleading with the soldiers as the music began again. Friars holding torches lit them, and waited until all the penitents, including the girl Esperanza had waved to and the woman who held her hand, had been pushed and crowded and tied tightly together. "Now comes the fun," the nurse exclaimed.

A roll of the drums drowned out the cries and prayers, and the friars bent their torches to the pyre. Smoke billowed and then flames rose around the feet and legs of the people tied together, climbing higher and higher until searing heat scorched the watching faces. The child Esperanza had waved to was engulfed in flames, and horrible sounds of torment filled the air as the people on the pyre twisted and writhed horribly, and then seemed to melt and sink down. Esperanza watched, transfixed with horror, until the wind suddenly fanned the flames and sent a cloud of thick smoke over the spectators, heavy with the stench of burning human flesh and carrying the unearthly screams of the dying. The plaza darkened with another cloud of smoke and Esperanza lost consciousness. When she woke in her own bed, the stink of roasting flesh was in her lungs, her hair, and on her skin, and she was violently, repeatedly sick.

Her father found Esperanza shivering in her own vomit, her eyebrows singed away, feverish and hysterical, and the nurse entertaining her guardsman in the kitchen. Normally the gentlest of men, Esperanza's father pulled the nurse up by her hair, and swung her against the wall like a madman until she confessed to the escapade, gibbering that she had treated the child to a joyous spectacle. He threw her from the house with terrible oaths and curses.

A calm and steady older woman took her place, watching over Esperanza while she slept and comforting her when the nightmares came. Now when Esperanza closed her eyes she saw the face of the child in the fire and screams filled her sleep. She was frightened of everything, barely touched her food, chewed her fingernails until they bled, and grew thinner and more nervous with each passing day. Her desperate father decided the only way to banish the demons from her mind was to occupy it with study.

He hired a roster of tutors and set his daughter a daily schedule that would have daunted a university scholar—Greek, Latin, French, Italian, astronomy, philosophy, and history. She would learn drawing, painting, and poetry composition. There were religious lessons, music, embroidery, and dancing. Even tailored for a small child it was rigorous, but it had the desired effect. Esperanza regained her appetite and fell asleep at night, too tired for dreaming.

Esperanza was no longer banished to the nursery. Instead she became her father's companion. They read and studied the stars, and over dinner he would quiz her about mathematics or philosophy. Afterward he would set up the colored pieces on the *alquerque* board and show her what moves would take his knights. Her father's old friend, a musician named Don Jaime, was often with them.

When Esperanza was thirteen, her father revealed a secret, against Don Jaime's advice—a secret inner room in the house filled with books forbidden by the church. There were the Qur'an of the Muslims and the Kabbalah and Talmud of the Jews, Moorish translations from Arabic and Greek of medical texts and natural history, the Persian Ibn Sina's great medical text *The Book of Healing*, and Al Masudi's history of a voyage to a distant land across the Sea of Fog and Darkness hundreds of years before the *Reconquista*. These books were works of art, bound in leather and gold, decorated in intricate patterns, with brass or silver clasps—exquisitely beautiful, and anathema to the Inquisition.

Esperanza and her father read these books together, especially the Ibn Sina, which held a special place in her father's heart. He taught her that these books contained knowledge and wisdom given by God, who revealed himself to people in different ways with the help of the blessed prophets of many faiths. Having witnessed the terrible auto-da-fé, Esperanza must never accuse anyone of heresy. She must never mention this secret library either.

Esperanza understood her father's views were at odds with those of her religious instructors, and that he particularly disapproved of celibacy among nuns and the clergy. She sensed this was somehow connected to her mother, but when she asked about her mother, her father only sighed and said he would tell her when she was older.

As Esperanza approached her sixteenth birthday, her father developed a racking cough and began to suffer fevers and breathlessness. Esperanza saw him pass whole days with *The Book of Healing*, trying one remedy after the next as he held a handkerchief to his mouth and coughed blood. She read it with him, memorizing symptoms and concocting medicines and poultices, but they helped no more than the doctors and apothecaries. When they played board games, she saw that his hands had grown thin and white and shook as he moved the pieces.

Her father reassured her he would not die yet. And sometimes he would eat and walk about and seem like himself again, and she would hope that he was indeed better. Then suddenly, he took a turn for the worse, and when she wanted to send a servant for the priest he shook his head. With his life fading, he took her hand and said it had once been a matter of regret that he had no son, but he had long since ceased to feel the loss. He gave her his blessing, told her she was the last of a distinguished family, and made her swear never to embrace a celibate religious life, but to marry and bear children that the family line might not die out.

Esperanza begged him to speak of her mother before it was too late, but her father signaled her to be still. Gasping for breath he held up three fingers to indicate he must tell her three things. One, she was heiress to all his fortune and must always remember the poor; charity was an obligation. Two, lest she be prey to fortune hunters, he had assigned her guardianship to a friend, a nobleman noted for his piety who had pledged to find her a suitable husband. Esperanza must promise to accept her guardian's choice and not be swayed by girlish notions conceived from reading chivalrous poetry and romances. With his last, rattling breath Esperanza's father whispered, "Three...your mother...Don Jaime...ask Don Jaime."

After her father's death, propriety obliged her to make her home in her guardian's house where she realized that her father's confidence in her guardian had been misplaced. Though a nobleman, outwardly pious, and a patron of many charitable institutions, he was both less wealthy than he appeared and less honest. Despite his obsequious condolences, Esperanza was uneasy.

She avoided him and his wife as much as possible, keeping to her rooms and immersing herself in her books, until one day a servant summoned her to her guardian's presence. Esperanza braced herself to hear of her betrothal. But when she and her duenna entered the salon her guardian was pacing furiously. Walking directly up to her he thrust his angry face close to hers, shouting and swearing so furiously that spittle flew into her eyes as he cursed Esperanza and her father as deceiving heretics. Shocked and astonished, Esperanza cried, "Sir, what do you mean? Who accuses us?"

"Do not play the fool, your father's secret collection of forbidden books is discovered. They accuse him *and* you. The infidel filth was consigned to the fire, as your father should have been and you with him."

Esperanza covered her face with her hands, feeling her father had died again. Those beautiful volumes, her father's treasures, all reduced to ash. By ruffians, fools, barbarous zealots! Rage flamed so hotly in her heart that she forced herself to keep her eyes down, lest it show. The rest of her guardian's tirade she heard in silence—that the books had been the property of her grandfather, a Muslim merchant, whose forbidden books proved him a false *converso*, whose son impregnated an infidel whore.

Esperanza looked up at him in utter disbelief. He thrust his face close to hers again, snarling that to arrange Esperanza's marriage, he had had to furnish proof of her *limpieza sangre*, only to discover she had none. Her mother had never relinquished the Muslim faith of her family, and had hidden a deceiving heretic heart beneath a nun's habit at Regina Coeli Convent in Seville and born another *converso's* bastard.

The ugly words rang in Esperanza's ears, the floor swayed from side to side, and everything grew dark. When she regained consciousness she was lying on the cold marble floor and her duenna was holding a strong-smelling pomander under her nose, looking at her with suspicion and dislike. "Your mother was a whoring novice! You can be no better!"

"But how can this be true?" Esperanza protested, in tears. "Nuns cannot leave their convent. My father was goodness itself. He would never...a nun would not..."

The duenna would not say more.

Alone in her bedroom, Esperanza paced, unable to sit still and badly frightened. She was trapped in this house. Then she recalled her father's last words: "Ask Don Jaime." There was certainly no one else she could ask. As the horrible day turned into evening Esperanza scribbled a note in Latin, worded ambiguously lest it fall into the wrong hands, beseeching the counsel of the mendicant Friar Jaime to whom she wished to make her confession. Esperanza had no one to trust with it but her page, who could not read and was devoted to Esperanza. She gave her little messenger a coin and some sweetmeats and sent him off.

The page returned safely, but Esperanza passed a sleepless night. Had Don Jaime understood? But the next day she was summoned to the hall where a filthy, cowled, barefoot friar waited, scratching himself for lice. As she entered, Don Jaime's deep voice boomed accusingly, "Repent! And make your confession to prepare your soul for what lies ahead." Esperanza burst into tears and led him to a quiet corner. She fell to her knees with her head in her hands. No one would object to a man of God in this hypocritical household.

Under his cowl Don Jaime murmured, "Keep your head bowed and listen. You are the child of a true marriage, a Muslim marriage, and a baptized Christian as well. But your guardian's information is partly correct. Your mother was a sweet and well-educated lady, whose parents and grandparents were forced to convert. Her family were forced *conversos* and an impediment to her marriage. When her parents died, your mother's fortune opened the doors of the Regina Coeli convent. It was known for its apothecaries and nuns skilled in medical matters, and she hoped to use her skills for good there.

"But seventeen years ago, before she completed her novitiate, a strange and deadly pestilence appeared in one of the poorest, most crowded quarters of Seville, near the docks where ships from America are loaded and unloaded. Two sailors just ashore from a galleon from Hispaniola were its first victims. They were drinking in a tavern in the docks when they grew ill, burning with fever. Within a day, their bellies had swollen to bursting point, they bled from the ears, and screamed with the pain in their heads until death ended their torment. Some whores with them fell ill soon after, with the same symptoms, suffered the same agonies, and also died. Soon other men who had lain with the whores were ill as well, and the disease spread like fire in dried timber through the quarter where so many sailors lived and beyond, killing many able-bodied seamen, then shopkeepers and butchers and others, then soon servants in the homes of the rich, and the rich themselves.

"It was the busy season when ships cross to and from America ahead of autumn storms, and the loss of sailors at such a time was a catastrophe. Spain expected an attack by Muslim forces gathering in North Africa, and maintaining its defenses depended on the wealth coming from the New World.

"The dead were soon too numerous to collect from the streets, and all who could fled Seville. Your father was one of the few with medical knowledge to remain to help. And he reminded a desperate official that a novice at the Regina Coeli convent was said to be skilled in treating New World diseases.

"Sor Maria Caterina was a skilled apothecary before she entered the convent, and afterward she came to the notice of the archbishop when she successfully treated returning missionary priests suffering from ailments contracted in the New World. These priests often recovered under her care, and from them she learned much of New World illnesses and native cures. Spanish doctors envied her success and called her an infidel witch, but the archbishop would allow no steps to be taken against her.

"Sor Maria Caterina would normally have given advice from the *locutio*, but the problem of the pestilence was too urgent for relaying messages in and out of the convent. Maria Caterina was ordered to treat the patients in person. By the orders of the archbishop, she was hurried into a waiting carriage with her chest of medicines on a stormy night when few were about to notice.

"It was a violent summer storm, with heavy rain and winds that sent debris flying, which spooked the horses. The streets were slick and wet, and finally a great clap of thunder caused the horses to bolt. The coachman lost control and Sor Maria Catarina had a terrifying ride as the plunging horses dragged the carriage sideways along the river. Just before plunging over a precipice onto the riverbank, the carriage uncoupled from the horses. The coachmen and outriders went into the river, but a passenger was thrown out. Your father witnessed the accident. He had gone out to observe the lightning and hurried down to assist the passenger—who, to his surprise, was a woman, shaken but uninjured, and concerned only to recover the medicine chest she had been carrying, and insisting she was bound for the quarter where the fever raged. Your father insisted on escorting her and her medicines to her destination.

"They were soon deep in a discussion about the pestilence. Both recalled Ibn Sina had mentioned similar symptoms, and they considered the distinguishing aspects of this new disease. It was only when the lady impatiently threw off her cloak to better see what she was doing that your father saw that his interesting companion wore a novice's gown."

"How did my guardian discover this?" Esperanza demanded.

"Since he receives a bequest from your father's estate when your marriage takes place, he wasted no time obtaining proof of your ancestry. When he could learn nothing by the usual means, your guardian offered a large reward to anyone who could provide the information. Your father's manservant was the informant, first disclosing the hiding place of your father's secret books, then what he had seen with his own eyes. That your father met a novice, alone and unchaperoned, that they spoke of the dark arts required to overcome the disease, how your father and Sor Maria Caterina waited to see if the protective measures the two of them had adopted would be effective. Their survival was proof that Satan protected them against the plague sent by God.

"They spent weeks caring for the sick and dying, snatching a few hours of sleep when they could. Sor Maria Caterina sent word back to the convent from time to time, but would allow no one from the convent to attend her, so as not to expose another nun, and possibly the entire convent, to the illness. It was improper, but these were difficult times.

"Finally a cold spell as Christmas approached ended the epidemic. Sor Maria Caterina knew she must return to the convent. Though she had not yet taken her perpetual vows, novices rarely obtained permission to leave. In desperation, your father conceived a bold and dangerous solution—Sor Maria Caterina would simply disappear. They would return to the Muslim faith of their ancestors, marry as Muslims in the eyes of God, and flee Spain.

"She and your father came to my house where they pronounced before me and two other Muslim witnesses, 'I acknowledge no God but Allah and Muhammad is his prophet.' As two Muslims they married. Your father gave your mother, in token of the contract, a very fine ring set with diamonds and pearls. But their looks of happiness exceeded the value of all the jewels in the world.

"When Maria Caterina failed to return to the convent, the quarter where she had worked was searched, but all that was found was a single slipper and empty medicine vials. It was believed that she had succumbed to the disease and her body had been thrown with other victims into a common grave. Instead, the couple was hiding in my house. I begged them to leave Spain at once, but the arrangements in his affairs your father believed necessary delayed them, and then Maria Caterina found she was expecting a child, and was too unwell to travel. She extracted a promise from your father that if she did not survive the birth, the baby would be baptized and brought up as a Christian, as your father's natural son or daughter."

"And my mother?"

"She died giving birth as she had feared, and your brokenhearted father resumed his life for your sake. Neither your mother nor your father ever turned from the Muslim faith they embraced, though your father kept his promise and brought you up a Christian. Only the valet knew the truth, and for years extracted money from your father in exchange for his silence. A lesser man than your father would have had the villain murdered. Your guardian is too greedy to hand you over to the Inquisition. Your fortune would be seized by them and he means to keep that for himself."

"And the valet...surely he remains a danger?"

"Ah, the valet...found in an alleyway with his throat slit. Thieves, no doubt hired by your guardian," said Don Jaime dryly. "Now, my dear, your guardian's wife is giving me suspicious looks. I will find a way to send help. Let the woman see me bless you."

Esperanza realized there was no one around her she could trust. She began to fear poison in every mouthful of food, every cup of wine, felt evil in the gloomy shadows of her guardian's house. Her childhood nightmares returned, and sleepless nights took their toll as they had when she was small. Her room was a prison. Unable to eat or sleep, she grew ill—at first lethargic, then feverish, first unwilling, then unable to stir from her bed. Days slid into nights. The fever worsened; her joints ached and burned.

Once she looked up and the guardian's wife hung over her with a razor, a lock of Esperanza's hair in her hand. Esperanza tried to scream and lost consciousness.

When she finally came to her senses, a sad-faced young maid with a crooked nose was sponging her face with rose water. Esperanza's head felt strange. Running her hand over it she realized her hair had been shorn. "Because of the fever," the maid whispered. "But it will grow again. I am Maria, your new maid. Don Jaime sent me. He has a plan, but first you must work hard to recover."

Astonishingly, it seemed Esperanza's guardian and his wife were determined she should get well. They sent for a prominent doctor who prescribed strengthening cordials and food. She was fed broth with eggs in it, bread made from fine flour, and wine mixed with spices and honey, and was continually asked what she wished to eat, and begged to name what dishes appealed to her. Strangest of all, her guardian's wife came each day to read aloud to her, from the most dismal book imaginable, Esperanza thought— a dull work on the nature of females and their path to virtue. It was a litany of women's imperfections as daughters of Eve, who had brought sin into the world, and whose inferiority and spiritual weakness rendered them unfit for anything except subjection to their fathers, brothers, and husbands. Her guardian's wife read out the section concerning the conduct and duties of Christian wives with emphasis and significant looks.

Finally her guardian's wife could not resist telling Esperanza that she was betrothed through the kindness of her guardian, and a noble man prepared to overlook the stain of her birth. Suspecting something amiss, Esperanza asked the name of her husband-to-be. Don Cesar Guzman, was the tight-lipped reply.

Maria, entering with a bowl of soup, whispered, "I will ask Don Jaime." She rolled her eyes at the door closing behind the guardian's wife. "Drink this."

A few days later Maria bent over Esperanza and hissed, "Don Jaime says better the Evil One for a husband than Don Cesar Guzman. He is old and has buried four young wives, all rich orphans, like you. He is cursed with a disease of his private parts, with pustules and swellings and a foul discharge, and suffers horribly in his efforts to beget a son. The need for a son has eaten his soul. He tormented his wives when they failed to conceive and within a few years, each died. Don Jaime says Don Cesar poisoned them. He believes your guardian has made a bargain, offering you to Don Cesar with a large dowry in return for asking no questions about your mother. Your guardian will keep the rest of your fortune and Don Cesar will let you live so long as you bear him children. Your guardian and Don Cesar are eager for the marriage to take place, and you must escape as soon as possible."

"Escape? How? The doors are barred, my duenna watches me night and day, and the guard at the gate would prevent my leaving. And where would I go?"

"Don Jaime devised a plan, but you must take me with you. Your guardian's wife is the cruelest mistress under heaven. She wears the barbed belt under her dress to mortify her body, and the pain makes her eager to mortify the flesh of others. She orders servants beaten viciously on the slightest pretense, especially the young ones, saying beatings do their souls the more good. She withholds food, then punishes us for stealing it when we grow so hungry we snatch a morsel. I long for the mountains and my mother and a boy...I promised to marry before my father sold me as a servant. I must return before he forgets me and marries another."

"But how can we go? And where?"

"Here is the how. You and I will dress as lads and make our way to the mountains. There is a convent not far from my village—women and girls, if they are beaten or treated badly, go to the nuns. To get their women back, men must give something to the Abbess in token of their good behavior. Men are in awe of the convent and treat women of our village with more care than other men do. The nuns will hide you from Don Cesar."

The duenna returned and heard the words "Don Cesar." Crossing the room with an angry step, she slapped Maria for gossiping and ordered her out of the room.

Escape seemed impossible. Thinking of it, Esperanza wept hopelessly for a time, then dried her eyes with the sheet. She had promised to accept her guardian's choice, but her father would never have wished her married to Don Cesar. In her predicament she had no choice. She must trust Don Jaime. And find some courage, or else her wedding would take place as soon as they saw she could leave her bed.

Provided her guardian's wife or the duenna had not taken it, she had a store of gold *reales* hidden in a secret compartment of the carved cedar clothes chest that had accompanied her to her guardian's house. That night when her duenna grew bored with the sickroom and left, believing she slept, Esperanza rose quietly and rummaged in her chest. The pouch of *reales* was there. She carried it back to bed with her. After that, each night she waited until her duenna left the room, then slipped out of bed to walk up and down the room until she heard the duenna returning, trying to regain her strength. She felt well again, but kept her recovery a secret and continued to languish by day.

One day in late spring Maria whispered, "Summer is the only time we can travel into the mountains, and we must go soon. I will bring a new chamber pot to hide under your bed. From now on, pour the sleeping draft your guardian's wife brings into it. I will collect it from you each day and save it. The night we leave, I will mix it into your duenna's wine when I bring up her supper. I will give drugged wine to the guard at the gate as well. He is always clutching at me, groping at my bodice! I will smile and refill his goblet, wear my bodice unlaced, and he will think I have relented. Then we will dress as boys—"

"Pages? Only my page is very small and I am..."

"No, idiot! Kitchen boys! If you give me something to pay our kitchen boy he will part with his ragged clothes—he is tall as you. I warn you, they stink, but that is all the better, and since your hair is already short all you need do is dirty your face and hands..." They both looked at her hands. White and thin, with pink nails. "Rub soot well into your hands and under your fingernails. Looking like that they would give us away in an instant, whatever our disguises," Maria advised. "And we will need money."

Esperanza triumphantly produced her pouch of *reales*, but Maria shook her head. "Country bumpkins with *reales*? We would be arrested as thieves!" She took one. "I never thought to hold a *reale*! Don Jaime will exchange it for small coins that peasants might have."

The duenna no longer watched as Esperanza drank her sleeping drafts. For ten nights Esperanza poured them into the spare chamber pot. On the tenth day, Maria slipped in with a bundle reeking of sweat and boy. On the eleventh day it was raining heavily, but cleared toward evening. That afternoon, Maria came for the chamber pot with the sleeping medicine and mouthed, "Tonight!" As night approached, Esperanza's teeth were chattering with fear and the duenna frowned and said she must be feverish again. The duenna's nose wrinkled at the smell of illness—the bundle of clothing under Esperanza's bed—and kept her distance.

The candle burned down to nothing by the time the duenna had her supper and drunk her wine and was slumped in her chair like one dead. Maria opened the door and whispered, "Hurry!"

Maria was wearing a filthy leather jerkin over a ragged linen shirt and patched trousers, and she had chopped off her braids.

Esperanza dressed quickly, disgusted by the filthy garments against her skin. "Wet your hands and face from the pitcher by the bed and wipe them with ashes from the grate," Maria ordered in a whisper. She tied the pouch of *reales* under the pantaloons so it bulged where Esperanza's legs met. Esperanza said it was uncomfortable, but Maria insisted it was a necessary part of a boy's disguise. And since Esperanza's accent would give them away, she must let Maria do all the talking in her country dialect. They were peasant brothers, returning to their village. Maria was the sensible brother; Esperanza was a simple fellow, unable to speak since birth. Esperanza crossed her eyes and scratched her pouch and Maria stifled a giggle.

They crept past the sleeping guard, opened the door and waited until a party of drunken men lurched past, then the night watchmen. "Now! Stay in the shadows," ordered Maria. They hurried into the night, knowing that when the guard awoke the alarm would be raised and a search for them would begin at once.

They soon found this was true. Everywhere they stopped for food or shelter, even when they begged rides on peasant carts, they heard talk of the stolen heiress and the reward offered to anyone who returned her safely to her guardian. Their closest call came at a tavern where they had been given a crust and a little stew out of charity. They were huddled in the shadows by the fire when a party of armed guards entered, asking if anyone had seen the heiress, mentioning an even greater reward than previously offered. The company fell silent and Esperanza was seized with terror that she would be handed over, especially when one of the rough fellows leaned over, guffawing and slapped Esperanza's back, saying, "Here she is, Your Worship! The reward is mine!" Then everyone laughed at the dusty simpleton drooling over his bread, nodding and smiling at the joke while he picked a louse out of his head and killed it between his fingernails.

But mainly the journey was hard. They had quickly worn holes in their shoes, and tied them on with rags as best they could. Esperanza was limping and they begged rides on peasants' carts when they could. But it was well into summer when they reached the foothills of the mountains, which had looked much nearer when they set out. They were two young hungry girls and their hunger at the end of the day was such that they invariably spent more than they intended on food. Their supply of coins was nearly gone, but Maria refused to let them use a *reale*. Now they survived on a little bread and oil and wild fruit.

Despite hunger and weariness, Maria grew more confident, pointing out the white stones that marked their way through the forest, encouraging and goading Esperanza. Higher and higher they went. The air grew thinner and cooler and there were eagles and falcons in the wide sky.

Esperanza lost track of time. Her feet were raw and she could think of nothing except putting one down after the other until the day's end. Only the charity of people in the villages sustained them. Esperanza's feet bled. Her fever returned. Finally she refused to go on, wanting nothing so much as to lie down at the side of the road to die. Maria left her collapsed on a rock and came back with a crust of stale bread and a half-rotted apple she had stolen from some pigs. Maria gave these to Esperanza, saying it was not much farther, Esperanza must try.

Two days later, numb from cold after a night in the open, they reached a terraced olive grove at what felt like the top of the world. Maria kicked and dragged and cajoled Esperanza up the terraces to the gates of a great stone enclosure, panting, "Here! Just a little farther! Another step or two"—then dropped her in the dust to reach for a bell rope. The last thing Esperanza heard was its clanging. She no longer cared whether she lived or died.

She awoke surrounded by nursing sisters cutting her ragged verminous clothes off. She struggled frantically to get up, crying she must escape before they married her to the Evil One. They fed her herbal broth and a calming cordial, and wrapped her in blankets warmed by hot stones, until she grew calmer. Finally she fell into an exhausted sleep so deep it seemed she had died.

"And they will kill me if they find me," she said, when she was well enough to talk.

"I know," said the Abbess.

Now Esperanza's hair has grown, her gaunt face has filled out and gained a little color, and she is content in the scriptorium. I depend upon her to write for me in the Chronicle when my hand and wrist are too swollen and stiff. It is good to have a girl by my side again, especially one who undertakes her tasks so efficiently.

And so we went calmly on in the scriptorium until the day soon after the swallows had returned and were filling the convent with the cheerful sounds of their nest making, and a new child arrived. This one was not an infant with a dowry and wet nurse, but one abandoned in rags outside the gate, though it had rained hard in the night. The Abbess sent for me, and, to my surprise, Esperanza.

CHAPTER 13

From the Chronicle of Las Sors Santas de Jesus,
Las Golondrinas Convent, Andalusia, Spring 1549

At first we did not see the child with the adult's head and face
on the footstool at the Abbess's feet. Luz does not speak, and
can sit so quietly for hours that she is almost invisible. To see a
dwarf child dressed in a ragged shift and broken shoes was surprising. The great households prize their dwarves, dress them in
fine clothes, and keep them like pet dogs for amusement, as if
they were not human beings with souls. It is a wicked custom and
Esperanza whispered hotly in my ear, "I would never have thought
the Abbess kept a dwarf! For shame!"

The Abbess snapped, "Do not stare at me with such disapproval, Esperanza! This girl was left at the gate this morning."

Esperanza flushed. Leaning over to the dwarf child, the Abbess
put her hand under her chin and raised her face into the light. The
child flinched, and reason for the Abbess's barely suppressed
fury was plain. There were traces of bruising around the child's
nose, and what looked at first like a harelip was a ragged scar that
must have been caused by a blow that split her upper lip. Her eyes
were big and terrified in a dirty face, looking from one of us to
the other, and her hair was matted and verminous. The Abbess's
expression changed and she said gently, "Child, you are safe here.

No one will beat you. But can you not tell us your name and how old you are?"

The child said nothing.

"Who brought you?" The dwarf girl reached into the pocket of her dress and pulled out a folded paper and handed it to the Abbess, then hung her head like an animal waiting to be kicked.

The Abbess unfolded it and read it out loud:

Esteemed Sisters, I have traveled a long way to leave my granddaughter Luz to your mercy and care. There is no one else I can turn to. I am dying and can no longer protect her. The child has been sadly wronged by the circumstances of her birth. It has long been a custom in our family for cousins to marry to preserve the family's fortune and estates, and my only child, my daughter, was married to a cousin who loved her since childhood. She was the darling of her husband's eye, a blameless wife, and a kind mistress to all the household servants—including her husband's mischievous dwarf, known for his lusty ways with the kitchen girls. Then she gave birth to their first child, who is as you see her. The moment the poor baby was born, my daughter's happiness was destroyed. When my son-in-law saw poor Luz he flew into a rage, convinced my girl had cuckolded him with his dwarf. My daughter protested her innocence, but was dragged by her hair from the birthing bed and locked away as an adulteress, allowed only a priest to make her confession, then left to die.

When I heard what had happened, I hurried to my son-in-law, to tell him that although it was never spoken of, women in our family had given birth to dwarves on other occasions; there had been instances in almost every generation, and the children were kept hidden from sight. He shut his ears and would not allow me to see my daughter. The poor girl died alone in her locked chamber in a pool of blood, according to the servants who found her. The unfortunate dwarf was never seen again.

I petitioned those in authority I knew to investigate the deaths of two innocent people, but all washed their hands of the matter, saying a man may regulate his family as he sees fit, and if he has behaved wrongly to his wife, that is a matter for his conscience; he should confess and do penance.

A woman is dust beneath men's feet, there is no justice for my daughter! I begged my son-in-law to let me take the child, but he is deranged by the supposed deceit and vowed he would see the creature suffer. He allowed me to remain in the household to witness it. I stayed, in the hope of protecting the poor baby from her father. I only sometimes succeeded. The man grew worse with time and has treated her like a dog—beatings and kickings and taunts, not taught so much as her prayers, sleeping in the straw by the fire, fed on slops. Yet according to family custom, as firstborn Luz will inherit the bulk of his fortune. He does not dare kill her, because he intends to marry her off to another orphaned cousin, and secure their joint fortunes to himself.

When my son-in-law left for a hunting party of several weeks, I took Luz and fled. I had heard that at the Convent of the Swallows, desperate women might find help and protection denied them elsewhere. For the love of God and the Virgin, have pity on Luz and give her shelter, and I will pray for you for the remainder of my life on earth and afterward before the throne of the Almighty.

The Abbess refolded the paper. "Terrible. Of course we will take the poor child in. We would take the grandmother, too, if only she could be found. But I have sent for you, Esperanza, as well as Sor Beatriz, because I wish you to record every word in the Chronicle, to bear witness to the inhumanity and cruelty that women suffer. But I am curious. You have told us you and your father read forbidden texts. The Moors were observant of the natural world and learned in the natural sciences. And so many of their works have been burned by the church." Book burning irritates the Abbess beyond measure.

"Yes," Esperanza said cautiously. "My father had many medical books he read to me and I studied those I could read for myself..."

"The infirmary sisters say that you...can you recall anything that considers the matter of dwarves?"

Esperanza thought for a minute. Then she said a Greek text about the breeding of animals had pointed to the result of inbreeding weak livestock, and the feeble calves or goats with three legs that resulted, and from that the writer deduced that inbreeding among small groups of people might produce weaklings and addled wits. He had then applied his observations about breeding animals to instances where human interbreeding had produced a similar result.

Pure heresy now. The church taught that observations of animal behavior had no application to humans who had been created in God's image. Esperanza's father, however, had agreed with the author of the treatise that it was the order of nature, and nature was a manifestation of God's laws. And the text had mentioned that a family that produced a dwarf or children with weak spines should avoid marrying any blood relation, no matter how distant. Esperanza added bitterly that the treatise had been burned along with the rest of her father's library. The Abbess screwed up her face and muttered an imprecation against ignorant fools who concealed knowledge and increased the sorrows of the world, causing innocent children like Luz immeasurable suffering.

"Thank you, Esperanza." Then she turned to Luz and said, "Child, your name means light, the beautiful light that shines in your soul and will now shine in safety. Go with Esperanza, who will see that you have a bath and fresh clothes. Then there will be a little bed for you. You must be hungry—ask the kitchen sister for some soup, Esperanza, tell them to strengthen it with an egg and to give Luz a little honey bread if any is left. Tell the sisters in charge of the children to find salve for those bruises. If Luz will not speak, we must have patience; it is not from obstinacy."

It is impossible to know Luz's age. The Abbess guesses between eight and ten or eleven. She cannot read or write, and is too frightened by everything to learn anything but sewing. But that she does very well indeed. While many girls fidget during the long hours of the sewing lesson, Luz hangs onto the sewing mistress's every word. She is delighted to possess her very own workbasket, with colored silk thread, a needle case, tiny silver scissors, and a thimble. She keeps it all in the neatest order and has mastered every stitch. She sits quietly at her work for hours on her stool, made low enough so her feet reach the floor, until called to prayers or meals or to walk in the cloister. Her stitches are beautiful, neat and almost invisible—unlike Esperanza's needlework. Esperanza, for all her cleverness, can scarcely sew a line that is not crooked and uneven. Luz is praised and held up as an example to the other girls, and this has done wonders. Little by little she has grown plump. Her bruises healed and she even smiles sometimes. She never speaks, however, and a sharp word or a loud noise sends her running to a corner in tears.

Esperanza has been made much happier by having Luz to look after, and brings her to sew in the scriptorium while the other girls are having lessons. "She's very quiet and good, aren't you, Luz? And look, Sor Beatriz," said Esperanza to me one day. She took a folded handkerchief from her pocket and spread it out, delicate as a moth's wing. "Luz worked this for me. Isn't it beautiful?"

Luz glowed with pleasure as I admired the handkerchief. It was very lovely, trimmed in lace around the edge and embroidered with a bird. "A *golondrina*!" Esperanza pointed out. "I showed her how they made their nests everywhere in the convent to sing to her because she feeds them crumbs. Isn't she a good, clever girl!" Luz blushed with pleasure and Esperanza gave her a hug.

The sewing mistress has now set Luz to work mending linen for the convent chapel. Normally she permits no one to touch it but herself. Meanwhile, the Abbess has received a letter on behalf of our patroness the queen, requesting prayers for the Christian conversion of the natives in Spanish America.

The Abbess told the sewing mistress to set a new task for Luz, an altar cloth for the queen's personal chapel, embroidered with religious symbols entwined with little *golondrinas*, the emblem of our convent. It will be sent with a respectful letter promising to pray as the queen commands, to assure her of our obedience to her wishes, the purity of our faith, and our respectful gratitude.

"We must take every opportunity to remind the queen that we look to her as our protectress," murmured the Abbess.

CHAPTER 14

Las Golondrinas Convent, Spain, April 2000

Having fought off sleep to keep nightmares at bay, Menina was groggy the next morning as she followed Sor Clara. She wished she had a whole pot of coffee. They passed the scriptorium and stopped before a heavy double door. "Here is *sala grande.*" Sor Clara fumbled for a bunch of keys at her waist and found the one that unlocked the ornate iron lock—but even though the key turned, the door refused to open, despite her shoves and mutterings and prayers.

Menina asked Sor Clara to stand aside, and gave it a good kick with her boot. The door scraped open—probably for the first time in many years, judging by the cloud of dust their entrance raised— and stuck halfway open. Menina sneezed and, looking around, saw they were in a room so long and dark that its ends were in shadow. She guessed it ran the length of the cloister. As her eyes adjusted she saw it was similar to the room with the iron grille where she had been yesterday, only much bigger. This one had the same dark carved wooden furniture, as well as a stiff horsehair settee with stuffing coming out of it, matching chairs, and a huge crucifix crooked on a wall. Then Menina caught her breath. The walls, which had just looked dark at first, were actually covered with picture frames.

Weak light filtered through the dust motes onto a threadbare Persian rug in the middle of the room. The arms and backs of the furniture were draped in rotting antimacassars, and an arm had fallen off one of the chairs. An embroidered runner with holes in it ran the length of a heavy table against the wall, beneath a dusty plaster statue of the Virgin Mary and two fat lopsided ecclesiastical candles in holders. The musty smell that permeated the convent was overwhelming, and the silence was so heavy it was tangible.

"How long since anyone used this room?" Menina asked, looking around.

"Many years. Is cold in winter. But I think the painting by Tristan Mendoza was in this room."

"Do you remember where, Sor Clara?" asked Menina faintly, looking up at the walls that held probably hundreds of pictures, all dark with dirt and age. Talk about looking for a needle in a haystack. Sor Clara tottered over to one of the stiff-looking settees, sat down, and waited expectantly.

"Sor Clara, do you know which wall it hung on?"

"Eh?" Sor Clara cupped her hand around her ear to hear better. Menina repeated the question, almost shouting. Sor Clara gave an expressive eye-rolling shrug.

"Why did I ask?" Menina said to herself. She chose a small frame at random, lifted it gingerly from the wall, took a piece of bread and began working it between her palms to soften it, then started pressing it gently onto the surface of the painting. The bread picked up dirt until it disintegrated. Menina stepped back and realized she could see a hand. She hastily pressed some more bread onto the surface until she recognized the same tonsured monk with a crooked nose and squinty eyes she had seen yesterday, only from a different angle. Menina took it to the middle of the room and searched for a signature at the bottom but could see nothing, no sign of writing or a bird. She wished she had a magnifying glass, but she didn't. Sor Clara was asleep with her rosary in her lap and her mouth open, snoring gently.

Menina propped the monk out of reach of the sun and picked another frame from the middle of the wall and started to work as quickly as possible. It would take months to get to every painting.

A couple of hours later, Sor Clara hadn't moved. Alarmed the elderly nun might be dead, Menina checked her breathing, then realized Sor Clara was probably tired because of the nighttime vigil. By now, half a dozen murky paintings of different sizes stood propped up against the wall. Menina stepped back and squinted at her handiwork. The monk kept drawing her attention, and the longer she looked at it the more uneasy it made her. She knew her reaction was probably due to being tired and disoriented—but it had an evil presence and she didn't like it. Finally, she turned it face to the wall.

As for the next four paintings…she peered, trying to see what they were about, looking for familiar themes and symbols and subjects that cropped up in religious art that would give her a clue about the painting. At college she always enjoyed the exercises where students had to "read" a painting, but at college there were textbooks and a library for reference. Now she was on her own, memory her only resource.

At Holly Hill the course on Renaissance methodology began with the same joke every year, that anyone brought up in the Bible Belt had a head start identifying the themes of Renaissance art. Menina had been astonished to find that years of Baptist Sunday School and coloring books of Bible stories had delivered this particular dividend. And while the methodology course was no more than the basics, Menina loved the process of hunting for clues to a painting's hidden meaning, unraveling the significance of light and shade and colors, the positioning of the figures, the symbols—like rays streaming through a window to represent the Divine Light illumining the world, or pomegranates to symbolize fertility and the Resurrection, dogs for fidelity, and parrots that people in the Middle Ages believed made the sound "Ave" as if they were about to pray to the Virgin Mary.

But the artist's perspective was only part of it. Painting was a dialogue between the artist and the viewer, and to interpret a painting you had to understand how the artist expected people of the time to understand it. And that depended on many things— the period when it was painted, politics, and religious ideas. The question you had to ask was, where were the painter and the viewer "at"? Maybe the painting was intended to link a donor or artist's patron to holy figures—where everybody was "at" was that the saint's holiness rubbed off on the donor by association. Maybe it was intended to generate awe in the viewer at the radiance of God's word, maybe it had a message of the power of life over death, or connected a king or queen to God, or illuminated a mystery everyone would have been aware of at the time, like changing the water and wine of communion into the body and blood of Christ—the possibilities were endless but it was important to search for a painting's message *to* the person looking at it.

Menina thought about all this while she opened her notebook and uncapped a ballpoint. She would be methodical and give each painting a number before she began cleaning it, then write a brief description of what she found. Then she could try the dialogue test.

She took down painting number one and narrowed her eyes. Where was everybody "at" with this one? The longer she looked, the uglier it seemed—a moon-faced Madonna whose hands looked like they had been painted on as an afterthought, sticking awkwardly out of her sleeves. Either the artist had no grasp of basic anatomy or it was an artistic statement. She would let somebody else worry about it. Just in case, she pat the corners looking for a signature, finding a *C* followed by something that might be "Lopez."

Painting number two was equally disappointing—insipid angels with open mouths, flat and lifeless against a brown sky. No signature. Menina put it next to the Madonna.

Number three was a still life of roses and lilies which she knew were a reference to the Virgin Mary, and might be valuable depending on the detail and colors under the dirt. She checked for a signature, found a *B.* and put it aside.

Number four was a stolid child carrying a lamb over his shoulder. Both lamb and child wore exactly the same dramatic pout and soulful expression. So awful it made her smile. She put it with the Madonna.

Three and a half hours later Menina was filthy, surrounded by two dozen paintings propped haphazardly against the walls. She wiped her forearm across her brow. None of it looked promising—maybe a cut above, or at least older than what was hanging in the corridors—but still she would bet nothing she had seen so far was worth much. She stood up to stretch her back and looked around the walls again. It was now early afternoon and the room was bright enough that Menina could see that a large black frame hanging at eye level had a lumpy pattern.

She looked at the frame closely, then scratched it with her nail, leaving a hairlike gray line. Menina spat on it and breathed on it and rubbed it with the sleeve of her sweatshirt, until her sleeve was dirty and the spot she had rubbed had a dull gleam. Not gilt as she had expected, but silver. Venetian? But a silver frame surely must be an indicator that the painting it held must be reasonably good. She looked at it closely. Under the tarnish was an ornate pattern of curling vines. Then Menina cried, "Oh!" Among the vines were small birds with forked tails.

She staggered under its weight as she lifted it down. Propping it up against the wall she set to work, until she could make out what looked like a crowd of people with no faces. No wait, there was a face in profile on the side. The others weren't faceless—it showed the backs of their heads. They were looking toward the center right which had something light, what looked like two figures…something was happening in the middle…she could see what looked like a bandaged leg. Was that crooked thing a crutch?

Unsettling faces, some in profile, some at an angle, emerged from the dirt—grotesque faces, syphilitic or alcoholic or something, noses too short and wide and nostrils twisted up, mouths open, sick and weary and mad faces, faces with features swollen and battered and distorted by hard lives and hunger, a crowd of suffering people all focusing on something. Someone lying on what looked like a stretcher. A skeleton. And something moving at the bottom of the painting. As the grime of centuries came away, demons with reptilian bodies, grinning humanoid features, and malevolent yellow eyes stared directly at Menina even as they scurried away between the legs of the crowd, away from whatever was taking place in the center of the painting.

She recognized the theme immediately—the story from the Bible of Jesus healing and casting out demons. She cleaned some more dirt off until she could make out two figures in the center. Two men in profile? No, it looked like a man and a woman. With the last piece of bread she dabbed the lower left-hand corner. And as the last bit crumbled, she thought there was a *T*. Then an *r*.

It wasn't possible, she told herself, turning the painting to get the light on it. But was that a *T*? And a capital *M*? At that point she would have licked the dirt off to find out if it wouldn't have done so much harm to the paint. In her excitement she gathered up dirty crumbs from the floor and rubbed, a little more vigorously than anyone should do on an old painting, and there—she couldn't believe it, she rubbed her eyes—was a little blob. Mustn't get over-excited, a blob was a blob...unless it was a swallow! She cleaned until she saw *T-r-i-s* then *M-e-n-d*, and stopped rubbing before she damaged it irreparably.

She stood up and took some deep breaths. She, Menina Ann Walker, age nineteen, had just made a discovery, a real art-world discovery, just like that! Bam! Art historians spent entire careers trying to do what she had just done. "I don't believe it," she muttered over and over. Then she punched the air with her fist and cried, "Yes!" Wait till Becky and Holly Hill and her parents heard! Yes! She was so excited she did a little impromptu victory dance, then "Sor Clara. Sor Clara? Wake up! Good news!" She patted the old nun on the arm excitedly and Sor Clara snored loudly and woke up, looking startled. "Eh?"

Menina said very loudly in Spanish, "I found the Tristan Mendoza! I found it! I found it! It was here! Just like you said! And I found it! Thank you! Thank you!"

"*Deo gratias...*" mumbled Sor Clara, rubbing her eyes.

There was a sound of footsteps, then Sor Teresa threw open the door and without preliminaries announced Menina's food was waiting for her and they must hurry. Sor Clara had to go to the vigil and she needed to get back to the kitchen because there were *polvorónes* baking. All the world wanted *polvorónes*, everything was late today, she had far too much to do, and Alejandro needed to speak to Menina at once.

"Sor Teresa, come look. I found the Tristan Mendoza! I found it!" Menina was almost jumping up and down with excitement like a five-year-old when she suddenly remembered Sor Teresa couldn't see. She started to apologize, but she needn't have bothered; Sor Teresa wasn't listening.

"We talk about it later. Come now!" she barked. Leading the way down the corridor to the *locutio* parlor, she was loud enough to be heard on the other side of the grate, complaining it was *Semana Santa*, and they were too busy to be always welcoming Menina's visitors. The captain said reasonably from the other side that he was the only visitor and it was necessary for him to speak to Menina on police business.

The two nuns hobbled off, Sor Teresa airing her grievances loudly as she went. Menina tried to stop dancing and bubbled happily. "Captain, you were right about the convent having a valuable painting, I just found—"

To her surprise he wasn't interested. He said, "Mees Walker, some people are looking for you."

The day was getting better and better. "Thank heaven! My parents obviously managed to galvanize *somebody*. I'm so reliev—"

"Your parents, eh? Though you do not believe me, I would have telephoned them if it had been possible, but I could not. So maybe is not your family who send them," he said slowly. "And maybe is more important than ever that you stay out of sight."

"What? Of course it's my parents! Who else? I called them from the airport to let them know I wasn't in Madrid yet, and that I was taking a bus. Obviously they got the police to trace the bus, and the bus driver explained I had been left here and—"

"No, it is a man and a woman who are following you, and whoever they are, they are not police. In fact they do not want the police to know they are looking for you. And because I do not want them to cause problems for me, I must get to the bottom of this now. You must tell me, who wants to find you?"

Menina's mouth suddenly felt dry and her elation evaporated as she remembered. "Oh God, please, not Theo!" she muttered. He had the money and connections to trace her, but surely the Bonners would be trying to put a spin on why the wedding had been canceled.

"Who is Theo?" the captain demanded.

"Um, nobody. My parents must have hired a private detective to find me."

"No, I do not think so. And I will tell you why I do not think so, and then you will tell me why they look for you, because it does not make sense to me. An old man, a retired policeman friend of my father, is driving from Malaga back to a village in the mountains where he lives with his daughter's family, and he stops for coffee. While he is drinking his coffee, a couple comes into the bar, a man and a woman, nice clothes, want to put a sign in the bar window, a picture of a girl, very pretty, and it says 'Menina Walker,' an American, is missing. Says big reward for information. My friend thinks I should know this...never mind why. But he, too, wants to know why so he listens to everything—old habit. And people do not think an old man in the corner with his pipe and his coffee is listening. He wants to see what this couple do next. He drinks more coffee, reads his newspaper. The couple order food, drinks, spend a lot of money for a small bar, and people at the bar say OK, they can put up their poster, but is better to fill out an official report at the police station. But, the couple say no, they do not bother police."

"Seems odd they said that! Why?"

"Is strange, no? My friend, too, does not like—"

"Oh for Pete's sake! *What* don't the two of you like? You should be thrilled someone wants to take me off your hands."

"You must listen...My friend understands why I cannot leave the village now, so instead of going home he comes to see me. While the people are eating, he goes outside, like he will make pi pi, to look at their car, memorize the number plate. Old habit. And then he is surprised, because he knows something most people, most police even, would not. A little symbol on the license means the car belongs to a Catholic organization, is like a *confraternidad*— brotherhood. But my friend knows this particular brotherhood is very old in Spain and very, very conservative, some say dates back to the Inquisition, dangerous because...how do you say it? It has fanatics, people who will do anything to protect the church."

"How does he know *that*? It sounds pretty far-fetched."

"You must understand something. You are from America, and for Americans yesterday is over, finished. In Spain it is not over. During the civil war in the 1930s terrible things happened that people do not forget today. My friend's family were Republicans, like my father. In 1939 the Fascists came to this village. They take all the men and boys, children even, and hang them in the square. They wanted to hang my father, too, but he was hunting because was no food, and when they come he hide in the hills, in caves.

"My mother, his wife, was sixteen, with a baby coming. She run with other women to this convent and the nuns take them in and lock the gate. Fascists very dangerous, but Fascist Catholics, don't burn convent. And the gate is very strong. My mother and the other women are safe. So later, because of the nuns, I have my parents and my family. My father's friend was not so lucky. The Fascists came to his village, too, killed his parents and raped many women, killed many people. For that, all his life he has hated the Catholic Church because Fascists are Catholics and the Catholic Church supports the Fascists. He has spent much of his life learning about the church and their secrets, and he knows things most people do not. The right wing of the church is very old-fashioned, everyone forget about them now, think they don't matter. But like this *confraternidad* they exist, and are powerful in the Vatican. Powerful in other places. And my friend knows, these people do not waste time looking for girls for no reason. So now you must tell me what that reason is. Do not play games."

Games? Menina just wanted to get out of here. "How should *I* know about Catholic organizations? I'm a Southern Baptist—the

Catholic Church can't be so desperate for converts that they chase tourists around the country!"

"There must be more you are not telling me if these people want to find you. They get instructions from a high level in the church, some say even the Vatican. And the Vatican has contacts in government, the police, everywhere. The church has great power today. You think religious fanatics are not dangerous? They are the most dangerous people in the world. Look at Northern Ireland, look at the Basques. Look at the Middle East. So I ask you once more, why are you in Spain?"

"I've told you and told you—I just want to go to Madrid!"

"Mees Walker, start with this Mendoza. Why is he important?"

Menina was beginning to feel like Alice in Wonderland. She had already explained about Tristan Mendoza, and while he was interesting if you were an art history major with a thesis to write, she didn't see how that justified this weird interrogation. "Look, I'm studying him because I have this medal, but it can't mean anything to anybody but me. Here!" She slipped off her medal and passed it through the grille, telling him how she was found with it and how the nuns wanted her to have it when she turned sixteen. "So it's important to me because it's all I have that connects me to my birth family. Now see the little bird on one side? The reason I'm interested in Tristan Mendoza is that he signed his paintings with that same bird under his signature. I wanted to research his work at the Prado—the only place with any of his work—to find out if that swallow meant something, what its history was, there would be a...connection to my birth parents. The Walkers are wonderful, and I love them, but if you aren't adopted you can't understand this terrible need to know about your birth family. It's like there's a hole in the middle of your life. I know the swallows may just be a coincidence, but it's absolutely all I have to go on."

"In Spain family is very important. I understand. The nuns helped my mother, my family. Now I must help Sor Teresa like I promise my father." He held the medal up and squinted, ran his fingers over the worn figures on both sides and thought for a moment before he handed the medal back.

Sounding less impatient he said, "In the mountains here, there are some old stories about a Jewish Christian community in this part of Spain, when the Romans were here. The first Christians were Jews, too; I think they do not say Jesus's mother Mary is a virgin forever, because she has other children besides Jesus. Then hundreds of years later, when Constantine is emperor, the church says yes, Jesus is son of God, so is like God and Mary is a virgin always. By then, who knows what is true about Mary? But Catholic Church is very powerful, and people must not ask what is true, must believe what the church says, and church says Mary is virgin forever, that is why she is powerful with God. And I think the old stories about the Christian Jews who were here when the Romans are here have swallows in them, but I do not know why. But never mind, you must tell me the rest of your story, so I know what I can believe about *you*. First, who is Theo? How is he involved?"

"Um, Theo's no one."

"If he is no one, why did you think he sent people to look for you?"

Menina felt anxiety rising. "Theo was...OK, we were supposed to get married."

"Supposed to? You are engaged to Theo? This is no one?"

"No, I'm not engaged. Not anymore."

"Why?"

Menina tried to keep her voice from shaking while she told him that they had a fight and called off the wedding. She tried to say calmly that people broke up all the time. But much as she didn't want to, she saw herself and Theo in the car by the lake and felt

Theo's hand across her mouth and her own helplessness…it all came rushing back, she couldn't banish it from her mind. Theo's hand stifling her screams so she couldn't breathe…it was like he hated her…and then…*what's the big deal*…she was hyperventilating. "And I…he…I came to Spain because…" *Shut up!* Menina told herself.

"But you will get married when you go home?"

"NO!"

"Why?"

It felt like her skin was slowly being peeled from her flesh. "Leave me alone! I don't want to talk about it!"

"It's better if you tell me."

"Look, it's none of your business, it's got nothing to do with the people you're describing or some argument in the church. It's got nothing to do with anybody but me!" She clutched the *locutio* and started to cry. "Now leave me alone!"

"Mees Walker, I am sorry, to break up, not get married like you want to…is painful. But maybe he is not a good man, or maybe not a good man for you. Sometimes we are lucky to find out in time we cannot trust the person we love."

Menina lost all her self-control. Fury took its place. She was angrier than she had ever been in her life. She grasped the grille with both hands and wished she could kill the man on the other side. "Trust? He raped me! And said it didn't matter, that we were getting married, and I think he wanted to get me pregnant, and I don't even know whether it's my fault—my mother would say so if she knew, so I can't tell her. I can't tell the police because I don't want to drag my family through a court case with all his fraternity brothers saying I'm…I'm a…I can't even tell my best friend! I'm trying to handle it and I was and I felt better and today I thought… now you…ruined that…you…you…arrogant bastard!" She heard herself shrieking words she had never used to anyone, until she was crying and choking too hard to go on.

The captain let her scream and cry until she was gasping for breath. "It is not good to say nothing when such a terrible thing happens to you." He sounded sympathetic. Reasonable. What a shit, she thought helplessly, hating him. "Is many bad people in the world, but you are not to blame if he is one of them." That made things worse. Menina didn't want his sympathy. She didn't want reasonable. She didn't want him or anyone to *know*! That he did was like being raped all over again. Menina kicked the *locutio* as hard as she could with her Timberland until the bars rattled and her foot hurt. "Damn you! You stupid…Damn you!" she screamed as loud as she could.

"You are angry," said the captain "This is good! Be angry at him. He deserves your anger, and to be angry at me because you tell me this, is better than angry at yourself for what is not your fault."

"Oh sh-sh-shut up you fuckwit! Just shut *up*!" Menina screamed again.

Suddenly Sor Teresa was there, scolding, "Alejandro! What is this? What have you said?" She put her arm around Menina, saying, "We go now."

Sobbing and gasping for breath, Menina was pulled away by Sor Teresa. The captain was calling something and then banging on the grille himself, saying it was important. Menina didn't care. She had almost felt like herself again for a while, but she'd been wrong. Her life was in ruins. The rest of the day was a miserable blur. She forced herself to wash her T-shirt and other set of underwear, rinsing them again and again in icy pump water until her hands were numb. Then she sat in the pilgrims' garden and tried to make notes about what she had found that morning. She couldn't remember a single thing. She picked up her guidebook and read the same paragraphs over and over again, then kept putting the book down because she was crying. That night a plate of small almond cakes were on her tray. "*Polvorónes*," said Sor Teresa and left.

Menina had no appetite for them or anything else. She lay down and stared into the dark. She remembered she hadn't brushed her teeth. She started to get up and do it, then decided that her life was going to hell, her teeth might as well rot.

CHAPTER 15

Las Golondrinas Convent, Spain, April 2000

The next morning Sor Teresa shrilled, *"Deo gratias!"* and Menina rubbed her swollen eyes, and pushed herself up. She hated the world and everything and everyone in it. Her head ached. Thursday. Three days till Easter. Then she remembered the humiliation of yesterday and nothing mattered.

Sor Teresa hobbled briskly out the door. Menina drank her coffee without tasting it, cringing at the way she had lost control the day before. She couldn't afford to do that again. She pulled on her clothes, feeling numb.

An hour later, she was following Sor Clara toward the *sala grande* when Sor Clara paused in the kitchen and, grinning broadly, pointed to a startling sight: a large basket of foil-wrapped chocolate fish, wrapped in layers of rainbow-colored cellophane, all topped with a huge bow of multicolored ribbon trailing elaborate ribbon curls. The label said: VALOR.

"Valor is famous, very nice, very expensive!" said Sor Clara, appreciatively. "Captain Fernández Galán brought it."

Menina eyed the rainbow basket. "Why?"

"Why? Because fish are a Christian symbol! In Spain there are chocolate fish for Easter; people give for presents, in the family, to friends." Sor Clara cast a sly glance at Menina. "Men give to girls. And a little note is here." She handed it to Menina and waited.

Menina unfolded a scrap of paper that said "Polizia" at the top, and read aloud.

Señorita Walker, Every year my older sister in Zaragoza sends these for Semana Santa, to remind me I am still her little brother. Please accept them for yourself and the sisters with my compliments.

Alejandro Fernández Galán

Menina normally loved chocolate. Now she ground her teeth, ripped the note in pieces, and was about to hurl the basket on the floor and stomp it flat with her Timberlands when the frightened look on Sor Clara's face stopped her. "You must take it," Sor Clara quavered anxiously, pointing at the basket. "Please, you bring it. Alejandro said he will see you later."

Oh hell! "Why?" She picked up the heavy basket.

Sor Clara shrugged and opened the door of the *sala grande*. "I don't know why. Is another of his girlfriends here last night." Obviously the old-lady grapevine didn't shut down over *Semana Santa*. "So many girlfriends. He should get married. He is lonely."

"Is he?" It came out a little sharper than Menina intended. Why didn't he give his girlfriend the damned chocolate, let her get fat! In the *sala grande* Menina slammed the basket down. Captain Fernández Galán was a pain in the ass! One minute he was rude, the next he was worrying about the nuns, the next prying out her secrets, the next…another red-hot girlfriend. She was sick of the captain.

In fact, she was thoroughly irritated by everything and everyone, including poor Sor Clara, the walls of dirty, stupid pictures, and the fact that she probably had only four or five hours of good light. She looked at the painting of the crowd and the demons in its tarnished silver frame, and the clean space on the wall where it had hung. So she'd found it. Big deal.

She looked around to see if any other frames caught her attention. There seemed to be four other paintings of the same size hung at the same height. She stepped up to the closest and felt the frame. Black and patterned and heavy. She yanked it down from the wall hard enough to snap the wire. Too bad. Yes, the same silver frame, same design. There seemed to be three more such frames, hung in a line. She pulled them down, too, and set to work on the first, scrubbing roughly with the bread. Right now she couldn't care less if she found a horde of lost Rembrandts.

Under the dirt a scene emerged of a group of women watching a boat on the horizon. Some were huddled in groups, some kneeling, stretching out their arms toward the boat. Bundles of spilled possessions were scattered around them. The only woman standing had an arm raised toward the ship; she was a small but central figure, wearing a cloak that billowed powerfully with the same wind filling the ship's sails. Men on deck had folded arms and were staring in the other direction at the sky. Definitely leaving the women. Theseus abandoning Ariadne on Naxos was the only classical subject that sprang to mind, but then Menina wasn't sure. The standing woman somehow didn't look like a Cretan princess. A couple of soldiers in the background looked Roman.

Menina examined it more closely—was it mold, or a dark cloud on the horizon where the blue sea and blue sky met? One of the sailors in the stern of the boat, a tiny figure, seemed to be pointing toward it. Now she noticed all the sight lines of the people in the painting drew the viewer's eye to the cloud. Funny, it was hardly noticeable at first, then the longer she looked at it, the seemingly insignificant cloud dominated the picture. And the cloud looked like a lot of tiny dots of paint, but the painting looked older than the nineteenth century when French Impressionists, the Pointillists, had also used tiny dots of paint. Her irritation began to dissipate. Just the tiniest bit.

The next painting was another group scene. Beneath the murk, women and children were sitting around a table holding cups. There was a wine jug like the wicker-covered one she had seen in the convent kitchen, and men in helmets peering through a window. There were loaves of bread and a large fish on the table, and a pot on a fire. At first she guessed it had been commissioned to show a solid burgher's womenfolk at dinner, and, yes, the fish was a Christian symbol. The clothes were plain—no jewels or fine robes, wimples, none of the elaborately wound turbans Renaissance women sometimes wore in paintings. Other than the fish and a candle on the table there was nothing to indicate the devotional nature of the painting—no saints, no flowers or other symbols she could associate with the Virgin, no angels or biblical references she could identify. In the eaves above the group around the table it looked as if birds were building nests. Swallows. What *was* with the swallows?

The next picture was another landscape, mountains. Then under the grime she discerned some tiny figures in the bottom right-hand corner. One appeared to be ahead of a group, and they were all on a path or a road or something that began in the lower right-hand corner and wound upward to the left, into mountains dotted with small white spots that looked like the distant white mountain villages she had seen from the bus. Someone—it must be a woman because she had long black hair flying behind her and she seemed to be naked except for a sort of transparent shift—was running from a group of...possibly soldiers? At the top of the highest mountain there was a dark cleft in the rocks. There was a storm cloud in this one, too, a dark mass in the distance that the viewer sensed was approaching. And the people in the painting didn't see it. Again, it didn't ring any biblical or classical bells.

She turned to the last, smallest one.

Another portrait, another dark-haired girl. But this one was not about to enter a convent. She was young and disheveled, as if she had just got up from bed. She had dangling earrings, a bright colored shawl slipping off one bare shoulder, parted lips, and a saucy, knowing, come-hither expression in her sleepy eyes. Her hair tumbled in elaborate curls that seemed to tickle her full breasts spilling out of an undone bodice. Menina thought she looked more like a hot sixteenth-century Playmate of the Month than something that belonged in a convent collection. She decided to call it "Captain Fernández Galán's Girlfriend."

Menina dragged the paintings to the window to catch the last light and, using the last of the bread, managed to make out "Tristan Mendoza" underneath the grime on each one. So the frames *had* been a clue.

OK. She had now found five works by Tristan Mendoza—two landscapes, an interior scene, and two portraits. Odd and ambiguous as they were, it was still a major discovery. Menina wished she could get excited about it, but all she could think was, so what? Still, it was good for the nuns. "Well, Sor Clara, I found all five paintings by Tristan Mendoza."

Sor Clara looked up from her rosary and held up her hand with the fingers spread out. Then she raised the other hand and held up one finger. Then she counted the fingers. "Was six by Tristan Mendoza. Six. Sor Teresa will come soon; time to eat lunch."

Lunch! Menina realized she was ravenous. She hadn't eaten anything since falling apart yesterday. She tried not to think about food. "Six? Are you sure?" She looked at the crowded walls.

"Six paintings." Sor Clara held her fingers to the light and looked at them dreamily. "One, two, three, four, five, six," she counted in Spanish.

Sor Clara must be as light-headed with hunger as Menina felt. She tried to revive her aggravation at Captain Fernández Galán and his stupid present, but was too wrung out now to care. She unwrapped layers of pale green, yellow, and lavender cellophane just to see what was in the basket. She wouldn't touch one of the fish if her life depended on it, but it was mean not to give Sor Clara any. She held the basket out to Sor Clara. Sor Clara smiled with delight as she picked a fish, peeled the foil off, and ate it slowly with a happy expression.

Menina looked at the basket, brimming over with shimmering foil-wrapped chocolate...OK, *one* stupid fish, thought Menina, picking a large one.

"Is good?" asked Sor Clara.

"Mmmm," said Menina grudgingly. They each took more. Then there were footsteps, the door banged open, and Sor Teresa exclaimed, "Aha!" Sor Clara started guiltily. Menina offered Sor Teresa a chocolate fish, which prompted a sharp lecture about *Semana Santa* when sweets were forbidden to the nuns. Menina thought it was a good thing she couldn't see all the bits of colored foil surrounding Sor Clara. Sor Clara sighed and lowered the hand holding a half-eaten fish.

Menina tried to tell Sor Teresa about finding the other paintings, but before she could, Sor Teresa said, "Alejandro is here again and says you must see him. I tell him he must behave, not upset you like yesterday. He knows I am very angry with him. Sor Clara! Come!"

Sor Clara surreptitiously popped her last piece of chocolate into her mouth, and followed Sor Teresa out.

With a sinking heart, Menina picked up the bits of foil and basket of fish and closed the door of the *sala grande*. The room had grown dark suddenly, as the sky had clouded over and it was going to rain. Next door the *locutio* parlor was dark, too, and she put down the basket, groped for the matches, and lit a candle. Today she would maintain a dignified silence, saying yes or no as necessary and nothing else. Only she was so nervous and self-conscious and embarrassed about yesterday's failure on the lady-like front that she immediately blurted out, "Alejandro...I mean Captain Fernández-um?" What was this man's name?

"Mees Walker," he said from the other side of the grille. "I like it better if you call me Alejandro."

Nervously Menina replied, "Oh. Fine, call me Menina; no one calls me Miss Walker either...Um, thank you for the chocolate. I've never seen a basket of fish. We have Easter eggs at home, you know, children dye them, and the Easter bunny..." Menina cursed herself. Here she went again! What happened to dignified silence? Why did she always have to sound like an idiot? "About the chocolate," she began.

"Oh that. Please. My pleasure. But I am here to ask you to do something."

"Look, I'm working as fast as I can," said Menina, "but with no electricity the light's not great when the sun goes, and I don't have night vision."

"It is nothing to do with paintings. I need your help."

Now what?

"What?" demanded Menina.

"I need you to open the gate and let someone in the convent, late tonight."

"You want me to *what?*"

"Yes. I will bring an Albanian girl. I think is Albanian. She is better with you I think than nuns. They will not like. She is about sixteen, maybe not quite."

The girlfriend Sor Clara had mentioned! A man in his thirties had no business with a girl who was practically a child. "Let me get this straight—you want me to bring a girl into the *convent*, an underage one, whom you obviously don't even know all that well because you aren't sure where she comes from?"

It sounded like the captain was saying he needed to hide her. He started to explain, but Menina erupted before he could finish. "I already know about your 'girlfriends'! Do you have any idea how fast gossip travels here? The old ladies who come to Mass watch everything everybody does in the village, and rush to tell Sor Teresa or one of the other nuns. The nuns are scandalized, think they're all prostitutes. I am the last person on earth to help you have sex in the convent with a teenager!" She paused for breath. This man was revolting, sordid, sleazy.

"Please, is not what you are thinking! The girls the old ladies see, yes they are supposed to look like prostitutes. I am a man; old ladies disapprove but not surprised. Is Spain—men are men..."

It was not the right thing to say. Menina, the good girl who had rarely argued with anyone or even raised her voice much in the course of nineteen years, heard herself shouting like a demented fishwife for the second time in twenty-four hours. "Men treat women like pieces of meat! How do men get so damn arrogant? And now, *now*, you've got this, this *kid*, she's maybe fifteen? You're nearly old enough to be her father! What's the matter with you?" she shouted. She was angry again, ranting about sorry-assed fuck-wit men. She sounded like...Becky!

Good!

"That is not...listen to me a minute, oh my God, you think I like children for sex...No, no, no!"

"Well, *what* then?" Menina's voice reached a decibel level she didn't know she possessed.

"Alright! You are not in a mood to believe me, is normal after what you have been through. Be quiet and I will tell you what is going on, what the police business is. I cannot tell the sisters, not even Sor Teresa, but now I think is more dangerous for too many people if I do not tell you. Girl is in big trouble so I need your help."

"No, I damn well won't help you! You're revolting!"

"Ay, and I thought your voice was so sweet! Listen first, then you can scream all you like. Maybe you wonder why I stay in this village? Here is quiet and old-fashioned, many old people. Maybe you think is because of my aunt, because my family was here? Yes, these things are important, but because my family is from this village and everyone knows I promise my father it is also my cover. I am here because of what I learn at the police academy in the US, surveillance. Several years ago, when I am coming back to Spain to live, I am recruited for a big surveillance operation with the Spanish authorities and Interpol."

"What? Here? In the middle of nowhere?"

"Yes, is because it is in the middle of nowhere. Today most people come here on the highway. Like you did on the bus. But before there is the highway, there is an old road that comes here from the coast, near Marbella, goes east through mountains to the Basque country, then to the border. This road has probably been there for two thousand years, and it goes even beyond this village into the mountains, toward France. Is bad road, hard to find, many trees, sometimes boulders fall from mountains, very dangerous, so nowadays no one use it. But is many old mountain roads, all over Europe, in good weather sometimes they are passable and there are people who use them."

"Who?"

"This is what I am trying to tell you. For years the police across Europe are watching these roads because people are using this route for smuggling from the old Eastern Bloc countries and from farther, from Iran and even Afghanistan. Is very big criminal operation and for a long time they are working carefully to make a trap. Here."

"Oh." This explanation made Menina feel a tiny bit sheepish for shouting at him. "Drugs?"

"Yes, drugs are involved. Drugs are a very big business. These men who come to Spain know the old roads are difficult for authorities to watch. They bring heroin and cocaine across Europe from Afghanistan and Turkey. Is big market for drugs here, many rich people on the coast in Marbella, Puerto Banus, other places in the south where there are big yachts, villas, much money. Criminals, too. They think they are safe, can do what they like. But they smuggle something worse than drugs. Maybe you hear, even in America, gangs traffic women from East Europe—Kosovo and Albania and Romania and Ukraine. People there are very poor, have nothing, no jobs. Men come and tell young girls they can go to France and Germany and England, rich countries, plenty of nice jobs, in restaurants, caring for children of rich families, be au pair, have a nice room, learn English, make a lot of money. Can send money home to families, save money to get married. So the girls go of course—sometimes they want to go, sometimes families force them, even sell them to these men, and sometimes they are kidnapped. Then they find the men lie about restaurant jobs and looking after children. They are locked up in trucks and taken to be prostitutes, like slaves. The men who bring them beat them up, rape them, give them drugs to make them work as prostitutes, take their money, and threaten their families back home if they try to run away or call the police."

"Oh." Menina put her forehead on the grate and closed her eyes, remembering the feel of Theo's hand clamped over her mouth, her terror, and, worst of all, the powerlessness. Like she had been reduced to dirt, to nothing. Her mouth was dry. Hearing about it happening to other girls made her want to be sick.

"The women that old ladies tell Sor Teresa are my 'girlfriends' are policewomen. Undercover. Like I say, is Spain, men are men. I am not married. Old ladies do not approve if I have prostitutes, but nobody thinks is strange. Old ladies are shocked. They make a scandal. This is what I need, because it is cover. The policewomen are helping me watch the men who come and go in the mountain villages.

"There is a lot of construction, new villas for wealthy foreigners in the mountains, jobs for foreign workers. The authorities cannot check all of them or stop them coming to Spain. And when they finish a job, they travel around looking for other work. You saw some of those men working in the village the day you missed your bus. Villages like ours hire them now to build the *Semana Santa* floats for the Easter procession, because is no longer enough young men who live here to build them. We know criminals mix with the gypsies who have always come at this time with their markets. Then they all help when the trucks bring another load of girls and drugs. The day you come to the police station, I am angry because I cannot decide if you are merely a stupid call girl who is in my way, or maybe you are a decoy or somehow involved—a kind of madam for the girls they are bringing. Your story about a college trip to Madrid sounded impossible. And yesterday when you say 'Theo' I think, I must know if he is involved."

"Oh! No, he's not. He's a...creep but he's not smuggling women or drugs."

"You did not know what a narrow escape you had that day in the square. They could easily take you like the other women. You are very pretty, sexy, young. You are worth money. But my father's friend worried when he saw the poster with your picture. He knows about this operation, and came to warn me that if people come looking for a missing American girl it will jeopardize our careful operation. We must keep the low profile until we catch them."

"Of course. This is all pretty horrible."

"Yes, and it gets worse. The people who buy drugs from these gangs buy women, too, and they pay more for very young ones. You were angry thinking I wanted a fifteen-year-old—there are men who want little girls even of twelve, sometime younger. Some yacht owners will buy several girls for a cruise, different ages but all young, all girls who thought they were going to a better life and find themselves in hell. If the girls they buy come back, they are sold again, but sometimes they do not come back. We are finding bodies in the sea. They throw girls overboard when they are finished. If you could see what has happened to them before they die...These men are animals. And men who have sold girls to the yacht owners bring more. Always more. And we must stop them."

Menina thought about the men who had circled her that afternoon she had missed her bus and closed her eyes. "And this girl you want me to let in tonight?"

"This girl is Almira. She cannot talk much—they broke her nose and her jaw, but she is braver and stronger than they think. I think she is a survivor because she is angry, angry like you yesterday. She managed to escape, and now she is an important witness; she can identify many of the men. Last week, just before you came, one of the undercover policewomen, one of my 'girlfriends,' brought her up here from the safe house where we have kept her, hiding in the back of her car. Almira told us that the truck that brought her there last spring had an air vent, and she pried it off and saw the sun setting between the mountains. We waited until the same time this year so the setting sun would be in the same position, and took her at the same time along the old road into France so she could show us where. When she did, nearby we found a fork of the road we did not know existed, and the road they used. She is a smart girl and risked her life to help. Even though she is very, very afraid.

"It was Almira who told us she overheard the men talking about bringing more girls at the time of the *Semana Santa*—we think either tomorrow, on Good Friday night, or on Saturday night, because those nights we have our traditional *Semana Santa* processions, and people come and walk in the procession with candles. Then there is a party, a crowd, very noisy. Everyone is looking at the procession; there is singing and people do not pay attention to a strange van coming out of the forest. Don't see girls tied up inside.

"But we have made a big mistake, the policewoman and I. When my colleague was ready to drive Almira back to the safe house where she is staying, Almira begged to have a ride in my car. She says it is so beautiful, she has never seen one like it. Poor girl, we are sorry for her. I told my colleague to wait for us a little way outside the village. I will bring Almira to her. We go for a drive and then head back to the village. Almira was laughing, playing with the stereo, pretending she is a movie star in Hollywood. Until we came back to the village and she recognized the men working in the square. She threw herself on the floor and started moaning they would kill her now. I said she would soon be back in the safe house, but when I got to the meeting place my colleague was not waiting for us. That is bad, and I cannot send a message or telephone for help. I cannot stop watching. I have no choice but to bring Almira back and keep her here. Almira is right—she is dead if they find her. She has been hiding at my house, but I do not like her there. It is safer if she hides inside the convent with you."

"Tell me what to do."

"I need you to be at the gate at midnight—they will ring the bell for the vigil at midnight—and open the gate to let Almira in, then close and bolt it. Walls are high, gate is very strong, the convent is like a fortress when it is closed. But it is better that the nuns do not know police witness is here. They will worry."

"Of course." Her heart sank. A million miles from anywhere and now caught up in a dangerous police operation. But she knew she had to help Almira. Almira was refusing to be a victim, despite terrible things that had been done to her—even worse than what had happened to Menina. OK, if Almira could do it, Menina would find some courage, too.

Menina wished with all her heart that Becky were here. Becky was the tough one.

"Wait! What about those people you said are looking for me? I can't think of any reason they'd want to."

Captain Fernández Galán sighed. "I think that is another problem and we must leave it till later." He cleared his throat. "And one more thing, you do not think bad things about me anymore? You know I am not a pedophile? I do not have the girlfriends?"

"I guess I have to believe you, but you fooled everybody." He'd had her wondering if she had been kidnapped to become a nun, but there was no need to mention that.

"Good," he said with a sigh. "And so you know, I am not really old enough to be Almira's father. I am thirty-three. See you later."

Menina called into the darkness after him. "Captain... Alejandro, please, can you bring some food tonight?" She hoped he had heard. Otherwise she and Almira were going to have to survive on chocolate fish and stale bread.

She felt her way back to her room, shaken by what she had heard about trafficked girls. Dinner was on the meager side on the Thursday before Easter. She ate bread and lentils and an apple as slowly as she could, and remembered what Sor Teresa had said about many girls coming to the convent. Well, they would never have expected girls in the kind of mess Menina and Almira were in. She really hoped she could keep Almira out of Sor Teresa's way.

CHAPTER 16

*From the Chronicle of Las Sors Santas
de Jesus, Las Golondrinas Convent,
Andalusia, Summer 1549*

Deo gratias, on this day of Salome's birth my hand permits me to write a little. She would be nearly forty-five now, an old woman. But God has sent girls to fill the hole in my heart—first Esperanza, then Luz, and now Pia. She is a striking creature, with silvery hair like summer moonlight, fine pale skin, clear blue eyes, and delicate features. She is fourteen, and though slender and willowy, having just begun her monthly cycles, is developing a woman's figure. Formidable Sor Sophia, who shows such courage in defying the enclosure rules to go abroad on convent business and is such a quick wit when challenged, has affected her rescue.

Pia is self-possessed, and her icy calm is unnerving in one so young. She told us a terrible story in a voice that was flat and without emotion:

My mother died when I was ten. She was very beautiful, and we lived in a fine house, with soft beds and silken hangings, and enough to eat—all things I did not think of until I no longer had them. I inherited my mother's hair, on which her fortune was built. Blondes were scarce in a land of dark-haired beauties, and my grandmother came from a place in the far north where the people have pale skin and hair like the sun and the moon. She had been traveling with her husband by ship when pirates attacked. The pirates killed her husband and took my grandmother captive, selling her into the harem of one of the last Muslim merchants in Seville, in the early reign of the *Reyes Catholicos*. But the merchant's mother learned that my grandmother was, like her, a Christian, one of the northern sects called Protestant. She took pity on this young widow who was in the early stages of pregnancy. The merchant's mother persuaded her son to free his captive, and my mother was born under the lady's protection. This lady died soon afterward and left my grandmother a generous gift of money to enable her to support herself and her child.

My grandmother's fine features and silver hair attracted many men, but marriage to an outsider who was neither Spanish nor Catholic, and whose family could not be vouched for, was out of the question. Yet as a woman her security and that of her child depended on the protection only a wealthy man could provide. My grandmother bought a house in Madrid and became a courtesan.

My mother inherited her northern beauty, and was raised in the Protestant religion that my grandmother stubbornly refused to relinquish. When my mother was seventeen, my grandmother accepted for her the protection of a handsome and charming young grandee, an only son who stood to inherit a great fortune from silver mines his family owned in the American colonies. He promised to provide her with a fine house, clothes and jewels and carriages and servants—everything a beautiful and vain young woman could desire. His only stipulation was that she bear no children. His family would countenance no bastards who, they feared, might make a future claim of their fortune. My mother told me only that for many years she "managed," that there were no children, though a shadow crossed her face when she told me this.

She became pregnant again and this time refused to "manage," believing my father would accept me. But he did not. He was furious and I was kept out of his sight as he did not wish to see me at all. Then news came that my father's family was ruined. Their silver mines in the colony had disappeared in a terrible earthquake, plunging the family in Spain into debt. In a desperate attempt to restore his fortunes, my father began to gamble wildly, only adding to the mountain of debts. My mother's jewels and carriage were sold, and our fine house was stripped of its furniture.

I was the focus of my father's rage. He would call me the Protestant whelp of a Protestant bitch, and say I should have been drowned at birth instead of living like a princess at his family's expense. He spent less and less time with my mother, taunting her that he preferred to court the ugly heiress his family hoped he would marry. Creditors descended, pressing my mother for money we no longer had.

She grew ill, and doctors could not save her. It was as if she had no more strength to live. My father sold the house but quickly gambled the proceeds away. The ugly heiress married another, and my father began to look at me in a strange calculating way. Though he hated me, he kept me with him. I was careful not to speak in his presence.

At court he tried to gain the king's favor and obtain preferment for a highly paid position, but was unsuccessful. He gambled more and more desperately. We moved from place to place, to lodgings that were ever dirtier and dingier. Though he could not afford to follow the court about the country, when the king was in residence in Madrid my father would put on what was left of his fine clothes and hover around the powerful courtiers, trying to wheedle their favor and influence. By then we lived in two dark and dirty rooms on a street that echoed with the shrill calls of prostitutes who hid their disfigured faces in the shadows. I was sent to a charity school by day, but otherwise was left alone for long stretches of time, cold and often hungry, save for the rare occasions when my father bid me put on the little finery I possessed and to comb my hair over my shoulders like a cape, and took me with him to court.

There I kept my eyes down and never spoke unless obliged to answer a direct question. I sensed that I had begun to attract attention. One day an older man, a grandee I had seen turning from my father's approaches, accompanied my father home. I was summoned into the cold room my father sarcastically referred to as the "salon." The man, who looked very old to me, had piercing eyes and wet red lips. I did not like him. "Make your curtsy!" my father ordered.

The man eyed me critically. He told me to walk up and down the room, then he called me to him and fingered my hair. His fingers crawled on my scalp like rats' paws. I shrank from his touch, but he wound a lock in his fingers and pulled it so tight tears sprang to my eyes. He smiled as I struggled.

"Like mother, like daughter," said my father. "You will not see such hair on many girls."

"Perhaps. But still, she is not worth so much as you think. How old?"

A sly look crossed my father's face. "Only eleven." This puzzled me, since I was fourteen. "To certain gentlemen, who prefer them young and untouched, she is worth a great deal. I have had several offers, but since you are a connoisseur I thought perhaps you would appreciate her youth. Either accept my terms or I shall take her to El Padron…"

I did not know until later that El Padron was the nickname of a great whoremaster in Madrid, but I sensed that whoever he was I did not wish to go to him.

My father's guest held his gaze for a moment and then shrugged. "Bah! Here is what I will give." He tossed a leather pouch on the table. My father could no longer pretend indifference and snatched it eagerly. Inside there was what looked like a great sum of money, but my father threw it back to the man. "El Padron has offered twice that sum."

The old man stared at me for a few minutes more as if considering, then he stood, nodded coldly, and left.

"Who was that man, Papa? Will he come back?" I ventured, but he growled that I would find out soon enough. And if I did not do as he said, the Inquisition had condemned Protestants, like my mother and me, and he would turn me over to them. At school I had learned enough to fear the Inquisition, even more than I feared my father.

The next day my father told me to dress in my best clothes and make a bundle of my other things. When I had done so, he produced a little pot of red cream and dabbed some on my lips and cheeks. We were putting on our cloaks to go out, when there was a knock and the old man from the day before stood there. He held out a larger pouch than before. My father hesitated, then opened the pouch. He gave a slow smile and shoved me in the man's direction. "Go," he told me.

"Where, Papa?"

"Where you belong," he said. By then he was hunched over the table, counting the *reales* from the pouch. "Take her," he said, without looking up. "Her things are in that bundle." I heard the clink of metal from the table as the old man thrust the bundle into my arms and pulled me out of the room. He had a hard grip that hurt my shoulder, and I did not like the look on his face.

"Get in and let's examine the pretty prize," he muttered, shoving me into a closed carriage. I was too terrified to ask where we were going. Then he was beside me, his body pressing against mine, and his hands tried to grope open my cloak, though I clutched it as tight as possible around me. "Let go!" he panted, his breath foul in my face, "or later I'll beat you until..."

I screamed as loud as I could and fought him with all my strength. He slapped me hard and pinned me to the seat with one hand ripping my cloak away, and was tugging my skirts with the other when there was a great commotion outside. The horses screamed and the coachman cried out, then the carriage jerked and lurched into motion, moving, faster and faster, rocking wildly. People in the street were shouting; things bumped beneath our wheels, and the man and I were flung from one side of the carriage to the other. The terrifying ride ended when the carriage listed and bumped sideways, then overturned with a sickening crash that threw my captor against the splintered roof onto the cobblestones with me on top of him.

It was as if his head exploded. He lay half in, half out of the bloody carriage, and when people pried open the door I huddled with my bundle, feeling something warm and wet on my face. I put up my hand and I looked at it, now covered in red. The horses were screaming, hooves thudding against the carriage. People shouted that they had bolted, and others shouted they were trapped in their harness, and someone cried they had bolted when a flock of small birds had darted out of nowhere and flown in their faces. Others shouted they had been spooked by a woman's cloak that had suddenly billowed and snapped under their noses.

The noisy mob fell on the coach. Hands were thrust through the smashed roof to search the corpse's pockets and, too frightened to scream, I watched a ragamuffin's dirty fingers steal a ring and the man's shoes.

Then hands pulled me from the wreck. Beneath the hood of a brown cloak a woman's voice said that I was safe now, then I felt her take my hand. "You can still walk. Quickly!" I was set onto my feet and concealed under her cloak as we hurried away. Then everything went dark and still.

Sor Sophia cannot explain what happened any more coherently. She had fallen asleep in her closed carriage and a voice told her of an accident—a carriage had overturned, an evil man was dead. Then Sor Sophia was awakened, as if shaken by an invisible hand, to hear a commotion outside. Suddenly the curtains were pushed aside and Pia was thrust in, kicking and shrieking hysterically. A woman's voice said sharply, "It is not a man but a nun. Get in! You are safe, I promise. The business can wait, Sor Sophia. Return to the convent!"

Sor Sophia is argumentative. She opened her mouth to ask questions and demand answers, but before she could utter a word the carriage door was slammed shut and bolted and the driver had turned around and set off from the direction they had come. Pia, finding the carriage door locked, had fainted.

CHAPTER 17

From the Chronicle of Las Sors Santas
de Jesus, Las Golondrinas Convent, Andalusia,
Late Summer 1550

Pia was not the last! The Abbess received a curious message that
the urgent removal of a "hidden girl" would require the personal
help of one of the nuns, a strong and forceful one, as the girl was
not an infant. There was little time, as the road would soon be
impassable in winter, so Sor Arsinoe was dispatched in a great
hurry, and returned with Marisol in a cold autumn hailstorm that
slicked the mountain road and soaked them both. Marisol looked
like a drowned rat, hair dripping down either side of her face, and
large brown eyes darting this way and that. She is only thirteen, but
even half dead with cold and terror, Marisol radiates something we
rarely see in the convent—defiance. "My mother may have sent me
here, but you will never make me into a nun! I will escape!" She
hissed between clenched teeth, as she was led away to be dressed
in a dry novice's gown.

   According to Sor Arsinoe's information, the girl is in danger
from the authorities and the court painter Tristan Mendoza is somehow involved. Sor Arsinoe believes the mother was dying in childbirth when she took the girl away from court. The girl's full name

is Maria Isabella Vilar d'Ascencion, but she insists on being called Marisol and scorned the idea that Tristan Mendoza is her father, insisting she is the daughter of Don Diego Vilar d'Ascencion, the commander of fleets to the New World. The Abbess said reasonably that if this was true, in justice to her father we should hear her story. Marisol is quick to argue but cannot withstand the Abbess's calm reasoning.

My mother and my father were descended from Old Christian families. My grandmother died when my mother was born, and Josefa, an orphaned sixteen-year-old cousin too poor to have a dowry, took over my mother's care and later accompanied her to convent school. When my grandfather died, his only living child— my mother—was heiress to his fortune. With no relatives to act as her guardian, she became a royal ward. At fourteen she left the convent where she had been educated and came to court, and lived with Josefa in apartments close to those of the queen.

Don Diego Vilar d'Ascencion was thirty years older than my mother when he saw her at court soon after her arrival. She was beautiful, well born, and rich, and he sought the king's permission to marry her. The king consented—Don Diego had commanded fleets to the New World many times and returned with riches. But when not at sea, Don Diego was a connoisseur of paintings and beautiful women, and he ordered my mother's betrothal portrait to be painted by Tristan Mendoza.

Josefa was scandalized. Tristan Mendoza's portraits of women were said to have some magic hold over men that drew men's eyes and excited their fantasies. Josefa told me Don Diego laughed away her protests, saying Josefa must guard my mother from anything improper.

Josefa would tell me proudly that Tristan Mendoza was irritated by her hovering and her refusal of his money when he tried to bribe her to leave him alone with my mother. My mother was always amused when she said this, insisting that the artist told her stories and made her laugh, so that sitting for the portrait was not tedious.

When the portrait was finished, Josefa said that Don Diego was delighted. It hung in my mother's bedchamber and my sister and I thought it very beautiful. My mother was far more splendidly dressed in the portrait than she was at home, occupied with a family and domestic matters. In the portrait, light danced up and down the folds of her silk gown with its wide skirt and her stiff white ruff. Her hair was caught up to frame her face with pearls and ribbons, her sleeves had lace, and the beads of her rosary were looped in her hand. Her dark eyes were wide, and though she looked shy, they seemed to smile just as she did in real life. Josefa said that before the wedding the portrait was displayed in one of the public rooms at court, to great acclaim, until it took the fancy of the crown prince, Don Balthazar.

At this point in the story Josefa would shake her head. She would murmur that perhaps an evil spell had been cast over him at birth. He had a harsh laugh that echoed down the palace corridors, and fits often robbed him of reason and he would howl and foam at the mouth, and wrestle imaginary foes, thrashing and lashing out at all around him until he had to be chained like a dog. Though he was heir to the throne of Spain, negotiations for Don Balthazar's marriage had come to nothing. My mother would tell Josefa to find a topic more suitable for young ears than court scandal about the poor prince. Josefa would frown darkly and say, "I know what I know!" but say no more.

After the wedding, my father took my mother and her portrait to his castle, an old Moorish stronghold high in the hills south of Madrid. One of my earliest memories is of sitting with Josefa in one of its windy towers, waving good-bye as my father left for a voyage to Spanish America.

My mother had five children to occupy her time—my three older brothers, a sister Consuela, then me. We lived quietly, beginning each day with Mass, then lessons. After dinner the boys disappeared with their hawks, saddles, and hunting dogs, while Consuela and I had our music and embroidery, practiced our dance steps, or played checkers. Consuela was three years year older than I, and by the time she was thirteen she resembled our mother. Josefa said I was like my father.

When we saw him in intervals between voyages, my father was kind. Consuela and I would sing for him, he would quiz my brothers on their lessons, and then give us marvelous gifts—jewels and soft shawls, gilded workboxes, and finely made boy-sized swords. He and my mother would retire early. After a few weeks he would be gone again.

The boys slept in one of the towers with their tutors, and Consuela, Josefa, and I slept in a small alcove at the far end of the apartment from my mother's bedchamber. Consuela slept soundly, but I was a light sleeper and small noises—the snap of dying embers in the fireplace, the hunting cry of a night bird on the plain, or Josefa's snoring—would rouse me. One night, a month after my father had paid us an autumn visit and departed, I heard the sound of horses' hooves clattering into the courtyard. There was an urgent command to "Open in the name of the king!" and then the sound of heavy feet and the servants being ordered away. My mother called sharply to Josefa to stay with the children. I said she sounded frightened, but Josefa shushed me in a way that meant she was frightened, too.

Many hours later, horses clattered away again. I asked Josefa who the mysterious visitors were. Josefa shook her head and said nothing.

The next morning I crept to my mother's bedchamber. My mother had dark circles under her eyes and a bruise on her cheek, and Josefa had an arm around her shaking shoulders. I heard her say, "But what could you have done that would not make it worse? He is the prince, and can order his way into the castle of any nobleman in the country. You say he had strongmen with him..."

"He is strong enough for ten and mad." My mother wept. "Obsessed...he had a copy made of my portrait! If he fathers a child, he insists the king will restore him as heir. And if he does not, that they plot to kill him. He was ranting, says my image in the portrait speaks to him, it promised to make him a...normal man! Now he believes it has! When he...was done he put his dagger to my throat and ordered me to say nothing, but to wait and see if I am with child! If I warn Don Diego, the prince will say I lured him to my bed and my husband will condemn me for destroying the honor of his name. If I do not warn him, I fear for my husband's life. Josefa, we are lost! Lost! My poor children!"

Then they both saw me, and Josefa shooed me away and later told me that if I loved my mother to forget what I had heard. But fear had entered our lives.

Not long after that incident, my mother received a letter from my father, with the signature of his secretary, ordering that my brothers be sent to school, to the Franciscans near Zaragoza at once. My mother did not like it, but of course she obeyed. The boys' chests were quickly packed and their valets prepared to accompany them. The boys were in high spirits as they kissed us good-bye, excited by this new adventure. Consuela and I waved our handkerchiefs from the tower until they were tiny specks on the plain below. My mother's eyes were red, and she looked worried.

A new serving maid joined the servants. It was she who now lit our candles and brought meals to our chamber. She had slanted eyes that looked in different directions at once, which I thought gave her an evil countenance.

As winter gave way to spring, both my mother and Consuela suffered from sickness of the stomach. Josefa and my mother seemed to share an unhappy secret concerning my mother's need to rest in the mornings and her desire for honey, while Consuela grew pale and thin and lethargic, with no interest in her lessons. Her eyes grew larger and larger as her face became drawn. She no longer wanted to sing or play checkers. "Nearly fourteen," murmured my mother anxiously, "perhaps she is beginning her monthlies—it often makes girls tired."

But Consuela grew too weak to leave her bed, and my mother would remain by her side all the day, coaxing her to sip a little broth when she was awake, and praying when Consuela slept. I hovered anxiously, wishing Consuela would wake in good health and join me in our lessons and games. Instead, Consuela's beautiful hair began to fall out, and her eyes sank into her head. My mother was ill herself with worry.

"Come," said Josefa loudly, pulling me from the sickroom one day as my mother and the slant-eyed maid were busy tending my sister. "You need fresh air and you shan't get out of helping me with the mending this time!" I hated mending, but it was a fine spring day after the cold of winter and I was glad to leave the sickroom. We took our sewing—Josefa her large mending basket and I the pretty painted workbox my father had given me to hold my thimbles, embroidery silks, and scissors—to the east tower where Moorish defenders had once rained arrows on the Catholic army below. Josefa had placed thick cushions in the window embrasure that made a wide stone seat.

Josefa fussed about threading my needle for me and pinning things unnecessarily, then taking the pins out again, clearing her throat as if to speak, then saying nothing. Finally she nudged me and said, "Look, the swallows are back from Africa." Above our heads the swallows were coming and going with bits of straw, and amid the chirping of the older birds there was a cheerful peep-peep of babies just hatching. For the next few days the weather stayed fine and we watched the parent birds fly tirelessly back and forth with insects in their beaks for their babies. Josefa watched more than she sewed.

"See," she said sharply one day. "A new male bird is flying around the nest above your head. Watch what happens now." The new male bird went into the nest and emerged with one of the babies in his beak. He then flew off and we saw a tiny speck fall from his beak to the earth. One by one, to my horror, he took the babies, flew a little way off, and dropped them.

"To attract the mother to be his mate, he kills the babies of her first husband," whispered Josefa, looking over her shoulder. Days later a messenger arrived on a lathered horse. There had been an accident at the Franciscan monastery where my brothers were at school. They had been seen sitting on the rim of a well in the cloister in their recreation hour. When a bell summoned them back to their lessons my brothers did not appear. Angry at their disobedience, a monk went to fetch them, but they were nowhere to be found. The entire monastery searched for them high and low, and finally a lay brother who went to draw water made a horrible discovery—all three at the bottom of the well, drowned. If they had cried out for help, no one had heard them. It must have happened very fast, one of them toppling in by accident, the others trying to help him and drowning, too.

My mother fainted.

A week later, as the summer heat rose from the plain below the castle, Consuela died, too.

My mother tore her hair and wept. Then she received a terrible letter from my father. He repudiated her utterly. My mother spent more and more time on her knees in front of her private altar. Josefa never left my side, and would allow me to eat nothing that she had not prepared with her own hands. The slant-eyed serving maid fell down the stone stairs to the kitchens, breaking her leg and cracking her head so badly that she could no longer walk steadily or serve at table. From her corner in the kitchen she mumbled she had been pushed, but the other servants, like Josefa, did not like her and she was ignored.

Uneasy months passed and my mother's waist had thickened. Another messenger came. My father had been lost at sea a week after leaving Seville. A freak wave, they believed, for all his experience it had taken him by surprise one night as he walked on deck. Masses would be said at court for his soul. The queen, who had always been kind, sent word that my mother should remove to the court for her lying in. Josefa said refusal was not possible, that we must take protection where it could be found. We began the slow hot journey across the plains to Madrid. When we arrived, the court was in mourning. The crown prince was dead. Rumors flew.

We were assigned rooms in the palace, but when autumn came they were drafty and cold despite fires and the braziers. My mother moved heavily from room to room, and then took to her bed. There were dark hollows under her eyes when she looked at me, and when she lifted her hand from the bedclothes to stroke my cheek her fingers were puffy. I was allowed to sit quietly beside her on the bed and play with the rings she could no longer wear that lay in a heap on the chest next to her bed. As the nights drew in, her bedroom was lit by two thick tapers, one on either side of her bed, which lit up an ebony crucifix on the wall above. Drafts made the candles flicker and the long shadow of the crucifix shifted as if Christ writhed in pain. My mother's rings glittered in the light of the candles like dragons' eyes—red and green. The rest of the room was deep in shadow. I imagined something was waiting there, holding its breath.

Each night when Josefa brought her supper my mother would ask, "Is there an answer yet?" Josefa would insist that first my mother must eat until, finally, she obeyed from tiredness and took a few spoons of soup, then a few sips from a goblet of Venetian glass holding sweet wine that smelled of almonds. Josefa would pat her mouth gently with a linen napkin. Then, night after night she gave the same response. "Perhaps tomorrow."

"Send him word again, Josefa! They say he alone knows how to go about it, to send the children. He is my only hope now."

Josefa told me to pray to help my mother get better. I took my beads and closed my eyes against tears, praying as hard as I could. My prayers had done Consuela no good. But Josefa at least came into the room with a happier expression one evening and bent over my mother to whisper something. I crept closer and caught the words, "He has set the matter in motion, sent for..." I could not hear the rest.

One gloomy night at the end of the month the rain fell heavily and the wind blew hard. Above my mother's bed, the head with its crown of thorns seemed to turn this way and that as the tortured body writhed in agony. I was startled to hear a strange cry from my mother's bed, like that made by the bird of many colors my father had brought home from his travels. The servants hated that bird, saying it shrieked with the voices of the damned, and it was left behind when we came to Madrid.

The cup of wine in Josefa's hand fell to the floor and smashed. A servant was sent running for the midwife, and soon after for the doctors and an apothecary who entered, tearing off wet cloaks. My mother made the noise again and again and I put my hands over my ears. A priest hurried past, accompanied by a sleepy boy bearing the Eucharist. A page tugged Josefa's arm to say someone was waiting.

She turned from the bed, pulled me from my knees, and dragged me toward the door. I pleaded to stay but Josefa shook me hard, and in a fierce whisper told me that I must be a brave girl; my mother's prayer for my safety had been answered. A tall nun was there, silent and still as a statue with a cloak over one arm. She unfolded it. "I am Sor Arsinoe," she whispered. "Make no sound and put this on."

I pulled away, but Josefa snatched the cloak and wrapped it around me so tightly I could not move. "Go with Sor Arsinoe!" Josefa ordered as I struggled and kicked. "If you love your mother, go at once! Go!" I was led down the darkened corridor and a back staircase that led to the kitchens and pantries, then through a small door used when tradesmen brought supplies. A carriage with the curtains down waited in the rain. The nun pushed me inside and here I am. Josefa and my mother turned against me and sent me here. I will never forgive them.

CHAPTER 18

From the Chronicle of Las Sors Santas de Jesus,
Las Golondrinas Convent, Andalusia, Autumn 1551

Marisol has sulked for the past year—it is how she keeps sadness from overwhelming her. And a fifth girl, Sanchia, has joined the others. She is nine and came after the swallows left and smoke was rising from the valley, where fires burned to clear the fields. How horribly apt. When she was lifted unconscious from the closed carriage, at first we thought she was ill, possibly dying. But Sor Sophia who brought her said she was only in a deep sleep. Because of the terrible pain of the child's burned legs and feet, she had been obliged to feed her dose after dose of a sleeping draft during the journey.

Now that she is healing and can walk again, Sanchia is restless. Her scarred legs and feet cause her pain and she cannot sit still long for her lessons. She skips, fidgets, and dances from the moment she rises until she is finally persuaded into bed for the last time. The Abbess coaxed the story from the child with the help of a plate of turrone, which she broke into little pieces and fed to her bit by bit.

The soldiers came when we were sleeping. They threw the furniture and our clothes about and ripped up the cushions. They said that where there were Jews, there was gold and jewels. They laughed when they found the candlesticks that my mother lit on Fridays when the curtains had been drawn. They were hidden behind a painting of the Virgin, together with Papa's prayer book in Hebrew, which he promised to teach me to read someday. Then they found the silver wine cups that belonged to Mama's family, with the six-pointed star that is a secret. Mama put her arm around me and said the soldiers were laughing and happy because they were playing a game, just like the game Papa and I played when I pretended to be the organ grinder's monkey. Papa would pretend to grind his organ and I would dance. Then he would look up and say "Where's the little monkey?" and I would run and hide quick as anything until my grandmother and grandfather coaxed me out with sweets, the way pet monkeys are coaxed with nuts.

And then the soldiers took us away, to the place where there were a lot of people locked together in the dark. Mama said that was a game, too. Soldiers took Papa and my grandfather, and when they came back Mama cried and I said it was a bad game and I was afraid and wanted to go home. Then they took Mama, and when she came back she did not speak to me. A man came to see Mama and Papa. They talked through the bars and Mama went down on her knees.

Mama got her voice back a little after that and told me that next morning she and Papa had a surprise for me: they knew a magic spell that would turn me into a real monkey. I would be hiding with them, and when she and Papa said the magic words, I would become a monkey and must scamper and dance away like I always did.

The next day the soldiers came again. In place of our clothes we had brought from home, they gave us horrible gowns that scratched. They made us take off our shoes and hold candles, and then everyone left the prison together. Outside there were crowds of people, pointing and shouting "Carrion!" and "Murderers!" and spitting at us.

Mama told me they did not matter because I was going to be a monkey, but the magic would not work until we were in the right place. Then she and Papa would say the spell, and I must not be afraid but scamper to the nun standing in the shadows. Mama pointed to a tall figure and said the nun would give me sweets and then change me back into a girl before I knew it. But I must not look back or the spells would not work.

She said there would be a fire and it might burn my feet a little, but a monkey could jump over it. She pointed the way I must go, and repeated what I must do over and over until I said, "I know! I know! Just there!" Then they tied Mama and Papa together with ropes, with me squashed between them. They didn't tie me, though.

My parents pushed toward the edge with me between them when the music started. People around us were crying and begging, but beyond them was noise and cheering. I heard my mother ask my father if he were certain, and he said in a shaking voice that all eyes would be on the fire; a child would not be seen if it were quick. He told me sternly not to lose sight of the nun's white wimple—look, she was kneeling in the shadows. "Wait for the magic spell," he said over and over, "then run straight to her."

"I know, I know!" I said. Then friars came with their crackling torches. When they lowered the torches to the place where we were standing I wondered why they were not more careful. Then there was a crackle. Smoke rose and people were choking and screaming, and suddenly fire was all around us. My parents were coughing, and my mother said, "Now!" and I heard my parents say the magic spell, "*Yit'gadal v'yit'kadash sh'mei raba!*" Like a monkey I scrambled over the flames, but still they burned my legs and feet so badly that I ran very fast to get away, coughing and choking in the smoke. The terrible screaming grew louder and louder, and then the nun came into the smoke and covered me with her habit and we hurried away. When she took the cloak off I was a little girl again and

I was crying because my legs and feet hurt so much. And she had no sweets after all!

The Abbess gave her the last of the turrone. Sanchia ate it, her troubled eyes darting from one to the other of us. Her legs and feet are horribly scarred, and she repeats the "magic spell," the Jewish Prayer for the Dead, constantly, believing it will somehow restore her to her family. Dear God, they are ashes scattered to the winds now. And if the Inquisition's investigator comes, asking questions and examining the children, if she repeats those words she will give herself and us away...we dare not think of it.

When Esperanza took Sanchia back to the *sala de las niñas*, the Abbess handed me the letter from the Inquisition. Las Golondrinas' turn is approaching. The Abbess touched the medal round her neck.

November 1551

As the first snow of autumn began, the Abbess came to the library in an agitated state and sent Esperanza on an errand. "Sor Beatriz, I have seen the Foundress! I was in the cloister as the snow began, praying for guidance about how to protect Esperanza and the others, thinking how snow masks everything. Suddenly she was there, her cloak blowing exactly as others have described! She said 'send them,' 'brides,' and 'Spanish America,' but I could not hear more. Just as suddenly she was gone."

I wondered if she had imagined it. The Abbess is quite old, older than I, under great strain, and very worried. She has insisted our five girls make themselves useful. To our surprise, sullen Marisol has proved to be very good at managing the children in the orphanage, and supervises in the *sala de las niñas* most days. Quiet Pia often sits with Luz, helping with the mending, and of course Esperanza works with me every day. The Abbess keeps Sanchia with her as much of the time as she can, trying to prepare her to face an Inquisition examiner without giving herself away. She tells Sanchia story after story of the saints, and makes her repeat them and her catechism and her prayers and the rosary over and over, so that Sanchia can give correct answers if interrogated. None of us think this will succeed, but we do not have the heart to say so to the Abbess.

We try to look forward to the Christmas celebrations, and after Lent is over, to the celebration when the novice Sor Serafina takes her final vows. There is to be a greater feast than usual to mark the day. Sor Serafina is the natural daughter of a rich widower with estates and silver mines in the New World. Unusually, she was not an orphanage girl, but entered Las Golondrinas from school in another convent. Sor Serafina is a lively girl who chatters constantly. Her older half brothers are fond of her. They send her letters with their news, and this year they made a special journey to the convent to visit their sister before the cold weather set in. They have traveled to the Spanish colonies on their father's business several times, and were due to set off again soon. They left money with the Abbess for a splendid banquet to celebrate their sister's profession.

The New Year
January and February 1552

On many dark winter evenings, when the mountain winds howl and we gather with our workbaskets and mending by the fire, Sor Serafina enlivens us with her brothers' stories of Spanish America.

She speaks so vividly that looking into the flames, we see flying serpents, gardens of gold and jewels, wide muddy rivers, endless green forests, bright-feathered birds, and in the midst of it all, the shining new cities that the Spanish settlers have built, with broad streets and churches and fine houses, and beyond them, haciendas that stretch to the horizon where mountains rise into the clouds. For us who are bound never to leave our convent, this is thrilling.

Sor Serafina also has a fund of more shocking stories, about the natives and their custom of taking many wives, and the Spanish settlers who, lacking Catholic Spanish women to marry, take mistresses and concubines among the mestiza women, who are very beautiful, and their children who go unbaptized unless the Spanish nuns or priests intervene. She insists brothels and divorce flourish. I scolded Sor Serafina for such frivolous speech, and she was silent for a moment, and then said that she had a better story, about nuns this time. I sighed and nodded. I have never been very strict with the novices.

She said that after Francisco Pizarro and his conquistadors captured and executed the emperor of the Incas, the Spaniards went rampaging, pillaging the great stores of native gold and silver and jewels wherever they could find them. Drunk on riches, they went farther and farther from the coast seeking more. Finally, in the shadow of the great mountains, the conquistadors sacked a palace belonging to the so-called Virgins of the Sun, whom her brothers said were a sort of pagan nuns. The Virgins disappeared, carried off as spoils of war to undermine Inca resistance, because people there believed the Virgins were sacred. But local people insisted that the Virgins had fled to a holy fortress in the mountains, where they passed through the portals of a magic gateway into the land of their gods.

The novice mistress interrupted to say that was quite enough about pagan nuns. Sor Serafina said she was coming to the part about Christian nuns and a mystery. This of course was too interesting to resist, and we put down our sewing to hear.

Surely God sent Sor Serafina to us. Her next words were like the sun blazing in a dark winter night!

Because the king and queen wished the natives would convert to Christianity to save their souls, a Spanish bishop with a party of Franciscan friars soon followed Pizarro. He approved of the destruction of the house of the Virgins of the Sun, and insisted that to purify the place of pagan worship, the stones be reused to build a convent, complete with a grand chapel at the gate. When the bishop traveled inland to consecrate it, he was astonished and angry to find that an order of Spanish nuns had already taken possession, without his knowledge or permission. He had no idea how this could have happened, but behind his back people said the ways of the church authorities were mysterious. The only explanation was that the nuns had been conveyed in a secret hold in a ship of Pizarro's fleet.

Pizarro never disputed the rumor. Sor Serafina's brothers said it was probably that Pizarro feared looking a fool. He was illiterate, and if there were documents that might have shed light on the matter, he could not have read them and he was too vain to admit ignorance. The bishop never protested either, lest people think he was not in the confidence of the ecclesiastical authorities. If anyone mentioned the nuns, he assumed a tight-lipped expression, and later died waiting for an official explanation.

But according to Sor Serafina's brothers, there was another reason for the nuns' presence. Older sailors in the seaside taverns said that once Moorish navigators from Spain had crossed the terrible Sea of Fog and Darkness, blown by storms to a strange land.

It did not do to speak of this in case the Inquisition heard of it. Catholic Spain wanted the triumph of discovery to belong only to Catholic explorers. But the sailors who knew the vagaries of the winds and the currents—the unpredictable and ferocious storms made the sea passage to the New World dangerous—believed such a thing could have happened to any ship that strayed into the Atlantic. Though nuns could scarcely have set sail themselves...it must remain a mystery!

Sor Serafina had laughed and called her brothers' suppositions fanciful nonsense. They protested that they had not yet told her the best part. By coincidence the convent on the site of the Virgins of the Sun's palace soon attracted great flocks of swallows, just as their sister Sor Serafina's convent. At first it was known simply as "the Spanish Convent" and the order of nuns, the Sors Santas de Jesus de Los Andes. But later, because of the swallows, the convent came to be known as Las Golondrinas. Sor Serafina was just excusing herself saying it was perhaps untrue but a charming story nonetheless, when I stood and let out a cry.

The workbasket in my lap rolled to the floor, and I stared at Sor Serafina as if the mountain itself had spoken. Then I grabbed her by the wrist and pulled her to her feet so roughly that her workbasket went flying, too, and the others looked at me with shocked expressions. It was unnecessary to discipline a novice so violently, even for such a ridiculous story. "Come with me, at once," I ordered and began to pull her out of the room.

There was a protest from Esperanza. She must have thought I meant to slap Sor Serafina, and cried, "No! Sor Beatriz, don't! Sor Serafina is not making it up. I, too, have read of such things..."

"Then you come also," I ordered and dragged Sor Serafina, now sobbing that she only repeated what her brothers had said and meant no harm. The three of us went straight to the Abbess's parlor. The Abbess looked up from her missal and frowned at the stormy interruption.

"Sor Serafina, repeat the story you told us."

Mumbling and tearful, Sor Serafina did so while Esperanza waited, fidgeting and nervous, too. The Abbess had Sor Serafina repeat it twice more, then Sor Serafina was assured she was not in trouble and dismissed. Esperanza went to follow, but I ordered her sharply to stay.

"Now explain why you believe Sor Serafina tells the truth."

While Sor Serafina is somewhat giddy and excitable, Esperanza is not, and her memory is both good and precise. And now she said that the tenth-century historian Al-Masudi wrote of Moorish sailors who had disappeared across the great Sea of Fog and Darkness. Years later, they reappeared with treasures and stories of a strange land where there were meadows of gold and quarries of jewels.

"And have you seen this book?"

"Of course. In my father's library," answered Esperanza.

"And therefore, what Sor Serafina said about conquistadors finding Spanish nuns already present in Spanish America, may be true? The ship carrying our mission party might also have been blown west?"

"If it is possible for some, why not for others?" Esperanza replied.

The Abbess dismissed her, too.

The Abbess looked as shaken as I felt. "Spanish nuns in New Spain? Our mission not drowned or captured by pirates. And the name—Sors Santas de Jesus? And the bishop knew nothing of it?"

We sat and considered the impossibilities. Finally the Abbess said that if it were true, it was a miracle. Such news, after thirty years of mourning! We dare not hope, and yet we do. As soon as the road is passable, the Abbess will send a letter to the convent that bears our name.

At Sor Serafina's welcome feast there was much rejoicing, and more wine than usual was allocated. And drunk.

Let all who read this pray for the Holy Sisters of Jesus wherever they may be. God is great!

CHAPTER 19

From the Chronicle of the Las Sors Santas de Jesus, Las
Golondrinas Convent, Andalusia, Spring 1553

It has been a year since the Abbess wrote to the convent of the
Holy Sisters of Jesus, Las Golondrinas in New Spain near the
Andes Mountains. The road is passable again after the winter.
Last week we celebrated Easter and now we are busy preparing
the convent to receive the pilgrims who come after *Semana Santa*.
The infirmary has been scrubbed from top to bottom, lay sisters in
charge of the hostels for men and women have a storeroom of fresh
straw mattresses, while pilgrims' cells with beds, fresh linens, and
candles are prepared for our more important visitors. The shutters
have been opened; the spring winds have swept the winter fug of
woodsmoke away and the convent smells of beeswax and lavender.
In the cloister, the herbs and roses have been pruned and the paths
swept. In the pilgrims' garden the orange trees are in bloom, and
the shell basin below the little spring has been scrubbed clean. The
jasmine that has grown over the fissure in the rock wall is in bud
and the rosemary and lavender are putting forth new green shoots.

Luz has completed the queen's gift that she worked on all
winter—a most exquisitely worked altar cloth on a fine piece of
linen, with swallows darting in flight, and a delicate swallow's nest
bearing the queen's initials and trimmed with lace. It was packed

with sprigs of rosemary and a respectful letter of thanks for Her Majesty's gracious patronage and assurance of our continual prayers for her spiritual and bodily welfare and for the conversion of the natives in Spain's American colonies.

The sister in charge of our chickens and goats rubs her hands with satisfaction at their increase, and many new lambs were fattened for the Easter feast. In the kitchen the smell of *polvorónes* mingles with the baking of our plain everyday bread. The silver in the chapel has been polished, the altar linen washed and mended, and the villagers have brought us two casks of last autumn's wine. A supply of communion wafers is wrapped in linen in the vestry. In the infirmaries the sisters have prepared a supply of clean bandages, salves, ointments, cordials, and tinctures. Illness in winter prompts many a pilgrimage in summer.

Today when I went to join the Abbess I was startled to find a very dirty and rather wild-looking man with shabby clothes held together by a rope around his waist on the other side of the *locutio*. I supposed it must be one of the hermits who make their way to us from time to time for a little company and proper food. The Abbess beckoned me to her side and murmured, "The portress opened the gate to him this morning, and he spoke wildly, insisting he must find someone, must tell the Abbess. The portress suggested he go first to the pilgrims' quarters, to have a meal and rest, and they would see what he wanted then, but he began raving that he must find a young girl who might have been brought here. At the same time he was unwilling to be parted from his donkey, which had a large pannier on its back. The portress was surprised to see it was full of brushes and paints and canvases. The man's accent and courtier's speech were at odds with his rough appearance, and she began to think he might be the father of one of the orphan children, returned to claim her. The portress made a bargain. A beata would take him to the Abbess if he would leave the donkey at the gate.

"I asked him the name of the girl and his reason for seeking her but—" The Abbess raised her eyebrows and tipped her head toward the *locutio*. Her expression indicated the man muttering on the other side was mad. And indeed, he was muttering about the crown prince Don Balthazar. Even before Marisol came, we knew of his rages and fits, and the rumor the king had changed the order of succession. But the madman was insisting that Don Balthazar had been killed on the orders of the king, and now some people were prepared to rally behind the martyred prince's heir.

"People grumble against the crown," the disheveled man said. Rumor flourishes where secrets are kept. Don Balthazar's supporters say that he sired a child, a girl—and she is the rightful heir to the Spanish throne. The child disappeared two years ago...The king has ordered her to be found."

"But what have you to do with this child?" asked the Abbess.

"I must find her before the authorities do. Because I am responsible. I must tell her the truth and ask her forgiveness," he answered. Behind the *locutio* all we could see of him were his wild eyes as he pressed his face against the bars. "And to warn her she is in danger."

"Forgiveness?"

"I have done a great wrong, Abbess. I was blessed by God with talent, but abused it. I loved women beyond anything and used my gift to paint their portraits in such a way that stirred desire. I was successful because making a portrait was like making love— women revealed themselves to me, confided in me, surrendered to me. Beautiful women have many possible likenesses, the countenance they wish the world to see, and usually, the face they keep hidden. Portraits, like love, demand an exposure of self. I could discern vanity and cunning and avarice, and disguise them as elegance or vitality. I knew of their lusts, their greed, and above all, who had a shameful secret child in circumstances that must never come to light. Because those were in my debt. I helped conceal those children. And took the payment I desired of them in return.

"I was commissioned to paint the betrothal portrait of a very young girl. She was shy and modest, untouched by an evil or calculating thought. I began intending to seduce her like the others, and instead ended half in love and anxious to do her no harm. But I felt obliged to paint her as sensual and desirable—her husband-to-be who commissioned the portrait was a man of the world, very powerful and rich, and himself a great lover of women. I used all my artist's tricks, a suggestive expression of the eyes, fullness in the lips to paint her as she might appear—if she were some other woman. The husband-to-be was greatly pleased and paid me double the fee.

"The portrait was much admired at court but it had the most powerful effect on the crown prince. When I was ordered to make a copy for the prince's private apartments I was uneasy but dared not refuse a royal command. I was relieved when the girl was married and gone from court to her husband's home, together with the portrait. But I could not forget her lovely face and trusting expression, and I began to regret painting the portrait in the way that I had, feeling I had betrayed her in some way. But I was to regret even more making a copy for the prince. I was unused to feeling guilt, and to avoid it, I threw myself into work and women. I painted and painted and became richer and more successful with each passing year.

"When I learned that the girl had become the mother of a family and lived quietly, that her husband was devoted to her despite his long absences, I was relieved. I had done her no harm after all. I do not know how the gossip started, that this lady was the mistress of the crown prince. True, he had lusted after the lady's portrait, but the lady herself was safely out of his way. But the gossip continued, spread by the prince's faction, who claimed despite the evidence that he was a normal man and fit to inherit the throne. Then they whispered that the lady's husband had repudiated her because she had born the crown prince one child and was about to bear him another. I believed none of the gossip, but knew my accursed portrait had fanned the lusts of the mad prince, enough to make him dangerous. Then I learned the lady's husband and most of her children had died in mysterious circumstances and the lady was again with child. The queen did not believe the slander and offered her protection, asking the lady to come to court for her lying in. There was no denying the queen, but fortunately for the lady, the crown prince died suddenly as she was on her way to Madrid.

"Months later I received a message begging my help for the usual problem—the discreet removal of an unwanted female child. I set the usual process in motion to have her taken away to the usual place, whose exact whereabouts I have never known. Only afterward did I learn that child had been the daughter of the only woman whose goodness ever touched my soul, the only woman I ever loved. She must have sought my help when she discovered I helped send children away and knew how dangerous her daughter's position would be if she died.

"She, poor slandered lady, died with her baby in childbirth, just as Don Balthazar's supporters fanned the flames of the rumor that Don Balthazar had been murdered on the king's orders, but had sired a child, a girl who was the rightful heir to the Spanish throne. They would rally behind her and claim her as queen of Spain in the name of the martyred prince. Two English spies were caught, tortured, and confessed to seeking the same child. They were executed, and the search for the girl intensified. The king orders her to be found before she becomes a weapon in the hands of Spain's enemies.

"I understood what I had done, bringing ruin and death to a sweet lady. My talent deserted me, my portraits ceased to breathe, and everything I attempted was flat and lifeless and dull. My commissions dried up; my debts mounted. I drank heavily until I did not know night from day, gambled desperately, and when I was no longer successful and the ladies began to shun me, I sought out prostitutes and embraced the meanest pleasures of the senses to forget what I had done.

"The burden of my guilt grew, until I could bear it no longer. I went to confession and repented of destroying a blameless woman and her family, save for one child. For penance, the priest said I must find the remaining daughter, obtain her forgiveness, and perform some act of contrition for her. I began to search for the convent where I had helped send so many unwanted girls. But although I had set the process in motion many times, the location remained a closely guarded secret, and try as I might, I could not penetrate that secrecy. All I could learn was that it was a convent in the mountains, a place of swallows. I gave away my possessions and what I had not squandered of my money to the poor, and kept only my artist's materials. I vowed that if God would guide me to the girl, I would paint a masterpiece for His glory. For two years I have traveled as a mendicant and a pilgrim from one religious house to another. But I am ill and I despaired of finding her and absolution before I die.

"Then a few weeks ago on the road, I saw great flocks of migrating swallows flying into the mountains, and the mountain people said they were returning to their home at the convent of Las Golondrinas. I felt hope for the first time; perhaps they had come to lead the way." He stopped for breath and his head sank into his chest. "I am the wretch Tristan Mendoza."

"And the child you seek?"

He whispered, "Maria Isabella Vilar D'Ascencion."

What the man said tallied with Marisol's account. "Yes," said the Abbess cautiously after a moment. "Yes, she is here. But I do not know if you may see her." The Abbess and I consulted—should Marisol be told? She is not so fierce as she seems. But it was for her to grant forgiveness if she could, and the poor man should not be denied the right to ask it. The Abbess decided to send for her.

Marisol flounced in, expecting a lecture for breaking convent rules, and emitted a startled "Oh!" when she saw a man behind the grille.

The Abbess told her to be seated and said bluntly, "Marisol, this man claims to be the painter Tristan Mendoza, who painted your mother's wedding portrait."

"If he is, beware," Marisol said rudely. "Josefa always warned that the painter was not to be trusted and women should look to their virtue in his presence."

Even Marisol squirmed at the Abbess's stern frown, though she subsided with a little exhale of breath meant to show us how little she cared. The man fell to his knees and cried, "A miracle!"

"What's this?" Marisol demanded suspiciously.

"My prayers are answered. I have come to confess my guilt and seek your mercy and forgiveness for the evil I brought upon you and those you loved. I am the murderer of your entire family. I have their blood on my hands, on my soul."

Marisol muttered, "This beggar is a madman. Allow me to go, Abbess."

"Be still!" the Abbess commanded.

The man clutched the *locutio* and repeated his story.

For once Marisol had nothing to say. She crumpled in her chair, looking small and vulnerable. She clenched her jaw and looked wildly at me, her spirited defiance gone. Tears welled in her eyes as she battled to recover the anger that is her shield against the world. "I did not know why I was taken away from her and Josefa, and I did not know she had died. I have hated them and hated them. And now, you tell me...I hate you, too, with all my heart and every breath in my body."

Marisol's hand reached out for mine. There was silence for a long time.

"Marisol, we are taught that when our forgiveness is sought we should grant it as we hope for God's forgiveness of our sins..." prompted the Abbess, kindly but firmly. "It is to the benefit of our own souls as well as for the glory of God."

Marisol nodded, while her hands twisted and twisted her handkerchief. "Poor Consuela," she whispered.

Tristan Mendoza said humbly, "I have vowed to use my gift only in God's service. Let me do so now. I wronged her mother with a licentious portrait—may I paint a spiritual portrait of Maria Isabella in her novice's gown to mark her transition into the life of a nun? Such portraits are often commissioned by the family of a girl taking the veil."

Indeed, just such a portrait of Sor Serafina had accompanied her when she arrived as a novice. "Premature!" the Abbess had grumbled.

Marisol raised her head. A little fire returned to her eyes. The Abbess said quickly, "*That* will be impossible. Marisol has no vocation."

Tristan Mendoza surprised us then. He stared at Marisol silently for a few moments, then said, "I can see there is perhaps no vocation, but her mother's goodness in her heart will do great things. She will act selflessly, though it will cause her pain, and be a strong force for good. She will be greatly loved by one and by many."

Marisol's eyes flickered up. "Really? Am I pretty, like my mother?"

The Abbess shook her head. "Marisol! Beware of vanity!"

"Oh please," begged Marisol. "There are no mirrors in the convent, and Josefa said I resembled my father. Even my mother took care with her appearance. And these novices' gowns we are forced to wear are so very *ugly*!"

The Abbess sighed. "Thank you, sir, for your offer. May I suggest that as your act of contrition, you paint Marisol and her inner... goodness together with some of our other girls? You will work from that side of the *locutio* of course and Sor Beatriz will act as chaperone."

"Gladly, Abbess."

"Thank you!" exclaimed Marisol.

The Abbess then sent Tristan Mendoza to the men's hostel and Marisol back to her work. I wondered aloud why the Abbess was willing to allow a man of such confessed carnality to paint five young girls.

"There are several reasons. It will take the girls' minds off this horrible Inquisition visit, and the man longs to make reparation. This is the only means in his power. If there is the slightest hint of anything improper, if he suggests one of the girls meets him elsewhere in the convent, he will be sent away at once. I do not think he wishes that.

"And I wish to see his work. He may have had the morals of a male cat, but he has the reputation of a master. The convent is unlikely to see many masters, and I have another idea which I will share when we see how the portrait goes."

Tristan Mendoza began the next day, rising early for Mass before turning to the task of grinding and mixing his paints. Though his face was horribly gaunt, almost a death mask, a little life returned to it as he mixed colors while the girls peered through the *locutio* and asked questions. When he was ready, he took some time instructing them to group this way and that on their side of the *locutio*. Marisol pinched her cheeks to give them color and fluffed her hair. Luz held her favorite doll, dressed as if for a consecration in a veil and flower crown, and would sit nowhere but at Esperanza's feet. Esperanza had brought a book and read while she waited. Sanchia fidgeted, and Pia combed out her hair to make a silvery waterfall down her back. Tristan Mendoza stifled a gasp at the sight. I gave him a sharp reprimand.

He was no longer the sniveling penitent. A note of authority had returned to his voice, and he told the girls they must keep still; he must work quickly because there was little time. He set to work on a canvas he had prepared the night before, while I worked at a table nearby.

A week passed. Then Tristan Mendoza turned the unfinished canvas to face the *locutio* so the Abbess and I might see it. The Abbess gazed through the grille and said, "It really is quite good! Unfinished, but I am amazed…look at Luz, with her doll. He has caught the sweetness of her soul exactly, just as he has captured Esperanza's intelligence, Marisol's impatience, Sanchia's demons, and Pia's detachment from the world, as if nothing can touch her! Now consider this. I have often prayed that God would send us an artist capable of painting our Gospel, perhaps as an allegorical cycle. Until now no artist here has been sufficiently gifted or could be trusted with our secrets. But I think Mendoza's gift has been tempered, not destroyed, by suffering and repentance. He may understand base human nature, but is capable of looking beyond it for divine grace, and I am more and more convinced the Gospel should be preserved here in painting even though we hope to find a means to send the Chronicle away."

Tristan Mendoza no longer looks quite so ill, and he talks of painting a work for the chapel once he is finished with the girls. He has asked the Abbess if there is any saint we wish to honor. The Abbess said that she had a plan she would discuss with him. But his premonition there was little time proved correct, though not in the way we expected, with his death. Before the portrait was finished, the bell at the gate rang loudly in the dead of night. Soon afterward a sleepy beata came to my cell saying the Abbess had received a messenger at the *locutio*, and that I was wanted at once. I dressed quickly and hurried along to the Abbess's apartments.

The Abbess held up the official letter. "The tribunal will arrive next week. All present in the convent are to be questioned—nuns, novices, beatas, servants, and now children over the age of four. Fr. Ramon Jimenez…they say he can smell a heretic, and gives his investigators great leeway in the manner in which they obtain information." Her voice shook a little.

The walls of the parlor suddenly closed around us. The convent, our refuge, had become our prison, a trap, a grave. A ringing in my ears drowned out the Abbess's next words.

"I said 'brides,' Sor Beatriz." The Abbess spoke sharply, exasperated at having to repeat herself. "Now I understand what the Foundress meant. Esperanza, Marisol, Pia, and Sanchia must go to find husbands in the New World! And take the Chronicle and the medal with them. I will make the necessary arrangements for them to leave as soon as possible. Write your last in the Chronicle, then give it to Esperanza. She can be trusted to continue it and seek out this convent in the Andes."

"Esperanza will read the Gospel!"

"Of course she will, Sor Beatriz! That is my intention! When she does she will understand why she must decide if Las Golondrinas in the colonies is our mission before she gives the Gospel to their care. But go, I know you wish to write a farewell…"

From the Chronicle of Las Sors Santas de Jesus, Las Golondrinas Convent, Andalusia, June 1552

It is midnight, but only the orphanage children sleep, unaware that last night a messenger came up from the valley to warn the Abbess. Like wolves slinking toward the sheepfold, the Inquisition tribunal draws nearer each day and will soon be upon us…

CHAPTER 20

From the Chronicle of Las Sors Santas de Jesus,
by the pen of Esperanza, July 1552

At Sea

Impossible though it seems even after the weeks of traveling to Seville, Marisol, Pia, Sanchia, and I have left the convent with Sor Emmanuela. We are on the open sea, bound for Spanish America and the convent known as Las Golondrinas de Los Andes. I am charged with discovering whether it was founded by a mission party of nuns of Las Sors Santas de Jesus many years ago. Sor Beatriz and the Abbess gave me a list of questions, the names of the mission party, and so on, and I must be satisfied by the answers before I part with the Chronicle and Sor Emmanuela parts with the medal. It is a great responsibility.

Sor Beatriz has told me about her daughter, Salome, who will either be a nun there or they will know of her death. Sor Beatriz believes this will be the test to confirm it is indeed the right place. But finding the convent is only part of our task. The other is to find husbands. I do not know which is the harder.

The Abbess and Sor Beatriz also wish me to keep a record of our journey. It began this way:

Late one night Sor Emmanuela came to the cell where Marisol, Pia, and I were sleeping and said we must come to the Abbess at once. We dressed quickly and hurried to her parlor as Sor Emmanuela went to fetch Sanchia from the children's dormitory. The Abbess, Sor Beatriz, and several other nuns stood by the fire, examining papers on the table bearing the Inquisition stamp. Pia gasped and silently gripped my hand. "They are coming!" cried Marisol.

"So," I whispered, "we are trapped! They will question us horribly and when they discover who we are the nuns will suffer for hiding us!"

"No, you girls will leave the convent at once," said the Abbess, "before they find you."

"Leave?" asked Pia faintly. "If you send us away, we will be hunted down. We may as well throw ourselves from the cliffs tonight!"

The Abbess said briskly, "Fortunately, Pia, we have made a better plan. You will leave tonight for Seville, and from there sail for Spanish America. One of the village men has gone ahead to arrange your passage on the first available ship, and two more are waiting to take you to Seville. You must be gone as soon as you are ready, and Sor Emmanuela will go as your chaperone. A convent in Spanish America was founded by missionaries from our order years ago. Las Golondrinas de Los Andes will give you shelter until you marry and I am sure will help find you husbands. The colonists are in great need of Spanish wives, and therefore less likely to look deeply into your families than men in Spain. We are providing dowries for each of you."

"But what of you, what of Sor Beatriz? And all the others?"

"That will be as God wills. I am not without hope that someone at court can influence the Inquisition inquiry, even at this late date. We have just sent the queen an urgent message begging her to help, hoping that Luz's beautiful gift will prove a reminder. But we are bound by our vows and will do our duty, whatever happens. And you must prepare to go."

"Sanchia is only ten—surely she cannot be married."

"Help each other as much as you can. The first to marry must take her into your home as a sister and find a husband for her when the time comes. Now make haste to pack...ah, here is Sanchia."

Sanchia came in rubbing her eyes, her curly hair unbrushed and her dress unfastened. Normally she bounced and bobbed restlessly, but in the middle of the night even she was too sleepy. "Child, wake up and pay attention. You are going on a journey with Marisol and Esperanza and Pia." Sanchia's eyes grew wide with fear. "Are there soldiers?" she quavered. "Will they tie us up?"

"No, my dear. There will be a ship with sails like a bird's wings, and the great sea and you will have an adventure."

We were all stunned at the sudden news, and I was overcome with sadness to think I must leave dear Sor Beatriz and the sanctuary of the convent. I loved our calm days in the scriptorium, with new books to discover, correspondence to be copied, or best of all, finding information required by the infirmary sisters. I had often regretted promising my father to marry, thinking how pleasant, how useful and fulfilling, it would be to stay and embrace a nun's life here. Had my mother felt the same when she entered Regina Coeli?

But there was little time for such reflections, and the Abbess sent us off to dress for the journey and gather our belongings. Sor Beatriz drew me away to the scriptorium where this Chronicle lay open on her desk. She told me that I was to take the Chronicle with us and aside from keeping an account of the journey I must read it all, including the order's Gospel in Latin, in the middle pages. Then I would understand why I must guard it with my life and be sure that it was delivered safely into the right hands. I swore to do so, then she told me to go and pack; she wished to make a farewell entry.

I saw Sor Beatriz one last time in the scriptorium when she laid the parcel with this Chronicle in my arms with as much sorrow and tenderness as if I had been her child. By then the convent had been alerted to the fact the tribunal had arrived suddenly in the darkness. With their horses and mules and carriages and wagons and servants causing an uproar, the bell rang incessantly, frightened beatas and novices and servants ran about, and all was suddenly noise and confusion.

The Abbess said the artist Tristan Mendoza had been dosed with powerful medicine and was in a deathlike sleep, bandaged from head to toe for good measure and hidden beneath the lepers' cell in the infirmary together with his painting materials. Still wet, the unfinished portrait of the five of us had been hung on a dark wall in the oldest wing. Perhaps in leaving the portrait, we leave a little of ourselves—that is a comfort.

I hope the Inquisition does not find it.

Having gathered the four of us girls in her parlor once more, the Abbess took the medal of her office from her neck and put it around the neck of Sor Emmanuela. The Abbess clearly expects the worst or she would not part with it. The sisters embraced, and then the Abbess hastily kissed each of us and gave us her blessing before opening a small door hidden behind a tapestry.

A narrow dark passageway, steep and all but invisible, led from the privy there down to the cellars where the wine casks are kept, then below them to the sewers. We stepped carefully down the stairs of the narrow passage, until we finally squeezed through a small window at the base of the convent, donned heavy cloaks, and hurried to a wagon that was waiting. Darkness was our friend. The village men had already loaded our trunks and muffled the wagon's wheels. They helped us in and we pulled silently away.

My heart ached for Luz. I had no time to say good-bye. What will she do without us? Without me? And the Abbess is pinning all her hopes of a reprieve from the tribunal on Luz's gift to the queen. I cannot bear to think of what will happen to them all! Huddled in the wagon we all wept, sniffling under our cloaks until the sky turned pink with the dawn and we slept.

We woke with a jolt as the wagon stopped and we feared the worst, but the drivers said we must get down and walk. A full wagon is hard going for the mules. Their orders were to shun the main road, and I could see we were on a faint track marked with white stones at intervals leading into the forest.

Our escorts took care to avoid villages, and if they spotted shepherds they would veer off to keep out of their sight. We slept in the open wrapped in our cloaks, surviving on dried fruit and mutton, almonds, and cheese, drinking from the mountain springs. Finally drawing close to Seville we were glad to be able to ride again, and to buy bread and oil and a little wine. Marisol looked eagerly at everything, saying how interesting the world was beyond the convent.

I was uneasy. To me, the familiar streets and cathedral towers of Seville meant only danger. Remembering how Maria and I had escaped, giddy with relief and daring, I wondered whether my guardian had appropriated all my fortune to himself or whether the Inquisition had clawed it from him. Every day I thought of Don Jaime with love and gratitude for engineering my escape, and said a prayer for his safety.

The city overwhelmed us with its noise and bustle. The convent sounds were bells and prayers and birdsong, the murmur of the schoolroom, the hush of the library by day and the mountain wind by night. At the docks, sailors shouted and swore and called orders, soldiers and priests and friars hurried in twos and threes, mules brayed, whips cracked, cargoes were loaded, sails snapped in the breeze, men drank and sang, and prostitutes called shrilly from the shadows. The other girls and even Sor Emmanuela exclaimed

with excitement at the sight of so many great-masted ships towering into the sky.

"Look!" cried Marisol. "The *Torre del Oro!*" We craned our
necks to see the great watchtower that guarded the docks, an aston-
ishing sight, dazzling gold in the afternoon sunshine. Marisol said it
was called the "Tower of Gold" because a lady with golden hair had
been imprisoned there by King Pedro the Cruel when she would
not love him. Sor Emmanuela said nonsense—it was called the
tower of gold because its yellow tiles reflected the light. Behind her
back, Marisol made a face.

Sor Emmanuela shooed us up the gangplank between the sailors so quickly that Marisol stumbled and nearly slipped into the
river. She muttered an oath. Down below, where it was very hot,
we saw the captain had curtained off a section of the dark hold
for us, with five small bunks that someone had attempted to make
comfortable with cushions. The bunks were only a plank in width
and the cushions left no room for our persons. Sanchia scrambled
onto the highest one and giggled as she tumbled off. Soon we were
all laughing, even Sor Emmanuela, pondering the best way to step
over and around each other in such a small quarters and lamenting
the lack of space for a chamber pot.

Then the porters brought our trunks and bundles. It appeared
impossible that space could be found anywhere for our small
trunks. But finally they were wedged in and we piled our bundles
containing a change of linen for the voyage and our prayer books
on top. Sor Emmanuela hung a crucifix on a nail protruding from
the wall. On deck above our heads we heard the sailors shouting,
then footsteps, and a great thump that Sor Emmanuela said was
the gangplank. We could feel the ship begin moving down the
river. We were away! And very hot, though a little fresh air comes
from the open hatch. Marisol was longing to go up on deck, but
Sor Emmanuela forbids it. Marisol is sulking.

We have said our evening prayers together, eaten some hard bread and dried meat, and shifted about to find enough space to lie down. But excitement keeps us all awake. That and the suffocating heat.

In the hot, light evenings at sea, I took the Chronicle from its wrapping of oiled wool and read the Latin Gospel. Now I have a new burden of dangerous knowledge that, considered logically, undoes any justification for Christian persecution of Jews and Muslims, and testifies to what we believe in common. And I cannot unknow it. It burns in my brain like the fire the Inquisition would throw me into, the fire I watched consume those poor people long ago.

The ship has begun to move continually with the swell of the sea, and Sor Emmanuela and Pia are violently ill. The hold smells of vomit, and water has leaked into the corners to make it damp as well as smelly. Sor Emmanuela was too sick to forbid Marisol to go on deck, and Sanchia and I followed her, desperate for fresh air. The salt breeze revived us and the endless sea is a marvelous sight, a world made of water. Stretching to the sky! It seems impossible that land lies beyond it.

At first the sailors eyed us warily, but grew friendlier as the days passed. They promised it would be an easy passage, and described the place we were bound. They said it was crossed by all the peoples of the world; Levantine and Genoese merchants, turbaned men with skins black as night, silk-clad Chinese, and grandees in cloaks worked with gold. In the markets we would find strange fruit, silks, spices, and fish with rainbow scales. We would know the grandees' ladies because they went veiled in black, attended by unveiled mestiza servants in bright clothes.

The sea air agreed with Marisol. Her eyes sparkled, her cheeks were pink, and she unbraided her hair to let it blow in the wind. The sailors vied with each other to make her laugh. After a few days Sor

Emmanuela came to sit on deck, too, to let the sun ease a bad cough and a chill caught from lying in the damp hold. Pia sat silently by her side, ignoring the sailors who gazed stupefied at her moonlight hair.

The floor of our quarters grew wetter and the bottoms of our trunks were soaked, but on deck the air was delightful, and the warm wind filled the sails. We spent as little time below as possible, saying our prayers and eating our meals on deck. Our hard bread, baked from salted flour, was dipped in a little olive oil to soften it, and we had olives and dried figs and sour wine from the barrels on board. The seagulls swooped and cried overhead and the world was an endless vista of water and light. How I wished my father could have seen it.

We were enjoying our meal on deck as usual one day, watching the horizon rise and fall, trying to imagine what sort of husbands we would find, when Sanchia cried, "Look." She pointed to the sky where little puffy clouds on the horizon were spreading across the sky with great speed. At first a thin haze dimmed the sun, and then became a dark canopy of cloud. The wind suddenly blew harder and colder. The sails snapped over our heads and the sea turned from blue green to black and the waves grew rougher. We watched this transformation anxiously, as did the sailors. The captain snapped orders that the men moved very quickly to obey. A sailor shoved us unceremoniously through the open hatch and down the ladder back into the hold as more orders were shouted and other sailors rushed about pulling in the sails and tightening ropes.

We could never have imagined anything so terrible as the storm that struck like a blow from the hand of the Almighty. Soon our ship was rocking, then heaving and plunging up and down through great waves and a half light through which nothing could be seen. A cold wave washed over the deck and poured down into our hold. The sailors cried out that we must not be afraid, and slammed the hatch shut.

The storm seemed to grow worse and worse. We were frightened and in the hours and days that followed, lost track of time as we clung together in the dark, bruised, dizzy, and sick with the pitching of the ship, unable to keep down dry biscuits or the brackish water, praying continually, sleeping fitfully to wake again to fear and cold...

Water sloshed ankle-deep around us. Our habits were soaked through and Sor Emmanuela could not stop coughing and complained of pain in her chest. A day or two later she was feverish. We took it in turns to sit by her side as we tossed, bracing ourselves upright to support her and sponging her hot face as best we could. Marisol managed to unpack some medicine, but it did Sor Emmanuela no good and she began gasping, saying she could not breathe. She grew worse, unable to talk, until finally, with great racking breaths, poor Sor Emmanuela died. On our knees, shivering and clutching each other for support in the rolling and shuddering hold, we commended her soul to God. We folded her rosary around her stiffening fingers and, having no winding sheet, wrapped her body in her beata's cloak. I managed to retrieve the Abbess's medal and for safety put it around my own neck.

Marisol crawled to the curtain that separates our quarters from the rest of the ship and called that it had pleased God to take Sor Emmanuela. Two sailors, whose turn it was to snatch a few moments of rest, struggled from their hammocks and, bracing themselves against the motion of the ship, swung the body up between them and staggered out. We knew Sor Emmanuela would be dropped into the sea. "We shall soon follow!" exclaimed Marisol through chattering teeth.

We all strained to hear the splash the body made when it went overboard. Just when we thought it must have done so, the wind howled ferociously and a great wave struck the ship so hard that it went onto its side, slamming us against the wall. Then we felt it carried up and up to a terrifying height and, as we clutched each other, plunged sickeningly down with such force it threw us apart and must surely have broken the ship in pieces. Sanchia screamed for her mother. I saw my father's face, and Pia and Marisol had buried their faces in each other's shoulders. Above the wind there was shouting on the deck above and a great crack and screams. There was a cry of "man overboard." We said a prayer for him and for ourselves, and Sanchia began reciting in Hebrew the same phrase over and over again. We looked at each other and whispered "farewell," as death approached in every groan, in every creak of the ship's straining, weakening timbers.

"They say drowning is quick," whispered Pia. Marisol whimpered.

Then there was another presence in the room.

"Can you see her?" gasped Sanchia and pointed.

Pia opened her eyes with an effort. "Yes!"

Marisol stared, past speech for once.

I thought it an apparition of the sea, like the half-woman half-fish creatures that lure sailors to their death on the rocks. But it was a lady in a cloak, just as the Chronicle described her, and I knew— as the others did not—who it was. The Foundress had come to succor us in the hour of our deaths, to speak words of comfort as I joined my father and mother in paradise.

I was mistaken. The Foundress spoke sharply, saying that in our present condition we would make poor sport for the fish, and that we would not drown. The storm had nearly blown itself out; we must trust in God and all would be well. Then she bent over me and said that the medal I had saved was a precious thing, a gift from her brother long ago. I tried to answer that I knew, but she held a finger to my lips and told me firmly to have courage, and someday the medal and the Chronicle would have a role to play in bringing peace in a time of trouble when Christians, Jews, and Muslims were at war with one another again. Then she was gone.

"They say that drowning people see strange sights in the moment before they die," said Pia faintly. This was not the time for explanations about what we had seen. Instead I said with as much force as I could muster, "She said we will not drown yet. Have courage, we must only have courage."

That evening, the storm abated and we could feel the sea grow calmer. The winds subsided, and the captain shouted through our curtain, "The sky is clearing and the lookout has spotted a flock of birds in the distance. That means land ahead. Land! God is great!"

"*Deo gratias*," we answered him automatically, and fell into an exhausted sleep in each other's arms.

Stumbling onto the deck next morning, we saw a thin line on the horizon, and as we drew closer we saw the outline of masts against the sky, then finally the port itself. Around us the sailors hurried about their tasks, laughing and slapping each other on the backs, talking of rum and women. Natives rowed out to us in long narrow boats, bringing strange yellow fruits that tasted sweet as honey, and fresh water that was sweeter still. We looked at each other, pale and thin, blinking in the daylight like underground creatures. "We must look like sea witches," said Marisol, tugging futilely at her soiled and crumpled gown. "These were hideous enough when clean. We'll never find husbands like this!"

My relief that we were not dead at the bottom of the sea became anxiety about more practical matters. What we would do once ashore? I climbed down to our cabin and calculated our resources. In Sor Emmanuela's trunk were our dowries, four pouches of *reales*. There was also a purse of coins for our expenses. I was counting them when the others called me to come; the gangplank was nearly down. I cannot write again until we are a little settled. Somewhere.

CHAPTER 21

*Of the Matter of the Holy Sisters of Jesus and of
the Matter of an Examination of the Convent of
Las Golondrinas for the Discovery of Heresy and
Enemies of the True Faith among Them*

Under the Seal of the Holy Office of the Inquisition

*This is the record of an investigation of the convent of the order of nuns known as
Las Sors Santas de Jesus, undertaken in the summer of 1552 Anno Domini,*

upon evidence presented by Count Jaime Defendor del Santo Sepulchre, who alleged that the convent in question shielded secret Jews and Muslims, and claimed the nuns were given over to heretical ideas, vice, and all manner of works inimical to the Faith.

The evidence in support of his allegations were a few remnants, scraps of parchment badly damaged and full of holes. Our investigators traced them to the possession of a certain serving maid at the convent. Interrogated by the Inquisition during their investigation in 1552, the girl admitted she had sold them to the count's servant. All the torturers could discover was that the women in the maid's family had served the convent for many years, that her grandmother had taken the scraps after cleaning the scriptorium after a plague of rats. Neither the girl nor any of her family could read, but the girl insisted the scraps came from the "book" of the convent. Learning that an unknown party would pay for information about the convent, she sold the fragments. The girl died under questioning before more could be learned, if indeed there was anything more to be learned. The fragment makes little sense, talking of visions and missions, a miraculous medal and swallows. Though the scriptorium, the nuns, and the convent were rigorously searched and examined, we found no other evidence nor any such medal as supposedly exists. Though interrogated in the manner prescribed by Fr. Ramon Jimenez to elicit correct information and expose heresy, we concluded that the Abbess and the scribe did not deviate from their most holy oath and duty to answer our questions truthfully.

There are special circumstances at work here that incline us to conclude the worthy count has been misled by the forces of darkness to cast suspicion and calumny upon a pious order of nuns. He is an elderly man. The Order of Las Sors Santas de Jesus found great favor with her late Catholic Majesty Queen Isabella for maintaining the convent as a beacon of Christian faith during the time of the Moors. It is common knowledge that Her Catholic Majesty made a pilgrimage to the convent in 1493 and the convent has been under the protection and patronage of the female members of the royal family ever since.

Her Majesty, our present queen, has been moved by the gift of an altar cloth worked by an orphan in the convent in token of gratitude to their royal patron.

HELEN BRYAN

Her Majesty urges that the gift pleads most eloquently for the purity of the faith there, reminding us of the venerable nature of the order, its valiant adherence to Christianity despite seven hundred years of Moorish rule. Erroneous suspicions weaken the authority of the church. Her Majesty emphasized the girls in the convent orphanage are a delicate matter because of the circumstances of their birth, yet tainted with the stain of illegitimacy, they enter upon a holy life. On the strength of this good work and yielding to the persuasion of those who beg us to consider the spiritual welfare of the girls, considering the merit and faith of the nuns who guide young women onto the paths of righteousness away from the eyes of the world and with due respect for those who would keep all matters relating to Las Golondrinas private, we judge that no further examination of Las Golondrinas convent is necessary.

Therefore we conclude that suggestions the Abbess experienced a "vision" may be ascribed to the weak and fanciful mind of our informant, who like all women are prone to folly at certain times of the month, being weak and inferior in mind as in all other things. There are other inaccuracies. There is no evidence a mission convent was established in Gran Canaria and, indeed, it is pure fantasy to imagine that a sequestered order of nuns in the mountains of Andalusia could undertake such a thing without our knowing of it.

We find that the document we were given is a forgery and a vile slander devised by Jews to cast suspicion on Christian nuns. Their evil design against these holy women has been thwarted. We could find nothing of substance inimical to the Faith and were persuaded there was no need to examine the orphanage children.

Although we do not discount the existence of an ancient heresy, we find no evidence of it in these papers or at Las Golondrinas. However, as our orders are to collect anything thought to be connected to the heresy, however insignificant, this fragment will now be delivered to the Papal archive for safekeeping.

266

CHAPTER 22

*From the Chronicle of Las Sors Santas de Jesus, by the
pen of Esperanza, the New World, October 1552*

My heart is so heavy with grief that, were it not for my promise
to the Abbess and Sor Beatriz, I would abandon the Chronicle. It
feels a lifetime has passed since we arrived in this strange place,
although it has been less than a month since tragedy struck. Were
it not for my promise to keep a record, I would write no more.

As the ship glided into the port, the air was heavy and damp,
with sort of a gray mist over everything. The quay was teeming.
Native men with broad dark faces were busy loading and unload-
ing ships, jostled by slaves and porters, food vendors and merchants, Chinamen and black women in turbans, all shouting at the
tops of their voices. There were native women with flat faces and
babies on their backs, water sellers with buckets on yokes, flower
vendors, carriages and sedan chairs bearing ladies in muslin gowns
that fluttered in the breeze, followed by servants trotting to keep
up. Caged parrots and monkeys squawked, mules and horses struggled to make their way through the throng, and over it all hung a
powerful smell of fish. Donkeys brayed, sailors shouted in a myriad
of languages, native porters called for customers, and in the town
church bells rang every minute.

Marisol was smiling. How painful to remember that!

As the gangplank was lowered the captain made his way through the sailors to us, beaming with relief the voyage was over, and I am sure, grayer in his beard than when we had left Seville. "Now young ladies, if you please, welcome to Spanish America!" With a flourish, as if he were master of the land ahead of us, he bowed and indicated we were to go ahead of him down the gangplank.

We hesitated. Then Marisol tossed her head and said, "Come, then!" and led the way. We followed her. But how full of men the world is! And what an attraction four girls make among them! Men eyed us boldly, and as it was far too hot and sticky to wear our veils, we felt uncomfortably exposed. "Surely these ruffians cannot be the husbands we have come for?" Marisol muttered, as swarthy young men flashed her a smile or a wink or bowed. How Marisol contrives to look so pretty after our ordeal I do not know. One impudent fellow even kissed his fingertips in her direction and called something we did not understand, but must surely have been impertinent. Pia followed close in her footsteps, eyes down. Fortunately Pia had taken the precaution of covering her hair or there might have been a riot.

Sanchia clung to Pia's hand, turning her head this way and that, staring at everything. I came last, feeling very beata-like in my brown dress and heavy shoes amid so much vigor and life and color.

We stood with our trunks and I took out the Abbess's letter of introduction we were to present when we arrived. "We must go to the Convent of the Holy Sisters of Jesus of the Andes," I said to the captain. "Can you tell us how we would find it?"

"Ah, so many convents," he replied, waving a hand in the direction of the town. "Often convents and monasteries here are known simply by their local name." He shook his head and shrugged. I steeled myself to ask one of the priests and friars making their way through the noisy throng, but just then someone roared, "Move aside!" and we were all four sent sprawling by a large wagon loaded with fruit, driven by a rough character waving his whip.

Two fine gentlemen in black silk hurried to our rescue, followed by their servants. We were helped to our feet and the men took in our shabby beatas' gowns and our disreputable appearances and I felt it best to explain that we were bound for a convent, and I asked if they knew the convent, known as Las Golondrinas.

The older of the two, a dignified man of about forty with dark piercing eyes, introduced himself as Don Miguel Aguilar and the younger as Don Tomas Beltran. Don Miguel was courteous, but the younger man was the impudent fellow who had kissed his fingertips to Marisol, and who now stared at her with open admiration and winked. Marisol fixed a disdainful gaze on the horizon.

"The swallows' convent, yes!" To my dismay he pointed into the distance where I could just see the mountains and white-capped peaks in the mist, explaining that the convent was in a fine new Spanish city a week's journey inland. Don Miguel said that if we would allow them they would escort us to another convent near the quay where we could stay while travel arrangements were made. It was dangerous for young women to be abroad without servants, and they could see we had none.

Of course we accepted their help. They summoned their carriage, saw our trunks put on, and gave directions to the convent of La Concepción. Don Miguel explained that he had two cousins who were nuns there, and when we reached it he sent a maid to fetch his cousins to the *locutio*.

His cousins were two sweet young nuns who welcomed us cordially, saying we must stay and rest, and that the convent would help procure us wagons and drivers and guards in a few days' time. We asked why the necessity for guards and were alarmed when they told us that the journey was dangerous. Travelers were often attacked by brigands, escaped slaves, or renegade natives, they said.

A young servant girl came and led us to a courtyard with a fountain where she pointed out a quarter for visiting women, with cells and rooms allocated according to wealth and importance. Wealthy ladies in the best apartments, narrow dark cells for women of lesser standing. There was also—she pointed to a barred section in the corner—a women's jail. The courtyard was full of women, children, servants, visiting female relatives, and lapdogs. In the shade by the fountain, two girls were practicing their music with a lute and a guitar.

We were given a plain whitewashed room big enough for three, with coarse linen on the beds. The maid brought water with rose petals for us to wash in, and insisted on taking our traveling clothes to be laundered. She wrinkled her nose as she carried them away. We washed and changed and the maid returned to lead us to a section of the refectory where other visitors were seated at long tables. We helped ourselves from dishes of fish, small flat cakes made of a coarse yellow meal, and strange vegetables in a spicy sauce. The sauce was so fiery it made us gasp and choke, but strangely, after eating it we felt less oppressed by the suffocating atmosphere.

Two older ladies at the table were looking at us with frank curiosity, so I ventured to speak to them and asked if they knew of our rescuers, Don Miguel and Don Tomas. This brought a flurry of eye rolling and exclamations. Don Miguel Aguilar, they said, was a wealthy widower. A very proud man, a *cacique*. We did not know what that was, but before we could ask, they were shaking their fingers warningly, saying to beware of Don Tomas Beltran, who was Don Miguel's godson. Don Tomas—their faces grew long with disapproval—has a dreadful reputation. "A rich young man but given over to vice and licentious ways," whispered one lady. "A frequenter of taverns and brothels. He is the despair of his mother."

"His father has been dead for six months, and Tomas is the eldest son. He should assume his responsibilities as head of the family," said the other, "but so far he has shown no inclination to do his duty. His mother is anxious for marriage to steady him, and she is a lady of some determination. They say she has arranged a good match for him, a girl from a Spanish family. Not pretty, but with a sound bloodline. It is Don Tomas's duty to get a legitimate heir. So far he has perpetuated the line only with mestiza bastards. A great many of them!" Here both ladies shook their heads and tutted again.

Marisol said nothing, but I could tell she was listening closely to this exchange.

A few days later, much restored, we thanked the kind nuns for their hospitality and set out in a hired carriage, our trunks following on a mule-drawn wagon, with armed outriders and a middle-aged laywoman from the convent accompanying us as chaperone. We began to climb above sea level to a plateau where the air was drier and it was clear enough to see the mountains. The guards told us the Incas had built the road, as they had built many others throughout their kingdom. We saw many Inca peasants on the road, wide-faced people with copper complexions burned by the sun and wind, leading long-necked beasts of burden. Their fields of crops were terraced high into the hills, and as we went higher still, great birds soared overhead in a bright-blue sky. "*El condor*," our guides said and crossed themselves.

We stopped the first night just before the sun began to sink, and the guards busied themselves making a campfire. The moment the sun disappeared it grew bitterly cold and we were quickly chilled to the bone. We were given heavy blankets that smelled of mutton and our guards brewed a drink over the campfire. "Chicha," they call it. Though we grimaced at the bitter taste, they insisted we drink it. Afterward we felt lightheaded and ceased to feel the cold. When we lay down to sleep, there was a haunting sound, like the music of the wind. Our chaperone told us it was the drivers' native pipes.

Three afternoons later we had reached a broad plateau and were dozing from the rocking of the carriage when a shout from one of the guards woke us. There was a sharp crack of his whip and we felt the carriage begin to go very fast. "Look, Marisol, that man from the quay is following us on horseback," exclaimed Sanchia, hanging out the carriage window. "The handsome one who bowed to you and laughed when you would not look at him. He is waving his hat. But I do not think he will catch us; we are moving too fast."

"Enough, Sanchia! Don't wave back or I'll box your ears!" Marisol pulled Sanchia inside. "Yes, I think he has gone," Marisol said. She looked out the window a long time to be certain.

On the fifth day we were approaching a narrow pass through some rocks. The carriage halted to let the baggage wagon go through. All the guards but one followed. Then *"Banditos!"* the driver shouted, and looking out we saw a party of mounted men galloping from behind the rocks toward us. The remaining guard drew his musket, but the bandits were upon us, throwing the guard to the ground and wrenching open the carriage door as their horses reared and plunged. They all had scarves across their faces and pushed Sanchia and Pia to the floor. Then their leader pointed to Marisol and beckoned. When she shook her head, in the blink of an eye he reached in and pulled Marisol from the carriage, shrieking, kicking, and biting. He flung her easily onto the front of his saddle, and off they all rode with Marisol's screams ringing in our ears. The guard took aim but could not fire lest he hit her. *"Banditos!"* he spat, and shook his head. "Very bad men!"

They had come and gone within minutes. The chaperone began to wail and supplicate the saints, one by one. The three of us burst into tears, stunned by the horror of what had happened. The guards who had left us came back to see why we had not followed. When they heard what had happened they swore and spoke of going after the bandits—though it was plain they were reluctant, and would not follow very fast.

In the following days we prayed sorrowfully for Marisol and kept an anxious watch for the brigands' return. The mountains seemed no closer, though we had been traveling for days. Finally Sanchia shouted, "I see it!" The driver pointed to a great gate with a cross above it rising above a cluster of buildings, against a background of snow-capped mountains and a very blue sky. "Look lady and young ladies! The convent of Las Golondrinas!"

CHAPTER 23

From the Chronicle of Las Sors Santas de Jesus, by the pen of Esperanza, the New World, Autumn 1552

I presented the Abbess's letter of introduction to the portress and she sent a servant to inform Mother Superior. Our chaperone was anxious to return with the driver and guards as soon as the mules had been fed, but two beatas came out to press her to come in for a meal and a rest first. A barefoot girl came to lead us across a wide courtyard, with a fountain in the middle decorated with patterned tiles, surrounded by earthenware pots with bushes of bright pink and orange flowers. The courtyard was even livelier than the one where we had stayed on our arrival. There the ladies and their servants had a decorous air. Here it was much noisier and busier, thronged with women and their servants walking here and there, calling to each other, stopping to exchange greetings, give an order, or deliver a scolding or quarrel loudly. Children scampered about. Several maids talked and laughed animatedly as they scrubbed clothes at the fountain. Nuns and novices went to and fro herding groups of chattering little barefoot girls from the chapel to the schoolroom.

We were led into a large room that was blessedly cool after the heat of the sun. The white walls were hung with great rectangles of woven stuff, like tapestries, with colorful patterns instead of pictures. There were heavy silver candlesticks as tall as Sanchia and thick as a man's arm, with fat beeswax candles and a large silver-and-gold crucifix on the wall. We should have been relieved that we had reached our destination, but we were too sick at heart about Marisol. A maid with a long braid down her back brought us a tray with hibiscus water and biscuits. We perched on the edges of our chairs sipping our water, feeling dusty and sad.

"Listen," said Pia suddenly, putting down her half-eaten biscuit. "Swallows!" And then we all heard the familiar chattering and scratching under the eaves. "Just like in Spain." I tried to think of something cheerful and encouraging about it being a good omen, but the words died in my throat. All I could think of was Marisol suffering horribly at the hands of the bandits and we were in the middle of nowhere, unable to help her.

There was a sound of footsteps on the other side of the *locutio* and we stood and curtsied to the commanding woman who appeared rather out of breath. A young nun hovered at her elbow. The commanding woman said, "I am Mother Superior and this is Sor Anna. I have read your Abbess's letter. My dear girls, welcome to Las Golondrinas! From Spain! What a journey you have had!"

Sor Anna had placed a high-backed chair murmuring, "Please sit, Mother," and we pulled stools over to the grille and sat, too. I meant to be circumspect about the medal and the Chronicle until I had asked the questions the Abbess and Sor Beatriz had specified. I could see they had been wise. There are so many convents here, and I had to be sure this was the right one.

After polite questions about our health, Mother went straight to the delicate topic of the purpose of our trip. "In her letter the Abbess explains that you are orphans, of good birth, and have come from Spain to find husbands. I hope for your sakes you will find men worthy of coming so far. But why are there only three of you? The letter says four; where is Maria Isabella?"

Sadly I explained what had happened to Marisol.

"Ah!" Mother was shocked, but less than I expected. Shaking her head she said the Abbess had been right to send us, that the civilizing influence of good wives was much needed. They would pray for Marisol. "And the Sor Emmanuela, who is mentioned here—where is your chaperone?"

"Sor Emmanuela, alas, died at sea. As the eldest, I assumed charge," I answered.

"You are most welcome here, of course, but there are many convents closer to the port. All, I am sure, would have given you shelter and helped you find husbands. I am curious to know why you chose to come here."

I asked if I might have a private word with Mother but before she could reply a bell began to ring and she stood. "Tomorrow perhaps. Sor Anna, show them the chapel. I must go now."

We went back across the crowded courtyard, attended vespers, then followed other women into the noisy refectory for a simple meal, again drowned in spicy sauce. Night came quickly and the chapel bell rang for compline, but we were too tired. We fell into our beds and slept soundly.

The next day I followed the girl with the long braid to the *locutio* parlor, where, to my surprise, she slipped a large key into the *locutio* lock, opened the gate, and led me to a parlor full of dark heavy furniture where Mother was waiting. She gestured I was to sit on one of the heavy carved chairs.

Mother wasted no time in pleasantries before saying, "Now Esperanza, tell me, why the need to speak privately?"

I nodded. "Forgive me, Mother, but may I ask you a few questions?" Mother raised her eyebrows but nodded.

"The names of the sisters who founded the order here?"

"Let me see, I think there was Mother Maria Manuela, Sor Inez, Sor Fidelia, Sor Anselma, Sor Blanca, Sor Lucia, Sor Emilia, and Sor Estephana."

Don Miguel had been so sure this was the one! I looked at her. The names were right, but they were hardly uncommon Spanish names, and there were not enough of them. Nine, not twelve. No Sor Salome. Oh dear, this was the wrong convent! My heart sank at the thought of setting out again.

Mother frowned and continued, "There were three more of the party. I cannot recall the names of the two beatas who died when their raft capsized crossing a river, and one novice chose to leave us and marry—the novice Salome."

I sat upright and exclaimed, "The novice Salome *married?*"

"She had not yet taken her final vows, and I assure you that she married with the convent's blessing. There were good reasons for her decision."

"*What reasons?*" I knew I should not sound so disapproving— my own mother had done the same thing—but still I was shocked.

Mother overlooked my rudeness. "I could explain, but it is a long story and it would be best for Dona Salome Aguilar to tell it herself. She is a great benefactor and patroness of our convent, and has donated generously to our school for Indian girls. She is in mourning for her husband who died a year ago. She rarely leaves the family's estate now, which is run by her eldest son, Don Miguel. Besides Don Miguel, the couple had a younger son, Don Matteo, and a daughter, Dona Beatris. Don Matteo Aguilar went into the church. Dona Beatris married a *cacique* and had seven children. Don Miguel Aguilar..."

Don Miguel, the gentleman on the quay who had picked me up...Salome's son! I interrupted to say that we had met Don Miguel when we landed. Mother looked surprised. I hastened to add this was because he and another man had come to our rescue and taken us to a convent where his cousins were nuns. *Cacique*, ladies at that convent had called him. What did that mean?

"It is the term for Inca noble," said Mother. "The Inca nobility are as proud of their *limpieza sangre* as any Spaniard with an ancient Christian family line. Generally convents only admit pure-bred Spanish girls, the daughters of the *hidalgos*, as nuns, but exceptions are made for *caciques*. Native women of other classes enter the convents as servants, sometimes beatas, never nuns. Much importance is paid to birth and blood and family honor here, my dear. A daughter who is a nun is proof of the family's importance, good breeding and faith. I think it is the same in Spain, no?"

I nodded.

Mother frowned. "His father was a descendant of the last Inca Sapa. Don Miguel inherited his blood and his pride, and broods over the iniquities of the Conquistadors, their cruel treatment of the Indians. There have been rumors that he is seditious, and has lent his support to rebellious factions in the mountains. That is a serious matter. There have been many revolts against the Spanish, God knows for good reason, and the landowners who live surrounded by slaves and Indians live in constant fear. Revolts are brutally suppressed."

I gave the medal to Mother, of course, as the gift of the convent in Spain. It was a great responsibility and I am relieved to have delivered it to its destination. Mother was very moved, saying that of course she knew of the medal, but had never expected it to come into this convent's possession. I told her about Sor Beatriz and the Abbess, about the Inquisition, at which she nodded and said that the Inquisition was also established here, but…She shrugged. Like many other things here, it sounds as if it may be less efficient than in Spain.

I told her of the periodic letters from the Holy Office and how they irritated the Abbess, and Mother said they had their own difficulties with the church authorities. However, the church relies on convents like Las Golondrinas for many useful functions, not least of which are the school and orphanage that absorb the embarrassing number of mestiza daughters fathered by Spanish soldiers and settlers. The governing authorities and the church fight a constant battle to prevent Spanish men succumbing to native vices, but are visibly unsuccessful, so both church and the civil authorities are anxious to teach the girls Christian values, in the hope they will eventually exert a civilizing influence as good Catholic wives.

I have many questions to ask, but a nun came to summon Mother to some emergency or other. Mother is rarely able to sit for long—the convent is an excitable place. I said nothing about the Chronicle because Mother mentioned that the convent has no scribe. I will keep this last link to Spain and to Sor Beatriz for the time being. I do not know whether it is wise to try and send a letter back to the convent in Spain. I cannot bear to think what may have happened.

CHAPTER 24

From the Chronicle of Las Sors Santas de Jesus, by
the pen of Esperanza, the Mission Convent of Las
Golondrinas de Los Andes, December 1552

The convent is celebrating the feast of Christmas in a manner
unknown in Spain. The flowers in the courtyard are blooming and
many women have come to stay in the convent. Inside the walls
all is chaos—hawkers of sweets and snacks and makers of toys,
children and visiting nuns, the widows and beatas and relatives
and servants and beggars, together with a great crowd of women
of the streets and bedizened mestiza mistresses and concubines
suddenly turned into what are called here "penitent women" for
the festival. The courtyard is thronged from early morning until
late at night! People push and jostle; small children howl on their
mothers' backs or scamper wildly everywhere. Some women spend
the entire holiday, others come and go on a daily basis. Every cell
is full, and the servants and slaves sleep wherever they can find
space.

In the middle of all this, something called a *santuranticuy*, or
"buying the saints," takes place, a kind of market selling small figures of saints and the Infant Jesus whom local people call *El Niño*.

Everyone must avoid stepping on the clay figures the sellers pile up for sale on native blankets, difficult in this crowded space.

A hot drink called "chocolate" is given out to the poor at the gates of the convent, with snacks. The convent kitchen, as crowded as the courtyard, produces a continuous supply of the local sweet bread with fruit, called *paneton*, and little spicy, savory meat pies paid for by wealthy ladies and some of the richer prostitutes. A great deal of wine and local spirits are drunk at this time. Men stumble about or lie drunk and unconscious in the streets, which may account for why so many women come here, where men are forbidden. Inside our walls there are female musicians and singing and dancing among the women, even the grander ladies.

The night before Christmas is called "*Noche Buena*." The bells rang wildly at midnight and the fiesta continued until dawn. Apparently these exuberant celebrations continue until the arrival of the three kings in January. The lapdogs and parrots are sleepless as everyone else. The dogs run madly through the crowds, tripping servants and barking continuously, while the parrots squawk until they are exhausted and drooping on their perches.

Pia manages to stay aloof and composed, but even she enjoyed many pies and licked her fingers. Sanchia disappeared with some other girls her age, and I glimpsed them prancing and whirling behind the dancing women. I huddle in the least-crowded corner I can find and write down what I observe, for want of something else to do with myself. I miss Marisol, who would have enjoyed it all, but oh for a little peace and quiet!

CHAPTER 25

From the Chronicle of Las Sors Santas de Jesus,
by the pen of Esperanza, the Mission Convent of
Las Golondrinas de Los Andes, May 1553

Mother has written to Salome, but has not yet had a reply. I must be patient. It is the custom here that widows do not receive visitors for at least a year and sometimes longer. Since Easter, Mother has received inquiries from possible suitors for us, though the prospect makes my heart sink. Meanwhile, much as I hate sewing, the three of us have undertaken the mending for the orphanage in return for our room and food, to save our dowries. The dry season has begun and the air is fresher, and we have a favorite shady spot in the bustling courtyard where we sit at our work. Sanchia grumbles that we have been here half a year and she wishes Pia or I would hurry and find a husband, or that she would, so we could leave the convent.

Pia, calm as ever, reminds Sanchia that she is only twelve and too young to worry about such things, but Sanchia, who has grown tall for her age, tosses her black curls and says that here girls younger than she are betrothed and sometimes married by twelve. Pia's friend Zarita, who sits with us most days, nods.

Zarita was such a child wife herself and is in the convent awaiting her divorce. Hopeful divorcees stay in the convent, for propriety's sake, until their petition is considered by the tribunal. Though
it takes a very long time, these petitions are usually granted, and
women go on to marry another husband they like better than the
first one. Sometimes husbands who are being divorced send messages or come to the gate and order or pitifully beg their wives to
come home, rarely with success.

We were scandalized at first. Now we are used to a constant
procession of disgruntled wives, often accompanied by children,
relatives, servants, and their pet birds or dogs. The richer ones
bring household goods that are essential to their comfort—candelabra, gold and silver plates, feather mattresses, and many dresses
and fans and shawls. Occasionally there is a public outburst of hysterics while a would-be divorcee establishes her place in the hierar-
chy of wives, widows, repentant prostitutes, and destitute females
who occupy the courtyard. It is a world of women we have never
seen before and is most entertaining.

Zarita is sixteen and as beautiful as Pia. When they whisper
and giggle with their heads together it is like seeing two flowers,
one fair and one dark. Zarita was married off at the age of nine
by her father, who is now dead. Her brother insists on a divorce
because he wishes her to marry his friend. When asked whether
she hopes her petition will succeed, she shrugs and sighs. Zarita
does not like her brother's friend any better than her first husband,
and would be happy to remain at the convent. She and Pia find
solace in each other's company. But in the end she will be obliged
to obey one man or the other, so she hopes the tribunal will not
hurry.

Pia is unconcerned about her unmarried state, content to pass
her days with Zarita. Mother says that as the eldest of the three of
us, I must be married first. She has made some inquiries on my

behalf, but has rejected several possibilities, saying I will not like the rough ways of many of the colonial men.

Would they like me?

Zarita has a mirror, and when she wasn't looking I picked it up. I have dark eyes, a long nose, long eyelashes, and heavy brows that make me look quite solemn. I tried out a smile. My teeth look very white, possibly because we are all a little brown from the sun. No teeth are missing. I bit my lips to give them a little color, and pinched my cheeks. Would a man like such a face? I am not beautiful like Pia or even pretty like Sanchia; perhaps I resemble my mother.

I told my reflection that I wish I did not have to be married.

There was a bustle and commotion in the courtyard, and I put the mirror down to see that it was caused by a well-dressed woman, veiled, as is the custom among the married women, with a nun and two novices at her elbow and two maids following with cushions and a sunshade and shawls. Clearly she was someone important to have so many people in attendance. The maids plumped the cushions on a bench, a footstool was placed for the lady's feet, and a servant hurried out with hibiscus water. When the lady was settled, a neatly dressed mestiza maid detached herself from the little group, made her way across the courtyard to us, curtsied, and asked our names. When I told her she smiled a little said, "As my mistress said...please come with me."

Pia and Sanchia and I exchanged surprised looks, but put down our sewing and smoothed our skirts and followed the maid to the fine lady's little court. The fine lady threw back her veil and we shrieked, "Marisol!"

"It is!" exclaimed Sanchia and threw herself into Marisol's arms.

I did the same, then Pia, and the four of us laughed and cried and hugged until we were breathless. As usually happens when there is any excitement, everyone else in the courtyard stopped what they were doing to watch. Zarita drifted over and joined us as we settled down around Marisol.

She looked very well. In fact, Marisol looked wonderful. Her dark hair tumbled around her shoulders, her cheeks were pink, and her eyes danced. Rings flashed on her fingers and she wore a great many necklaces. Her face had somehow softened, no longer overcast with anger and impatience. She was also unmistakably pregnant. Clearly much had happened since the terrible day that she was abducted.

She blushed. "It was not so terrible after all. In fact, it was quite romantic."

"Marisol!" We waited in suspense. "Tell us!"

"When the bandits carried me away, I was terrified. But angry, too, that anyone would attack women in this way. The man who seized me was very strong, but fury sustained me, and as we galloped away I determined that when we stopped I would fight, kick, and bite with all my strength. It was the only way not to let the fear overwhelm me.

"We rode and rode, until at last we reached a deserted tumbledown settlement with a few houses that were crumbling and empty, and some sort of chapel with a cross on top. The riders slowed their horses, and though I knew I could count on no help here I decided to fight to the end. I looked up at the villain who had snatched me, and tore the scarf from his face to find it was the impertinent fellow, Don Tomas Beltran! He was laughing and looking rather pleased with himself.

"'Don Tomas!' I exclaimed. 'How dare you treat ladies so!' and slapped him as hard as I could. He looked surprised but caught my wrists before I could strike him again and held them fast, forcing me to listen to him. 'I have an honorable proposal. I need a wife of my own choosing. At this very moment my mother is arranging my wedding to an older woman from a good Spanish family, who is very fat, ugly, and devout, who smells bad, and who is very bossy and will, my mother thinks, succeed in recalling me to my family responsibilities. You, on the other hand…I could not let such a pretty and spirited girl waste away in a convent.'

"This was outrageous of course. But flattering in a way." Marisol smiled. "Then he went on, 'With my father's death I am saddled like a mule with a huge estate and its responsibilities, not least of which is to marry and provide heirs. Legitimate ones, not my others…never mind. I am summoned home to be officially betrothed to the fat dragon, and as my godfather has sworn to have me jailed and taken home by force unless I obey, it is best to marry you now and court you later. It is the only escape I can devise, but I flatter myself that being my wife will have its compensations—I court charmingly. You will be the mistress of a great house and the queen of my heart. You will have many servants and clothes and jewels and everything you desire. Your children will be Beltran heirs. And not least…' He drew a hand down my bodice and I shivered, imagining how it would feel if his hand slid farther. 'Unless, of course, you are too holy to be troubled by carnal thoughts… but somehow I think you are not. For that I love you already. Conveniently,' he pointed to the hovel with the cross on top, 'we are near a priest. And here, as a token of my good faith and our betrothal, is a ring.' He bowed and held it out to me.

"A ragged, rather wild-eyed figure in a priest's cassock shuffled out of the church, squawked like a surprised chicken, raised his hand in benediction and muttered to no one in particular, shuffled back and forth in the dust, as if waiting for worms to appear. The situation was ridiculous—a kidnapping, a pompous proposal in the middle of nowhere, now this human chicken…but the ring was a very large emerald with diamonds. And there was no help to be had in the deserted settlement.

"I said, 'And if I refuse your gracious offer, Don Tomas, this hermit or vagabond or priest, or...chicken...will marry us anyway?'

"He smiled. 'Oh, yes. I will marry you now whether you agree or not, that being the only way I can avoid my mother's plan. But once we are married you will be put to the trouble of swearing to the ecclesiastical court that you were abducted and married against your will. My formidable mother, who I can promise you will be furious, will give you every assistance in your divorce. But consider this—it is also possible that once you are married to me you will not wish to seek an annulment. How else will you know?'

"Arrogant but very handsome. Rich. And his arms carrying me on his horse had been strong. Looking at him I thought, why not accept? The nuns would only find me someone older and duller. I held out my hand and he slipped the ring on my finger. 'Let it be the shortest of betrothals,' he said. The old priest led us into the hot little chapel and married us. Afterward the men who had accompanied Tomas wished us joy, left a horse for me, and rode off. Don Tomas gave the priest a gold coin, leaving the man blinking at such generosity, and led me by the hand into one of the little empty houses as the sun was setting. He unpacked food, spread our blankets on the ground, and built a blazing fire that soon matched our passion that night.

"The next morning, Tomas said I was a married woman, Dona Maria Isabella Beltran de Vilar d'Ascension, and when he brought me home as his bride he would insist his family not call me by my childhood name but Dona Maria, as befits the heir's wife. We needed all the dignity we could muster between us—when I met his mother, I would understand.

"Tomas led my horse by the bridle to keep it from running away. I had never been on a horse before and it was thrilling to be so high up, though it made my back stiff and legs sore at first.

We rode along together as husband and wife, talking and talking, sometimes arguing, often laughing, as if we would never stop.
Tomas told me about the country, how his family had come with
the conquistadors and been granted a vast tract of land with many
silver mines and *encomienda* rights."

"What are those?" asked Esperanza.

"It is what has made the Beltrans rich. The natives that live on
the land must make payments to us with a proportion of their crops.
It is like the feudal system in some parts of Europe, I believe."

"And what crops are those?"

"There is a kind of nut in the ground, not like the almond trees
we had in Spain, and roots called "manioc," a beautiful reddish-
gold fruit with even more beautiful sweet flesh inside, and a green
fruit called "avocado" that is very pleasing to eat when peeled and
sprinkled with salt and chilies. Tomas also told me about the family.
He has three younger sisters, but since his mother has decreed that
the two younger girls are to enter a convent, he is only responsible
for finding a husband for the eldest, who has had to wait until Tomas
was married. He told me about the peasants who worked his family's
land, and the way his mother controlled them and her family and
even the local priest with an iron hand. She is also very, very devout.

"I told him a little about myself, mainly what I thought would
interest his mother—that my father had commanded a fleet, that
my mother had been a royal ward, that both had died. I did not
say anything about Consuela and my brothers and the evil gossip
about the crown prince that destroyed our family. And while we
were far from Spain, there were Spanish administrators here—
who knew what these authorities might do with the information?
My life had taken an interesting turn and I did not want to attract
their attention.

"Finally on the eighth day, Tomas pointed to a cluster of buildings on the horizon. 'The Beltran hacienda,' he sighed. As we rode

very slowly toward it he warned me to say nothing to his mother of the way he had abducted me. His mother's views on etiquette are as rigid as those on everyone's duty to her.

"After days of traveling I knew I could not look particularly fresh, not to mention being in a state of dishevelment because Tomas kept stopping the horses and pulling me down to the blankets with him. I made him stop by a stream and I did my best to wash off the dust and smooth my hair, and Tomas straightened his clothes and brushed himself off as best he could. Then as we were dressing I saw he was eyeing my bosom again and I was about to protest that this was not the time, but he said only that I should button my bodice to the top and draw my shawl tightly round my shoulders. A note of anxiety had crept into his voice. After that, our progress toward the hacienda slowed to a crawl. Tomas seized every excuse to stop, pointing out trees and bushes as if they were the most interesting objects in the world, or saying he had spotted a snake here or a puma there as a boy. He swore he saw the wild creature *La Llorana*, who killed her own children and is doomed to walk the earth seeking them, snatching human children whenever she can. Tomas said she had tried to take him once, but he had a lucky escape.

"I said that if she had succeeded, *La Llorana* would no doubt have returned any child who talked as much as Tomas. Finally we saw a large cluster of buildings with blue shutters, and in the distance a boy left the fields and ran for the gate of a large sprawling house.

"By the time we rode up to the house, waiting for us on the veranda was a fat, beetle-browed woman dressed in black who looked like a human thundercloud. Three dark-haired girls younger than Tomas peered from behind her with interested expressions. The woman pointed at me rudely and asked how her son dare parade his harlot before his mother and innocent sisters. When Tomas introduced me as his wife, she looked stricken, then raised her hands to heaven and emitted a loud piercing wail. She struck her breast dramatically—quite a large one that looked as if it could take a great many blows without the least damage—and called on the Virgin and the saints, one by one, to witness a mother's trials while her daughters patted her ineffectually and whispered 'Mama, hush!' When she finally calmed down she looked at me as if I were some putrefying tidbit one of the mongrel dogs had brought home, and launched into an insulting diatribe. It was plain to see that I was a slut of no birth, no dowry, and who knew what kind of mongrel blood. It was not enough to rut with the peasants and people half the hacienda with his bastards; now nothing would do but to import prostitutes from the cesspool of the city to bring grief to his mother's heart and kill her in her old age. God would punish him! And this so-called marriage he had been tricked into would be annulled at once.

"She ranted in this vein for half an hour, not letting Tomas get a word in, swearing to disinherit him unless Tomas divorced me immediately. I simply stared at her unmoved, thinking, 'So this fat toad is my enemy?' What a great many bad words she knows.

"Tomas's family is too wealthy to need my dowry. When my new mother-in-law came to that particular issue Tomas finally spoke up, pleading that he had thought to please her by bringing home a true Spanish bride of *lipienza sangre* which she has taught him was better than any dowry. He added that I was a model of piety, had been at school in the oldest and holiest convent in Spain. And had traveled to Spanish America with a party of nuns bound for Las Golondrinas convent. Our marriage had been sanctioned by the church, and if she did not accept it there would be a scandal. And now that he was married, it was possible that a legitimate Beltran heir would appear in the next year. This only partly satisfied Tomas's mother, who continued to rumble with bad temper like a large volcano about to erupt.

"I knew I must establish my rightful place in this embattled household at once or the dragon on the veranda would make my life intolerable. After all, Tomas was master of the estate now, and as his bride, mother-to-be of his children, and mistress of the hacienda, I must make it clear that I was in charge and I would never be bullied. I raised my head as high as I could, and looked her haughtily straight in the eye—something I had noticed her daughters and even Tomas avoided. Then I looked around me and sniffed disdainfully, as if the hacienda had a bad smell. 'The estate is smaller than I expected. Much smaller. And the family *far* less well-bred than I had been led to believe. I am disappointed.' Holding her gaze, I held out my hand imperiously for Tomas to help me dismount. I strode up the veranda steps, back ramrod straight, staring coldly at her as I gave her a curtsy so perfunctory it was an insult. 'Dona Maria Isabella *Beltran* de Vilar d'Ascension, at your service.' Then I swept silently into the house ahead of her, head held high like the royal princess some believed me to be. This rude little performance left the three girls gasping, and silenced my mother-in-law. I think she expected me to cry and wring my hands and beg forgiveness. Señora Beltran and I now have a daily battle of wills but I usually win. Tomas is in awe of us both."

"And Marisol," Sanchia exclaimed, "we will call you Marisol when we are together, not Dona Maria Isabella. You're expecting a baby!"

"Yes, even Tomas's mother is pleased he will have a *legitimate* heir." A shadow crossed Marisol's face. Her expression changed fleetingly and I saw that something gives her pain and that she struggles against it. Her big emerald-and-diamond ring on her finger sparkled and we all leaned over to admire it.

Marisol said that she would stay several days with us, that Tomas had business nearby. She returned the bows of several other wealthy women of her acquaintance also staying in the

convent—evidently as the wife of Don Tomas Beltran she is someone to be bowed to.

"I must tell you a story," she whispered, turning back to us
after her bowing. "The ladies over there have built at their own
expense a special chapel in town for repentant fallen women. As
you know, there are many brothels and prostitutes and concubines
in the city but"—she giggled—"men here are notoriously generous, and fallen women often live very well. So"—she giggled even
harder, and nodded in the direction of a group of finely dressed
young women fanning themselves in a far corner—"*those* fallen
ladies are reluctant to abandon their lifestyles permanently. They
come to stay at the convent for the festivals or just to have a rest.
None, however, will set foot in the new chapel, because it would
be embarrassing for them to declare themselves fallen so publicly.
So the new chapel stays empty."

We were all surprised to hear such easy talk of brothels and
concubines, but Zarita looked unconcerned. "Yes, the men have
many mistresses among the mestizas, and live openly with them as
if they were married. The women have children and go about very
finely dressed, even to church." Zarita leaned over to tuck a stray
lock of hair behind Pia's ear and the two smiled at each other.

I, too, had a great many things to tell Marisol, beginning with
the fact that Sor Beatriz had had a daughter who was among the
nuns who had founded the mission over thirty years before.

"No!" Marisol exclaimed. "Do you suppose they sent her here
to keep her existence a secret? I mean, a nun with a child? It must
have been awkward for Sor Beatriz. I wonder who the father was."

And so we passed the next few days very pleasantly, gossiping
in the courtyard between prayers and meals, speculating on who the
father of Sor Beatriz's child might have been, and wondering what
sort of person Salome is. I told the others her story and said that
I was determined to meet her. Finally Don Tomas sent a servant

to say that he had completed his business and they must leave. In parting Marisol said she was rich enough and we must divide her dowry between us. She also promised to send the carriage soon so we could pay her a visit before the baby came. Mother was as happy as we to learn that Marisol's kidnap ordeal had ended well, though she shook her head over Don Tomas's scandalous behavior.

CHAPTER 26

From the Chronicle of Las Sors Santas de Jesus, by the

pen of Esperanza, the Beltran Hacienda, July 1553

Marisol kept her word. A servant brought an invitation to visit and Mother sent for a dressmaker because our gowns were shabby and ragged at the hems. The dressmaker, an impoverished Spanish widow, was to make us each three new gowns—one for morning, one for afternoons and visiting, and one for evening parties. We accompanied her to the market where she bargained hard with the merchants for fabrics and lace, and a shoemaker took the measure of our feet for new leather slippers. Mother said that her price was fair, though our new finery ate up an alarming amount of our dowry money. Mother herself purchased Chinese fans as gifts for us, saying all ladies carried them nowadays.

Mother said that the Beltrans have a large circle of acquaintances among the local landowners, many of them single men.

The Beltran carriage arrived, with two armed outriders and a maid to look after us. Our trunks with our new dresses and laces and fans were tied on the top. My trunk also contained this Chronicle. Though I should give it up to the convent, I cannot bring myself to part with it yet and dare not leave it for others to find in my absence, especially as the length of our visit is uncertain. Here people seem to be very casual about their visits, and Mother expects we will stay with the Beltrans for weeks. Pia and Zarita were sad to part, but Zarita assured Pia that divorces always took a long time and that she would still be at the convent when Pia returned. They embraced farewell, like two flowers kissing in the breeze.

The Beltran hacienda is a four-day journey from the convent. We have been here for two weeks, and Mother was right, Marisol and Tomas have invited a number of men to call on one pretext or another. In the gloomy *sala* with its heavy furniture and holy images and crucifixes crowding every available space, we sit silently on display every afternoon, sipping sugar water, our eyes modestly cast down. The fine clock Tomas's father brought from Spain at unimaginable expense ticks loudly in the background and keeps the wrong time. The men drink a fiery alcohol made of some local plant and talk among themselves, walking up and down the *sala* like prize cocks, looking us over haughtily, as if we were livestock.

It is horrid!

The men circle Pia like wasps around a honeycomb. Dona Luisa, Tomas's mother, watches us like a hawk, and if we so much as speak to one of the men, purses her lips and complains that we are shameless hussies. Dona Luisa especially disapproves of Pia, possibly because Tomas's eldest sister Rita is not only the same age as Pia, but is considerably plainer. Dona Luisa makes sure they do not sit next to one another on the settee when we have callers.

Pia is genuinely indifferent to the men, although they write her poems and bring her flowers and languish pointedly in her presence looking sick with love. Marisol points out the advantages of this one or that one and tries to arouse some interest, but with no success. Pia misses Zarita.

Sanchia has suddenly become quite pretty. She has grown tall for her age, and quite graceful, with a lovely complexion and dark eyes full of mischief. She looks much older than thirteen and does her best to flirt with Pia's suitors. The child should never have been allowed a fan—she has found she can summon a man to her side in minutes simply by fluttering her eyelashes over the top. I am alarmed to see that they do not regard her as a child, and Tomas has been forced to remonstrate with several inflamed young rascals that Sanchia is not yet old enough to marry. This makes Sanchia very cross. She loves attention.

Marisol has offered to have Sanchia live there. But Sanchia, much as she loves Marisol, does not wish to live where there is so little excitement. Especially in the same hacienda as watchful, censorious Dona Luisa. She wants to return to the convent with Pia and me and see what the future brings. She means she will see whom we marry and make her decision then.

We had been with Marisol a month and should have gone sooner, but there was to be a ball at the regional governor's home and all the local landowners for miles around were obliged to attend with their wives and daughters. Marisol was very large now, but over-rode Dona Luisa's objections and insisted on going to chaperone us. She would not hear of the two younger Beltran girls staying behind as their mother wished, either, much to their joy. A social outing was a rare treat for them.

The day of the ball we rose very early to bathe and dress and Marisol unlocked her leather chests of jewelry and said we must all borrow what we liked. Tomas has given her a king's ransom in jewels and we spent an entire morning playing with the glittering pile, trying pieces on and debating about what would suit our new dresses or match our eyes.

There is a tall looking glass with a gilded frame in our room, and when we were dressed we took turns scrutinizing our reflections, amazed at our own and each other's transformations. I am tall, like my father, but the seamstress was skillful and my new dress disguises my awkward height. I think it is very pretty—deep-blue silk with an underskirt of pale yellow edged in lace. My hair was braided and coiled round my head, with waxy white flowers that smelled heavenly, and a pearl-and-sapphire necklace and earrings grand enough for a princess. I picked up my fan and practiced furling, unfurling, half-furling it over the lower half of my face, leaving only my eyes visible over the top—this is how Sanchia does it. The girl in the looking glass staring back at me over her fan is not the least beata-like.

By the time the eight of us were crowded into the carriage early that afternoon, even black-clad Dona Luisa could not dampen our spirits with her lecture about proper behavior that she kept up all the way to the governor's.

The journey seemed endless, but finally we arrived to a splendid, festive scene. There was a garden filled with tall sweet-smelling plants, a fountain, and torches everywhere. There was a group of musicians and a troupe of performers making a display of lively peasant dancing and singing. We followed Marisol and Dona Luisa inside to make our curtsies to the governor's wife. The house blazed with candles, and servants in elaborate livery and bare feet handed around trays of delicious cordials. Around us the women were sparkling with jewelry. Everyone seemed to be talking at once. Sanchia's eyes flashed as she flirted over her fan when she thought I wasn't looking, and even Pia was laughing at a story a young man was telling her.

When the ball began there were so few unmarried girls we were engaged for every dance and did not sit down once. Dona Luisa took a chair among a group of other dowagers close to the dance floor where they could keep a close watch on all the girls. Every time there was a break in the dancing, Dona Luisa grabbed poor Rita and hurried her off for a lecture.

Later, after a splendid supper had been served at midnight, I was sitting alone waiting for Dona Luisa to return with Rita when a gentleman stopped and bowed and wished me good evening. I looked up. "Don Miguel!" I exclaimed. Don Miguel Aguilar—now that I knew whose son he was, I tried to discern a resemblance to Sor Beatriz in his face, but I could not. His native blood has shaped his features. He has heavy brows and piercing dark eyes, and his brown skin is set off by the whiteness of the ruff around his neck. He was dressed in black with many gold chains and looked very distinguished.

I said that I understood we had him to thank for Marisol's unusual marriage, that had he not sworn to drag an unwilling Don Tomas home for the betrothal arranged by Dona Luisa, Don Tomas would never have carried off Marisol the way he did. Don Miguel unbent and smiled a little, saying that courting in the colony was conducted in a different manner than in Spain. "Evidently," I said, laughing, "but Marisol is very happy all the same."

Don Miguel is serious, rather intense and proud. I was surprised that he continued to sit by my side, but then he is very courteous. I was grateful to him for not leaving me to sit alone without my friends. I asked him to tell me more about the country and he grew quite passionate in telling me. It became clear, as the ladies said on our first evening in the country, that he resents Spanish treatment of the natives. He is very eloquent on the poor souls forced into the silver mines, slaves and peasants alike, and the massacres and looting by the Spanish. It is shocking to hear such stories, and he must have seen it in my expression because he fell silent.

Then I said that Mother had written to his mother to ask if I might visit and pay my respects when her mourning was over, if that would not be too great an intrusion, because I had messages to deliver from the nuns in Spain. He said that he was sure she would be delighted to receive me. I wondered if he knew he was Sor Beatriz's grandson, whether Salome had ever told him of the circumstances of her birth. Most of the fine Spanish ladies speak and act with exaggerated propriety, so perhaps Salome has said nothing.

Then Doña Luisa interrupted us and thrust Rita toward Don Miguel, elbowing me out of the way. Don Miguel stood, bowed, murmured his compliments, and withdrew. Dona Luisa *humpffed* indignantly. "He should marry again," she said, looking after Don Miguel's retreating back. "Only half Inca, but his father was a prince. A good Spanish wife would soon put an end to his nonsense about the natives. You might have said something to make him notice you, Rita! Don't stand about like a donkey! He was taking enough notice of Esperanza when she talked to him."

Poor Rita is completely under her mother's thumb, at her beck and call day and night, and would willingly marry the devil himself if it would take her away from home. "Yes, Mama." She sighed.

I thought Rita and Don Miguel would be a most unfortunate combination. There is a sense of contained anger and power in Don Miguel that is somehow at one with this place, the vast mountains, the brightness of the light, the great plateau. He is fiercely proud of the fact that his father was a descendant of the Inca emperors, the sun gods on earth they called them. A heathen deity and a cruel one by all accounts. Giving sweet, inoffensive Rita to such a man would be sacrificing her, just as they say the Incas once sacrificed maidens.

As the dancing began again Dona Luisa whisked Rita away as Pia hurried over to me with an alarmed look on her usually placid features. "Sanchia has disappeared," Pia whispered. A cluster of young men hovered nearby, waiting to ask Pia to dance, gazing at her like a herd of lovesick llamas. She ignored them completely.

"Sanchia was dancing, and while Dona Luisa was busy trying to get Rita a partner and not watching, Sanchia and her partner escaped onto the veranda. Now I cannot find her."

Pia and I edged away from the throng of adoring beaux to look for Sanchia. Perhaps she too had been kidnapped—a willing victim if ever there was one. God help her kidnapper! But at last we discovered her behind the stables with the musicians and their dancing girls. Her face was flushed and her skirts hitched up. She said she had been learning native songs and dances.

Pia and I kept her between us for the rest of the night.

It is September and we know we should return to the convent, but news has reached us of an outbreak of smallpox. Marisol wishes for our company and will not allow us to return until the danger is past. She is so large and round now she can barely move, and we have all felt the baby kicking vigorously. Tomas waits on her hand and foot, and even Dona Luisa grumbles more quietly. Rita is to be the baby's godmother and Don Miguel to be godfather—Dona Luisa's idea. She hopes it will bring them together.

Marisol dreads the coming ordeal. She remembers her mother. Though I do not say so, I, too, think of my mother who died giving birth to me and feel frightened for my friend. Pia and I are saying a novena for Marisol.

Life has grown very quiet on the hacienda as every hour we expect a sign the baby is coming. There are few visitors, so Sanchia has prevailed on Tomas to send for the musicians and the dancing girls she befriended to amuse us in the *sala*. They are installed in the servants' quarters, to Dona Luisa's annoyance—but Marisol enjoys the way they enliven our evenings after dinner, so she countermanded Dona Luisa's order they leave. Sanchia now dances as well as any of the troupe, as she demonstrates at every opportunity.

Pia is anxious about Zarita. We get little news here save for the fact that the epidemic has been very bad and many have died.

Marisol has been screaming for two days in her darkened room. I take my turn to sponge her face and hold her hands, until I cannot bear it any longer! Tomas paces to the stables and back, unable to be still for a moment. There are many children on the estate who are plainly his. How many times has he been responsible for this agony? I begin to hate Tomas. And all men. Dona Luisa says the natives and peasants do not feel pain in the way that high-bred Spanish women do. At mealtimes she regales us with *her* descriptions of childbirth—what Marisol suffers is nothing in comparison, she insists.

Marisol has a son *and* a daughter, both healthy. *Deo gratias!* She, however, was frighteningly white and weak, bleeding heavily, and feverish after the birth. Nothing I could remember from the medical texts was efficacious and I was in despair until one of the native women servants pushed her way into the room with a poultice and an herbal drink that stank horribly, and refused to move from Marisol's side to make sure Marisol drank a little throughout the day. Otherwise I am sure she would have died. Dona Luisa has kept a priest at the ready, for baptism and last rites. Tomas has dark circles under his eyes and looks much older suddenly. The babies have been christened Marianna and Teo Jesus. When Dona Luisa told Marisol what names she had chosen for them, Marisol only opened her eyes for a second and closed them again, too weak to argue.

Dona Luisa has found a wet nurse for the babies. We sit by Marisol's side and feed her broth, alarmed at her lethargy and pallor, though she is recovering, we hope. I heard Tomas's younger sisters whispering that they were glad they were going to be nuns and avoid the torments of childbirth.

A month after the birth Marisol can finally leave her bed and sit on the veranda. The twins are large lusty babies and thrive on their wet nurse's milk. Sanchia, Pia, Rita, and I take it in turns to walk them up and down, while Dona Luisa complains that we will spoil them. Don Miguel has paid us a visit to see his new godchildren and brought each a small golden cup. He and Tomas rode out for the day and went hunting, which did Tomas good. Marisol is well enough to argue with Dona Luisa about the babies' feeding schedule and contradict Dona Luisa's orders about what the cook was to prepare for dinner.

It is time to return to the convent.

CHAPTER 27

From the Chronicle of Las Sors Santas de Jesus, by
the pen of Esperanza, the Mission Convent of Las
Golondrinas de Los Andes, October 1553

They said the smallpox had abated. But when we entered the gate,
a funeral procession was gathered around a bier in the courtyard.
The last victim, said the portress, one of the ladies waiting for her
divorce.

"Which lady?" faltered Pia.

"A young one," said the portress. "The epidemic had slowed.
There had been no new cases, then suddenly she contracted the
diuuuuu und it plouuud God to take her from the hands of men.
Now neither her brother nor her husband nor her would-be husband may have her."

"No! Not Zarita!" Pia stifled a scream and before we could
stop her, jumped down from the carriage and ran toward the bier.
Like a madwoman she pushed the startled priest and sisters around
it away and tore off the shrouds, crying "Who is it? Who?" Then
a great scream echoed around the courtyard. "Zarita! Zarita! No,
no, no! I was not here...I did not know...come back! Do not leave
me! Live again, Zarita! Oh, Zarita!"

Sanchia and I caught hold of a frenzied Pia to drag her away, but could not help seeing the horrible dead thing on the bier. Poor Zarita, so beautiful in life, was hideously swollen and disfigured in death and, most grotesquely, was beginning to putrefy.

It took all our strength together with two strong beatas to pull Pia away and get her to our chamber, where she collapsed in hysterics. Sanchia and I sat and tried to comfort her all night, but Pia sobbed and moaned and shrieked "Zarita!" like one possessed. Sometime in the night Sanchia and then I fell asleep, worn out from the journey, sorrow for Zarita, and for poor Pia.

The next morning Sanchia and I woke to the sound of scissors. We rubbed the sleep from our eyes to see Pia standing naked, her silvery hair covering her feet. She had cut it as close to the scalp as she could and her head was bloody in places. Her eyes had sunk into their sockets and blazed with a strange light. "All flesh decays, all beauty, even Zarita. Only the spirit remains and things of the spirit. God has opened my eyes and my vocation has been revealed to me. I must go to Mother at once and tell her."

Sanchia and I exchanged frightened glances. "Yes, we should go to Mother at once," agreed Sanchia, thrusting her feet into her shoes while I quickly hid the scissors. "But please, put on your shift first."

Mother insisted we leave Pia alone with her. We hovered outside the door, listening to Mother's measured tones and Pia's keening response, an unearthly sound that grew louder and louder, then turned to deranged shrieking. Sanchia rushed to summon help and four strong beatas came running from the infirmary. Mother called them to enter, and between them they held a struggling, kicking, snarling Pia and took her away. Pia's high-pitched screams of anguish followed us until we put our hands over our ears and ran, in tears, for our room.

Afterward we learned that Pia somehow managed to snatch the *golondrina* medal from Mother. No one can find it. Sanchia and I visit her each day. She presses her face against the grille and whispers hoarsely that she is an anchorite and will pray for us all. The infirmary sisters say Pia stays on her knees and will take no food, only a little water. In this convent the nuns never wear the cilice— it is discouraged as excessive, but she has somehow procured one and wears it around her waist under her shift, which is now spotted with blood. Pia insists that when she wears it she is visited by angels who look like Zarita. Other times she says demons enter her cell and torment her. She screams her prayers and has bitten the sisters who nurse her.

In our distress over Pia I had forgotten Salome. A servant arrived with a note inviting Sanchia and me to visit her. Don Miguel's doing, no doubt. I was reluctant to accept but Mother said we must go, that Salome is a great benefactress of the convent and having sought the invitation it would be ungracious not to accept. I confess it will be a relief to be away. The convent is a sad place, in mourning for all who died in the epidemic, while those who caught the smallpox and survived are badly scarred—a constant reminder, Mother says, to guard against vanity.

A carriage pulled by beautiful white mules and emblazoned with the Aguilar arms came for us, with a coachman, two footmen, a maid, an armed guard and a Spanish captain's widow to act as chaperone. Sanchia and I again packed our dresses, though our hearts were too heavy to take any pleasure in our finery.

CHAPTER 28

From the Chronicle of Las Sors Santas de Jesus,
by the pen of Esperanza, the Hacienda of the
Sun and the Moon, January 1554

Salome's home, the Hacienda of the Sun and the Moon, lies three days away. Like Salome and her Inca husband, it is a house of two worlds, Spanish and native. It stands on the ruins of an Inca palace, and Salome tells me that it was one of many palaces belonging to her husband's family. After it was destroyed by a great earthquake the stones were used to rebuild it in a kind of Spanish style, around a courtyard with a fountain. She is not at all a fine Spanish lady like the colonial wives, but a handsome, reflective woman at one with the house, with the place.

Beside the gate there is a family chapel with a stone altar and a dazzling gold-and-silver altar screen and wooden statues of the saints with native faces. The house itself is very large and low, filled with the tapestry-like hangings of wool dyed beautiful colors that caught my eye in the convent, earthenware pots and other fine native artifacts, as well as silver candlesticks and the heavy carved furniture that is common here. Her house is tranquil, comfortable, and well ordered. Her slaves and servants go quietly about their work, with less of the excitable ways I have seen elsewhere. Inside the rooms lead one into another around a tiled courtyard with a fountain and many flowers. When we admired it, Salome said there was once a garden made of gold and silver, with jeweled flowers. But, she said with a smile, she prefers living things and oversees the garden herself.

There is nothing of the fashionable colonial lady about her. Salome wears a kind of native tunic of fine wool over a longer, plainer dress of cotton, which suits her very well. Her hair is nearly gray now, and her sad eyes are beautiful and deep. She is very like Sor Beatriz in looks and manner. When she speaks, it is in a considered and intelligent way, like Sor Beatriz.

One of the rooms is a small library with a splendid view of the mountains in the distance. She spends much of the day here, reading, praying, and writing to her daughter, Beatris, and son Fr. Matteo all the news of the hacienda, births and deaths and marriages of the servants and natives and slaves on the estate, the crops and animals, her garden. The library was made especially for her by her husband. She bears her widowhood stoically and does not speak of her grief, but she does not need to. It hovers about her.

She welcomed Sanchia and me very kindly. The morning after our arrival, Sanchia went off to watch the excitement in the garden where the gardeners were trying to catch a large poisonous snake. In what would become the pattern of our days there, Salome saw to her housekeeping and gave orders for meals, then drew me into her study to talk until dinnertime, as Sanchia rode or explored outdoors. We spoke easily of many things.

I told her it had come as a shock to learn Sor Beatriz had a daughter, and gave her all the news of her mother and the convent. I told her how kind Sor Beatriz had been to me, how she had trained me as her assistant. "It sounds like you took my place," said Salome. "I am glad. And the Inquisition? We hear a little. Is it really as bad now as they say?"

I said it was, and she was alarmed to learn that a tribunal had come to Las Golondrinas just at the time we left, although I did not explain why the Abbess did not want it to find us.

It took a long time to tell Salome all the convent news. It had not been possible for her to send or receive letters from Spain until the conquistadors had come, and after that she had written many times to the convent but never received a reply. I assured her that no letter from her had come, and that it wasn't until Sor Serafina repeated her brothers' tales of the colony that the order realized the missionaries had not drowned or been taken by pirates. Once Salome asked, "I don't suppose my mother ever spoke to you of my father? No? She would never speak of him to me either. I believe she had her reasons for keeping that secret."

She looked so pensive and sad that I changed the subject, telling her about Don Tomas Beltran and how he had abducted our friend. This made Salome laugh. She said it was very like Tomas to do such a thing, that as an only son he had been dreadfully spoiled until he believed he must have his own way in everything. Don Miguel had become his godfather when Don Miguel was only sixteen. Since then he had gotten Tomas out of many scrapes, placated many an infuriated husband and father, and he now hoped that Tomas would be content with one woman for the time being. Salome patted my hand reassuringly and said that Marisol sounded as if she had a mind of her own, and she understood Dona Luisa took the birth of Marisol's twins as a personal compliment—twins ran on her side of the family. Poor Rita, who had finally been married, was now expected to produce twins, too.

Another day I told Salome about Pia.

I woke each day hoping it might bring Don Miguel to the hacienda, but there was no sign of him. Salome said that he lived in his own wing of the house, but family business often obliged him to be gone for long periods of time. She was clearly uncomfortable speaking of his absence. I understood what she did not wish to say. Don Miguel lives with a mistress, probably with their children as well, as is the way here. I said nothing more about Don Miguel. It was her turn to tell me her story. There was so much I longed to know. It took the better part of a week for her to tell me, and I recorded it as she did.

I left Spain over thirty years ago on what I believed was an adventure to build a mission in Gran Canaria. The Abbess had obtained permission from the church to send missionaries to establish a convent and a school for native women and girls there. I believe the church authorities agreed because Muslim traders in Gran Canaria had begun building mosques and the church and Spain wanted to forestall the Muslim presence there.

I was longing to go, and my prayers were answered when the Abbess chose me. My mother and I wept when we parted, but we expected she would come with a second party of nuns when the new mission was established. I can still remember how exciting the trip to Seville seemed. The world beyond the convent walls was vast! Mountains and valleys, farms, villages and peasants, castles, the rivers and plains—then Seville itself! Sor Maria Manuela, who was in charge of the party, was continually telling us to lower our veils.

The ship and the sea seemed wonderful at first. It was agreeable flying over the water with a salt breeze on our faces, though the sailors pointed to the horizon and told us that was the Sea of Fog and Darkness, where sea djinnis dwell and prey on ships blown their way. They reassured us that Gran Canaria was less than ten days away and there was nothing to fear. But next morning the sky had turned dark, and suddenly there was a terrible storm with lightning and howling winds, and we were locked into the hold as waves crashed across the deck.

I can still remember that terrifying ordeal. It was dark in the hold and we lost track of whether it was day or night as the ship shuddered with the pounding of the waves. We were violently ill, seawater had soaked into our cabin and everything around us was foul and cold. Worst of all, we knew we had been blown into the awful Sea of Fog and Darkness whose perils the sailors had described to us. As the miserable hours, then days passed, I thought of my mother and prayed she not blame herself for giving permission. We realized that we would never reach Gran Canaria, and tried to encourage each other to meet death bravely. Then as suddenly as it had come, the storm died, and the captain threw open the hatch and shouted, "Sisters! The storm has passed and Gran Canaria lies ahead!"

It seemed a miracle when air and sunshine poured into our hold. We crawled up onto the deck and saw land ahead and the sailors prostrated in prayer in the Muslim way, abandoning all pretense of Christianity after deliverance from such an ordeal. We knelt, too, and gave thanks. When we finished we saw that the closer we drew to land the more puzzled the captain looked. It was certainly not the busy harbor the sailors had described. After we anchored in a deserted cove he tried to work out where we might be from his charts. The sailors set about assessing the damage to the ship and found freshwater on land. That night we feasted on fish roasted over the fire and strange fruits growing on the edge of the forest. In a few days we had all regained strength and the captain and a few of the older sailors sat awake late into the night trying to determine where we were by the stars.

Then one afternoon painted men appeared out of the forest, and attacked us with bows and arrows, wounding the captain badly. We hurried back onto the ship and sailed on along the coast, as close as the sailors dared, our party now taking turns to watch for reefs under the water.

Having avoided death at sea, it began to seem we would perish near land, though no one knew what land this might be. Some thought India and some thought China. Different tribes along the way met us with hostility each time we tried to pull in to shore, and the captain's wound festered. He grew feverish and drifted in and out of consciousness in his cabin. We had our medicines and treated him as best we could, but the poor captain finally died in great agony. After they dropped his body overboard next day, a row blew up between those who believed we should go forward and those who were determined to turn back. The argument was decided as we saw we were approaching a narrow isthmus and the plan in favor of turning back was agreed, when, just as the ship came about, we saw a great mass of water swirling around itself on the way we had just come. The lookout shouted the alarm and an order to come about again at once—it was a trap of the devil to suck ships and men straight down to hell. Sailors rushed to the ropes and pulled with all their might to change the sails. Just in time, our ship changed course and swung back toward the isthmus at such a speed that there was no choice except to sail through.

We went slowly along another coast until we were woken at dawn when the ship ran aground on a submerged rock and water poured in through a hole in the keel. We all bailed as best we could, and waited most of the day before going ashore to see if our presence had attracted any natives. It had been many days since we had eaten more than a few bites of fish; we were in need of freshwater and we were exhausted from bailing.

We found a stream beneath the trees at the end of the beach. The trees were hung with vines and the air was full of shadows and silence, the calls of strange birds and the sounds of animals or reptiles moving in the undergrowth. Though we saw no one, we felt some presence near the stream so we drank quickly, filled our skins with water, and hastened back. The sailors were busy building a fire and catching fish, discussing how best to mend tears in the sails and patch the hole in the gunnel. The damage was worse than they had thought and they said unhappily that repairs would take days. They unloaded our bundles and chests and we spread their mildewing contents to dry and air in the sun. Beyond the shore, there were snow-covered mountains one behind the other against a bright-blue sky. Had we not been frightened, lost, and hungry it would have been a magnificent sight, but by this time our spirits were very low.

The sun began to sink, and we women hurried to collect firewood from the edge of the forest. We did not notice the warriors approaching. By the time we looked up they had surrounded us.

They were well made, tall and muscular men, with dark hair and deep-brown skin, beardless. They wore a sort of uniform or livery, identical tunics with lengths of cloth wrapped about their heads, much like the Muslims wear. Their commander was the tallest of the group. He had strong, handsome features, and a helmet fashioned like an animal's head, its mouth bared in a snarl. The light of our fire flickered on their bronze skin, their shields and spears with gold tips, and the great gold discs like the sun that hung from the commander's ears. They were a frightening sight, but they simply stared, making no move to attack or harm us. Instead they pointed at the ship and conversed among themselves, yet when the commander looked at us huddled together I sensed restraint and courtesy. His eyes were dark and deep, and his chest very broad. Sor Maria Manuela finally nudged me and snapped, "Do not stare so, Salome! Close your mouth!"

The commander and his men gathered around the terrified sailors, who with signs and pointing, attempted to explain where we had come from. The commander pointed at us, and the sailors shook their heads and gestured violently to explain that we were not their women. One of them pointed to us and then to the sky, over and over. "Kneel and say prayers; show them," one of the sailors called out. So we did, making a great show of folding our hands and bowing our heads. There was more pointing at the heavens.

The natives pointed up, too, directly at the setting sun. The sailors nodded and pointed at us, then at the disappearing sun. They pointed at themselves, then at the other men, and shook their heads. They made signs of small people—children we supposed—with their hands, pointed at us, and then shook their heads. The natives looked bewildered, and it would have been amusing if we had not been so frightened. Finally one of the sailors pointed to his codpiece, and made a crude rocking motion with his hips, then shook his head no and pointed at us. Then he pointed at the setting sun again. The commander gasped, stepped back and snapped an order, and to our relief, the warriors disappeared.

On the beach the sailors made a fire and sleeping place for us some distance from theirs. At first glance the sailors had seemed so much rougher than the few men, priests and pilgrims and beggars, that we saw in the convent that we had been nervous about our situation with them, but as we became better acquainted we learned most were from *converso* families and they boasted Muslims made the best sailors. They insisted that honor obliged them to regard us as their sisters.

That night we overheard them discussing what to do when the repairs were finished, whether to sail on in the hope of reaching some known place or whether to turn back and brave the Sea of Fog and Darkness again. And was it safer for the women to stay behind while they sought the best passage, to return for us later, or was it preferable if we took our chances with them? All agreed they could not leave us here alone, and decided to draw lots to select three to remain behind with us.

As they debated, we huddled together for warmth and had our own discussion. There were already too few sailors to crew the ship.

It was not right to separate the men and jeopardize their chance of a return to their families. We finally agreed they must leave us here. Sor Maria Manuela said that the natives had not harmed us; perhaps we could obtain shelter from them. The other three nuns agreed, saying we must trust God and stay. The beatas, one by one, said that they would abide by the decision of the nuns and that the novices should do the same. The other novices, however, wept and wished to go back. I was prepared to trust the commander.

We all fell quiet. I kept my book by my side at all times, with a pen and the last cake of ink wrapped in the pocket of my habit. I hugged the book to my chest and folded my hands in the sleeves of my habit, trying to meditate on something besides the memory of the commander's handsome face, muscular arms, and broad shoulders. The sailors finally slept and we watched on, turning our backs to the fire for warmth. Hunger makes us feel the cold sharply. We had eaten so little in recent weeks that our teeth were loose in our mouths.

Then, without our hearing a sound, we looked up to see ourselves surrounded. A silent group of native women in tunics stared curiously at us. Like the men earlier, they were handsome, straight and tall and with bronze skin that glowed in the firelight, dark haired, with steady gazes and calm manners. They were not armed, but carried cloaks in their arms. They pulled us to our feet and put the cloaks around our shoulders. These cloaks were made of some wonderful material, miraculously soft and warm.

Then the women put their arms around us and drew us away. Befuddled with cold and sleep, we did not call out to the sailors until it was too late, and by then the women had taken us into the forest, where we came to a low building of stone whose entrance was lit by great torches. It seemed to be a kind of native palace. Inside many fires sent light dancing on objects of gold and silver placed around the rooms. The walls were covered with hangings woven in many colors and patterns, and the same cloth covered some low divans in an inner room where we were seated. The sensation of warmth was almost painful to our aching limbs.

They brought us bowls of gruel with strips of what appeared to be leather, which was dried meat, like mutton—strange but delicious, though we sucked it instead of chewing on account of our poor teeth. There were brightly colored fruits, sweet and starchy, and silver bowls of some warm bitter drink that made us feel lightheaded, yet revived. "Chicha," the women murmured. We did not know if this was the name of their tribe or a kind of welcome— later we learned it was the favorite drink of the place.

We were unsure whether to be cheered or frightened by these attentions. Finally we were led to a room with couches piled with more finely woven coverings and left to sleep, which we did at once, deeply. Such splendor to find among the native people! The last thing I remember is thinking how fortunate it was that I had been clutching the book in my arms when the native women appeared. I still had it when I fell asleep.

The next day we could not tell if we were prisoners or guests. We tried to communicate in signs, but the women's response was to point to the sky. We nodded vigorously and pointed to the sky and then to ourselves, trying to indicate that we served God who lived in heaven. The women nodded some more and spoke to each other in their language. For the next week we submitted to being cared for, sleeping much of the time.

After a week we were restored and anxious to return to the sailors. Covered litters arrived, born by men who averted their eyes in fear while we were made comfortable. The litters were lifted onto their shoulders, but we soon realized that instead of returning to the sailors we were traveling toward the mountains! We went on for days, stopping each night at houses, like *refugios*, where the women who walked behind our litters had hurried ahead to build fires, and prepare food and bedding. We reached the foothills of the great white-capped mountains, where the slopes were terraced for orchards and gardens, just as they were in Andalusia, and strange long-necked beasts stared with human eyes as we passed. We were now worried and frightened.

Finally we saw buildings in the distance. As we approached the outskirts of what appeared to be a native city, a great procession of women in finer garments than those who had accompanied us came singing toward us. As we alighted, the singing grew louder and we were led into the building, which curiously seemed made of one solid piece of stone. However, when we examined it, we saw blocks of stone marvelously cut to fit seamlessly together. Inside, there were the same kinds of beautiful hangings we had seen in the first house, and fine gold and silver ornaments everywhere. As before, there were many women to wait on us. Then came a tall, beautiful woman with two pretty, graceful girls of about eight and ten who resembled her, all finely dressed and wearing a great many gold ornaments and feathers.

We guessed that we were being honored by a lady of standing—a queen or a princess perhaps. This elegant lady spoke for a long time, and though we could not understand the words, their graciousness was plain. She waved her hands to indicate the palace and its contents. Then she and her daughters withdrew in a dignified manner, all the native women and slaves prostrating themselves as they went. Our bows seemed inadequate in comparison.

That night, after a very large and fine meal, we said our prayers and settled on our couches to sleep. All through the night we heard each other turning restlessly and sighing—we were uneasy and very worried about the poor sailors.

Then God sent us a sign. The next morning after our prayers, we heard the familiar chirping. *"Golondrinas!"* we exclaimed joyfully. Following the sound we discovered a garden where the dear, familiar birds hopped between glossy plants and vivid flowers, like none we had ever seen, lush and oddly glittering. A novice bent to pluck a flower and drew her hand back quickly with a shriek. The garden was made of silver and gold and precious stones!

"No food for you here," said Sor Maria Manuela briskly to the swallows. "We must scatter crumbs for you. And here I think God teaches us a lesson, sisters—if these birds cannot subsist on gold and jewels, we cannot do God's work if we give way to luxury and comfort. God must have led us here instead of Gran Canaria to establish our mission. We must return to a lifestyle proper for nuns, learn the natives' language, and make ourselves useful in this place."

Her bracing words recalled us to our duty. Our first attempts to assist with the tasks of the household were rebuffed by our scandalized serving women and slaves. Plainly anxious to fulfill our wishes, they nevertheless tried to prevent our putting a hand to any task, however light. To their dismay we persisted, and in the days that followed, working side by side, we asked the names of things—women, water, food and animals, cloth, washing, sleeping, sunlight, rain, and so on—in the language we came to understand was Quechua. After our evening prayers we shared what we had learned and little by little were able to converse with the women. The most important word in the language seemed to be "Inca," meaning the country, the people, and their king, all of which are one.

We had left our belongings airing on the beach and despaired of seeing them again but one day, to our joy, our serving women carried in our trunks. To our surprise our spare habits and shifts and shoes and missals and rosaries, together with our medicine chest, pens and ink, the book on herbs and the medical treatise, were all there. We hung Sor Maria Manuela's crucifix on the wall of our central room at once, and felt that we had established ourselves a little. We thanked the women and tried to express our relief that our things had not been stolen. The native women were unable to understand what "stolen" meant. When we managed to explain, they were shocked, insisting that in the Kingdom of the Four Quarters of the Earth, as they called the country, no one would take what did not belong to him.

Our ignorance was a source of wonder to the serving women. Little by little we learned that the Inca people worshipped many gods, of whom the sun was the supreme ruler, and the natives' king was called the Sapa Inca. They believed he was the all-powerful son of the sun god, and revered him beyond expression. The novices scoffed at this as heathen superstition but one of the beatas remarked, "Think how quickly the cold descends as soon as the sun sets, even on a hot day. It is not surprising that their religion looks to the sun, and that they believe without it all the world would remain as cold and dark as the nights we spent on the beach."

But it was some time before our conversations with the women allowed us to understand our extraordinary reception by the people here, and how best we might serve God in this place.

We learned there are native nuns, the Virgins of the Sun, dedicated to the sun god from childhood. Those of noble birth lived a life of strict seclusion in their great house between the royal palace and a great temple, just as convents are often located near a church. Each year there was a great ceremony honoring the sun, with religious processions led by the Sapa Inca himself, followed by feasting and dancing and sacrifices. Virgins of the Sun devoted their lives to weaving the exquisite cloth for the royal garments and making the mead drink on ceremonial occasions, living only among other women, served by virgin servants, and never allowed to see a man or leave their house. They belonged all their lives to the Sapa Inca, their emperor and the sun on earth in human form.

Of all men, only the Sapa Inca may see these virgins face-to-face, though by custom he did not exercise this privilege.

For any other man, setting eyes on a virgin offended the sun and carried dreadful penalties. The maiden was buried alive and the offending man hanged, his family and neighbors killed, all animals destroyed, the village razed, and their fields and crops plowed up.

These rules were relaxed in the regions into which the land is divided, where there are lesser houses of virgins who also live secluded from men and work for the Inca royal family, but from time to time the Sapa Inca chooses concubines from among them or gives them as wives and concubines to his allies. Usually these lesser virgins serve for a period and return to their homes, with much honor, and often marry.

Our party seemed to fit into a category of virgins somewhere between the two. In our first encounter with the warriors on the beach, the sailors' rude gestures not only conveyed the information that we were virgins of the sun god, but also that it was he who had sent us across the water to the Kingdom of the Four Quarters of the Earth on great wings, with superhuman guardians in the form of ordinary men. The commander had ordered the women to welcome us as befitted the sun's handmaidens, and the warriors not to kill the sailors. Instead the commander sent food and slaves to repair the ship, after which the sailors had departed. We prayed they might find themselves safely home.

We were objects of curiosity and reverence, and we hoped, not suitable concubine material. The handsome woman who visited us with her daughters was not the queen but the commander's wife. Both had royal Inca blood and it was the custom for such women to maintain close ties to the virgins of the sun, just as the Spanish queen was patroness of Las Golondrinas.

But despite the hospitality shown to us, we learned this is not a gentle land. Many people were sacrificed during the great ceremonies, especially captives of war, and in times of famine or other hardship, their priests would choose the most beautiful children from among the noble families and take them away to the mountains, where they were anointed and blessed, then sacrificed to act as intermediaries with the gods and plead for the humans down below.

Sor Maria Manuela came to believe God's purpose in bringing us here was to end this practice. We knew we must set an example of virtuous living before we could hope to exert any influence among the people. She ordered the women who served us to forego the daily banquets on golden dishes, insisting we would eat as simply as the peasants, maize porridge with vegetables and fruit. The gold and silver ornaments and cups and plates were exchanged for simple pottery bowls, though we kept the beautiful wall hangings for their warmth. We fashioned new wimples of plain native cloth, and mended our habits. Our days had structure and purpose.

Our preference for plain living met with approval. The next step was to let it be known through our serving women that our virgins were required to serve God not by weaving cloth but by teaching and helping the sick, caring for the poor and crippled and orphans, devising medicines and cures, and instructing girls in these ways of helping others. We gathered that our unusual behavior as virgins was tolerated because the sun god permitted us a certain license not allowed to native virgins.

This emboldened us to take another step we had decided was necessary if we were not to be enclosed against our will. We sent word to the commander's wife that it was the custom of our virgins to go about among the people, as God protected us and no harm had ever come to any man from gazing on us. We asked her to intercede with the priests. After a time, a message came back that as we had so far demonstrated our virtue, our customs, though unknown to the Inca, would be honored. Little by little we cautiously ventured outside the building.

We arranged one of the rooms as our chapel. We filled it with the finest wall hangings of the house, made an altar of a carved block of stone from the garden, and hung a crucifix above it. We used a beautiful hammered native silver bowl as a font for holy water, and torches of the kind the natives use in place of candles. Like the Abbess, Sor Maria Manuela heard our confessions, and the natives referred to her as *mamacunya*, the term given to the novice-mistress of their virgins. We decided that she should be formally consecrated as the first Mother Superior of the Holy Sisters of Jesus in the Land of the Four Quarters of the World in the Year of Our Lord 1526. It was the first service held in our little chapel, and the ladies of the royal household, including the commander's wife and daughters, were invited to attend.

The Inca ladies came dressed for an important ceremonial occasion, in beautiful embroidered robes with trains and jewels and feathers, and watched and listened attentively, gratified to see that our virgins had ceremonies. We had new habits and sang the psalms, anthems, and the prayers of the consecration. The visitors seemed to appreciate our choir, though they were puzzled by the lack of instruments and dancing, which always accompany their ceremonies. When the moment came to consecrate Sor Maria Manuela, we all gathered around her and one at a time laid our hands on her head. She is officially Mother now.

Afterward the queen and all the ladies withdrew and did not join in our simple feast of celebration. But we all felt deeply satisfied, as if we had somehow established our presence in an official manner. We had turned two rooms into an infirmary and soon it slowly began to fill with cases beyond the patience or competence of the local doctors—mostly children who were disfigured or feeble-witted, a few who were lame, and several elderly childless widows. In a land where all were responsible for the welfare of others, our efforts met with approval.

Yet we proceeded cautiously, judging our words and actions against the orderly way things were done here, before the Spanish came. The people lived in a way that reminded us of the bees the nuns kept in Spain, with their workers and their queen bee. Peasants worked hard at their fields for the Sapa Inca. The local authorities ensured that every family had enough for its needs, and if one family fell ill or could not work, others looked after their fields until they recovered. Authorities were punished if any in their supervision were hungry or naked or unprovided for. Young couples received what they needed to marry. Our care for the chronically ill or lame or elderly or those too infirm to work was a contribution to the general welfare, though we had to avoid anything that could be construed as an attempt to usurp the priests' authority.

After two years we could survey our progress with satisfaction. We had laid out an herbary and begun to study the native medicines and illnesses that prevailed in order to expand our apothecary. We had set aside a room for a school, had a small flock of goats, some ducks, and had begun digging a vegetable garden when scandalized local women arrived to insist on doing it for us. They planted seeds for gourds and maize and shoots of the tuberous vegetable called "potatoes" that are delicious when roasted in the coals. The swallows made nests in the roof, and sang to us of Spain.

We tried to persuade the local nobles to bring their daughters to our school, but were only successful with the commander's two daughters because their father wished them to learn to read and write in our language. They were delightful girls, very pretty, quick to learn, and sweet natured. They could calculate and do sums rapidly using an intricately knotted piece of string, and we taught them to read and write in Spanish using lives of the saints—they were fond of stories of the martyrs, the more gruesome the better.

An alcove in the schoolroom held our six precious books from Spain: three missals that had survived their soaking and, except for a few pages, were intact; one illuminated prayer book; one on the distillation of herbs; and another on the treatment of diseases. I used the book on herbs to teach them Latin.

Although we had consecrated Mother Maria Manuela, we had yet to conduct a similar ceremony for the four of us novices to take our final vows. My heart ached when I remembered how I had expected my mother to be present, but that could not be helped. We had begun our preparations and were only awaiting the return of two of the beatas. They had left us to travel to a distant village where a peculiar sickness the local doctors did not understand had caused many deaths and debilitated the entire populace to the point that they could not plant their crops.

We consulted our books and thought it sounded like something brought on by the constant rain and cold of the time of year, and to our surprise had been given permission to try one of our herbal remedies. It was a sign that we had advanced in local trust, and the beatas took the medicine and departed.

But our consecration did not take place as we had hoped. Alas, the two beatas drowned when their raft overturned as they made their way back. It was a sorrowful blow to our little community and we had no heart for joyful celebrations. We remembered them in our prayers and hoped that in time our shrinking numbers would be swelled by local girls who felt a vocation. The commander's daughters were joined in the classroom by five other noble girls. Noble or not, there was much giggling, and with the loss of two pairs of hands, we were even busier than before.

We continued to postpone the service of profession. The death of the beatas was followed by another disaster, a terrible famine. For an entire year the rains did not come and it was terrible to watch the unripened maize wither. The tubers that are a main foodstuff were diseased, and game disappeared. The people began to suffer as the storehouses emptied. The people shared what food there was, but many died. Another bad year followed. All grew thin and weak. Children had swollen bellies and hung listless in slings on their mother's backs. Animals perished in the road for want of fodder.

Then we began to see and hear processions of priests going into the mountains. Our serving women confirmed they took children to be sacrificed to plead with the gods to end the famine.

Before the famine we had attempted the delicate task of persuading the priests and officials to end this horrible practice, on the grounds that rather than sacrifice girls to the gods, it would be more useful to give the girls to us to intercede with heaven. Although the priests were generally well disposed to us, this time they grew angry and warned that our insolence would offend the gods further. It was terrible to stand by and do nothing.

Then the commander's wife came to give us the news, and persuade us that this was an honor, that the priests had selected the commander's daughters for sacrifice. The poor mother! The girls were to be permitted a last visit to us on their way to the mountains and she begged that we would support them, to strengthen them for what lay ahead. This was the way of their land and their god. Faced with our reaction to the news, she, proud woman, nearly broke down. She and the commander had no other children.

We waited sadly for the farewell visit of these two dear children. It came soon. On a long dry day we were working in the garden, attempting to kill the weevils that eat the little the drought had left us, as always keeping an eye on the road, waiting. It was unnaturally quiet that day; even the swallows ceased their chatter. We were all uneasy, then we heard the awful drums in the distance and knew the priests and the commander's daughters were beginning their walk into the mountains. The procession with banners flying came into view, with the two girls in the middle. In the unnatural silence the drums and singing were as harsh and cruel as if they welcomed Satan himself.

Outside our house the singing stopped and the two girls stepped away from the procession to us where we waited for them. Smiling, they embraced us one by one. Their eyes were bright and glittering and they seemed in a trance. We knew they had been given the special drink that prepares the victims. We were almost overcome with grief at such a terrible parting, but tried to do as their mother wished. The Incas love flowers, and despite the drought we had managed to find a few to give the girls when this moment came.

Mother Maria Manuela turned to take them from a clay pot of water. She was lifting them out when the pot began to shake of its own accord. As she exclaimed and started back, it fell to the ground and smashed, and suddenly the ground began to shake and the silence was broken by a distant rumbling sound that became a horrible roar. The earth heaved up and down with a sickening force so violent that we were thrown about the garden and the procession scattered, priests and people screaming as rocks began to tumble down from the mountain above us.

Clutching the drugged girls we ran for our house. Just as we got inside, the ground heaved and shook again, followed by rattling showers of pebbles, then the thunder of boulders crashing down, and avalanches of earth and rocks. The terrified serving women pushed behind us into our little chapel where we had dragged the girls and were kneeling in prayer around Mother Maria Manuela. She held her crucifix high so we all might rest our eyes on it in the moment of our death. Outside, landslides thundered and we knew people and animals were trapped and crushed and buried, and every minute we awaited the same fate as our house shuddered and shook. Part of the roof gave way and things crashed against the walls. Then the ground steadied beneath us, but just as we began to look around at each other, marveling at our deliverance, there was another movement that triggered more landslides.

This occurred at intervals during that long and terrible night, so that we dared not leave the chapel to see what help we might give. We stayed tightly packed together, the girls between us and the servants praying to their gods, we to ours.

When we ventured outside again the next morning, a horrible sight met our eyes. Houses and empty granaries and stables and fields—whole villages had disappeared, buried under a ton of rocks and earth. There were bodies or parts of bodies of people and animals, and tattered remnants of the banners carried by the priests the day before. We did our best to find survivors, but were not strong enough to do much. A day later a party of soldiers arrived to carry on the rescue, but it was slow work, and though some were dragged alive from the destruction, most were dead of horrible injuries. We learned even the great temple and house of the virgins of the sun had been damaged, killing many.

Our servants and slaves who had pressed into the chapel with us described how we had passed the night, and word spread of the power of our prayers and our God's protection. A week after the earthquake, it began to rain, and the crops that had not been buried recovered somewhat. We took the injured into our infirmary and kept the commander's daughters out of sight. The priests did not return for them, to our great relief. But they had been chosen for the "honor of the sacrifice" as people here would have it, and what would happen to them concerned us greatly.

A few weeks later the commander himself arrived. He was a kind of viceroy of the region and had been assessing the extent of the damage. We went to receive him, prepared now to argue against his taking his daughters back to the priests to be sacrificed.

He greeted Mother, calling her *mamacunya*, and congratulated us that we were favored by our gods who had prevented our destruction. He spoke with dignity of the fact that the priests had chosen his daughters for a sacrifice, but the gods had not willed it. We all began to breathe easier and I looked up quickly at him and realized that although warriors and princes would suffer the most horrible and bloody torments without admitting pain or weakness, his daughters are precious to him. Only the terrible discipline of this place and what was demanded of the royal family if chaos was not to engulf the kingdom prevented his showing the relief he felt.

I was touched by the vulnerability I had glimpsed behind the warrior façade. It affected me so deeply I had to force myself to keep my eyes down, away from his. He was married and heathen and of a people who practice the most dreadful cruelty, but his presence dazzled me. I stared hard at the ground, as if a miracle were about to take place at my feet. Though somehow my eyes strayed of their own accord from the ground to his legs, strong and bare under his tunic. I forced myself to rejoice on his wife's account that her children had been spared.

And he, too, was speaking of his wife, to say she and his concubines all lay dead after the earthquake! There were exclamations of sympathy from all of us. We felt grief for them all, especially for his graceful and gracious wife.

Then he said something that sent the blood rushing to my head and set my heart pounding. Because our gods kept us safe while so many others had perished, he had come to take a concubine from among us, as was permitted to a prince of royal blood. I gasped and lifted my head. He was looking straight at me and his dark gaze was like a spear into my heart. A concubine? But his wife was dead—and I had an idea.

Mother Maria Manuela was saying with tact but unyielding firmness that his royal rights did not extend to us. *"Our* virgins," she began, and I knew she was about to say "would be obliged to choose death instead," so before she could do so, I sprang to her side and whispered urgently that I had not yet taken my vows and could abandon the novitiate if the commander chose me.

"Certainly not, Salome! Has lust made you mad?" hissed Mother.

"No Mother, wait," I begged. "God may have sent this opportunity to achieve what we cannot accomplish otherwise. I think the commander is bargaining, one of us for his daughters. You, the *mamacunya*, must bargain in turn, to demonstrate the value of what he seeks." Mother looked so shocked I rushed on. "First, you can truly say that Christian virgins may never be concubines. Their God permits them the status of wives, provided they are given to men in accordance to our laws and ceremonies, and never where there is another wife or concubine. And a man who would have one of our virgins as his wife must observe our custom, which is to grant her a wish, otherwise…er, otherwise to dispense with this formality will incur the wrath of her powerful God."

Mother Maria Manuela snapped, "Salome, you are talking nonsense!"

"No, Mother. If the commander agrees to leave his daughters with us, the priests may follow suit and send girls here to intercede with God instead of sacrificing them. And a good Christian wife might persuade her husband that many wives and concubines are…unnecessary." I blushed when I said that.

Mother gave me a look that said I was a demon's changeling, sighed, and turned back to the commander to explain her conditions. He nodded and dispensed with any pretense about which of us he preferred. He pointed to me and asked what wish I had, promising that his honor demanded he grant it. When Mother told him about giving the sacrificial victims to us it was his turn to look shocked, as if he had been tricked and betrayed. I held my breath. The power of his religion and his obligations as a royal prince warred mightily with his inclination, and even more with his sense of personal honor, which would not permit him to revoke his word. But only for a moment. Then he nodded and held out his hand to me. I stepped forward, and clasped it.

That same day a heavy rain began, as if heaven approved our union, although it would be months before the crops that were hastily sown would flourish. With the famine not yet over, would the sacrifices continue? The answer came a few weeks later when three beautiful girls of different ages were taken into the house from the hands of the native priests who delivered them with inscrutable faces.

The commander and I were married a month after the earthquake, by Mother of course—there was no one else to officiate at a Christian wedding. She conducted the ceremony with lengthy prayers begging heaven's blessing on our union. There was nothing else to do. I wore a plain linen shift hastily made for me by the sisters, over which, in the native style, I wore a wedding gift from the commander—a fine tunic of beautiful native embroidery, clasped on the shoulders with gold serpents' heads with emerald eyes. My hair had grown and I washed and brushed it out to hang down my back, tucking a large red flower over my ear. I could feel my face flushed with happiness and knew my eyes were bright with joy. I hoped the commander would approve.

We were married before as many people as could travel gathered to watch. After the sisters had sung every psalm, every hymn in their repertoire—Inca ceremonies are not official without music, sometimes many days' worth—Mother blessed us. Then it was time for the Inca part of the ceremony the commander insisted upon, saying people would not accept me as his wife otherwise. He bent and put new sandals made of vicuña wool and gold thread on my feet. I took a new tunic I had made from fine soft wool, and placed it over his shoulders. One of the members of the royal family joined our hands to signify that we were one.

He led me away to this Hacienda of the Sun and the Moon, which was badly damaged by the earthquake. Servants carried my few possessions, including a crucifix my husband particularly wished to hang in our home. There was another sparse wedding feast at our hacienda—corn beer and a few vegetables with the spicy sauce that accompanies everything. I could eat nothing. I was very nervous about the step I had taken, yet very happy on my wedding night. And I wished my mother could give us her blessing.

Salome's face had softened as she spoke—even now the memory of her wedding to the commander warms her heart. She quickly had three children, the boys, Miguel and Matteo and a girl she named Beatris in honor of her mother. She took care to have them all baptized immediately with as much ceremony and singing as possible, to claim them for the powerful Christian God. The youngest, Beatris, was eight before the stonemasons and workmen finished repairing the hacienda. Salome said proudly that the commander insisted the peasants' houses, the terraces for the fields, and the roads be repaired before his own home. She praised him as a just man, devoted to his duty to the people and the Sapa Inca, fearless, and good to her and their children. He sought her advice as an equal as well as her intercession with the Christian God. The commander's daughters passed through the novitiate and took their vows two years later, the first native nuns. The commander and Salome attended their service of profession, and she had the satisfaction of hearing Mother Maria Manuela tell her privately that she had been wise to follow her heart.

Salome followed the example of the commander's first wife, taking food and blankets woven by the servants, often helping in the school, the infirmary, and the orphanage that had been filled after the earthquake. While orphaned boys were taken to be raised as soldiers, it quickly became established that orphaned girls should be brought to the nuns. From time to time the priests left beautiful girl children at their gates when they wished to supplicate the gods. In due course these little girls became nuns just as the orphans in Spain did. There was no other option for girls who would have been sacrificial victims—once selected, they could no longer remain among ordinary people.

Then Salome drew her story to a close, describing the night that changed their lives forever. A runner had come with an urgent summons for the commander and his soldiers to hurry to the capital. Men with carapaces of metal and strange beasts that breathed fire had flown over the sea with great wings, and there had been signs and omens in the sky to warn of the strangers who had brutalized and slaughtered many of the people en route to the capital. The messenger said the leader was Francisco Pizarro and she was afraid. It was a Spanish name.

Revulsion was plain on Salome's face as she described the events that had happened as if she had become more Inca than Spaniard. The Sapa Inca, Atahualpa—a ruler so powerful the people did not dare look at him directly—was captured by trickery and executed, garrotted—a "mercy," since at the last hour he recanted his faith and accepted baptism. Otherwise he would have died at the stake. His death had sown terror among the Inca. They believed that now the sun would withdraw, the world would grow dark and cold, and all would perish. When the sun continued to rise every day, resistance to the fearsome invaders crumbled. The harvest was plentiful, a sign that the gods favored these ruthless invaders.

The Spanish claimed this Kingdom of the Four Corners of the Earth for Spain, sacking and killing and looting all the while. The nuns sent messengers to the nearby house of the virgins of the sun to offer them the protection of a Christian convent. But the messengers found the virgins gone, carried off like prizes, the great blocks of stone still tumbled about by the earthquake. A bishop sent slaves to rebuild it for use as a Christian convent, and the Holy Sisters of Jesus, being terribly crowded in their old house, seized the opportunity and swiftly moved themselves and the children into the rebuilt part.

Salome was sickened by the Spanish and frightened for her husband. She persuaded him to accept baptism for the sake of the region, and the Spanish conquerors thought it advantageous to appoint a member of the Inca royal family and a Christian convert acting governor of the region. It was in the course of his duties as governor that he died last year in a distant province. Salome clings to the part of her life that is Inca and has little to do with the Spanish colonists.

It seemed that Salome had welcomed the opportunity to tell her story, but at the end of three weeks I could see that she becomes tired easily and we thought it best to go. In fact, she seemed almost eager for us to go, and something she let slip made me think her anxiety for us to leave was connected to her expectation of Don Miguel's return. I tried to put the disappointment of not seeing Don Miguel out of my mind.

CHAPTER 29

From the Chronicle of Las Sors Santas de Jesus,
by the pen of Esperanza, the Mission Convent of
Las Golondrinas de Los Andes, March 1554

When we returned to the convent we learned that Pia is calmer but will not leave her cell, even when the beatas open her door and try to coax her out. She does not sleep for the battles waged by angels and demons for her soul. She is so thin her skin is translucent. It makes Sanchia and me cry to see her.

I have delayed writing to the Abbess and Sor Beatriz. It is impossible to know if letters reach their destinations, or whether letters from me will pose a danger to the convent, or whether they will be able to write back. I long to know if Luz is safe. I have her handkerchief still.

But to business…Mother called me to her parlor to discuss my future. After our visit to Marisol there were more inquiries about Sanchia, Pia, and me, especially Pia, with a view to marriage negotiations. Pia was in no state to marry anyone and I was reluctant for the three of us to be separated, so I managed to avoid the issue.

However, when we returned from our visit to Salome, Mother said someone has particularly inquired about me. I experienced a moment of foolish hope that it might be Don Miguel but Mother said, "Don Hector Santiago. He is sixty and has never married, so you would not have to manage stepchildren. He is a distant cousin of the Beltrans. He was very particular about selecting a wife—so long as she is Spanish he is prepared to consider one with no dowry, provided she is plain, devout, modest, submissive, quiet, not given to fine dressing, and likely to breed. Preferably a simple girl not educated beyond reading her prayer book."

I tried to match the name to one of the haughty land-owners. When I did my heart sank. "Oh. I remember him, Mother—a little pinch-faced, sharp-nosed bantam of a man who thinks highly of himself, with dreadful breath, as if his teeth were rotting."

"He is very rich—the family own many silver mines," said Mother severely. This news makes him even less appealing. Don Miguel told me how natives are worked to death as slaves in the mines.

"His grandfather was one of Pizarro's generals. Naturally the family will consider your background before a formal offer is made, but I trust they will find no obstacle?"

Worse and worse, I thought.

I had already told Mother as little as I could about my family, saying only that my mother had died when I was born and that my father had been a scholar. But now I protested vigorously that I did not fit Don Hector's requirements as I had been rigorously educated at home.

Mother made a dismissive motion with her hand as if to say, "Let us ignore that." She is anxious to have our futures secured, and I feel sure she will set this information in the best possible light when she replies to Don Hector. She told me to think Don Hector's proposal over seriously. The idea made me shudder, though it would enable me to keep another promise—to give Sanchia a home before she gets into serious trouble.

Sanchia grows more and more restless in a way that alarms me. She slips out of the convent from time to time to join troupes of traveling players and musicians and dancers who entertain on platforms in the public squares and the new theaters. This is dangerous behavior. There are too many men, too many adventurers and drunkards, who think all women and girls are theirs for the taking. Especially the dancing girls that she befriends. She insists that the performances are religious in nature, morality plays to educate and Christianize the natives, but they draw unruly crowds all the same.

Sanchia has also begun to speak of her family, very painful memories that make her cry, but she says that now she is growing up, it is her duty to remember them, however terrible it is, "or they will die again, Esperanza. I understand that they died horribly because they were Jews. I want to be a Jew, too." I shushed her and said that whatever we think, we must be careful what we say.

"Don't be such a prig, Esperanza! You have a secret of your own. Anyone who has a secret can tell when others do also," retorted Sanchia.

This is true.

In addition to her newly acquired performing skills Sanchia surprised me by taking a studious turn. And a dangerous one. On one of her illicit excursions she has acquired a printed Old Testament in Spanish from a mestiza bookseller who they say deals in forbidden merchandise. It is very beautiful. Sanchia spent half her dowry on it—without my knowledge—and reads it assiduously. She tells me it was the work of Italian Jews. I warned her that these Bibles in the vernacular are banned by the church. I cannot reason with her and carelessly said that she had no inkling how dangerous they are. Sanchia retorted, "Oh, but I have." She pulled up her skirt and peeled down one stocking. The purple scars are terrible. "These remind me that I must find a way to be my parents' daughter. That is why the Almighty has allowed me to live. I do not know how yet, but I will think of something. In the meantime, I will learn the story of my people."

Meanwhile Don Hector is pressing Mother for my answer. Mother grows impatient that I do not give one. I would have delayed until the sky fell into the sea, except that last night Sanchia narrowly escaped being caught by a night watchman. Today I have agreed to marry Don Hector on the condition he is willing to have my sister to live with us. His answer was that he is willing to have Sanchia provided she is a godly and obedient young woman. Fortunately he knows nothing of Sanchia or he would refuse. How I shall manage them both when we are married, I have no idea.

I make Sanchia hide the Bible in her mattress. I told her of my decision to accept Don Hector's proposal and that she must come with me to my new home. Sanchia looked at me in horror. "Not the one with breath like rotten fish! Ugh. And he is old, like a desiccated beetle. Imagine those dry little beetle hands all over you! Even Dona Luisa did not push Rita his way. Esperanza, you cannot!"

But I must. My own dowry is nearly gone, and I do not know what else to do.

I must not think of Don Miguel now, but oh, how I wish he had been present when we visited Salome.

The banns are posted for my marriage. Sanchia is gone *again*, the wretched girl! I am put to great trouble concealing her absence, which is a strain just now. My wedding day approaches far too quickly. I should prepare my trousseau, but my heart is too heavy and my hands too unwilling for such work. Mother has reminded me to pack a nightdress at the top of my trunk. I will never survive my wedding night!

I went to tell Pia of my marriage. Pia only responded in a dreamy voice that she is married to a heavenly bridegroom. The beatas who look after her persuade her to eat a little by telling her it is heavenly manna. She pointed to the jug of water in her cell and whispered it was God's tears. At least she seems calm.

I pray for strength and remind myself that at least I will fulfill my promise to my father. Sanchia and I have few choices. We cannot stay at the convent indefinitely without embracing the religious life in some form. Our money is nearly gone. We can neither of us become nuns; it would involve too much pretense and betrayal of what we are.

I hope Sanchia returns in time for my marriage. I need one friend by me.

CHAPTER 30

From the Chronicle of Las Sors Santas de Jesus,
by the pen of Esperanza, the Hacienda of the
Sun and the Moon, Late October 1554

I spent a sleepless, wretched night before my marriage to Don Hector was to take place, and the dawn came too quickly. Sanchia had not returned, and Don Hector's carriage waited outside the convent walls. I had a wreath of flowers and a new gown as a wedding present from Mother, and as I dressed I wished with all my heart it was my burial shroud instead. My trunk was waiting by the gate, packed with my small trousseau, and I had put this Chronicle—my friend and confidante—in the bottom, wondering if I would ever have the heart to write in it again.

Suddenly there was a great commotion outside the walls, and the Aguilar carriage and a host of outriders stopped at the convent gate. Nuns and even Mother hurried out to welcome our patroness, who to my amazement entered the gate demanding a word with me. When I ran to see what Salome wanted, she begged me to come with her to the Hacienda of the Sun and the Moon at once. She would explain on the way.

Mother protested that I was about to get married, point-ing to my trunk ready and waiting to be put in Don Hector's carriage. Salome looked surprised, then gave me a piercing look and raised her eyebrows slightly as if to ask if this was what I wanted. I shook my head. "Then come, I beg you," said Salome. Her coachman flung open the carriage door and she pulled me in, ordering the two female servants with her to fetch my trunk. In front of the chapel Don Hector spluttered furiously while the servants tied my trunk behind Salome's carriage and shook his fist as we drove away. I collapsed in tears of relief at my escape.

Then I heard a giggle and looked up to see the imp Sanchia.

Relieved to see her alive and unharmed, and furious with her for the worry she had caused me, I shook her hard, demanding to know where she had been.

Sanchia has been my deliverer! She had slipped out of the convent and made her way to Salome, going most of the way with her friends the traveling players, and the rest of the way alone. Such a perilous journey for a young girl along a road where bandits lurk that I cannot think of it. Besides viewing Don Hector with distaste as a possible husband on my behalf, Sanchia says that she would sooner be buried alive than have to live in his house as his sister-in-law. She had begged Salome to help. "I did not want to worry you, Esperanza, and you would have found a way to stop me. And there is a good reason, now, for you to come with us." She wouldn't tell me what it was, and I almost did not care. It was enough to be rescued from Don Hector.

Salome was quiet and on edge. She ordered the coachman to drive through the night and was impatient when we stopped to change horses. We arrived in less than two days and I wondered at the anxiety she could not hide as we approached her hacienda. A servant hurried to open the carriage door and muttered something in an urgent voice. Salome turned to me and said abruptly, "Thank God he is still alive! Don Miguel needs your help."

I felt my heart quicken. "Of course," I said.

Salome led us inside and into the quarter where Don Miguel lived. "Here," said Salome over her shoulder, and we entered a bedroom, where candles burned on either side of a bed, and a person whose beaten disfigured face I did not recognize lay moaning. The Indian servant sitting at Don Miguel's side glided away. "Sanchia says that you are skilled in medical matters, that you may know something I do not. Please, help my son if you can!"

If anyone ever looked as if he could not live from such injuries it was Don Miguel. Salome turned back the covers to show me a gaping suppurating wound in his side. It was an ugly color. I could also see he had many broken bones—there was terrible swelling around some of them and his body was a mass of bruises. I looked at Salome with horror. "What happened?"

"Miguel is his father's son, and the Spanish treatment of his people roused him and his cousins to action. Some of the Inca princes, his cousins, raised an army in the mountains and led an uprising. They killed a Spanish governor and many of his soldiers, but in the end the Spanish crushed the rebels brutally. Those who were captured were flung off a high precipice, and only because Miguel was badly wounded and fell out of sight of the Spanish did he escape the same fate. One of his cousins managed to drag him away into the darkness before he was recognized and executed."

I stared at him helplessly, my mind a blank.

"Esperanza!" It was Sanchia's turn to shake me. "I told Salome that you had knowledge of old medical books. You told me yourself that you and your father read them. You must remember something! Think!"

I shut my eyes and thought hard...the beautiful Moorish texts that had been fed to the flames...Ibn Sina the Persian's *Book of Healing*. In my mind I opened it, saw the Arabic words flowing across the page...My father's voice as he read aloud...The connection between mind and body...the pharmacopoeia...the careful treatments...I had no book. I must force my memory. What treatment for wounds and fevers and broken bones? And for who knew what damage inside?

I asked for water and sent Salome and Sanchia for clean linen and herbs, ashes and smooth splints. I said, "God is great," and begged the spirit of my mother to guide my hands. Then I set to work on the man I loved.

Splints on the broken bones, not too tight—there was a danger of putrefaction. Native ointments on the wounds before bandaging lightly to let the air through...aromatics on a sponge under Don Miguel's nose. Cool compresses for the fever.

We sat by his bedside for four long days and nights, and his fever did not abate, but it grew no worse. He was a mass of splints which I checked continually to make sure they had not grown tight with swelling. I changed his dressings and sponged his face. We made infusions to ease the pain and dripped them into his mouth. I knelt by his side and spoke into his ear, begging him to summon his great strength of will and recover. On the fifth day he was quieter and I feared he was dying. On the sixth day he opened his eyes as I changed his bandages. On the seventh his fever seemed less. On the ninth day he took some broth and I fell into an exhausted sleep by his side.

When I woke Don Miguel's eyes were open, watching me. I held his dark gaze, and his expression changed. He smiled. I put out a hand and touched his cheek, now cool instead of feverish. He turned his head and kissed it.

We looked deep into each other's eyes and I knew my fate as surely as Salome had known hers when she saw the commander.

Salome is pleased in her dignified way. She kindly says that as her mother's protégée I am dear to her already. Our wedding will not take place for many months, until after Easter to allow Don Miguel to recover. Word of his injuries must not get about. But he continues to mend. God is great.

Salome's younger son, Fr. Matteo, will perform the ceremony, and her daughter, Beatris, and her large family will attend. In the meantime I am learning to weave. I want to surprise Don Miguel with the traditional Inca bride's present to her groom, a fine tunic woven by her hands. Sanchia teases me incessantly, saying my weaving is crooked. Alas she is right.

The day has come and we are married. Fr. Matteo is a very genial priest and Dona Beatris is as graceful and lovely as her mother. When Fr. Matteo had finished, Don Miguel performed an Inca marriage rite, putting new sandals on my feet. He bent stiffly, still feeling the aftereffects of his injuries, but the touch of his hands sent a shiver up my body and looking down I saw him smile at my reaction. He was pleased and surprised by the cloak I had woven, though I told him any other Inca husband would have scorned it and the bride who wove it so inexpertly. Fr. Matteo joined our hands in the way Incas do to symbolize the marriage has taken place. We all stood quietly for a moment. Salome thinking of the commander, I thinking of my father. But when I looked up, I could see that Don Miguel was thinking only of me.

Then one of Beatris's children said he was hungry and we had a great feast that I could scarcely taste, thinking of the night to come. I feel very happy and only wish my father knew. Perhaps he does. God is great.

CHAPTER 31

From the Chronicle of Las Sors Santas de Jesus, by
the pen of Dona Esperanza Aguilar, the Hacienda
of the Sun and the Moon, March 1555

I am with child, and frightened, remembering my mother and
Marisol. Salome takes great care of me and Don Miguel will
scarcely let me move. I used to think him rather forbidding. Now I
see only dignity and passionate pride that he strives to keep under
control. I pray he will not return to the mountains where they say
the spirit of resistance to the Spanish lives on. A mistress would
have been far less dangerous—almost preferable.

A year to the day we married I have a daughter. *Deo gratias*, the birth
was easier than I dared hope and we are well. The baby is named
Maria Caterina after my mother. Don Miguel dotes on her, and
small as she is he tells her stories—how the god Viracocha rose
out of a lake and created the sun and the stars, how he created the
Inca to be lords, how the flute-playing herder of white llamas fell
in love with the daughter of the sun. Swaddled to her chin, Maria
Caterina stares at him with eyes as dark and steady as his own.
Salome laughs at him and says the Incas were much harder on their

children than he is likely to be. Don Miguel says there is time for strictness later.

Sanchia is devoted to the baby, and dances her round and round, humming and singing, until Salome and I protest she will be sick. Sanchia seems happy here, and Salome and Marisol are matchmaking by messenger and letters, but Sanchia seems uninterested.

The Hacienda of the Sun and the Moon, December 1557

I have little time to write in my beloved Chronicle! Salome is often tired and able to do less and less here, so I assumed her role as patroness of the convent's orphanage and school for Indian girls. I have written to Marisol to say that she must set up a similar school on her estate. She and I both know—everyone knows—that Don Tomas is the father of many children there, as many born after his marriage as before it. And whatever her feelings, Marisol has a duty to see they have enough to eat and wear, and are taught to read and say their prayers. Between the convent, the household, Maria Caterina, Don Miguel, and Sanchia, the days pass before I realize they have begun.

Don Miguel is settling a portion of his estate on Maria Caterina to prevent more Inca land being snatched by the Spanish settlers.

Sanchia is gone! She accompanied Don Miguel to the city on some errands, then disappeared. Don Miguel was beside himself thinking she had been snatched, and tried everything and everyone he knew trying to find her. When he returned, exhausted, I told him about the note she had left on her bed, saying that she has not forgotten what she owed her parents. Sanchia's Old Testament is missing, too, along with her best shawl, some silver hair combs, and my Chinese fan. I fear for her. I am also with child again.

The Hacienda of the Sun and the Moon, October 1560

It has been almost three years since Sanchia left. Don Miguel has sought her everywhere, and each time he travels to the city he asks the convent if any news of Sanchia has reached them. So far none has. He also brings back word of Pia, but the news is no happier. She has never left her cell, prays night and day, mortifies her flesh, and eats and drinks almost nothing, only a little bread and fruit. The last baby, little José, has begun to walk and I am with child again, and this time, wretchedly ill.

The Hacienda of the Sun and the Moon, April 1561

Isabelita was born after Christmas, much sooner than expected. It was a long and difficult birth. Isabelita is not well, not thriving as our other children did. She is listless and weak and rarely cries, looking at me with large suffering eyes. I love her all the more, so little and so sweet, but my love does nothing to help her. I hold her constantly, and try to get her to feed a little. It breaks my heart to hear her sad little wail, see her small hands curl and uncurl as if all her energy is concentrated in tiny fingers, clutching at life.

I hold her close to my heart, as if its beating will keep her alive. Don Miguel has aged and his hair is white. Salome says he looks more and more like his father. Salome herself is ill, gaunt, and in pain though she tries to hide it. I do what I can for her, but she can scarcely eat or drink or leave her bed.

As long as I do not allow tears to come, Isabelita and Salome will live.

And now, on top of everything, I must leave the hacienda. I received a message from the convent that Pia is dying and has asked for me, begs me to come. They write that she has a disease eating at her from inside, that she has suffered terribly without complaining. Salome insists that I go. I fear the journey will kill Isabelita, but I dare not leave her behind with a nurse. What if I never saw her again?

CHAPTER 32

*From the Chronicle of Las Sors Santas de Jesus, by the
pen of Dona Esperanza Aguilar, the Mission Convent
of Las Golondrinas de Los Andes, April 1560*

There has been a miracle. I could write the words over and over.
A miracle.

When we reached the convent a novice led me to Pia's cell. I
carried Isabelita with me—I hold her tightly always so that Death
cannot wrest her from my arms. I had forgotten how small and dark
Pia's cell is, with only one narrow barred window. It was morning
but a candle burned on either side of her narrow bed. Pia's face was
as white as the sheet that covered her and her rosary was wound in
her fingers. For a second I thought she was already dead, but then
she gestured to the nuns praying on either side of the bed to leave
us. I could tell from her eyes that she knew it was me.

I bent down to kiss her and she looked at Isabelita who lay in
my arms, listless as usual. "Oh Pia," I said. I could not stop the
tears now.

Pia reached up and touched my wet cheek. Then she labori-
ously unwound the rosary from the thin fingers of her right hand.
Twined with it was a gold chain, and at the end of the chain, the
Abbess's medal!

"You took it from Mother the day that you…Zarita…Oh Pia, have you had it all this time?"

"Mother wishes me to be buried wearing it," Pia whispered. "But this is a better use for it." The ghost of her old serene, otherworldly smile crossed her face. She slipped the chain over Isabelita's head with frail fingers and said, "A gift for you, little one."

The baby's eyes fluttered open and she turned her head and looked at Pia curiously. Pia smiled at Isabelita and they held each other's eyes for a long moment. And then…my baby did a terrifying thing. She arched her back and kicked vigorously with her little feet. She waved her arms, threw back her head and began to howl. Such a sound from a tiny bundle of bones! Terrified she was having a fit, I rocked and shushed her. Her pale little cheeks grew pink, then her whole face turned red from crying. If it had been one of my other children I would have said this meant she was indignant at not being fed quickly enough.

"Feed her," whispered Pia, "feed her at once. All will be well now." She closed her eyes, the smile still on her face. "Farewell. The demons are gone. I have vanquished them. Feed her."

I put the baby to my breast, and to my astonishment and joy, Isabelita suckled greedily, smiled at me and fell asleep, milk dribbling out of her little pink mouth. When I looked up again, Pia was dead.

That night wonder and grief denied me even the terrified half-sleep that was all the rest I had known since Isabelita's birth. That and the baby herself. Isabelita woke often, demanding to be fed. At the requiem funeral Mass three days later, Isabelita was quiet but alert, holding her head up from my shoulder and looking around her with interest. I held her up to see Pia's coffin, and the incense made her sneeze and kick and wave her arms, squawking in protest. Then she suckled again until I was dry, and that night she and I slept soundly for the first time since her birth.

So soundly, in fact, that when I woke I was terrified to hear none of the wheezing sound her breathing makes when she is asleep, or the sad little fretting noise she makes when awake. Had I had been mistaken about her recovery? Had she died in the night? But instead she lay beside me sucking her thumb contentedly, medal still around her neck. She looked at me, her thumb slipped from her grinning mouth, and she gurgled and waved her arms and kicked.

At home again she feeds constantly and smiles and crows with delight at her sister and brother. She chews anything she can grasp, laughs when someone catches her eye, and has become a plump, naughty monkey. When Don Miguel looks at Isabelita and smiles, I see how deep the lines on his face are, like crevasses in a rock.

The Hacienda of the Sun and the Moon, September 1563

Isabelita comforts us. Salome has died. The Hacienda of the Sun and the Moon feels empty. I can write no more.

CHAPTER 33

From the Chronicle of Las Sors Santas de Jesus,
by the Pen of Dona Isabelita Beltran de Aguilar, the
Hacienda of the Sun and the Moon, 1597 AD

I hope that my dear mother, Esperanza, would feel it is fitting
and proper that the final entry in this Chronicle is being made
by the same Isabelita whose life was saved by Pia's medal so long
ago. My mother had not written in the Chronicle since that event
but now that the Chronicle is to leave the Hacienda of the Sun
and the Moon, I will take it up to explain where it is going and
why.

I will begin with the letter my mother received from La Flor
six months ago. Of course everyone has heard of La Flor, the legendary temptress who famously danced and sang her way across
New Spain for many years, leaving a trail of broken hearts. Her
career ended in a blaze of scandal in Mexico City, when two prominent admirers dueled over her one night outside the opera house
where she was performing, and crippled each other. But until my
mother received her letter from Mexico, I had no idea that La Flor
was one and the same person my mother always spoke fondly of
as Sanchia. Sanchia/La Flor wrote that she owed my parents many
apologies, that she hoped they could meet once more in this world

so she could deliver them in person, and if they would permit her, she intended to pay us a visit.

Her letter asked if my mother still kept this Chronicle. If so, she would like to see it to refresh her memory before traveling "home." My mother said Sanchia/La Flor had always been restless. By "home" Sanchia meant Spain, where she intends to go on one of her husband's ships.

To avoid being thrown into prison for loose morals, La Flor married one of her admirers, a widower and wealthy merchant named Vaez Sobremonte, who died a few years later. He was one of the suspect "New Christians"—a Jew, in other words. They say that beyond Mexico City there are whole settlements of these New Christians who practice their religion secretly, and this is where the Sobremontes made their home. My mother replied to Sanchia that we would welcome her with great pleasure, that she had not opened this Chronicle in many years, and how good it would be to look over it together.

Saying that she must show me the Chronicle Sanchia's letter referred to, my mother went to a leather chest in her room, bound in silver. I had never seen her open it but she did now, and lifted out the only contents, a silk bag inside a rougher woolen one, holding thin book and a medal on a long chain, wrapped in a beautifully embroidered handkerchief that looked very old. She unwrapped the chain and held the handkerchief against her cheek, whispering "dear Luz." Then she held up the medal and slipped it over my head.

"Isabelita, you were Pia's miracle," she said to me. "And when Salome died, I lost track of many things. I had been so busy nursing her and caring for all you children, helping the convent...so much was happening that at one time I feared the medal had been lost. After a frantic search I found it again and put it away with the Chronicle for safekeeping."

That was not surprising. All sorts of objects in this house would disappear, resurface, and disappear again. My mother, Esperanza, had nine children who lived, and the house was always overflowing with babies, cousins, nurses, animals, servants, endless visitors and their children. My mother was strict about our education and refused to entrust it to tutors, preferring to teach us herself. It left her little time to oversee the housekeeping and I can well understand her safely putting away anything she wished to keep.

My mother tapped the medal and said, "This was meant to belong to the convent, and I gave it to Mother Superior not long after we arrived from Spain. But then Pia took it and gave it to you and said you were meant to keep it. Who knows, perhaps it will save another child." Then we sat in the old schoolroom and she read the family stories again; that of my great-grandmother in Spain, the scribe who began this record; my mother's account of her voyage to Spanish America; the story of my grandmother Salome.

As my mother turned the pages she grew pensive. "Alas, I have neglected my duty. I never honored a promise I made to the Abbess of the convent in Spain. I must do so before it is too late." She handed this Chronicle to me, and made me promise to see that Sanchia delivered it to the Mother Superior at Las Golondrinas de Los Andes. I protested that she should tell Sanchia herself, but she shook her head.

I believe she had a premonition. A month before Sanchia came, my mother died in her sleep. Sanchia spent the first hours of her visit at my mother's grave. She returned with red eyes and had me read the parts of the Chronicle about the four girls, and then insisted I write this last chapter before she delivers it to the convent, as my mother had wished.

My mother's old friend has proved a consoling distraction for my husband, Teo Jesus Beltran, and my grieving father. There is nothing of the temptress about Sanchia now, just an old woman who talks incessantly of past times, about her husband's grandchildren, the charities she patronizes, and what she will find in Spain.

Vaez Sobremonte's widow has very fine diamonds to enliven her mourning clothes, elegant gowns of silk trimmed with black Belgian lace. She arrived in a well-sprung, cushioned carriage, with a coat of arms on the door followed by a great many wagons loaded with things she is taking back to Spain. A large ship will be necessary to hold everything. In addition to her personal baggage there are several paintings she commissioned at great expense, and one of Marisol, that Marisol's husband, Don Tomas, had painted to mark the twenty-fifth anniversary of the school for girls which Marisol established on the Beltran hacienda. Poor Don Tomas has not been the same since Marisol's death, but still, Teo Jesus cannot understand how Sanchia managed to persuade him to part with it. Sanchia also has with her a portrait of her husband Sobremonte, a strong-featured, intelligent-looking man in a skullcap and a kind of fringed shawl. She takes it with her everywhere she goes on her travels.

Sanchia spoke of her intention to pay her respects at the cell where Pia lived and interceded for my life. That cell has remained empty since Pia's death and they say the nuns hear voices coming from it in the night, that it is visited by spirits—a lady in a dark cloak, and two beautiful young women, one with silver hair and one with dark. The bishop does not know what line to take about this, but fears to upset the local people who believe Pia is a saint.

Sanchia wished to know about us. I told her that we are all married and have families of our own. My eldest sister Maria Caterina is married to one of our *cacique* cousins. I am married to Marisol's son, Teo Jesus, and our brothers have also chosen *cacique* wives, educated at Las Golondrinas. My other sisters married Spanish husbands and two of them died in childbirth. Between us we have many children and a few grandchildren. My father views our increase with great satisfaction, saying that it comforts him to know that through his children Inca will remain on the land until the earth joins the sun.

Sanchia leaves tomorrow at dawn, and I decided to add one more item to her consignment for the Spanish convent. Tonight, Teo Jesus helped me take down a portrait from the *sala* wall. It is of our youngest child Maria Salome, who entered Las Golondrinas de Los Andes as a novice by her own choice—her demand, I should say—the instant she turned sixteen. She is a strong-willed girl, who in temperament resembles her fearsome grandmother Dona Luisa Beltran. It is a fine portrait, I think. Maria Salome is dressed in a handsome new tunic woven specially on our hacienda, and insisted on wearing all her jewelry, and some of mine and her sisters'. Her expression says it all. She is a formidable nun, young as she is. We intended to give the portrait to the convent here as is the custom, but since Sanchia does not mind how much baggage she travels with, Teo Jesus and I would like to send it back to Spain to hang in the convent where our mothers found shelter.

I am about to close this Chronicle forever. It will finally go to Las Golondrinas de Los Andes where it belongs. I dedicate this last entry to the memory of my mother, Esperanza, and her parents with a prayer I heard continuously on her lips, "God is great."

CHAPTER 34

Las Golondrinas Convent, Spain, April 2000

After letting Almira in, Menina managed to pull her boots off before collapsing on her bed, but despite being more tired than she had ever been in her life, she slept badly, waking every few minutes imagining that the men looking for Almira were climbing over the walls. As the first light of dawn came through the window she got up quickly and went to check. But Almira was still snoring, curled in a ball.

Too nervous to go back to sleep, Menina was on edge listening for gunshots, but except for the swallows it was quiet. She brushed her teeth, then went to intercept Sor Teresa, who was just then hurrying to open the gate to the chapel. Menina delivered Alejandro's warning to keep the gate locked. Sor Teresa was predictably outraged. She went off into a tirade in Spanish. Did Menina not realize it was Good Friday?

"It's not my idea," Menina tried to interrupt over and over. "Alejandro says it is necessary. We must trust him...There's a police operation going on. It's very dangerous. Dangerous for him and for many people if we do not do as he says. There are very bad men involved. Please."

Finally Sor Teresa calmed down enough to focus on what Menina was saying. "Dangerous for Alejandro?"

"Yes, for many other people, too. There are criminals, probably with guns. Alejandro has a gun, and there will be other police with guns..."

In distress Sor Teresa cried, "No! Guns evil! People had guns in the civil war, very bad!"

"Alejandro needs you to help him, by not opening the gate for any reason. He wants the gate to the convent to be kept closed and bolted." Menina tried another tactic. "If the gate is locked and he doesn't have to worry about you and the other nuns, he will be safer. You don't want him to get shot, do you, while he is worrying about the nuns and not paying attention to his job?"

"Is for the police what he is doing? Not for anything else, not because these criminals are paying him money?"

So Sor Teresa *had* been worried he was on the take!

"No, it's not like that, not at all. He will tell you about it later. It is a long story and Alejandro is very brave. But first he needs to catch the criminals."

"When we can open the gate again?"

"He will tell us when it's safe."

"Alejandro is a good man. He take care of people, he help us in the convent, he help you, that is why I do not like to think of him and his too much money, his prostitutes. Or dead from the men with guns."

Menina sighed. "I never thought I would agree but I do now."

"Alejandro like you."

"I'm not so sure but that doesn't make any diff—"

"Yes, I tell you I see with my ears, hear what people think when they talk. I hear Alejandro when he say he want to talk with you, he is nervous, like a boy. I think he is combing his hair and straighten his uniform."

"I don't think he..."

"He is lonely. So many girlfriends but is lonely. He was in love with American girl. In California. She was *novia*. But she did not come here. So he does not get married and he waste his life on bad girls."

Menina couldn't enlighten Sor Teresa just now about the girl-friends. "Really that's none of my concern."

"He should get married. Settle down. Have children."

"No doubt you've told him so many times. I'm sure he will when he meets the right woman, but it's none of my business."

"You are not married!"

"No—"

"Why not?"

"Sor Teresa, that's—"

"Something bad make you unhappy. Two days ago you were crying."

"I am *not* unhappy!" Menina was appalled to hear herself snapping at a nun. She just managed to stop herself saying that it was none of Sor Teresa's business.

Sor Teresa shrugged and changed the subject. "Alright, I do not open the gate today. I will tell the others. Sor Clara she has a cold and a little fever. Is windy in the *sala grande*, she get a chill there." Menina was guilt stricken by this parting shot. If Sor Clara was ill it was Menina's fault. What if it turned into pneumonia? A doctor ought to see her, maybe she needed antibiotics…So now the nuns were *her* responsibility? Menina slumped against the wall and rubbed her temples where a headache was starting.

Menina kept listening and waiting for something to happen, but all was quiet. She found an apple from the mesh bag for breakfast. Almira wouldn't be able to eat it with her broken teeth. She paced the corridors restlessly while she ate it. Then she walked back to the refectory and took the last of the stale bread. Let the chickens find worms. She was so twitchy, she'd go look at more paintings.

In the *locutio* parlor she pulled the tapestry hanging across the broken window and looked around to see what else was there. On the wall with the portrait of the girl entering a convent was a portrait of a well-dressed middle-aged woman and another of a man in a black gown and skullcap with a jewel around his neck. They were grouped together over the chest that had tripped her on her first day.

There was a tarnished plaque underneath the middle-aged woman—she breathed on it and rubbed off tarnish until she could make out the name "Dona Maria Isabella Beltran" and something about a school. The portrait was a gift of…Dona Sanchia de Sobremonte. Like the portrait of the girl entering a convent, there was something *primitif* about the painter's style, and yet it was an arresting portrait—the matron had a lively face with expressive dark eyes, and under a black lace mantilla, a mass of brown hair graying at the temples that looked as if it had been neatly arranged earlier in the day but had now slipped from its restraining combs. She had many bracelets, pearls around her neck, and diamond earrings dangling from her ears. Her dress was high and decorous at the throat, and black with a froth of lace trimming. She held a fine white handkerchief, a book, and a riding crop, and something about her pose made it seem that she had only paused briefly and turned her head to look at the painter. A portrait of a rich and busy woman, who had made a hasty if elaborate toilette, impatient to get on with her tasks.

Menina rubbed the plaque under the man in the skullcap. "Vaez Sobremonte, gift of his widow." Who were these people and why were their portraits here? Menina was interrupted.

"Aha! You are here like I thought," said Sor Teresa.

Menina turned and begged, "Sor Teresa, it would be so helpful if you had any idea where the inventory of the paintings might be."

"Is somewhere of course…many things in the convent is somewhere."

"I bet. But what about in an office?"

Sor Teresa's reply was drowned out by a rumble of thunder and Menina realized the morning had turned dark. "Is storm," said Sor Teresa. "Big storms in the mountains." There was another clap of thunder, followed by a flash of lightning, and Menina knew she had to get back to Almira, who would panic when she found Menina was gone—and Menina didn't want to have to explain if the nuns found Almira wandering the empty corridors. She was glad Sor Teresa couldn't see her grab two half-burned church candles and a handful of matches.

Hurrying back she found Almira pacing the corridor, tearful and scared to the point of hysteria.

"It's OK," said Menina soothingly. Almira clutched Menina's arm, saying something over and over but Menina could not understand her. "Don't worry," said Menina, and put her arm around Almira's trembling shoulders. "It's going to be alright. We have to hang on a little longer. The police will get them and you won't have to be afraid anymore." She hoped.

Lunch was bread and watery lentil soup. Menina gave half to Almira and slipped her share of the bread into her pocket, hoping she could resist the urge to eat it until later. Sor Teresa said it was the nuns' habit to mostly fast on Good Friday and Saturday, only drinking a little water until Easter. She said it in a way that made Menina feel in the wrong for thinking of food at such a time, but by now she could think of almost nothing else.

Almira wouldn't let her out of her sight, and Menina was frustrated and bored. At least the storm blew over and the sky cleared. She and Almira went to sit in the wet pilgrims' garden in the sun. Almira seemed to like it there, but it was boring to sit and listen to Almira chewing her nails. Menina finally went back to her room and fetched the old book. She'd try the Spanish part again...

The writing was spidery but neat, and though the ink had faded it was legible.

I, Sor Beatriz of the Holy Sisters of Jesus, servant of God and scribe of the convent of Las Golondrinas, make my last entry in this Chronicle I have kept for over forty years.

She had to skip Spanish words she didn't know. When it grew too dark to see, Menina looked up with a start, her mind thousands of miles and four centuries away, lost in the stories of Esperanza and Sanchia and Pia and Marisol and Luz. And it seemed that all of them—Menina hardly dared believe this, it seemed such an odd coincidence—had been at a convent called Las Golondrinas in Spain. This very one, unless she was terribly mistaken. And if she was right, there had been a portrait of the five girls that Tristan Mendoza had painted. Was it possible that still existed somewhere in the convent? What had happened to the girls?

All this was interesting enough to distract Menina from the present, but she came back to it with a start when Almira shook her arm again and rubbed her stomach. They ate the last of the food Alejandro had brought for supper. By now it was cold, greasy, and unappetizing, but Almira seemed to enjoy it. Almira finally went back to sleep in her cell, but Menina was too keyed up to sleep. She tossed and turned, thinking about the Chronicle, listening for gunshots and police helicopters, but nothing was happening. And she was hungry. At dawn on Saturday she had an idea—maybe the portrait of the five girls was in the *sala de las niñas*. She got up and made her way through the silent convent to the kitchen where she found a stale *polvorón* in the chickens' basket along with some stale bread, which she took.

Menina didn't dare stay away long. Quickly examining frames in the *sala de las niñas* she had decided that what she was looking for probably wasn't there either. The room was getting light, and a painting that had obviously slid off the wall to the floor caught her eye. She picked it up and ran her fingers over it. The swallows, definitely. This painting was in better shape than the others in similar frames. She could make out the composition despite the dirt. Then she sat back, baffled. This frame had fooled her. It was a painting of children alright; that was why it was in the *sala de las niñas*. But not of five girls.

Instead there were small boys playing at the edge of a stream. At first sight it looked like the Christ Child and John the Baptist and some cherubs. But the longer she looked at it, the less certain she was. None of the children had a halo. They just seemed to be... playing in the mud by a stream. Ordinary children, making mud pies. In fact, that was the disconcerting thing about all five of the paintings in the silver frames—at first sight they looked as if they should have Christian themes, then the longer you looked the less they did. Menina couldn't point to a single biblical reference or religious theme here. But it was in the convent, it must have one.

Though as she looked there were some incongruous details—a child's pale foot sticking up out of the water—at a disturbing angle, like a child was drowning. And one of the boys was holding a lump of mud, while in front of him sat a little girl in a semicircle of...more lumps of mud. And there was a flock of swallows with their forked tails playing above the boys' heads. She didn't have time to check for a signature, but maybe it was the sixth Tristan Mendoza Sor Clara had mentioned.

It wasn't a picture of any Bible story or myth she knew. She looked at her watch and hurried back to check on Almira and give her the last *polvorón*.

In the pilgrims' garden Menina and Almira ate the last of the chocolates and drank some water from the spring. Almira began to chew her nails again and hum tunelessly.

Menina got back to work on the book. The four girls were leaving the convent one step ahead of the Inquisition and there was something about a Gospel. Wait, the Gospel had been copied into the Chronicle. It must be the Latin part in the middle. It seemed to be important. If she understood correctly, they wanted to hide it from the Inquisition. She got her small Latin-English dictionary out of her backpack and opened the book to where the Latin part seemed divided into sections, or small chapters.

She began copying what she could make out onto one of her pads. The Latin wasn't as difficult as Cicero's speeches or the *Aeneid*. This was church Latin, sort of basic and literal. She found she could manage a fairly literal translation, perhaps what the writer intended. Hours passed and the shadows grew long. Her eyes hurt. Her brain hurt. She persisted and wrote it all down, but decided her translating skills must be rusty. It seemed to be a peculiar story about the child Jesus. It made absolutely no sense. Who on earth had written this? Then she wondered if the painting in the *sala de las niñas* was telling a similar story.

She wrote what she could. Dusk fell and they went back inside. Almira had dragged her mattress and blankets into Menina's room, where she fell asleep and began to snore. No supper appeared and the first fat church candles burned down. Knowing she wouldn't sleep, Menina lit the other candle and kept working, pausing to rub her eyes or go to the bathroom to splash icy water on her face.

Concentrating, she didn't notice when the bell tolled its mournful hours, or hear the distant bang that caused Almira to open her eyes and shriek. Then she heard what sounded like an explosion, a rattle of gunfire followed by a screeching of tires and sirens and then shouting and the roar of helicopter engines. More gunfire. Almira screamed and she and Menina clutched each other as it came closer, and Menina thought surely the dark corridors were full of armed men who had somehow scaled the convent walls. The bell at the convent gate began to clang, as if someone was pulling the rope hard.

Menina shook free of Almira's grip and ran toward the gate. What if the gang was breaking in? There was no hope of getting out; all she could do was try to barricade the gate. Almira scrambled after her, jabbering hysterically and tripping on the loose tiles. Menina reached the gate where someone was pounding and pounding on the door, and there was more gunfire in the background. "Who's there?" she cried, and to her relief Captain Fernández Galán shouted, "Open the gate! Now!"

Menina lifted the heavy bar and pushed the gate open. There was a frenzied group of young women holding up two of their number covered in blood and Captain Fernández Galán behind them waving a gun and signalling to a policewoman with a medical bag while pushing the women inside.

"The driver tried to shoot the girls in the truck; three died but we rescued these. Take care of them till I get back." The girl bleeding from a wound in her shoulder collapsed to the ground and the medic bent over her. Almira began to scream and grabbed at his jacket, but Alejandro pushed her hard back inside the gate and disappeared.

Menina pulled everyone in and locked the gate. They all sank down, sobbing and wailing around the two wounded girls. The medic was injecting the first with something, and then turned her attention to the other one who had gone into shock and was shaking uncontrollably.

Then a furious Sor Teresa was there, demanding to know why the ungodly din was disturbing the peace of Easter. The older nuns believed the Falangists had returned. Menina sprang to her feet and explained it was the police operation she had mentioned, and very quickly, told her some girls had been hurt in Alejandro's police operation, and that Alejandro would come back and explain later. Sor Teresa wrung her hands in distress. Menina put her arm around Sor Teresa's frail shoulders and said that everything would be alright—the best thing Sor Teresa could do was go and explain to the other nuns. Maybe say a prayer for the injured girls and Alejandro.

The next few hours passed in a blur of tears and noise and bloody dressings. The two injured girls lay quietly, sedated and bandaged, and the medic said she had done all she could for the time being, that someone would come as soon as the way was clear to take all the rescued girls to the safe house under a police escort. The two wounded girls would go to the hospital then with police guards. "Will Captain Fernández Galán go, too, or will he come back here?" asked Menina tentatively. "I mean, he needs to talk to his aunt."

"Oh, I think he is coming here as soon as he can," the tired medic said, and grinned. "Keep these two still; they should be alright. Now I must go in case anyone else needs me."

Menina bolted the gate behind her.

Menina and Almira found beds for everyone. The two dozen or so girls pulled their mattresses together to crowd into the corridors huddled together. Nobody wanted to be alone. At dawn the chapel bell began ringing to welcome Easter, and sleep was out of the question. Menina, who had been awake the better part of two nights, thought her head might explode.

Then Sor Teresa appeared again, this time to shoo everyone down to the kitchen where there were cracked, mismatched cups of thick hot chocolate and some fried sugared things she called "churros" to dip in it. A little color returned to the rescued girls' tearstained faces. Menina noticed the kitchen was full of food and good smells—the village had obviously provided for the nuns' Easter celebration.

Then the bell over the gate was ringing and there were medics with stretchers for the two wounded girls, followed by the police and an armed policewoman who took the rescued girls away. After hugging Almira a long good-bye and telling her that she was safe, and everything would be fine now, Menina went to her cell and collapsed on the bed, utterly drained. She couldn't remember what the piles of notes next to the open Chronicle were for. She couldn't remember what day it was. She didn't care.

She fell into a deep sleep until a persistent ringing noise penetrated her consciousness. She ignored it, but it was a very loud bell. It rang and rang until Menina reluctantly opened one eye. She closed it again. Let it ring. And she did, until it felt like it was ringing between her ears. Crossly she realized the only way to stop it was to answer it herself; obviously the nuns weren't going to.

She staggered out of bed and made her way to the gate, lifting the crossbar to give whoever was ringing a piece of her mind. It was Captain Fernández Galán, gray with exhaustion. She was not too tired to feel relief he was unharmed. "Did you get them all?"

"Yes. I wanted you to know we got them all alive—except for one idiot who tried to shoot his way out. He is dead. There are no words bad enough for these people. I am not sorry. The rest, they will try to make a deal, give us names. But you, you are alright?"

"Only tired. But you must be more tired."

"It doesn't matter. Now, what I came to say is, when I have made my report and cleaned up, will you come with me to the village? Always in this village, Easter is a holiday, at the bar they make a fiesta, lambs on a spit...the whole village is there, is very nice. To say thank you before you go?"

"Oh! I'd love that if Sor Teresa will let me out. I'm starving! I almost forgot I'm going tomorrow. The bus *is* coming, isn't it?"

"Yes, yes it will be here." He sighed. "Leave Sor Teresa to me; the owner of the bar always sends food from the fiesta to the convent."

"And I must tell you what I found."

"I see you in two hours." He turned and she watched him walk down the terraced olive fields she had followed him up so warily less than a week ago. It wasn't a date; he was only being polite. And she did need to explain about the paintings. No, it wasn't like a date at all.

Still, she had to freshen up.

CHAPTER 35

Las Golondrinas Convent, Spain, April 2000

Menina used the last scrap of soap and the dregs of the shampoo and scrubbed herself in the icy water until she was numb but relatively clean. She brushed the dust off her clothes and boots and tried to smooth the wrinkles out of her sweatshirt. Without a mirror she couldn't tell whether she looked any better. Probably not. As long as she smelled better.

She met Alejandro at the gate where he and another man had delivered a huge basket to Sor Teresa, food sent by the village café for the nuns' Easter celebration. Menina carried foil-wrapped dishes that smelled heavenly to the nuns' kitchen and left Sor Teresa rubbing her hands in satisfaction. Then Menina and Alejandro walked down to the village. Halfway there, the aroma of lamb and herbs roasting over coals rose to meet them. The plaza was noisy, crowded with people sitting around old wooden tables, whole families together for Easter, all talking all at once. Children ran about, and from time to time one or another of the old black-clad women gossiping by the fountain stopped midsentence to chide a child in a shrill warning voice.

As they walked past, men rose to slap Alejandro on the back and shake his hand. "You're a hero," said Menina as he detached himself from yet another group of congratulators.

"No. Just a policeman. Doing police work."

"You're a hero to those girls," she answered firmly. "You saved them and who knows how many others from a living hell."

"And you helped. Almira says you were so brave; she will never forget you." Alejandro pulled out a chair for her.

"Almira's the brave one," said Menina with feeling. People were talking to them from other tables and staring at her, but right now all she cared about was food. A little plate of deep-fried something appeared, to be followed by more little plates—of almonds, olives, shrimp, peppers stuffed with salty cheese, thin slices of dark-red ham, and a carafe of red wine. Menina tried to be ladylike and eat slowly, but she was so hungry it was hard. Before she knew it she was polishing off the last bit of ham. The rest of the little dishes were empty. She looked up and saw Alejandro watching, amused. She blushed. "Sorry," she mumbled. "I think I ate most of that. It was so good I got carried away."

"No, is good. I see you like Spanish food," he said, grinning broadly. He had been up and down, standing to greet people who stopped at their table, all wanting to congratulate him, ask after his family, and wish him happy Easter, clucking with dismay over the fact his brothers and sisters and their families had not come home for the holiday. Alejandro said firmly that he had told them to stay away this year, and everyone said, "Ah!" knowingly and nodded. "The police operation. *El Sting.*" A woman asked if Alejandro's sister still sent him chocolate fish.

They all studied Menina with undisguised interest. She guessed they were asking each other where Alejandro had met a girl who looked such a mess after his string of hot girlfriends. Alejandro introduced her as an art student, and said she had been working at the convent, looking for paintings the nuns could sell. There was an approving murmur as this information was passed from table to table. Everyone seemed to know she had been there, and she soon learned that most of the older people had a story about Las Golondrinas and the civil war to tell her. Alejandro pointed out those villagers at the tables nearby who chopped wood for the nuns or took food or bought *polvorónes*, or who still had relatives among the nuns.

Several people told Menina that it was a scandal the bishop wanted to close the convent. It was part of the local history, since before the *Reconquista*. Did Menina know that once this village had been part of a great estate in the valley, owned by a wealthy Moorish family? They pointed out this person and that person as being their descendants. "Even Alejandro, his ancestors lived in the valley once, must be Moorish many years ago." There was a chorus of agreement.

"Ah yes, it is true," said Alejandro nodding. "On my mother's side." An elderly man leaned over from the next table. Did Menina the American know what the *Reconquista* was?

They talked about the *Reconquista* like it was yesterday. Just like the way older people in Georgia talked about the American Civil War, or "the Late Unpleasantness," as some of the older ladies in Laurel Run called it. When Menina nodded and said she did know about the *Reconquista*, about 1492, wasn't it? Word of her response seemed to pass from table to table. Again, people nodded approvingly, and the elderly man at the next table stopped eating and shifted his chair closer to tell her that, with all the trouble in the world today between Jews and Muslims and Christians, Menina should know that at one time the Moors and the Christians and the Jews all lived together in peace in Andalusia. Menina said she was reading an old Chronicle of the convent that said the same thing.

An old lady, one of the grandmothers, said that whatever people said against the Catholic Church, there was something good and holy about the convent.

That would explain why the church wanted to close it, the old man snapped back. Roars of laughter.

Menina laughed, too. She was having a good time. More wine, then bread arrived, followed by lamb and artichokes and rice. The shadows lengthened and plates of small pastries appeared. Someone began to play a guitar. Alejandro shifted Menina's chair so she could see the guitarist. "I think now it is better to eat dessert slowly," he said with amusement.

"Yes, I know. I've overdone it. But everything was so good!" said Menina. The waistband of her jeans felt tight. A thin cat curled itself around her ankles and she fed it a scrap of lamb. Somehow Alejandro's chair had moved so they were sitting side by side, watching the musicians, and people singing spirited songs that she couldn't understand all the words to but were apparently very funny, and this old man or that grandmother leaping from their chairs to perform a little flamenco to general applause.

It grew dark. Small lights came on in the orange trees. Coffee came and went, along with small glasses of some fierce brandy-like spirit that took Menina's breath away just smelling it. More plates of small sweets. More coffee. Alejandro's arm hovered casually on the back of her chair, not quite touching her shoulders. Menina thought she would like to sit like this forever. It felt peaceful and safe. She felt good.

Someone lit a bonfire. "I am thinking something and I am just going to say it," said Alejandro, looking straight ahead. "I am glad you missed your bus. Don't go tomorrow. Stay a little longer. You have another two weeks before your flight. I know you will want to go back to America, but maybe you can stay a little." Menina drew away. What exactly did he mean? With him?

Alejandro saw surprise and alarm in her eyes and said quickly, "Sor Teresa says it is good to have a young person in the convent. Especially a well-brought-up girl who is respectful. There you have many chaperones, and here," he swept a hand at the square of celebrating villagers, "are more. The village is very old-fashioned. Every one of these people will be watching every move you make, just like they watch me, and it will be the main topic of discussion until you leave. So you are very safe here." He smiled.

"I can believe that! But..." Only a few days ago she had thought she wanted to leave more than anything in the world. But now she had found the paintings, and the part of the Chronicle she had read had whetted her appetite to read the rest and see if things fit together as she was beginning to think they might. She would really like to be here when Professor Lennox came. But—OK, it was impossible to ignore—Alejandro sounded like he was holding out another reason. Not pushing, asking. Testing the water. She had thought she never wanted to have anything to do with a man again. And she wasn't sure she did. Yet. But...did she want to go through life wondering if she had been too much of a coward thanks to a bad thing, to miss her chance with a good one?

It was her decision. Menina decided to dip a toe in the water. "Maybe I should stay a bit longer if you really think Sor Teresa won't mind?"

He shook his head. "Believe me, she won't!"

Menina hastened to say, "I mean, I should because I never told you about the paintings I found. Or what the Chronicle says. You said something about 'old stories about the convent,' and I wondered if maybe they're actually in the Chronicle, maybe that's why the nuns gave it to me with the medal...oh, it's too long to go into tonight. I'm too tired and full and sleepy to make sense and you're probably too tired to listen. Besides, you haven't told me about the people from the *cofradia* or whatever you called it, who were looking for me...look, when I can get my head together we still have to talk about a few things before I go. There'll be another bus."

"Yes, we are not finished talking," he said.

"But if I stay I have to call my parents. First thing. OK?"

"Of course, no problem now. To find a telephone with a good connection we must drive down to the valley. First thing in the morning we will go. And then we can stop for lunch. But now I will take you back to the convent, because you are right, I am tired." Alejandro pulled her to her feet and they climbed the terraces still hand in hand. Menina didn't notice that until he let hers go. The gate had been left a little ajar. They both yawned as they said goodnight and went their separate ways.

The next morning Alejandro drove—very fast—a long way down the twisting mountain road until they reached a roadside café that Alejandro said had a reliable phone. He dealt with the operator, and when the Walkers finally picked up he started to walk away. Menina called him back. "I might need your help here."

Later, over coffee, Menina was still red-eyed from an emotional conversation with a frantic Virgil and Sarah-Lynn who said the Spanish police hadn't been able to tell them much, and they had been told to stay put in case Menina contacted them. Now that they knew where she was, they would take the next flight to Spain. Menina assured them over and over she was perfectly alright but they weren't going to believe it till they saw her.

Then when Sarah-Lynn was about to hang up she said they'd let Theo know where she was. He had been more worried than anyone—the papers had got hold of the story that his fiancé had disappeared and reporters were driving the Bonners crazy trying to find out if she had been kidnapped and if the kidnappers were demanding a large ransom.

Oh hell! Menina thought. She told her parents firmly not to talk to reporters or tell Theo where she was; she never wanted to see him again. From now on, what she did was none of his business. When Sarah-Lynn tearfully urged her to think twice about what she was throwing away, Menina said, "Mama, I'm thinking

371

about what I get back by living my own life. Something really interesting has happened—I found some old paintings, it's kind of exciting, a really big deal actually. I need to see what happens next with that. If I married Theo I couldn't do that. I'd live his life, not mine. I don't love him, for one thing. No, I don't think he loves me, not at all. Really, Mama, I don't care anymore what people will say! They'll just have to say it and then we'll all forget about it. I'm sorry to upset you, but I've made up my mind about this." Menina was shaking. Her mother was convinced she ought to marry Theo, and for the first time ever she was standing up for what she wanted. She had never spoken to her mother so assertively. "I told you, Mama, I don't want a last chance to change my mind!"

At that point Alejandro held out his hand for the phone and introduced himself as the local police captain. He assured them Menina was fine, and he was looking forward to meeting at the airport in a couple of days. Just let them know what time. He hoped they would have a pleasant flight. Then he hung up. Menina was tearful after her outburst and suddenly a lot less assertive, and wandered off to the restroom to splash cold water on her eyes. Sitting down again she said, "Talking to my parents makes me feel like I'm twelve years old again and messing up."

"But you are not twelve—you are a grown woman. Something terrible happened to you, but you still found strength to help other girls to whom bad things were done also, things that were not their fault either. You help the nuns because you have a good heart. But instead of thinking 'I am a strong person, a good person, a clever person who can do many things' you let other people decide for you because you want to please them. But in life you must take responsibility for what you do. If you are having second thought about Theo, if you are sorry you say you do not want him…then you should go back to him."

No way! Menina raised her head, looked him in the eye and said firmly, "I meant what I said. I'm finished with Theo. And even though you say I mustn't blame myself for...for...I was carried away by who he was, what my mother and other people thought of him and his family. It blinded me to the fact that he and his family wanted a nice presentable Hispanic wife to get Hispanic votes. One they could control. I think I was just too stupid to see it. No. I wasn't stupid, I just...hoped everything was the way people said it was."

She took a deep breath. "If I had married Theo it would have turned bad eventually and been an even bigger mess, probably with children involved. What he did showed me how despicable he is. But when I felt so shattered, what helped most was when you said it wasn't my fault and that it was good to be angry. And I was so angry at Theo then. Well, you heard me! Then when you asked me to help Almira and told me what happened to trafficked girls, I realized you knew what you were saying about being angry at the right person. And that's when I started to think *maybe*, like you said, I didn't bring the rape on myself. It changed the way I looked at things."

Menina managed a painful smile. "And you know what else helped? The fact that you disliked me, that you thought I was stupid to get my bag stolen, that you called me a prostitute. If you had such a poor opinion and still thought it wasn't my fault, well, I could trust that."

"I am sorry. I was a bully, but I was worried about Almira and the whole operation. I couldn't let anyone jeopardize that. But I did not choose my words well." Alejandro held out his hand, palm up, and Menina hesitated, then put hers into it and they sat looking at each other, holding the moment, neither saying anything because each of them knew it was important to choose their next words very carefully.

A man cleared his throat and broke the spell. "Alejandro? Excuse my interrupting, but you did ask me to come and meet— Ah, is this the lady? *Encantado, señorita!* You are even more beautiful in the flesh than in the missing-person photo."

"Ernesto! I told Menina about you." Alejandro sprang to his feet and embraced a little nondescript gray-haired man with a pipe in his hand and a paper under his arm. They sat and exchanged pleasantries while Alejandro ordered coffee. Alejandro told Menina to start at the beginning. Ernesto lit his pipe and sat back to listen.

"I better start with this." She put the velvet bag on the table. "Ernesto, Alejandro says he told you about my medal and how I got it." Then she withdrew the book from its velvet bag along with two notebooks. "I told Alejandro that the nuns in the convent where I was adopted also gave me an old book. See, swallow on the medal, swallow on the book cover, you can just make it out. Beyond taking a quick look inside I never tried to read it, really. It's an old Chronicle and you know, a sixteen-year-old couldn't care less. I brought it to give to the Prado since it was old and in Spanish and I hoped they'd help me with research on the medal in exchange. But since I've been at the convent with nothing else to read, I dipped into it. And what's odd is, I think the Chronicle and this medal actually came from Las Golondrinas, a long time ago, and wound up in the place where I was rescued in South America, I think to hide them from the Inquisition. Most of the Chronicle is in Spanish in old-fashioned writing, and I may have gotten some of it wrong, but that's the gist.

"But it mentions a 'Gospel' over and over until I wondered what had happened to the Gospel. But there's a part of the Chronicle in Latin and while I was stuck in the convent I had a look at it, and I began to think, hey, that *is* the Gospel. And I think the reason the nuns wanted me to have the book is that the Gospel tells the story of where the medal came from."

Ernesto kissed his hand to her. *"Hermosa e inteligente!"* he exclaimed. Beautiful and intelligent.

"Still the ladies' man, Ernesto," murmured Alejandro.

"Listen, you two! There's more. I get the impression the Gospel dates back to Roman Spain in the early days of Christianity, though the Chronicle says it was recopied, so maybe the Latin's been simplified. And I kept reading and rereading it because it was such an odd story, and I wanted to translate it right, but it says Jesus had a sister named Salome and that she came to Spain and founded the order that started the convent up there." She pointed in the direction of Las Golondrinas. "She looked like Jesus, according to eyewitnesses, and she even acted like Jesus. And this medal"—she held it up—"was hers. Jesus gave it to her. And one way of looking at the Gospel, if you put it all together, is that it says women are just as close to God as Jesus was. And I guess it also means that Mary was never the virgin the Catholic Church says, or that she even needed to be."

Ernesto's expression had changed to one of horrified alarm. He put his hand on Menina's protectively. "My dear, you have done an excellent job, but you do not understand the significance of this Gospel you have found. The Catholic Church says the Virgin Mary is the link between man and God, that she is the ever-virgin mother of God...this is doctrine decided by the bishops in a theological conference called by the Emperor Constantine in the fourth century! Council of Nicaea, that was the one. By that time, who knew what the truth was. But by making the matter one of faith it was beyond challenge. If there is evidence Jesus had a sister, the church was wrong, the Virgin Mary was not a virgin forever. I am sure that in the past anyone suggesting such things would have been accused of heresy."

Ernesto shook his head and continued. "I am an old Republican and a nonbeliever, but this is serious! The couple who were looking for you, the missing-person poster...Now I know why! They want this book and this medal, and they will do anything to get it so that no one will find out what is in the Gospel. What I do not understand is how they knew Menina had it."

"I can tell you," said Menina. "There was a story about me in the paper when I got engaged, and there was a picture of my medal and the Chronicle and a bit about why I had them."

Both men were plainly worried now. Alarmed, Menina looked at Alejandro. He had risked his life for the Albanian girls and from the grim look in his eye she knew he would do the same for her. "I have my gun," said Alejandro. "I'll see what we can do about police protection—"

What have I done? For a moment the old Menina, the good girl, quailed to think this new mess was her fault—but a new Menina told the old Menina to shut up and think. And the answer came to her. Call Becky.

Menina pushed her chair back and said firmly, "Guns and police won't be required, gentlemen. I know exactly what to do. The last thing to do is hide the story; better to publicize it as much as possible. Alejandro, please help me make another call. My best friend is...a journalist who would love to get a story this big. And I owe her; she's the reason I'm in Spain at all. And if Ernesto would contact Professor Lennox." She pulled Professor Lennox's card from her pocket. "She's a specialist in sixteenth-century Spanish art and the organizer of my tour. I didn't make a good first impression, but I bet you could charm her into coming up here and taking a look at what's at the convent. She's very attractive, by the way." Ernesto picked up the card and said that it would be a pleasure.

"And I'll keep working at the Gospel translation. What I would really like is a desk and a chair."

"I can manage that," said Alejandro.

For the next two days before everyone arrived, Menina walked down the hill to the police station, carrying the Chronicle, her dictionaries, and the notebooks. After huddling on a stone bench and squinting in candlelight, it was luxury having a desk and a decent lamp. She polished and checked her translation and transcribed different versions in longhand while Alejandro completed a long report about the weekend's operation. Telephone engineers finally came and repaired the telephone connection. Alejandro took calls from Interpol and Ernesto, and Menina spoke to her parents and Becky.

At the end of the second day, Ernesto came to join them for dinner and over coffee Menina read them her day's work:

The first story of the Gospel of our Foundress Salome,
told by Salome to our scribe

On a hot afternoon in Judea, Jesus, the son of Joseph the Carpenter and his wife, Maryam, led his younger sister Salome to join a group of boys laughing and splashing on the banks of a stream. The boys fell silent as Jesus sat Salome on the bank and waded into the stream to join them. No one dared splash or jostle him. In the Temple rabbis called him a strange prodigy, a boy who knew the alphabet without being taught, knew the law, and who boldly lectured the rabbis instead of the other way around. Children sent to fetch water from the well said that when Jesus did so he carried it back to his mother in a cloth instead of a jar. Accidents happened to playfellows that angered him—he had cursed a boy who pushed him and the child's hand had withered. A child who had taunted him unkindly, as children do, dropped down dead. It was said that when a neighbor accidentally severed his foot from his leg with an ax, Jesus picked up the twitching foot and joined it back onto the leg while the injured man stared at his bloody ax in shock. Some claimed he had restored life to a man who had fallen from a high roof onto his head, although those who had not been present disputed this, insisting the injured man must have merely been

377

unconscious and not dead. Witnesses insisted the roof had been very high, the man's head was smashed, and blood had trickled from his ears before Jesus approached, then he had sat up and walked away, shaking himself. When questioned about these things, Jesus only shrugged and said, "It is God's will these things happened."

People whispered the boy was an infant sorcerer or a demon, and parents ordered their children to give the prodigy a wide berth. So the boys didn't ask Jesus to join in their play, and after a minute Jesus shrugged and walked alone down the stream looking for minnows.

Salome kicked off her sandals, too, but the water was deep so she sat and dabbled her dusty toes up and down.

"What are you making?" she asked the boy nearest her. He was slapping wet clay into a high mound.

"Girls belong indoors. Go home!" he muttered.

"A fort," said another boy, scooping up more muddy clay and shaping it into a wall around the mound. "One that's too strong for the Romans." He looked over his shoulder as he said this. "Judas Maccabeus and his army are waiting inside for the enemies of Israel to come close, then they will burst out and kill them to the last man. Their blood will soak the ground." As he said the word "blood" he slapped on handfuls of mud so violently that Salome was splattered. She wiped her face with her forearm but knew better than to complain.

"Death to the Romans. May they bury their children," said the boy building the fort loudly, and spat with contempt. Jesus stood up straight and frowned at the speaker. The boys stopped what they were doing and held their breaths until Jesus went back to his minnows.

Two older boys came splashing over to tell their friends building the fort to be quiet. One slipped and fell, knocking down the fort's walls and provoking angry shouts from the builders. The rest of the boys gathered around, shouting and arguing about who was at fault. Suddenly there was a tussle and the knot of shouting boys slipped and shoved and slid on the muddy bank of the stream, trampling the last vestiges of the fort and knocking Salome into the water. She tried to get out of the way but they knocked her down again and again. Her head went under the water. Choking and frightened, she struggled for a foothold in the streambed but it was too slippery and she couldn't stand up. Then a boy's foot went into her stomach and she felt the boys on top of her no matter how frantically she tried to push them off. Trapped, she tried to call her brother, but muddy water filled her mouth and nose and she couldn't breathe…The boys' shouting grew fainter. There was no sound but a gurgling bubble.

When Salome opened her eyes she was lying on the bank, still unable to draw breath. Her chest hurt and Jesus was shaking her. Finally she turned her head and vomited dirty water. The boys stood at a distance terrified, only held back from running away by a greater fear of what might happen to them and their families if they didn't pacify Jesus first.

"Don't cry," said Jesus to Salome, ignoring them. He pulled her to sit upright and patted her back.

"Is Salome alright?" asked one anxiously. "We didn't see her."

"We're sorry!" muttered another sullenly. "Say sorry," he hissed at the others.

"Sorry, sorry. It was an accident, Salome," they mumbled, keeping wary eyes on Jesus. "Little girls should stay home with their mothers and sisters," said the bravest one, though he didn't say it very loud. "It's where girls and women belong. Then they wouldn't fall in the water…"

"Stupid girl!" muttered another.

Jesus ignored them. Salome rubbed her eyes with her fists. She coughed some more to get the mud out of her throat.

"Watch." Jesus took some wet clay from the bank and rolled it in his hands. "Look, a swallow!" he said. Salome was dubious. It looked like a ball of mud.

Jesus set it on the ground. "Here, we'll make some more."

He made a circle of lumps around Salome and gave her one to hold.

"Now watch!" Jesus clapped his hands and Salome felt the cool clay in her hand grow warm and soft and feathery, then it began to chirp and move its wings. She shrieked with surprise and delight. "You made a bird!" she exclaimed.

"No, I only shaped the clay; it is a bird by Jehovah's will," said Jesus, and the swallow flew out of Salome's hands and into the air. Jesus clapped his hands again and the other lumps began to flutter and chirp as well, hopping about on the bank around Salome before flying into the air. "All things that happen, happen by Jehovah's will, Salome."

The watching boys were rooted to the spot, terrified first by what they had done. Salome had been lying under the water with her mouth and eyes open when they had finally noticed her under their feet. Dragging her body onto the bank they knew she was dead, and the look on Jesus's face when he came splashing from his minnows to push them away promised a terrible retribution. Now the drowned girl was alive and laughing and clay swallows were flying around her shoulders. With one accord, the boys scattered, running for home, wailing that the boy Jesus had a sister touched by sorcery, too.

Menina read the story to Alejandro and Ernesto as they sat in the café waiting for the café owner to bring them supper. "There's a painting of that, in the *sala de las niñas*," said Menina.

"Serafina Lennox is going to be very, very surprised," muttered Ernesto as their food came.

"And there's more," said Menina

"Don't keep us in suspense!" exclaimed Ernesto.

"Wait till I've eaten!" Menina laughed.

The second story of the Gospel of our Foundress Salome,
this is dictated by our first Abbess, of blessed memory, who wit-
nessed these things and later dictated them to our first scribe.

The Coast of Hispania, 37 AD

Two Roman centurions in a harbor tavern watched as the merchant's ship pulled into the harbor among the fishing boats and dropped its anchor. It belonged to a

Palestinian merchant named Joseph, from Arimathea, who came several times a year to take on provisions before sailing on to Britannia where he traded spices and wine for tin and lead from the Britannia mines.

The centurions sometimes purchased a ribbon or a few cheap silver bangles from him to give Flavia, the youngest of the port's whores. She loved trinkets. At fourteen, Flavia preferred the younger soldiers who would compete for her favors, but if older men gave her a pretty present she would favor them.

Joseph's boat pulled into shore and dropped anchor. A group of women and their belongings were bundled roughly off the boat and dragged through the shallows toward the shore. "New whores." The centurions looked at each other and smiled. "Flavia will scratch out the eyes of any more beautiful than she is."

Sailors strode through the water, dragging women who were hampered by waterlogged skirts and cloaks. The younger ones shrieked and stumbled and the older ones pleaded. From the boat, bearded men watched from the stern with folded arms and pursed mouths. Only the last woman, carried roughly ashore between two sailors, did not beg or protest or cry. She spat and fought.

She kicked the sailors who deposited her roughly on the shore. She had a handsome face, tanned from the Levantine sunshine, with dark eyes and heavy brows that met over a long nose. She threw back her head and her head covering fell off to reveal a tumble of black hair almost to her waist. She raised her fist and shook it at the men in the boat. In a clear voice she shouted, "For shame, Joseph! Shame on you all, to treat women so! We have traveled with you and endured the same hardships. We have softened the hearts of those who would have thrashed you for your arrogance and your squabbling. Now, to lure us here with lies...saying there was need of us in Britannia...Deceiver, miserable carrion! May your sails rot and your cargo spoil and the winds carry you out of sight of land until you repent." She ignored a sailor who flung a small bag of coins at her feet and hurried out of kicking range.

Joseph leaned over the gunnels and shouted back, "Look to yourselves now, women! We warned you, beware of Salome!" He shook his fist back at her. "She has led you astray from the law and a Jewish woman's duty, to her home and family. Was Moses a woman? Were the prophets women? Can women study Torah? It is written that the synagogue and study house are the province of men. A woman's voice in the Temple is like the braying of an ass. You think of a community of women and scholars, bah! Stay there until you come to your senses!"

A breeze spun the woman Salome's long hair out around her head as she shouted something back. Her cloak billowed behind her and she shouted angrily and shook her fist as the sailors lifted the anchor, raised the sails, and began to tack back into the Mediterranean. Salome stamped her foot angrily. "A vixen!" muttered the first centurion. "No, a witch or a sorceress, the wind bears her curse after them…see that cloud on the horizon? Has she conjured a storm to sink them on the Bicaien Sea?"

But the cloud was only birds, returning from Africa after the winter was over. Headed for Hispania, flying low. For a moment the boat was in shadow as they passed overhead.

Onshore, Salome picked her veil up and threw it over her head. She retrieved the coins and turned to the other women. "Come, have courage! It must be God's will. We will go and find our brother Titus and our sister Octavia. It is something to be on dry land again. It will be a comfort to enjoy the fellowship of others besides those stiff-necked fools. Come." She began to pull the women to their feet.

A young girl with painted eyes and ringlets emerged from the door of the tavern. She sauntered slowly down to the beach to stare at the women. She pointed, arm jangling with cheap bracelets, and cried shrilly that she needn't bother scratching anyone's eyes out after all.

"Child," said Salome.

"Flavia," said the girl. She pointed to the medal Salome was wearing. "Pretty," she said, leaning close enough to flick it insolently with her fingernail. "Sell it to one of those fellows—they'll give it to me." She pointed at the centurions. Then she walked back to the tavern with a deliberate sway in her hips that was not lost on the two men.

A year later the same centurions watched as Joseph and the men sailed back into the port. They were met on the shore by Titus, the husband of Octavia, the deaconess. "Welcome," said Titus, rather sourly. A small crowd gathered to see what would happen next.

"Greetings, Titus! Have our women learned their lesson? Keeping modestly indoors, are they? Ha ha!"

Titus stared at Joseph. "You old fool! All the women here, Octavia my wife and my daughters among them, have taken themselves to the mountains. They...they have a community of women, with no men, the mountain...I hold you responsible for bringing that woman, sister or not..." Titus's speech could not keep pace with his anger.

"You mean Salome?" ventured one of the new arrivals.

"Who else would cause so much trouble, idiot! The women hadn't been here two days before she began preaching. What set her off was the prostitute Flavia. Salome found her weeping over her rough treatment at the hands of a centurion—nothing out of the ordinary for those girls, that's what they're for. But Salome was angry, and became angrier when Flavia told her she was with child. She began preaching against those who use women ill by selling them. Whores stopped working, and gathered to hear her instead. And when she was done, Salome insisted Flavia join the Sabbath meal at my house—imagine! Octavia defied me and welcomed her!"

"Why didn't you order Octavia to send the harlot away instead of allowing her to defile the Sabbath meal? Is she not your wife to command? Is it not your house?" asked a man.

Titus shuffled his feet. "You have no idea what they're like when they get something in their heads. One or two, you can beat into submission, so many..." He shrugged. "But that's not all...someone asked Salome if she had her brother's powers. She insisted her brother Jesus was a prophet who claimed no powers. He and she were ordinary Jews, servants of God seeking to do God's will on earth. The women began shouting they were servants of God as well. Just imagine! Even the whores! And they would no longer serve men but God."

Within days the commander of the Roman camp was threatening to punish the entire Jewish community unless they silenced Salome. The whores were refusing to work and demanding to be baptized, and the whore master was busy flogging them.

Joseph stared at him aghast. "Where are the women now?"

"There." He pointed toward the mountains. "Most of the women have gone—our wives, daughters, sisters, and the whores. The women claim they will live in the mountains like the Essenes—no husbands, no children—a religious community. Of women!"

"The mountains? Essenes were in the desert!"

"That's not the point! Wherever they are, it's against the law, against nature. Even Octavia has gone, saying they will need women who are educated as she has been. I blame her parents—why teach a girl to read and write? The camp commander sent soldiers to bring them back, with Salome in chains."

"Have they returned yet?"

"No. Because something else happened."

Menina, Alejandro and Ernesto had reached coffee and dessert by this stage. The café owner had brought plates of the small sweet pastries left over from Easter and the table was littered with crumbs that Menina was gathering up with the tips of her fingers as she spoke. "I can't wait for you to see the paintings themselves. One of them is a painting of the women on the beach—the curious thing about it is a cloud in the corner that looks like an accident or mildew. You hardly notice it at first, then it starts to draw your eye until it's the most important thing in the painting. There's also a portrait of Flavia—well obviously as Tristan Mendoza imagined her," said Menina. "My guess is, he got a last chance to paint a sexy woman and he went for it. And now that I've read this I think one of the pictures is of the Sabbath meal Flavia was invited to. Now here's the last part…"

Here is the third story of the Gospel of our Foundress Salome dictated to our scribe Octavia by our first Abbess, of blessed memory, who witnessed these events with her own eyes.

I, Flavia, left the town in search of the other women as soon as I could escape. I had been locked up by the commandant to prevent my joining the other whores and was used so mercilessly by the soldiers, because the other whores had gone, that I thought I would die. Still when God opened the way for me to go I found strength to flee for my child's sake. And by mercy I was able to join the others. All of us were anxious, fearing husbands and fathers and soldiers and the whoremaster.

Every night Salome gathered us and repeated her brother's teachings about a good life, through serving God and sharing and kindness among ourselves. Is there hope of finding something beyond the cruelty of men in this life? Her words are like warmth and sunlight. But to think of women going all alone into the mountains to live! Away from men! My heart lifts even though our lives will be hard, if we survive at all. Following the swallows we found an old road marked with white stones. Local people pointed to a mountain where they say there are caves inhabited by an old settlement of Carthaginian women, and we used Salome's fund of Roman coins to purchase bread and porridge, woven baskets for catching fish, and even goats until we were driving a small herd. A few women who grew tired were persuaded to stay behind by men needing wives in the little settlements we passed through, but most of us kept on.

After weeks of walking, living on wild fruit and catching fish in the mountain streams, tired and footsore, we reached the place where the caves are. We saw no sign of any living person, but found terraces of untended olive trees full of fruit, with a broken press and more terraces where grapevines and fields of wild beans flourished. There was a stone enclosure with the remains of huts where goats must have lived, fruit trees, and many mountain springs with fresh water. We found old combs, a few chipped pots and water jars, small sharp bone tools, some rotting blankets, and a small stone altar with a goddess and an inscription even Octavia cannot decipher. We drove the goats into the enclosure and barricaded it against wolves, then set about making our homes in the caves. We all worked hard, knowing that winter was coming; getting firewood, drying fruit and fish and wild beans, which we ground into a kind of paste to make bread, repairing the press as well as we could and taking turns yoking ourselves to a kind of harness to press oil. We made cheese from the goats' milk, gathered wild herbs to dry in the sun, and one of our women found hives of bees and managed to remove the honeycombs. We all long for salt, but there is none. Still, our rough encampment is habitable. If others have survived here, we may survive, too. Salome leads us in prayers each morning and night.

Then one day at the end of summer, as the evenings were turning cold, and we were hastening to collect as much firewood as possible before winter, a boy arrived from one of the villages below with terrifying news—a party of centurions was coming. Many wept and I swore that I would not go, but would throw myself from the cliff first. Salome said we must have faith in God and above all not be distracted from our tasks.

Though we expected the centurions every minute, still they did not come and we were relieved to think they had turned back and ceased to worry about them. One day Salome stayed below while the rest of us ventured a longer way up the mountain than usual to collect fallen branches after a storm. We heard angry shouts below, and leaving our piles of wood we began hurrying back to camp. To our horror, from above we could see Roman soldiers rushing into our camp, and the first ones were advancing on Salome. One clutched her gown and ripped it from her shoulders. Another tore her shift from her body. She turned this way and that trying to run, naked save for the medal round her neck, and they blocked her way and taunted her to prolong her fear and the moment of retribution. There were cries of "Teach the witch a lesson first, then teach the others" as they closed in for her. We stumbled down toward her crying, "No!" and saw Salome look up beyond us. Then the swallows came, their shrill cries, louder and louder, and a dark mass of birds descended on the soldiers, pecking at their eyes and helmets. The soldiers slashed with their swords, wounding each other and cutting many birds into pieces.

Then the mountain rumbled and shook beneath our feet, and a terrifying sound like the roar of God threw us and the soldiers to the ground. The rock behind Salome split open. As boulders rained down from the mountain Salome ducked her head and slipped inside the crevasse. The earth shook again and the fissure closed behind her. Those soldiers still alive cried out in terror that the place was the preserve of some goddess and fled, dragging the wounded.

Trembling and weeping we climbed down to see the place where Salome had disappeared. The ground was covered with blood and the bodies of men and swallows, and among them something glittered. I picked it up. Salome's medal. I slipped it over my head. "We will not go back" I vowed. "Salome is here... Here we will stay." The swallows flew off the next day. And where Salome had entered the mountain, a spring appeared in the rock.

The yawning café owner had gone home to bed. It was after midnight and he left the keys and an open bottle of wine on the table. Alejandro muttered his thanks, saying he would lock up and drop the keys in the café owner's letter slot.

"There's a painting of the third Gospel, too," said Menina. "Put the six Tristan Mendozas together and you have a religious cycle. Really, it's so extraordinary I keep thinking I must be mistaken about everything—I'll be relieved when someone else has a look at it."

"But if you go back to the beginning of the Chronicle, this was what the nuns hoped would happen, that someone would bring the medal and the Chronicle back to the convent and put it all together. Only I think—though I can't be sure—that Tristan Mendoza must have painted the cycle after the four girls left the convent. Because between the time he arrived at the convent and the time the four girls left, he painted a group portrait of the five that were here. So maybe that's still in the convent somewhere."

There was silence in the café. Ernesto took off his glasses and rubbed his eyes. "Beyond a doubt you have made the discovery of a lifetime in this Chronicle. The paintings, the key to their meaning, the history of the convent..."

"And maybe a little of my own family history. Reading the Chronicle I think this medal might have been in my birth family for a long time, maybe even been connected to another miracle. And I have this weird feeling, like maybe on account of that connection I was meant to find all this and put it together."

"You are...I cannot find the words to tell you what you are," said Alejandro. "No words to say what you have done." This time he did take her hand across the table, not caring if Ernesto saw.

"I have a feeling this is just getting started," said Menina. She smiled at him. "I think...like the poet said, 'the best is yet to be.'"

CHAPTER 36

Las Golondrinas Convent, UNESCO World Heritage Site,
Tristan Mendoza Foundation and Museum,
Directors Menina Walker de Fernández
and Alejandro Fernández Galán,
June 2013

Becky had been the first person to grasp that things were indeed "just getting started." What Menina had found was a huge project waiting to get off the ground. When she arrived in response to Menina's phone call saying she had to drop everything and come to Spain and get the story of a lifetime, Sor Teresa allowed her to stay in the convent where she was given a pilgrim's cell next to Menina's. Sor Teresa reluctantly agreed to unlock the gate so Becky and Menina could come and go to the café for their meals. "But no mens," she said as sternly to Becky as she had to Menina. Becky followed Menina around the convent, beside herself with delight at having an exclusive news scoop. She foresaw a series of newspaper features, then maybe a book. "Oh Child of Light! If any male reporters get wind of this, it's just too bad! They won't be allowed in the convent!" she exclaimed gleefully, and within a day had sold a series to the *New York Times*.

"Things are just getting started, probably. I mean, look at this place! I started off trying to help the nuns a little," said Menina. "Now I'm wondering how to make everything come together—it keeps nagging at me."

"The place is a mess. Interesting, but a mess. That bathroom is evil," said Becky. "Good thing Alejandro asked your parents to stay with him—his place is fabulous. You can tell it's an old house, but he's had a lot of work done so it's comfortable. He's got good taste for a man. Anyway, he said we can come over and take showers whenever we want." She had looked sideways at Menina, trying to gauge her friend's take on the handsome police captain. Becky's take on him was that he was macho but good news. He gave Menina space. Becky was definitely getting signals that something had been started between them.

When Serafina Lennox came to the convent the first time and saw what Menina had discovered she was speechless, and hyperventilated until she had to sit down, while Menina brought her some water and assured her they were just getting started.

For Menina and Alejandro the phrase "things are just getting started" became a mantra. Over the years it preceded statements like, "maybe this is a crazy idea, but what if we could turn the convent into a museum" to "how can we ever raise that much money?" to "let's try it" to "Dear God, what were we thinking!"

Menina and Alejandro said it when experts arrived to look at the Chronicle and medal. They said it when Menina wondered aloud if it would be possible to keep and display the Mendoza cycle alongside the Chronicle and the medal, to have a gallery in the convent and a shop selling copies of the medal and Chronicle and reproductions of the paintings. They said it hopefully to teams of architects and conservationists and heritage bodies who trooped around the convent, shaking their heads at the impossible job of restoring and repairing a building that ancient, historic, and huge.

They had said it to insurers and museums and charitable trusts. They said it, talking themselves hoarse, giving speeches and networking and chasing official bodies for funds. And when they told Sor Teresa that the very first work to be done was new quarters for the nuns and a live-in care team of lay sisters. This provoked exclamations and warnings and a flood of advice from Sor Teresa, so Menina left it to Alejandro to explain to his aunt that in fact they were "just getting started."

They said it when the first tentative fundraising efforts bore fruit, and then to describe the state of perpetual upheaval—fundraising, dignitary-visiting, building work, repairs, renovations. Alejandro said it when he asked Menina to marry him. Only when Menina, who seemed to be immune to every method of birth control, announced she was expecting their fifth child did they look at each other and say, simultaneously, "Don't, whatever you do, say we're just getting started!" And when his wife was tearing her hair out over yet another crisis, Alejandro would put his arms around her and remind her the best was yet to be.

And when it was suggested that Alejandro, a local hero for his part in breaking up the smuggling ring and rescuing women from the traffickers, should run for election to the Spanish parliament, the *Cortes Generales*, they had sat up late into the night, discussing it. Menina could see her husband was interested. "I guess just getting started—again," she said. "It'll be interesting! But you're a good man for the job." And then she told him she had some news as well, they were expecting baby number six.

Today was one of the rare occasions when Menina had time to think about anything that had happened longer than five minutes ago, and she thought about that conversation and smiled. They must have been insane thinking they could let life get any fuller, but somehow it was working. Menina had become quite good at living calmly amid chaos, just dealing with the most essential things. She had had plenty of practice. And the one thing you could say for being pregnant was that you got to sit down occasionally.

Today Menina, dressed in a pink maternity sundress, big pearls, and espadrilles, sipped orange juice as she sat in the shade of a huge umbrella out of the scorching midday sun and took stock of her life. She watched her parents enjoying a game of ring-around-the-roses with four of her daughters—Pia, Esperanza, Marisol, and Luz—in the old walled pilgrims' garden. One-year-old Sanchia was taking her prelunch nap in her stroller.

Today she had a full house of the people she loved best, and the remaining one, her husband, was driving back in time for what promised to be a lively Spanish family lunch. The table was set in the arbor, she had postponed two urgent meetings until the next day, her parents had the children, and her assistant, Almira, was dealing with the lunch. This left her time to concentrate on the most essential and pressing matter of the moment—Becky, whom she hadn't seen for years.

When Becky had walked through the door the previous evening Menina had to mask her shock at Becky's appearance. Sarah-Lynn had been less reticent. "What on earth happened to that child?" she had whispered to Menina almost as soon as Becky left the room. From a distance, Menina thought Becky looked her old self. Up close, Becky's face had fine wrinkles from a hot Iraqi sun. There were dark shadows under her eyes, her cheekbones were sharp, her nails chewed to the quick. Becky tended to hit things angrily with her crutches. Menina wanted to hug Becky and cry, which Menina knew would be a terrible mistake. So while trying to smile and chat like everything was fine, Menina was racking her brain trying to think how to help her troubled friend. Years ago the convent had helped her deal with the aftermath of rape. Maybe it would somehow help Becky just to be here. Menina should remain calm and patient and give Becky time. If Becky didn't explode first.

Becky had written a series of brilliant pieces about the convent, the paintings, and the proposed gallery, paving the way for Menina and Alejandro's efforts to get the huge project they envisaged off the ground. But still determined to follow the lure of adventure, she had literally been through the wars. After graduating from journalism school she had somehow finagled press credentials that took her to Afghanistan then Iraq. She had reported from one hellhole after another, getting addicted to the adrenaline rush of danger, and the crazy living-on-the-verge-of-death high that lent an intensity to everything, from relationships to a cold beer.

When Menina had tried to ask how she was, Becky had snapped that the counseling her paper had insisted on hadn't worked and she didn't want to talk about it. OK?

Sitting on a deck chair across from Menina, Becky was halfway through a bottle of wine and her right foot was jiggling. Immobilized in a caliper, her left leg lay heavily on the chair and her crutches were in reach. "So peaceful," muttered Becky, then jumped like a scalded cat when from somewhere in the depths of the convent there was a loud clash of scaffolding poles, and the rattle of pulleys, then workmen shouting over a blaring radio.

Menina bit her tongue so she wouldn't blurt out what she was thinking, that thank goodness the paper had enough sense to refuse to send Becky back. Becky had wanted to go. Iraqi women with horrifying stories to tell, things they would only tell a woman reporter, were her speciality. That was what she had been doing when the bomb detonated and blew up the café full of widows and children she was interviewing. Becky was struggling with the fact she was alive.

Menina kept her tone light, as she tried to decide whether to tell Becky that Hendrik was joining them for lunch, instead of springing it as a surprise as planned. No surprises, she decided.

"Remember the UNESCO architect, Hendrik? Swedish, glasses, tall, looks like an owl? Sweet guy, you kind of liked him."

Becky nodded and made a noise that sounded like "mmmf" or like "the married one," depending on how closely anyone listened.

"He's having lunch with us, and I wanted to tell you that he's div—"

"Whatever's cooking for lunch smells fabulous. I'm starved." Having changed the subject, Becky ate the last of the olives and started on a dish of baby artichokes.

"Almira cooked it—it takes about twelve hours. Lamb stuffed with herbs."

"It's been too long since I've seen you." Becky's foot jiggled and tapped like it had a life of its own. "I miss us meeting up in Paris or Venice for a week like we used to when you first got married."

"So do I, but as you know I've been the size of an elephant and unable to fly for most of the past nine years." Menina patted her stomach. "Nice of Muhammad to come to the mountain this time. By the way, how's your mother?" It seemed like a neutral question so Menina changed the subject and asked it.

Becky took a deep breath and tried to grin. "She says teaching kindergarten would have been so much more *ladylike*—well, you can imagine. She was ecstatic when I told her this assignment was a story on you and the foundation. She still thinks you're the good influence in my life."

"Not that we're not glad to see you, but I didn't get the whole story on the phone about this interview when you called two days ago. The phone connections aren't wonderful and I've got diaper brain."

"It's ostensibly one of those 'how does a modern woman cope with her partner's political career, her own career, and a family' things. I know, I know—gag! Finger down throat. But I had to pitch it that way so the paper would agree. What I really want to write about—to tie it in with religious divisions since 9/11—is the interfaith conferences here. I know you want to keep politics out of it, but Child of Light, if there's one thing I learned covering wars, it's that you can't keep politics out of religion. So I kept nagging about doing a story on you and the foundation because I've written about war. And it occurred to me I need to write about someone trying to start a peace."

"Any excuse to stay sitting down with my feet up."

"OK if we do a little work now, then?" Becky reached down and fiddled with her recording equipment and swore, then angrily banged it with her fist, swearing. Menina flinched.

A little red light came on. Becky snapped "testing" into the microphone, and when she played it back it repeated "testing."

"Finally! Now just start with what made you think about having interfaith conferences. We'll edit later." She pressed a switch and put the microphone between them, and Menina said what she had said many times before.

"Well, by 9/11 people from different religious groups had been meeting on what they saw as common ground here, because of the special history of this place. But it was after 9/11 we had another idea. There's so much unused space, and if we could get the funding, we thought, why not use the cycle as the focus of an interfaith center. It made sense when you think about the parallels—religious intolerance today, and religious intolerance in the sixteenth century. People are still as anti-Muslim, anti-Semitic, and anti-Christian, anti-Catholic, and anti-Protestant as ever. UNESCO finally declared it a World Heritage Site and we held the first interfaith conference about the time you went to Iraq. Word spread and more and more groups are connecting with us, and our conference center is a neutral meeting ground for everyone.

"I really like your phrase 'starting a peace'—it's exactly what we'd like to do and we need more funding to do it. A lot of basic work ate up the first grants—supporting walls, plumbing and electricity, and new quarters for the nuns. Things still collapse, and some new artifact turns up from time to time—there was a Roman lady's comb the other day, for example. They finally got the special room to display the medal—it would take a nuclear bomb to open that display case—and magnified and mirrored so you can really see it. Same for the Chronicle. We need security like the Pentagon and it's expensive. The shop sells translations of the Chronicle and the Gospel in different languages and copies of the medal and reproductions of the paintings by the thousands, so that provides income to take care of the nuns that are left. We have nurses and a resident doctor who are all nuns, willing to respect their wishes not to leave the convent, even for medical care."

Becky shifted and switched off her machine.

"And Sor Teresa?"

"She looks frail but she's indestructible. She still insists on getting up at dawn to make *polvorónes* for the café. She refused cataract surgery—believes it's God's will she can't see and in return God seems to have given her a second wind. The children think she has magic powers because she told them she sees with her ears. Grumpy as she is, they adore her so I take them to visit for a few minutes most days." Menina sighed. "She has a lot of advice about raising children."

"I bet she does! I'll go say hello later," said Becky. "Now I'm going to have to write a few words about adorable you." She switched her machine back on. "People are interested in how busy politicians' wives with jobs and families manage, with all the extra demands on them, to look good, stay informed, and be supportive. You run this enterprise as your full-time job, Menina—how do you get everything done?"

Menina groaned. "I have no idea because I have never yet gotten everything done for just one day. I prioritize chaos. There are always workmen and architects arguing, wanting me to look at plans or arbitrate or making a huge mess just as an important delegation is due and we need to make a good impression. I visit the nuns every day, see if they need anything. Leaving aside the fact that I have five children and another due any minute, there's correspondence and putting people in touch and speakers to organize for conferences. If we didn't stop for lunch and a siesta I'd collapse. But if it weren't for Almira being my assistant I would give up. She's the efficient one."

"But you make speeches and stuff, you're the face of the institute. How do you manage to look so good?"

"Fortunately, being pregnant softens people up. Alejandro and I keep being overtaken by events. And Alejandro laughs and says big families are normal, and I always wanted a big family—probably the adopted-child syndrome—but he's promised to have the snip after the next one. Very un-Spanish male of him. Oh Lord, don't write that!" Menina leaned over and switched off the machine. "Without Mama's help I'd look like something the cat dragged in. My dad won't go shopping with her any more, says all he does is sit on the husbands' bench."

"I'll get some photos of the kids, too; they're adorable."

"They need to get out of the sun now anyway. Girls, come give Mommy a big hug and have some juice," she called.

Four little dark-eyed girls of seven, six, five, and nearly four in identical smocked sundresses raced across the courtyard, followed by their grandmother.

Becky picked up her camera and aimed it at the children. "You've got your work cut out for you, Mrs. Walker." The little girls and Becky made silly faces at each other while Becky took photos.

"Yes, I do, honey. I'm blessed having so many."

There was the sound of an engine coming up the new gravel drive through the convent gates. Menina closed her eyes and smiled happily, seeing a dark-eyed man in a blazer and an open-necked shirt, who had driven much too fast to return home, get out of the car with a big bunch of flowers for his wife.

At the bottom of the steps leading up to the old pilgrims' garden that was now their private one, Alejandro smiled, too, as he heard his daughters' laughter on the terrace where Menina and her mother and her friend were waiting for him, and his father-in-law calling "get ahold of yourself" to one of the children. He smelled lamb and knew his mother-in-law had set the table under the grape arbor with their wedding china and that a lazy lunch in the shade surrounded by his family and his wife's best friend would be followed by a siesta. Pregnancy increased Menina's appetite for sex, and then she would sleep, entwined in Alejandro's arms while the baby kicked them both. They would visit the nuns' quarters to hear whatever advice Sor Teresa felt was called for today. And neither of them would have traded this for anything on earth.

Alejandro was halfway up the steps to them when there was a terrible boom like an explosion, and a rumble of collapsing masonry deep inside the convent. He swore, dropped the flowers and leaped up the last stairs shouting, "Menina!"

At the top he nearly collided with Becky swinging past on her crutches propelling herself toward the explosion. She looked more than upset, she looked dangerous, face white and shrieking something incomprehensible. Alejandro quickly counted his children to be sure they were safe and gave his hand to Menina who was struggling out of her chair with a worried expression. He wrapped his arms tight around her. "Thank God!" "It's alright, darling, it wasn't a bomb. Hendrik warned me they were pulling a wall down in the old pilgrims' quarter and it might be loud, but Becky's a little shaky—I didn't know till I saw her how badly she'd been injured. I think she's got post-traumatic shock and she needs help. We have to get her before she kills Hendrik with her crutch." She pulled her husband toward the cloud of dust billowing from the convent. "She's been holding it together, by herself, for too long. She needs professional help and peace and quiet. I was so glad she was coming because I thought being here might help, but listen to her, screaming at poor Hendrik! See what I mean? And I'd asked him to join us for lunch because Becky liked him when they met before, but he was married. I didn't have a chance to tell her he's divorced now. I hoped meeting him again would remind her there are good guys out there...I'm an idiot."

Steadying his pregnant wife, Alejandro muttered, "*I* thought it was a bomb. Not surprised she did as well. But Hendrik and Becky? Ice and fire."

They listened and could hear Becky's voice, high pitched and hysterical now. Coughing and waving dust away so they could see, and stepping carefully over pieces of broken wall, they went inside toward the screaming. Which suddenly stopped.

"Do you guess Hendrik's still alive?"

Alejandro peered into the dimness then nudged Menina as the dust slowly settled. "Maybe you were right." At the end of a long dark corridor a tall blond man in glasses had his arms protectively around a short woman with hair so sun bleached it was white in the dim light. The woman's face was muffled in his shoulder and he was murmuring soothing indistinct words into her ear, rocking her gently back and forth. "We'll go back and let them be," advised Alejandro.

"Oh!" said Menina. She stopped and panted, leaning on her husband's arm. "Oh, Alejandro, I think that was a contraction. Just a little one."

"Thank God I'm home! I thought you weren't due for another two weeks."

"Babies don't keep very good time. But it is early. Probably a false alarm."

"Papa?"

Their four-year-old stood silhouetted in the entrance.

"Wait there, Marisol, it's a mess in here. Too dangerous for you. Mommy and I are coming out."

Marisol stamped her foot. "Hurry because I want to tell you! There was a lady in the garden. She came after the big bang and told me not to be scared. She had a long dress on and it blowed in the wind and I showed her my new tricycle and was ringing the bell and she smiled and went '*Shhh*.' So I did *shhh*. Then she showed me a swallow nest hidden in the vines. It had little eggs in it. She asked did I want to know a secret. Guess what? Aunt Becky's going to get married and live here. Then the lady said she lives here, too, that she was goned away but she came back. I told Granma but Granma said the lady wasn't really there but she was, Mommy, she *was*!"

Menina stared at her daughter, and bent over clumsily to give her a hug. "Marisol! Oh, sweetie..." She stared up at Alejandro. "Salome?" she mouthed. He shrugged.

Then there was a snuffle and slow footsteps. A man cleared his throat. Hendrik looked at them solemnly through his horn-rimmed spectacles. "Careful," he said. He was carrying a large rectangle that seemed to be wrapped in ragged old material. Becky, looking tearstained and drained, limped along behind him. "I was just telling Becky, that we are finding something hidden in the wall that we knocked down. This is a very interesting thing to find, I think. Come, we must see it." Alejandro went to help him.

In the kitchen Almira hastily cleared the large refectory table and Hendrik laid the object down. Menina said, "It looks like it's a painting. Behind the wall? Like it was hidden?"

She felt another unmistakable sensation. It was a long drive to the maternity hospital in the valley, but first she had to know what this was. She carefully pulled away rotted material, blew the dust off, and underneath they could see the faint outline of a group of people. "What on earth...hand me some bread." Almira grabbed the breadbasket ready for lunch and passed it to Menina. Everyone gathered around expectantly as Menina dabbed a little dirt off here. Then there. Even Becky looked curious.

They could see the outlines of five heads.

"Oh!" Was that another contraction? Menina tried to ignore it; she needed to know if it was what she hoped it was—the missing piece of the puzzle. She grabbed more bread and worked as quickly as possible until the sitters were visible enough for the others to see. "Esperanza gets to sit on Grandpa's shoulders. I want to see, too; pick me up, Papa!" demanded Marisol. Alejandro swung her up. She shrieked and pointed at the figure on the right of the portrait. "Mama! There's you!"

"She's right!" exclaimed Becky with Hendrik at her shoulder.

"Sure enough is," Virgil agreed. Almira's eyes were wide. She crossed herself. The resemblance was unmistakable.

"That's Esperanza," said Menina. "And...and the others." She pointed them out, identifying each one easily. Sanchia, Marisol, Pia with the hair like moonlight, and the dwarf Luz.

"But that's *my* name!" Esperanza protested from Virgil's shoulders.

"Yes, it is, just like the Esperanza in the picture who is probably your great, great...I don't know how many great, grandma. Maybe you'll look like her too one day when you're older. And when you are, I'll tell you all about them." About these girls, and about Isabella who had become Sor Beatriz, and Salome and the Inca commander, how Esperanza had married Salome's son Don

Miguel...everything she knew about her ancestors, which she would tell them made her no less the Walkers' daughter.

She was distracted from her musings by another contraction. A stronger one. Probably time to go.

"I'd love to eat lunch first but this baby," she announced, "is going to be born on this table, Alejandro, if we don't leave for the hospital at once!" There was a flurry of consternation, Almira ran to phone the hospital, Sarah-Lynn was telling Virgil where Menina's suitcase was, and the little girls began jumping up and down. Alejandro searched his pockets frantically for his car keys, and Sarah-Lynn was giving instructions to everyone.

Menina pointed out the keys where Alejandro had put them on the kitchen table and holding his arm said, "But before I go, we've decided what to name her. Or actually, I think the name chose us a little while ago, when Marisol was in the garden." She raised her eyebrows at Alejandro to see if he agreed. He nodded.

There was a chorus of "What is it? You can't go until you tell us!"

"It's Salome, of course," Menina said, patting her stomach. "Salome is finally coming home."